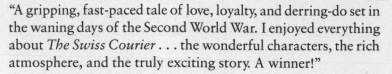
"A gripping, fast-paced tale of love, loyalty, and derring-do set in the waning days of the Second World War. I enjoyed everything about *The Swiss Courier* . . . the wonderful characters, the rich atmosphere, and the truly exciting story. A winner!"

Christopher Reich, *New York Times* bestselling author of *Rules of Deception* and *Rules of Vengeance*

"What I love about *The Swiss Courier* is its gutsy heroine Gabi. Willing to take risks for the higher good, yet vulnerable, Gabi is a wonderful portrayal of the tender strength of womanhood. Add that to a twisting plot, the raging of World War II, and a kindling love story and you have an enjoyable read."

Mary E. DeMuth, author of *Daisy Chain*

"Fabulous! Filled with heart-stopping suspense and fascinating details of life in WWII Europe, *The Swiss Courier* is an unforgettable story of faith and courage when faced with the highest of stakes. I loved everything about this book, from its riveting first scene to the surprise denouement. Bravo, Tricia Goyer and Mike Yorkey. This is more than a page-turner; it's a keeper."

Amanda Cabot, author of *Paper Roses*

"The Swiss Courier sizzles like a 24 episode with a World War II twist. The pulsating action and plot twists will keep you riveted."

Bob Welch, author of *American Nightingale* and coauthor of *Easy Company Soldier*

"A tense, fast-paced thriller that takes the reader on an exciting ride. *The Swiss Courier* is a masterful blend of history and intrigue; above all, it's a reminder that God is present even in the most dire of circumstances."

Kathleen Fuller, author of The Royal Regency Mystery Series and *A Man of His World*

"'This was a time of war, not love.' That statement from the beginning pages of *The Swiss Courier* sets the tone for this gripping, fast-paced story of honor and duty set in 1944 against the backdrop of World War II. With an intensity that builds to the very end, this book is compelling, chilling, and fascinating."

Lenora Worth, author of *Code of Honor*

"There is something fascinating and heroic about the stories from this historical period. Tricia Goyer and Mike Yorkey have added to that list. Each character hooked me into their world and agenda. I couldn't wait to see how all the threads would weave together. *The Swiss Courier* is a unique look at the front lines of World War II and what everyday people sacrificed to stand up against the evil surrounding them. Farmers, shopkeepers, and soldiers alike risked their lives to do what was right. This was an unexpected and thrilling adventure. I highly recommend this book for readers ages 16 and up."

Jill Williamson, author of *By Darkness Hid* and reviewer at Novel Teen Book Reviews

"Outstanding! *The Swiss Courier* is a fast paced, tightly plotted thrill ride. It packs plenty of masterful twists and turns but does not skimp on character development or historical accuracy. Goyer and Yorkey spin a terrific tale."

Rick Acker, author of *Blood Brothers, Dead Man's Rule* and *Devil to Pay, Inc.*

The
Swiss Courier

The
Swiss Courier

A NOVEL

TRICIA GOYER AND MIKE YORKEY

Revell

a division of Baker Publishing Group
Grand Rapids, Michigan

© 2009 by Tricia Goyer and Mike Yorkey

Published by Revell
a division of Baker Publishing Group
P.O. Box 6287, Grand Rapids, MI 49516-6287
www.revellbooks.com

Printed in the United States of America

Library of Congress Cataloging-in-Publication Data
Goyer, Tricia.
    The Swiss courier : a novel / Tricia Goyer and Mike Yorkey.
      p.   cm.
    ISBN 978-0-8007-3336-0 (pbk.)
      1. Women intelligence officers—Fiction. 2. Nuclear physicists—Fiction.
    3. World War, 1939–1945—Switzerland—Fiction. I. Yorkey, Mike. II. Title.
    PS3607.O94S85 2009
    813'.6—dc22   2009022229

Scripture is taken from the King James Version of the Bible.

This is a work of historical fiction; the appearances of certain historical figures is therefore inevitable. Names, characters, places, and incidents are the product of the authors' imagination or are used fictitiously. Any resemblance to actual persons, living or dead, is coincidental.

To the Reader

In the early afternoon of July 20, 1944, Colonel Claus Graf von Stauffenberg confidently lugged a sturdy briefcase into *Wolfsschanze*—Wolf's Lair—the East Prussian redoubt of Adolf Hitler. Inside the black briefcase, a small but powerful bomb ticked away, counting down the minutes to *der Führer*'s demise.

Several generals involved in the assassination plot arranged to have Stauffenberg invited to a routine staff meeting with Hitler and two dozen officers. The one o'clock conference was held in the map room of Wolfsschanze's cement-lined underground bunker.

Stauffenberg quietly entered the conference a bit tardy and managed to get close to Hitler by claiming he was hard of hearing. While poring over detailed topological maps of the Eastern Front's war theater, the colonel unobtrusively set the briefcase underneath the heavy oak table near Hitler's legs. After waiting for an appropriate amount of time, Stauffenberg excused himself and quietly exited the claustrophobic bunker, saying he had to place an urgent call to Berlin. When a Wehrmacht officer noticed the bulky briefcase was in his way, he inconspicuously moved it away from Hitler, placing it behind the other substantial oak support. That simple event turned the tide of history.

Moments later, a terrific explosion catapulted one officer to the ceiling, ripped off the legs of others, and killed four soldiers instantly. Although the main force of the blast was directed away from Hitler, the German leader nonetheless suffered burst eardrums, burned hair, and a wounded arm. He was in shock but still alive—and unhinged for revenge.

Stauffenberg, believing Hitler was dead, leaped into a staff car with his aide Werner von Haeften. They talked their way out of the Wolfsschanze compound and made a dash for a nearby airfield, where they flew back to Berlin in a Heinkel He 111. When news got out that Hitler had survived, Stauffenberg and three other conspirators were quickly tracked down, captured, and executed at midnight by a makeshift firing squad.

An enraged Hitler did not stop there to satisfy his blood-lust. For the next month and a half, he instigated a bloody purge, resulting in the execution of dozens of plotters and hundreds of others remotely involved in the assassination coup. The Gestapo, no doubt acting under Hitler's orders, treated the failed attempt on the Führer's life as a pretext for arresting 5,000 opponents of the Third Reich, many of whom were imprisoned and tortured.

What many people do not know is that Hitler's manhunt would dramatically alter the development of a secret weapon that could turn the tide of the war for Nazi Germany—the atomic bomb.

This is that story . . .

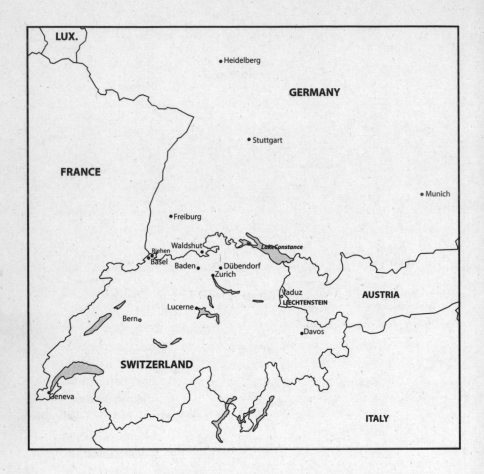

List of Major Characters

(in order of appearance)

Jean-Pierre: a Swiss male in his twenties who participates in underground activities in Germany and Switzerland.

Gabi Mueller: the twenty-four-year-old daughter of an American father and Swiss mother working in the translation pool at the Basel office of the OSS (Office of Strategic Services), the American intelligence-gathering operation in Switzerland during World War II and the forerunner of the CIA (Central Intelligence Organization).

Ernst Mueller: Born in New Glarus, Wisconsin, to Swiss parents, Ernst met his wife-to-be, Thea, at a missionary conference. They married and have three children: Gabi and the twins, Andreas and Willy. They live in Riehen, Switzerland, just across the border from Germany. A furniture maker by trade, he is also a part-time pastor of a "free" church in Switzerland.

Thea Mueller: A native of Switzerland, she is Gabi's mother and a full-time homemaker.

Dieter Baumann: a Swiss in his late twenties who's working for the Americans at the OSS office in Basel, where he is in charge of operations.

Allen Dulles: the American spymaster who opened the Office of Strategic Services (OSS) bureau in neutral Switzerland in 1942 to collect information on Nazi Germany and run a spy network. He runs his nascent espionage network from Bern, the Swiss capital.

Sturmbannführer Bruno Kassler: the fast-rising head of the Gestapo Regional Headquarters in Heidelberg, Germany, where he established a reputation as a fierce hunter of Jews.

Corporal Benjamin Becker: the young aide-de-camp for Bruno Kassler.

Reichsführer Heinrich Himmler: the feared chief of the Gestapo, the secret police of the Nazi regime.

Werner Heisenberg: A winner of the 1932 Nobel Prize for his discoveries in quantum physics, Dr. Heisenberg was in charge of the research program behind the construction of an atomic bomb at the University of Heidelberg.

Joseph Engel: a twenty-seven-year-old physicist working under Professor Heisenberg at the University of Heidelberg.

Eric Hofstadler: a Swiss dairy farmer in his mid-twenties who's in love with Gabi Mueller.

Captain Bill Palmer: a U.S. Army Air Corps pilot who managed to land his damaged B-24 Liberator in Switzerland instead of being shot down over Germany. He is being interned with other American and British pilots in Davos, away from the population centers and high up in the Alps.

Andreas and Willy Mueller: the younger twin brothers of Gabi and guards at the internment camp for American and British pilots in Davos because of their fluency in English.

1

Waldshut, Germany
Saturday, July 29, 1944
4 p.m.

He hoped his accent wouldn't give him away.

The young Swiss kept his head down as he sauntered beneath the frescoed archways that ringed the town square of Waldshut, an attractive border town in the foothills of the southern Schwarzwald. He hopped over a foot-wide, water-filled trench that ran through the middle of the cobblestone square and furtively glanced behind to see if anyone had detected his presence.

Even though Switzerland lay just a kilometer or two away across the Rhine River, the youthful operative realized he no longer breathed free air. Though he felt horribly exposed—as if he were marching down Berlin's Kurfürstendamm screaming anti-Nazi slogans—he willed himself to remain confident. His part was a small but vital piece of the larger war effort. Yes, he risked his life, but he was not alone in his passion.

A day's drive away, American tanks drove for the heart of Paris—and quickened French hearts for *libération.* Far closer, Nazi reprisals thinned the ranks of his fellow resisters. The young man shuddered at the thought of being captured, lined up against a wall, and hearing the *click-click* of a safety being unlatched from a Nazi machine gun. Still, his legs propelled him on.

Earlier that morning, he'd introduced himself as Jean-Pierre to members of an underground cell. The French Resistance had recently stepped up their acts of sabotage after the Allies broke out of the Normandy beachhead two weeks earlier, and they'd all taken *nom de guerres* in their honor.

Inside the pocket of his leather jacket, Jean-Pierre's right hand formed a claw around a Mauser C96 semiautomatic pistol. His grip tightened, as if squeezing the gun's metallic profile would reduce the tension building in his chest. The last few minutes before an operation always came to this.

His senses peaked as he took in the sights and sounds around him. At one end of the town square, a pair of disheveled older women complained to a local farmer about the fingerling size of the potato crop. A horse-drawn carriage, transporting four galvanized tin milk containers, rumbled by while a young newsboy screamed out, *"Nachrichten!"*

The boy's right hand waved day-old copies of the *Badische Zeitung* from Freiburg, eighty kilometers to the northwest. Jean-Pierre didn't need to read the newspaper to know that more men and women were losing their lives by the minute due to the reprisals of a madman.

Though the planned mission had been analyzed from every angle, there were always uncertain factors that would affect not only the outcome of the mission but who among them would live. Or die.

Their task was to rescue a half-dozen men arrested by local authorities following the assassination attempt on Reichskanzler Adolf Hitler. If things went as Jean-Pierre hoped, the men would soon be free from the Nazis' clutches. If not, the captives' fate included an overnight trip to Berlin, via a cattle car, where they would be transported to Gestapo headquarters on Prinz-Albrecht-Strasse 8. The men would be questioned—tortured if they weren't immediately forthcoming—until names, dates, and places gushed as freely as the blood spilling upon the cold, unyielding concrete floor.

Not that revealing any secrets would save their lives. When the last bit of information had been wrung from their minds, they'd be marched against a blood-spattered wall or to the gallows equipped with well-stretched hemp rope. *May God have mercy on their souls.*

Jean-Pierre willed himself to stop thinking pessimistically. He glanced at his watch—a pricey Hanhart favored by Luftwaffe pilots. His own Swiss-made Breitling had been tucked inside a wooden box on his nightstand back home, where he had also left a handwritten letter. A love note, actually, to a woman who had captured his heart—just in case he never returned. But this was a time for war, not love. And he had to keep reminding himself of that.

Jean-Pierre slowed his gait as he left the town square and approached the town's major intersection. As he had been advised, a uniformed woman—her left arm ringed with a red armband and black swastika—directed traffic with a whistle and an attitude.

She was like no traffic cop he'd ever seen. Her full lips were colored with red lipstick. Black hair tumbled upon the shoulder epaulettes of the *Verkehrskontrolle*'s gray-green uniform. She wielded a silver-toned baton, directing a rambling assortment of horse-drawn carriages, battered sedans, and hulking military vehicles jockeying for the right of way. She looked no older than twenty-five, yet acted like she owned the real estate beneath her feet. Jean-Pierre couldn't help but let his lips curl up in a slight grin, knowing what was to come.

"*Entschuldigung, wo ist das Gemeindehaus?*" a voice said beside him. Jean-Pierre turned to the rotund businessman in the fedora and summer business suit asking for directions to City Hall.

"*Ich bin nicht sicher.*" He shrugged and was about to fashion another excuse when a military transport truck turned a corner two blocks away, approaching in their direction.

"*Es tut mir Leid.*" With a wave, Jean-Pierre excused himself and sprinted toward the uniformed traffic officer. In one quick motion, his Mauser was drawn.

He didn't break stride as he tackled the uniformed woman

to the ground. Her scream blasted his ear, and more cries from onlookers chimed in.

Jean-Pierre straddled the frightened traffic officer and pressed the barrel of his pistol into her forehead. Her shrieking immediately ceased.

"Don't move, and nothing will happen to you."

Jean-Pierre glanced up as he heard the mud-caked transport truck skid to a stop fifty meters from them.

A Wehrmacht soldier hopped out. *"Halt!"* He clumsily drew his rifle to his right shoulder.

Jean-Pierre met the soldier's eyes and rolled off the female traffic officer.

A shot rang out. The German soldier's body jerked, and a cry of pain erupted from his lips. He clutched his left chest as a rivulet of blood stained his uniform.

"Nice shot, Suzanne." Jean-Pierre jumped to his feet, glancing at the traffic cop, her stomach against the asphalt with her pistol drawn.

Suzanne rose from the ground, crouched, and aimed. Her pistol, which had been hidden in an ankle holster, was now pointed at the driver behind the windshield. The determined look in her gaze was one Jean-Pierre had come to know well.

One, two, three shots found their mark, shattering the truck's glass into shards. The driver slumped behind the wheel.

As expected, two Wehrmacht soldiers jumped out of the back of the truck and took cover behind the rear wheels. Before Jean-Pierre had a chance to take aim, shots rang out from a second-story window overlooking the intersection. The German soldiers crumbled to the cobblestone pavement in a heap.

"Los jetzt!" He clasped Suzanne's hand, and they sprinted to the rear of the truck. Two black-leather-coated members of their resistance group had already beaten them there. Jean-Pierre couldn't remember their names, but it didn't matter.

What mattered was the safety of the prisoners in the truck. Jean-Pierre only hoped the contact's information had been correct.

With a deep breath, he lifted the curtain and peered into the truck. A half-dozen frightened men sat on wooden benches with hands raised. Their wide eyes and dropped jaws displayed their fear.

"Don't shoot!" one cried.

The sound of a police siren split the air.

"Everyone out!" Jean-Pierre shouted. "I'll take this one. The rest of you, go with them." He pointed the tip of his Mauser at the men in leather jackets.

The sirens increased in volume as the speeding car gobbled up distance along the Hauptstrasse, weaving through the autos and pedestrians. An officer in the passenger's seat leaned out, rifle pointed.

Jean-Pierre leaned into the truck and yanked the prisoner's arm. Suzanne grabbed the other. "Move it, come on!"

Bullets from an approaching vehicle whizzed past Jean-Pierre's ear. The clearly frightened prisoner suddenly found his legs, and the three sprinted away from the speeding car.

Jean-Pierre's feet pounded the pavement, and he tugged on the prisoner's arm, urging him to run faster. He could hear the screech of the tires as the police car stopped just behind the truck. Jean-Pierre hadn't expected the local Polizei to respond so rapidly.

They needed to find cover—

More gunfire erupted, and as if reading his thoughts, Suzanne turned the prisoner toward a weathered column.

Jean-Pierre crumbled against the pillar, catching his breath. The columns provided cover, but not enough. Soon the police would be upon them. They had to make a move. Only ten steps separated them from turning the street corner and sprinting into Helmut's watch store. From there, a car waited outside the back door.

Another hail of gunfire struck the plaster. Jean-Pierre mouthed a prayer under his breath.

"Suzanne, we have to get out of here!"

She crouched into a trembling ball, all confidence gone. "They're surrounding us!" The terror in her uncertain timbre was clear. "But what can we do? We can't let them see us run into the store."

"Forget that. We have no choice!" Jean-Pierre raised his pistol and returned several volleys, firing at the two policemen perched behind a parked car.

"Listen to me," he said to Suzanne, taking his eyes momentarily off the police car. "You have to go. You take this guy, and I'll cover you. Once you turn the corner, it's just twenty more meters to Helmut's store." His hands moved as he spoke, slamming a new clip of ammunition into his pistol.

"But what if—"

"I'll join you. Now go!"

Jean-Pierre jumped from behind the protection of the column and rapidly fired several shots. One cop dared expose himself to return fire—not at Jean-Pierre but at the pair running for the corner.

No!

Jean-Pierre turned just in time to see Suzanne's body lurch. The clean hit ripped into her flesh between the shoulder blades. She staggered for a long second before dropping with a thud. The gangly prisoner didn't even look back as he disappeared around the corner.

I can't lose him, Jean-Pierre thought, remembering again the importance of this mission. Yet to chase after the prisoner meant he'd have to leave his partner behind.

Suzanne . . .

He emptied his Mauser at the hidden policemen, ducking as he scrambled toward his partner. Sweeping up her bloody form, he managed to drag her around the corner to safety.

"Go," Suzanne whispered.

"I can't leave you. Stay with me—"

18

Her eyelids fluttered. "You need to go . . ." A long breath escaped, and her gaze fixed on a distant point beyond him.

Jean-Pierre dropped to his knees and ripped open Suzanne's bloodstained woolen jacket. Her soaked chest neither rose nor fell. He swore under his breath and brushed a lock of black hair from her face.

Jean-Pierre cocked his head. Incessant gunfire filled the air. His colleagues were apparently keeping the German soldiers and local Polizei at bay, at least for the time being. He knew only a few valuable seconds remained to escape with the prisoner.

He planted a soft kiss on Suzanne's forehead. "Until we see each other in heaven," he whispered.

Jean-Pierre darted to a trash can, where the shaken prisoner had hunkered down, covering his head. The resistance fighter clutched the man's left arm and hustled him inside the watch store, pushing past two startled women. The rear door was propped open, and a black Opel four-door idled in the alley. With a few quick steps, they were inside the vehicle.

Before the rear door was shut, the driver jerked the car into gear, and the Opel roared down the tight alley. The door slammed shut, and Jean-Pierre glanced back. No one followed. The car merged onto a busier street, and only then did Jean-Pierre sink in his seat and close his eyes.

Soon they'd arrive at a safe house pitched on the Rhine River. And later, with the dark night sky as their protection, a skiff would sneak them into the warm arms of Mother Switzerland—a skiff piloted by the mentor who'd recruited him. His *nom de guerre*: Pascal.

Jean-Pierre's mission would soon be complete, but at what cost? Another agent—a good woman and a friend—had been sacrificed.

He had followed orders for the greater good, to save the life of a nameless prisoner. He only hoped this mission was worth it.

2

The scent of fresh-baked bread drifted through the cracked door to Gabi Mueller's bedroom. Her mother hummed softly as she stirred the diced potatoes cooking in oleomargarine, and the increased creaking of her father's rocking chair told Gabi dinner would soon be announced. Her father always rocked faster, in anticipation, as her mother set the food on the table.

Gabi frowned, flipping stray locks of her blonde, shoulder-length hair away from her eyes.

"Don't be late, Andrietta," she muttered to herself. She straightened her full skirt over her lap and readjusted her collar. Then she mindlessly picked up a sandpaper nail file from the pine desk her father had made for her when she was ten years old. She used the file, then glanced out her bedroom window, which provided an idyllic scene of green pasturelands. "She'll be on time—she will," she stated with feigned confidence.

The only way, though, that she could tell if Andrietta Lansel was indeed strolling down the country road would be to look out the kitchen window—something Gabi wasn't about to do since that would only raise her mother's suspicion.

"Gabi, supper! Hurry now, we don't want the potatoes to get co—" The bang of the heavy oven door closing overwhelmed her mother's words.

Timing is everything, Andrietta. Gabi closed her eyes and

felt the fine grain of sandpaper slide over her already tender fingertips. Not her nails, but rather the fleshy pads—as if she were attempting to sand away her very fingerprints, preparing them for the work ahead.

She'd been dressed and ready to go for the last half hour, but her stomach had rumbled all afternoon since lunch at work had been rather sparse: a simple *grüner salat* and turnips from the garden garnished with a slice of day-old *Roggenbrot*. What she would give for a feathery tuft of Parisienne baguette topped with a dollop of creamy butter and backyard honey. Ever since the federal government ordained rationing in 1941, staples had been in short supply—or hoarded by certain families. Meat, cheese, milk, eggs, sugar—even chocolate—could only be purchased with monthly ration coupons and Swiss francs in hand.

Now, the scents of fresh bread and cooking potatoes caused hunger pangs to grip her tender stomach. Anxiety rose in her throat. All afternoon, she'd fought against thinking about her first "black" assignment, which she couldn't reveal to a soul. Even Andrietta had no idea that the initial step of the plan began with her.

"Gabi! *Mir chönned ässe!*"

"Coming," Gabi replied in English as she set the nail file on her dresser and exited her room. She rather liked replying to her parents in the opposite language they addressed her. It was a game she played, and one she was verbally adroit at since she had grown up as the daughter of an American father and a Swiss mother.

"Hello, Papi," she said brightly. He held the front section of the *Basler Zeitung* chest high. "Anything new in the war today?"

Her father set the afternoon newspaper on his lap. "There are rumors of mass executions following the assassination attempt on that mongrel Hitler. Says in this article that the border guards have noticed a recent influx of refugees, political or otherwise, trying to get into Switzerland."

"I heard that at work too."

Ernst Mueller cast a disapproving glance her way. "You know you're not supposed to tell us anything you hear at work. Loose lips sink ships, and all that."

She stayed in English. "I-I didn't mean anything by it. After all, i-if it's in the papers—"

"I'm just giving you a hard time. But you . . . me . . . everyone has to watch their tongues these days. Spies are everywhere."

Her father had that right. She mindlessly brushed her fingers through her hair. *If he only knew . . .*

"Dinner's on the table," Thea Mueller sang out—this time in English.

"Was git's z'nacht?" Gabi slipped into Baseldeutsch—the Swiss-German dialect favored by those living in the Basel region. *What's for dinner?*

"Still playing your silly game, I see," her mother teased. "Well, if you don't sit down, I'll feed your potatoes to Seppli." Thea petted the family's Yorkshire terrier on the head. "You'd love to eat Gabi's dinner, wouldn't you?"

"Mami, don't!"

"Of course not." They sat down at a rectangular table with bench seating built into the wall—more handiwork from her father's capable hands. Her mother set a bowl of steaming potatoes in the center and warm Brötli rolls from the oven. A rectangular bar of yellow butter sat on a ceramic bed of painted flowers.

"We have butter!" Gabi exclaimed. "I thought—"

"Your friend Eric dropped it by this afternoon while you were at work." Her mother attempted to hide a smile. "Said they had plenty at the farm."

"Oh," Gabi replied nonchalantly as her parents exchanged knowing looks. "That was kind of him."

"He sure seems sweet on you."

"Mami! Quit teasing!"

"I'll say the blessing." Her father offered a sly grin, then bowed his head to pray. "Dear heavenly Father, I thank you for the wonderful meal tonight, especially the fresh rolls and butter, because we know there are many people going hungry. We ask that you watch over Andreas and Willy as they continue to serve this country. Keep them safe, Lord, as we live in these perilous times. Amen."

Thea opened her eyes and passed the salad bowl. "I'm just glad they got transferred away from the border. Too much action for a mother's heart, I can assure you."

Gabi slid her cloth napkin out of a silver ring and set it on her lap, smoothing it and resisting the urge to look over her shoulder toward the door. "Did we receive a letter from one of the twins today?"

"Not today. They must be awful busy up in the mountains, guarding those American pilots." Her father took a large bite of bread and slowly chewed. "It seems like every other day a B-17 nicked by German flak manages to limp to one of our airfields. At least Andreas and Willy's English skills are coming in handy."

"Guard them from escaping?" Gabi flattened a potato with her fork. "Why aren't the pilots free to go?"

"Because of Switzerland's history of neutrality. Our policy is to intern downed Allied fliers 'for the duration'—as they say—because the Swiss government doesn't want to antagonize Berlin. We import half our food from Germany, you know."

"I wish we had some more butter in those imports," Gabi said lightheartedly, despite her aching gut that churned with worries about Andrietta.

"Let's not complain," Thea interjected. "We're not due another five hundred grams until next Tuesday. I used my last ration coupon to make that chocolate cake for your brothers."

"No complaints, Mami. I know that's just the way things are. Besides, it was nice to see the boys, if only for one day." Gabi recalled how Andreas's face lit up when he saw his favorite *Schoggichüche*.

Her father spread raspberry preserves on the fresh bread. "Your mother spent days picking wild berries to make this jam, and the rolls are very good, even without Eric's butter. I don't think Andreas and Willy are having fresh bread and jam in the Alps tonight."

"Papi, I wasn't complaining!" Eager to change the subject, she smiled at her father. "Anything happen at work today?"

For as long as Gabi could remember, her father had pastored a church that met in the back of a local restaurant on Sunday mornings. To support the family, he constructed wood furniture during the week with painstakingly precise craftsmanship that was much sought after.

"Two more orders for bunk beds came in. I guess some families are taking in refugees. Our justice minister in Bern keeps telling the newspapers that 'the lifeboat is full,' but how can you turn away desperate Jews when they land at your doorstep? It's horrible that our authorities escort families back to the border and hand them over to the Nazis. A shame."

"What about us, Papi?"

"Take in a family? Good question. If we ever got a knock in the middle of the night, how could we not? Remember Jesus' story of the Good Samaritan? We should do no less when somebody's life is in danger."

Gabi's fork penetrated her second potato when a heavy pounding sounded at their front entrance.

"Maybe I spoke too soon." Ernst Mueller stood from the dinner table. He opened the front door to the sight of a lanky young woman in a black skirt and white dress shirt. A long braid of brown hair flipped over her shoulder.

"Andrietta, so good to see you. You've come just in time. Won't you join us for supper?"

"Sorry, Herr Mueller, actually I was hoping Gabi could join me at the Hirschen." Andrietta swayed from side to side, the hem of her skirt brushing against their doormat. "I got a promotion at work today and can't wait to celebrate."

"Nonsense. Why spend a few francs on food and drink

when a fine meal waits. I insist you join us." He motioned toward the table, set with china and sterling silver.

"Thank you for the kind offer, but I've eaten already." Andrietta's eyes sparkled. "We had something special to-night—bread and potatoes."

"Then I guess you wouldn't want what Thea's serving," he muttered with a smile. "But come in anyway."

Gabi stood to greet their guest. Her heart resumed its quickened pounding.

"*Hoi*, Andrietta. How are you?" Gabi bussed her friend once on each cheek.

"So nice to see you." Andrietta fingered her braid. "But I see I'm early."

"No, you're not. I'm done." Gabi pushed aside the plate after finishing the last few bites of food. "Ready to go?"

"Aren't you going to give us a hint of what time you'll return?" her mother asked.

"I'm twenty-four years old." She smiled, glancing at her father.

Ernst Mueller cocked an eyebrow. "This is true, but you know that your mother and I still worry, and we always will—even when your hair is as gray as mine."

"Papi, please. We're fully grown women with stressful jobs who just need a little time off every now and then. I wouldn't be out until dawn. I promise. Besides . . ." She wrinkled her nose and peered up into her father's soft brown eyes. "I promise to ask Eric to walk me home. Deal?"

Pastor Mueller patted her shoulder. "Fine. Go. Have fun. But next time make plans so we don't have to rush through dinner."

Gabi poked her father's slight stomach paunch, attempting not to wince as her raw fingertips caught against the rough wool of his shirt. "Oh, I'm sure you'll take care of that." She placed a kiss on his bearded cheek.

"Don't wait up," she called over her shoulder, hurrying out the door.

25

With quickened footsteps the two women hustled down the pathway to the road in silence. When they reached the pavement and rounded the first curve, Andrietta paused, glanced up into the sky, which just hinted of dusk, and made the sign of the cross.

"Mercy. Jesus, Mary, and Joseph, I swear I've never seen a finer performance in any of those American films you insist on me watching with you at the *Kino*. Lying to your Reverend father, of all things!"

"Lying? I don't think so. You did get a promotion, and I *will* ask Eric to walk me home, later." Gabi intertwined her arm with her friend's as a truck rumbled past. "And it *is* a celebration that we are grown up enough to venture out on our own for the evening. How many nights did we hide under the quilt and whisper about the day when we'd be able to spend a night on the town?"

"Yes, but while I'm sitting in a dark restaurant, you'll be off meeting up with a handsome admirer. I just wish you'd tell me who he is."

Gabi patted her friend's arms. "In due time, Andrietta, I promise. Have I ever had a secret that I didn't eventually confess to you?"

3

The Schlagerkapelle band had finished their second set when Gabi patted her friend's hand. Mouthing a *merci vielmol*, she slipped away from their table. She stepped aside as a heavyset waitress rambled past hefting three foamy glasses of Warteck in each hand. The Swiss government knew better than to ration beer, she thought.

Gabi glided into the lobby, then slipped outside unnoticed. The summer air remained warm at this hour. A few shafts of muted moonlight managed to maneuver into the narrow alley between the theater and the business offices next door.

With cautious steps, she hurried toward the back of the building and unbuttoned her skirt at the waist as she moved along. Looking back to ensure she hadn't been followed, Gabi ducked into a small alcove and slid off her skirt. Her sweater quickly followed, and then her white-collared blouse, revealing the slim, black slacks and black undershirt she'd purchased just for this mission.

With a kerchief she'd knotted around her leg under her skirt, she quickly tied up her hair the best she could. A stocking cap would have done better, but for the life of her, Gabi hadn't been able to figure out how she could have hidden one on herself without drawing attention to the extra lump of fabric.

Letting out a slow breath, Gabi tucked one last strand of hair into the kerchief and stepped into an alley.

"Identification papers, *bitte*," a gruff voice demanded from out of nowhere.

Gabi spun on her heels, only to see the smirk on the face of Dieter Baumann.

"I thought I was supposed to meet you around the corner, Herr Baumann."

"You were. I was just checking up. In fact, I was nursing a half liter of *Bier* at the Hirschen while you yapped away with your girlfriend. I hope you weren't talking about work."

"She doesn't even know I work for the OSS."

"Good girl. That's the way Mr. Dulles prefers things. But he must have seen something special in you to give you this assignment. I can't recall someone from the translation pool ever being involved in a covert operation before. But that is to your credit." Dieter Baumann flashed a toothy smile.

Gabi frowned. One moment he spoke to her as a child; the next he poured on the charm like Clark Gable. Dieter Baumann kept a desk vis-à-vis the translation pool, but he had ignored her until the day Allen Dulles, the head of the Office of Strategic Services, paid a visit from the American Legation in Bern. Dulles had invited her into a private office and proceeded to interview her about her background, her political leanings, and yes, even her religious beliefs. She explained that as the daughter of an American father and a Swiss mother—and holder of dual passports—she felt a deep allegiance to the Allied cause. If she could be of help in the translation pool, translating whatever was handed to her in German and typing up the English translation on a well-used Krupp manual, then that work suited her fine. If there were other duties asked of her, she would willingly comply.

She recalled the way Allen Dulles, who looked like he was in his early fifties, leaned back in his leather chair and turned his gaze to the window overlooking the Rhine River that wended its way through Basel. "Miss Mueller, you understand that our job is to provide Washington with information we deem important."

Gabi nodded, wondering what was coming next. She knew all along the OSS—Office of Strategic Services—was, for all intents and purposes, a spy organization. She didn't really feel like she was involved in espionage since her low-level job involved shuffling papers and typing up reports, but nonetheless, the organization she worked for was trafficking secrets— ones that could determine the war's outcome.

"The rumor walking the halls is that you have an overlooked talent."

Gabi blushed and glanced away.

"Now here, Miss Mueller, there's no reason to hide your talent under a bushel. Perhaps there is a way we can tap into it. I must state at the outset, though, what I'm suggesting will be more dangerous than your translation work but eminently more satisfying."

And that's how she found herself in the company of Dieter Baumann, the dark-haired man assigned as her handler. Dieter had to be one of the most handsome men she knew. Not only was he tall and broad-shouldered, but his light blue eyes spoke of passion for his work that Gabi envied. From first hearing of this meeting, she'd secretly wished Dieter had offered to meet her inside, in full view of Andrietta. What would her friend think of her keeping company with such a man?

"My car is around the corner. You can leave your extra clothes with me." Dieter's words interrupted her thoughts.

Ten minutes later, they arrived in Basel's Altstadt, or Old Town. Since the spring of 1940, when German Panzers and Nazi shock troops stormed into the Lowland countries and France, Basel had been under nighttime blackout restrictions. Now only a few muted lights escaped the shuttered windows.

"You have the key?" Baumann asked.

Gabi reached into the top of her shirt and pulled out a silver key hanging on a piece of string. The enormity of her first mission suddenly weighed on her shoulders. She inhaled and blew air through her lips. "I'm not sure I can do this."

"Listen, everyone gets the jitters first time out." Baumann's smile caused the knots in her shoulders to loosen.

He handed her a canvas bag with a flashlight. "Remember how we brought four safes into the office for a big test—and you cracked each one? I'm sure you can do it again. You have plenty of time. We tailed the German this afternoon but lost him when he crossed the border. His usual pattern isn't to return for twenty-four hours, so you shouldn't be bothered." He patted her hand. "If you take longer than a half hour, though, I'll check up on you."

Gabi nodded, taking in the strength from her handler's cause. "Sorry. I'll hurry."

She alighted from Baumann's car and walked purposefully to the front door of the modest home. She grasped the door handle, then felt for the keyhole and found it. A hefty shoulder would probably bust the door wide open, but signs of forced entry would compromise the mission.

Gabi's fingers trembled slightly as she unloosed the key from her neck, noticing the key was still warm from her flesh. Then silently she slid the key into the keyhole and turned, unlocking the door with a small click.

That was the easy part.

Gabi slipped the key back around her neck and stepped inside, closing the door behind her and relocking it. She waited a few seconds, then reached inside the canvas bag for the flashlight. With barely a sound, Gabi moved through the maze of desks and cabinets, wastebaskets and chairs, to a rear bedroom with windows overlooking a quiet street. Outside, through the thin curtain, she could make out a couple walking their dog. A shiver traveled through her shoulders at the realization of where she was and what would happen if she were caught. She turned off her flashlight.

A nosy neighbor could spot her rummaging around at any time. Then what a mess would she be in? Gabi swept those fearful thoughts from her mind and continued with her jaw set in determination. Her work mattered—besides, Dieter was just outside the building, backing her up.

Gabi turned the flashlight back on and set it on the desk, pointing to the safe. She then moved to the back wall. Cautiously, she removed a framed print of a pastoral mountain scene—a kitschy rendition of the Matterhorn—and turned her attention to the safe hidden behind it. She was familiar with this safe—a case-hardened, wrought-iron TL 6 with anti-blowpipe protection. Most safecrackers would need sixty minutes to break into such a safe with tools and drills. She planned to take a lot less time by "manipulating" the combination lock.

Her eyes fluttered shut, and she placed her tender fingertips on the dial, turning ever so slowly. Her fingertips listened for subtle clicks and bumps—any change in tension. Her whole concentration focused on the tactile edges of her fingers. In her mind's eye she pictured the slip-clutches catching and the wheel lock lining up in grooves. Slowly to the right—there it was, so slight the slip. Then to the left, then right again.

Her eyes popped open in surprise at the final click and the swinging motion of the safe door opening. Sweeping up a stack of papers, she moved back toward the large wooden desk and slid underneath, grabbing the flashlight from the desk and setting it on the floor. Her cupped hand directed the beam as she glanced at her booty.

Bank statements.

Mortgage deeds.

Certificates of authenticity.

Everything's here.

She paused at a sheet of paper that listed two columns of words, handwritten. Gabi scanned several printed words in the first column.

Schnitzel

Brass

Garden

Helmut

Mincemeat

The words—twelve in all—continued on, yet they made no sense.

"Oh, well," she whispered. "If they think this is worth me risking my life for, it must be something good."

She slid the paper on the top of the stack and read through the words until they were committed to memory. She knew that her mission wasn't to copy them down. Not here. Not at home. But tomorrow in the safe room in the OSS offices.

First, though, she needed to get out of there. Gabi returned the papers, shut the safe, and readjusted the framed print to the wall. *Oh, yes . . . and to think of some romantic story to keep Andrietta at bay.*

"*Guten abend.*" A German-accented voice spoke from the shadows.

A chill traveled up her spine and she turned quickly—just in time to see the form of a large man lunging at her. A shoulder plowed into her chest, and a cry escaped with her breath. Pain exploded through her, and she felt herself falling as the power of the large man propelled her to the ground. His full weight pressed on her stomach, knocking the wind out of her.

Breathe. Fight. Breathe, she urged herself.

Her arms and legs flailed, but the attacker clasped both wrists and flipped her over on her stomach, pinning her arms behind her back. It all happened so quickly. He wrenched her arms, causing a searing pain to rush through her shoulders.

Don't give up. Fight. Fight. The faces of her family members flashed through her thoughts, and she knew she could not give up. Where was Dieter?

She continued to thrash about, attempting to free herself, when a leather-clad hand covered her mouth. Panic shot through every cell as a second hand reached around and clasped her throat. The man's fingers tightened, choking the air from her lungs. *Dear God!*

Gabi bit into one of the fingers over her mouth, sinking her teeth deep.

"Aagh!"

The grip released.

She turned long enough to see a swing of his right arm. Gabi buried her face in her hands, preparing for the blow. His fist ricocheted off her skull and slammed into the parquet floor. The man screamed a second time.

Pain shot through Gabi's head, and a rush of nausea rose in her throat. She jerked back, preparing to fight him off, when she heard another pained cry. This one louder than before. Her assailant stumbled above her, a stunned look on his face.

Gabi lifted her gaze, and her heart leapt as she noticed Dieter standing just behind the man. Raised over Dieter's head, a tire iron glimmered in the dim glow from the flashlight.

She watched as Dieter swung again, and the second blow slammed against the assailant's back. The large man staggered once before crashing against the desk. Dieter advanced, swinging wildly and making contact with the man's shins. Another scream split the air, followed by curses, as the man sunk to his knees.

"Let's go!" Baumann extended a hand to Gabi, then he windmilled the tire iron toward the man in a threatening manner, as if daring him to make a move.

Gabi rose from the ground, ran out of the room, out of the house, and sprinted for the car. As clear as the pain radiating through her, she knew her life as a simple pastor's daughter would never be the same.

4

Sturmbannführer Bruno Kassler glanced at the framed photographs on the beige walls of his high-ceilinged office. The steely gazes on the portrait of Himmler to his left, and the autocratic Führer to his right, prompted the Gestapo bureau chief to wonder if the walls also had eyes . . . or ears.

He figured they did.

He reached for the top folder from one of the large stacks on his desk. Each folder contained sensitive material, and it was his job to find yet another traitor to be pruned from their midst. The bureau chief rubbed his eyes as the words before him blurred. How many hours had he pored through them? How many more would it still take?

A distinctive rap sounded on his door. Kassler cocked his head, knowing his underling, Corporal Becker, waited on the other side. The pause between the second and third knock was characteristic of the twenty-year-old Heidelberger whose Adam's apple stuck out so far that Kassler wondered if his throat did the knocking.

"Come in," Kassler grunted.

Corporal Becker swung the door open and struggled to roll a mahogany table inside Kassler's rectangular office. Becker shoved the table inside and worked it in next to his superior's Biedermeier three-drawer desk and trio of lacquered chairs.

"*Guten morgen*, Major." Becker patted the sturdy lockbox that sat on the rolling table. "As you requested, I have pulled the remaining dossiers of those working at the University of Heidelberg." The corporal straightened his shoulders with pride.

Kassler surveyed his desktop, noting the dossiers he still had to go through. "There's more?"

Kassler ran both hands through his slick black hair and considered mentioning he hadn't allowed himself the luxury of a Sunday off since Stauffenberg and his band of murderous turncoats had unleashed their violent attack on the Führer. Yet complaining would do little good.

He wearily reached for several dossiers. "Let's see what you've found." The top two were of no interest, but the third was marked *Bonhoeffer, Karl Friedrich*. The Gestapo chief opened its contents and scanned the report. *Midthirties. Professor of physical chemistry at the University of Heidelberg. Recently transferred from the University of Leipzig.*

"Hmm," he muttered. The name Bonhoeffer rang a bell.

"Think of something, sir?" Becker swallowed, his Adam's apple bobbing.

"This name Bonhoeffer. Do you recognize it?"

Becker relaxed. "Karl Bonhoeffer has a brother named Dietrich who was arrested last year for helping Jews escape to Switzerland. He also played a key leadership role in the Confessing Church."

"The what?"

"Surely, you remember, Major. Members of the clergy who've opposed the policies of our Führer—especially the National Socialists' treatment of the . . . *Juden*." Becker spat the last word.

"*Ja*, of course." Kassler glanced down at the dossier. His weary limbs gained strength as zeal to please Berlin surged through him. "Does this Karl Bonhoeffer share the same views?" He sat straighter in his chair.

Becker stiffened to attention, locking his arms behind his back. "Apparently not. He was questioned thoroughly by the Sicherheitsdienst before he was allowed to work under Herr Doktor Heisenberg and—"

"Heisenberg?" Kassler interrupted. His heartbeat quickened as he recalled the name. Just three months ago, Heisenberg and his brainy scientists had moved from the University of Berlin to Heidelberg because of intense Allied bombing raids. According to a colleague in the German capital, Heisenberg's team was secreted away to the University of Heidelberg because they were working on a *Wunderwaffe*—a wonder weapon—that would guarantee a victory for National Socialism. With the American and British forces breaking out of the Normandy beachhead, and the Eastern Front getting closer to the Fatherland, the need for such a weapon increased by the day.

"And these dossiers . . . are they all for those working under Doktor Heisenberg?" Kassler patted the pile.

"Yes, sir."

"Yes, well, perhaps they may be slightly more interesting than the others. Although, I doubt they'll amount to much." Kassler steepled his fingers, leaning forward on his desk, and feigned boredom. But he could tell Becker wasn't fooled. The young man leaned forward, as if hoping to gain a glimpse into Bonhoeffer's file.

Kassler shut the file and waved the young corporal away. "Thanks for your help. You are dismissed. I'll glance over these while you retrieve the next set."

Becker clicked the heels of his leather boots and snapped a stiff-armed salute. "Heil Hitler!"

Kassler half-raised his right arm. "Heil Hitler," he said, as his subordinate turned on his heels.

The door closed with a loud thud and a click, and Kassler's shoulders tightened. A huge lump formed in his throat as he returned his attention to the stack of dossiers. He knew as a Gestapo major that digging out the dirt on possible opponents to the Führer was his duty. But more than that, due diligence could also lead to his glory.

His chest swelled at the remembrance of the crowd's roar at the last rally, lifting their voices and their arms in high salute. Heat expanded within Kassler's chest even more as he imagined being one of the men chosen to stand by Hitler's side. Surely, someone who discovered a high-level traitor would receive such an honor, even someone as young as him, not even in his thirties.

If he could not unlock the power of the Führer, at least he could hold the keys for a while and feel their weight.

Kassler flipped through Bonhoeffer's file once again, seeing nothing of importance. He set it down and perused the next set of folders. Something in the third dossier caught his eye.

Engel, Joseph
Born 7 April, 1917
A1918

Kassler buzzed his young assistant, who stepped in right away.

"Yes, sir?" Becker inquired.

"This A1918? What does it mean?"

"May I take a look?"

Becker walked around to the side of the desk. "An *A* before the year means that the person was adopted that year."

The hair on the back of Kassler's neck lifted. His mind clicked into a higher gear, and he had a strong hunch there was more to this adoption—more that needed to be uncovered. His co-workers often called Kassler's intuition pure luck, but he believed he'd been gifted with a sixth sense to know when something was amiss. And so far, following this sense had yet to lead him astray.

"So Engel was adopted in 1918. Do we have any information on that?"

"No, it appears not." Becker took the liberty of flipping through a few pages of the dossier. "It states here that he attended Spandau Schule for kindergarten and the primary grades. That is in western Berlin. His parents were Thomas and Eva Engel."

"I can read. And I know where Spandau is!" Kassler waved Becker away, and the younger man hurried from the room, again closing the door behind him. Kassler picked up the phone. "Fräulein, get me the Recorder's Office in Spandau. *Schnell!*"

Kassler set the handset on the broad-bottom black phone and waited to be patched through. Twenty seconds later, the Phillips phone rang.

"Hello?" He impatiently drummed his fingertips on his desk.

"Sir, did you ring? This is Fräulein Huber from the Recorder's Office."

A smile tipped his lips, and he softened his tone. The woman on the other end sounded young, beautiful, and impressionable—his favorite type. "Ah, Fräulein Huber, Sturmbannführer Bruno Kassler from the Gestapo bureau in Heidelberg. Tell me, are you able to look up adoptions in your district?"

"Yes, but my search will go faster if you can provide a name and date, sir."

"I have a name, but no exact date." He clicked his tongue. "But surely that will be hardly a problem for someone such as yourself."

Kassler heard the slightest intake of breath on the other end of the line.

"Yes, sir, and the name?"

"I would like you to look up an adoption of Joseph Engel, sometime in 1918."

"Very well, sir. I will call you back when I learn something."

Kassler set the phone back on the cradle, straightened in his chair, and continued reading Engel's file, confident that his instincts were leading him down a rewarding path.

• • • • • • • • •

University of Heidelberg Research Lab
Basement Room
10:04 a.m.

Joseph Engel readjusted his clipboard in hand, jotting down notes, as did the other half-dozen, white-coated junior physicists who circled Professor Heisenberg in rapt attention, even on this Sunday morning. To any outsider, the metallic cylinder before them, standing upright in meter-deep water, would appear as nothing of importance. But as Joseph peered into the wooden tank, his eyes widened with expectation, knowing today's events could change the history of nuclear science forever.

"Gentlemen, German physics is poised to take a momentous step forward in our research," Heisenberg began. "For months, we have worked under the assumption that slow neutrons do not have the energy to blast a nucleus apart. We are about to conduct an experiment to see if two atoms will be slightly lighter than the parent uranium atom by the equivalent of one-fifth of a proton."

Deutsche Physik. How many times had Engel heard Dr. Heisenberg proudly insert that phrase into his speech? German physics—like German literature—was the envy of the world. It was German physicists, Heisenberg lectured, who filled blackboards with mathematical symbols that won Nobel prizes. Brilliant theorists like Max Planck, Philipp Lenard, and Johannes Stark had developed quantum theory and unlocked the fundamental discoveries of atomic processes. And Joseph hoped one day his contributions would equal theirs.

Professor Heisenberg's lecture about slow neutrons droned

39

on, interrupting Joseph's thoughts. "I once heard a colleague say, 'Intellectuals solve problems, geniuses prevent them.' Gentlemen, we shall put that idea to the test today."

Joseph snapped to attention. He'd heard that quote before. Whose words were those? Then he remembered: Albert Einstein, the celebrated physicist.

Of course, Joseph thought, *Heisenberg didn't dare attach a name to the quote. Einstein was Jewish.*

Whispers in the hallway claimed Heisenberg maintained back-channel contacts with several Jewish physicists and mathematicians who'd fled across the Atlantic and resettled in America. These distinguished scientists had lost their teaching posts shortly after Hitler became German chancellor in 1933. With a stroke of a pen, all Jews were banned from government posts within days of Hitler's installation. Since universities were state institutions, anyone Jewish was driven off like an uninvited guest.

Many of Germany's best and brightest—scientists like Victor Weisskopf and Fritz Reiche—quietly fled with their families to academic institutions like Oxford University outside London or Princeton University in New Jersey, where they resumed their research on atomic particles. Of course, Joseph had also heard that those who—for one reason or another—had remained behind until Germany invaded Poland now found different work at "relocation" camps like Auschwitz-Birkenau and Treblinka. Camps that had whispered rumors all their own.

Joseph shook those stories from his head and turned his attention back to his professor.

"This morning, we are continuing our experiment with atomic piles," Heisenberg noted in a professorial voice. "This aluminum cylinder, which we are calling C-12, contains powdered uranium metal set in heavy water from Norway, which is acting as a moderator."

"The water appears to be quite hot," a junior physicist piped up. Joseph couldn't remember his colleague's name, but he could see excitement in the man's eyes. Joseph peered closer into the cylinder and discovered the man was right. Joseph's heartbeat quickened at the thought that today *could* be the day his career had prepared him for.

"Yes, the temperature has been rising steadily over the last twenty-four hours, which is why I've called everyone here." Heisenberg's voice rose with enthusiasm. "I've asked Doktor Schumann to look into it. This morning, he tested the escaping gas from the cylinder and found it to be hydrogen. We concluded water must have leaked inside."

"What do you propose to do?" another junior physicist inquired, pushing his glasses up the bridge of his nose.

Heisenberg's lips curled with the slightest hint of a smile, and he ran a hand through his sandy hair. "What else can we do? We will remove the cover of the C-12 cylinder and inspect the uranium oxide. Perhaps there has been some type of spontaneous fission. Doktor Schumann?"

Schumann put on heavy gloves, attached a chain-link pulley to the aluminum cylinder, and turned a crank. Centimeter by centimeter the cylinder rose. The room was silent. Every eye fixed. Every ear cocked. As Schumann swiveled the cylinder, a sudden hiss escaped.

Next to Joseph, Heisenberg removed an unlit pipe from his mouth, jaw dropping.

"Must be air rushing into a vacuum." Gingerly, Schumann maneuvered the cylinder to the edge of the tank. Eager to see if their guess had been correct, he unscrewed the cylinder top. Licks of blue flame shot out, and gasps filled the room.

Even bigger gasps erupted as the flames were followed by uranium particles spewing from the cylinder, landing on Schumann's white lab coat.

"Watch out!" someone called.

With a gasp, Schumann looked down. "No!" Releasing the chain, his hands fumbled with the buttons on his coat.

"Don't let go!" Joseph reached for the chain, but it was too late. With a splash, the aluminum cylinder crashed into the tub of heavy water. Steam rose from the tank, and the water turned from clear to a yellowish hue. Joseph's colleagues glanced at each other with wide-eyed looks of concern.

"Oxygen must have seeped into the sphere before Schumann uncapped it." Heisenberg stepped up to the tank and peered into the water. "And—" The hissing of steam rising and the quivering of the aluminum cylinder interrupted his words.

Everything within Joseph told him to run, but his scientific curiosity got the better of him. For several moments, the gentle shaking persisted until it suddenly turned violent. The precious heavy water splashed over the edge and onto the floor as if an earthquake rumbled beneath the wooden tank.

"*Los jetzt!*" Schumann shouted. Joseph didn't have to be told twice. He sprinted for the heavy metal door separating the basement laboratory from the hallway and stairs. The others tailed him.

Joseph yanked hard, pulling the door open, and waved the others past.

Heisenberg looked more perturbed than worried. Still, Joseph noticed he didn't mince steps. The professor and Schumann rushed out, and Joseph ducked through the door, shutting it hard. While the others sprinted up the stairwell, Schumann reached for a set of keys inside his lab coat.

"You go ahead!" Schumann called in the mayhem, waving Joseph on.

Joseph raced for the stairway, but just before he took the first step, he glanced back and noticed Schumann scrambling to find the right key for the lock.

Joseph motioned to him. "Leave it. Leave it. We have to get out of here!"

After several precious seconds, Schumann stuffed the keys into his pocket and sprinted toward Joseph.

Schumann had nearly reached the stairs when a concussive blast flattened the metal door and knocked Joseph to his knees. Schumann sprawled to the floor. Noxious smoke filled

42

the hallway. Joseph labored for air and rubbed his stinging eyes.

"Schumann, Engel, *raus*!" Professor Heisenberg called from the flight ahead.

"Coming!" Joseph jumped to his feet. Schumann regained his footing. They scurried up the stairs two by two until they caught up with Heisenberg at the top of the landing.

"What happened? What caused that, sir?" Joseph panted, hands on his knees. He glanced up at his professor.

"The only thing I'm sure of is, we're closer to smashing an atom!" Heisenberg's voice rose with excitement. "Can you believe it? We're closer than ever!"

Joseph whistled through his teeth, stuffing his quivering hands into his pockets. Being the first to harness nuclear fission meant victory on the battlefield—and salvation from surrender.

5

The phone call from the Recorder's Office in Spandau came after lunch.

"Excuse me for the delay, Major Kassler, but I found the adoption certificate for one Joseph Engel attached to the back of his birth certificate." The clerk's voice hesitated slightly.

"And—" Kassler's fingers tightened around the receiver.

"The certificate notes that the boy was originally named Joseph Cohn—C-o-h-n."

A Yiddish surname. Kassler tapped his finger on the top of the file. "Can you tell me who the mother and father were?"

"Abraham and Hena Cohn," the clerk said.

"If the boy was adopted, what happened to the parents?" The Gestapo major flipped through the file with his free hand.

"I anticipated your question, Herr Major. I searched Vital Records and found death certificates for Abraham Cohn and Hena Cohn. They died within a week of each other in April 1918. Cause of death: Spanish flu."

Kassler was too young to personally recall the worldwide influenza pandemic of 1918–1919 that killed many more soldiers than the gruesome trench warfare of the Lost War, but he'd learned about the epidemic in primary school. Some

44

of his classmates had even lost a parent to the deadly viral infection.

"Fräulein Huber, I'm quite impressed with your efforts, and I will make note of that to your superiors. In the meantime, I need one more bit of information. Can you determine if the Cohn parents were members of a synagogue while they were still alive?"

"I don't think that should be a problem, Herr Major. I will need a little time, however."

"Very good. Please call when you have retrieved the information. And may I remind you that this request needs to stay confidential. It could be vital in the war effort."

Kassler gently returned the handset and allowed a satisfied smile to blossom. If his hunch was correct, this Engel character was as Jewish as the Twelve Apostles.

* * * * * * * *

University of Heidelberg
Main Lecture Hall
1:58 p.m.

Joseph Engel found a seat in the second row of the cavernous lecture hall as others streamed in, scurrying to their places. The small "blast" generated in the basement that morning had been the raging topic at the canteen. The lecture hall buzzed with junior physicists debating how it happened and what it meant to the future of the atomic research program.

Joseph glanced up as Professor Heisenberg strode to a desk situated in front of two blackboards—one of which contained equations from yesterday's lecture. Wearing his customary beige tweed suit, white shirt, and thin blue tie, Heisenberg set his glasses on the table and ran his right hand through his sandy hair. He looked up from his notes; the cue to cease chatting produced an expectant hush.

"Gentlemen, we move forward," proclaimed Professor

Heisenberg. "Our long-range efforts to separate plutonium from the parent uranium took a step backward today, but until we can build a suitable reactor, that will always be the case."

Heisenberg knitted his hands behind his back and strode across the room. "Nonetheless, our experiments in the last month have clearly established that a uranium machine is capable of multiplying neutrons, taking us closer to nuclear fission."

Joseph opened a notebook and glanced at several quantum equations the team had been working on.

"This afternoon, I would like to discuss *Energiegewinnung aus Uran*, a report prepared by Herr Engel regarding the energy production of uranium and the details of plutonium production necessary to produce ten to one hundred kilograms of fissionable material."

Joseph glanced up, surprised to hear his name.

"After reading this remarkable report, I am convinced that we are within a year of producing a Wunderwaffe. If we can successfully separate isotopes of pure U-235, that is. Herr Engel, would you please come forward and share your remarkable revelations?"

All eyes turned in his direction, and Joseph Engel rose, humbled by the recognition. As he walked to the front, his shoulders straightened as excitement surged through his limbs over the possibility that his mathematical work could bring the team closer to harnessing atomic energy.

All eyes were on Joseph as he paused before the professor.

"Herr Engel, your equations on the start of a chain reaction intrigued me. Would you care to discuss how you arrived at your revelations with the class?" Doktor Heisenberg held out a long piece of chalk and pointed the young physicist to the empty chalkboard.

Joseph hesitated, but only for a moment. This was the first time he had been singled out, but he remembered what

Professor Heisenberg had said to him the day before: Joseph's string of theoretical equations—if borne out in the laboratory—could mean the start of a "chain reaction" leading to an energy release twenty million times stronger than a single stick of TNT. He still found the truth of that hard to believe.

He accepted the white chalk from his mentor and cleared his throat before addressing his colleagues.

"Thank you, Herr Doktor, for your gracious words as well as your confidence. Let's start with the elementary theory that each fission of an isotope of uranium-235 will produce two secondary neutrons, leading to an enormous release of energy."

Joseph turned his back to the class and looked down at his notebook, although he needn't have bothered. He had memorized the equation string, which he began writing in careful script on the blackboard. "You will notice that I've included the use of cadmium as an absorber of neutrons," Joseph said as he continued the string of numerals and variables. "I'm confident this will commence a runaway chain reaction—"

"You mean bomb," interjected a colleague from the third row. Murmurs erupted around the room.

Heisenberg stepped forward. "Herr Klein, need I remind you that our scientific research is much wider in scope than military purposes. The ability to harness the power of the atom has untold civilian applications. For example, Herr Engel has already shared with me his thoughts on the possibility of a reactor large enough to supply the power needs for a city like Berlin."

The room fell silent, and Joseph's thoughts raced. While a fancy electricity-producing plant was certainly a feasible and worthwhile goal, everyone knew that the German High Command had given Professor Heisenberg a budget to develop what was known in Berlin as an "atomic bomb." The Führer was said to be enthusiastic about a secret new explosive so powerful that it could throw a man off his horse at the distance of ten kilometers and would have such colossal force that all human life could be destroyed within a four-kilometer radius.

The professor's voice interrupted Joseph's thoughts. "Please continue, Herr Engel. Would you care to show us how you arrived at this equation?"

"Certainly, sir. Now, as I was saying . . ."

* * * * * * * *

Gestapo Regional Headquarters
Heidelberg, Germany
2:45 p.m.

Kassler gazed out the narrow window of his office, watching the passing of automobiles, the movement of people, the gentlest swaying of the trees lining the boulevard. The summer sun slanted rays of light through the window, making a rectangular pattern on the floor.

Yet even the dazzling summer afternoon couldn't brighten his dark thoughts. Deep in his gut something told him that traitors threatened the reign of the thousand-year Reich. Traitors in his power to stop . . . if only he'd get the break he needed.

He stood, paced to the window, and watched a beautiful example of an Aryan woman cross the street below. But even she did not hold his interest. He returned to his chair and flipped open the file he now knew by heart.

There has to be more to this Engel guy . . .

Though Kassler's informants at the University of Heidelberg relayed snatches of information they'd tracked down about the work being done on the wonder weapon, it wasn't much help. The rudimentary descriptions of their quantum equations dulled his brain. Still, Kassler wasn't ready to give up.

Kassler's phone rang, and he answered, tapping his fingers on the file.

Becker cleared his throat. "A young woman identifying herself as Fräulein Huber from the Recorder's Office is on the line."

"Put her on." He leaned back in his chair and let out a slow breath.

Following a click on the phone line, Kassler spoke with aloofness. "*Ja*, Fräulein Huber. Were you able to find more information?"

"I'm afraid our office doesn't hold the *Juden* files, Major Kassler. Locally, that comes under the Schutzstaffel. I made a call, but they wouldn't release the information." She let out a sigh. "I'm sorry I could not be of more help. Would you like the phone number?"

"Of course." Kassler reached for a pencil.

Within minutes, Kassler had the Spandau SS office on the line.

"I was expecting your call," a corporal said. "We have our procedures that we must follow before giving out this level of information—"

"Understood." Kassler leaned forward in his chair. He could tell from the level of formality in the corporal's voice that he'd indeed found something of interest.

"Very good. Abraham and Hena Cohn were married May 18, 1917, at the Temple Rykerstrasse in Spandau."

"Did they have any children?"

"Only one. A son Joseph was circumcised on his eighth day by a *mohel* named Rabbi Horowitz."

So Joseph Engel was a vermin after all.

Kassler willed himself to remain calm. "Very good. Is there anything else you can tell me?"

"No, sir. I could investigate the disposition of this Cohn clan. If they were shipped to the camps, we would have a record."

"That won't be necessary, Corporal. I know their whereabouts, thank you."

Two dead, one lives . . . but not for long. Not for long.

Kassler hung up the phone and leaned back in his desk chair, looking first at the portrait of the Führer and then the Reichsführer. As much as his enthusiasm propelled him to call for a crack SS unit and truck, he hesitated. Joseph Engel had no suspicion his ruse was up.

Time was on Kassler's side.

6

OSS Branch Office
Basel, Switzerland
Monday, July 31, 1944
9:45 a.m.

Gabi refused to rub the lump on the back of her head despite
the low-level throbbing. Refused to roll up the white sleeves of
her blouse in spite of the sun's rays falling on her shoulders,
lest the curious gazes of her co-workers look too closely.
The woman who'd dared to break into a safe, to put up a
fight against a man twice her size, seemed like someone in a
dream. Were it not for the bruised evidence from the man's
hands, Gabi would think the spy in the night was someone
other than herself. Instead, she continued with the job she
was hired to do, working with the intensity of one whose
employers required nothing more than her daytime hours.

With ramrod posture, Gabi consulted her dog-eared copy
of *Langenscheidt's German-English* dictionary and thumbed
through the alphabet. Ninety percent of the time, translating
the intercepts was fairly mundane and predictable: battalion
strength, petrol supplies, troop movements, and battlefield reports. But this communiqué from an informant in Heidelberg
contained a German word that she wasn't familiar with—
Strahlung.

It took her ten seconds to locate the noun in her Wörterbuch.
The definition read: *Strahlung:* n. 1. radiation. 2. rays.

"Radiation" was a word she wasn't familiar with. "Rays,"
of course, were what the sun emitted. She wasn't quite sure

which word usage was correct. It would help if she could read the entire message to gain context. But on this occasion, the message was judged too sensitive to put in the hands of just one translator, and Gabi had been given random paragraphs. She looked around the room, wondering who else was working on the Heidelberg communiqué.

Gabi returned to her notepad and fiddled with the syntax of a long phrase preceding *Strahlung*. She hesitated typing the words, knowing how much could be riding on her translation of this sentence.

She remained lost in thought when her supervisor, Frau Schaffner, dropped by her desk. Since intrusions were rare in her section, several typists in the room stopped clacking their keys as they glanced her way.

"Herr Baumann asked if he could see you for a moment," Frau Schaffner whispered. "And don't forget to lock up your work."

"Of course, Frau Schaffner. I'll be right there."

Gabi pulled out the center desk tray and inserted the teletype message into the drawer, then locked it. She reached into her purse for her rosewood hairbrush, then quickly stroked it through her blonde hair before striding down the hall to Dieter Baumann's corner office. Through the plate glass window separating Dieter's office and the typing pool, she could see him working behind his desk. She even caught a glimpse of the Rhine River beyond Dieter's hunched shoulders.

She'd been in his office enough times to appreciate its view overlooking the Rhine and Basel's north bank, but she had to admit she appreciated the man behind the desk even more.

If it hadn't been for Dieter saving her . . . a chill traveled down her shoulders at the thought. She owed her life to him.

Dieter stood to greet Gabi, casting a handsome smile. "Please take a seat, Fräulein Mueller. How are you feeling?"

Gabi instinctively rubbed her left shoulder, still tender. "Sore, but I'll be fine," she said in an upbeat tone, hoping

Dieter focused on her smile rather than any nonverbal cues revealing that she was still shook up. Instead, she hoped to project an eagerness for a second mission even as she battled apprehension.

"I'm concerned about your welfare. You got roughed up a bit—"

"Nothing a good night's sleep couldn't fix. Really, I'm fine."

Gabi settled into a wooden chair, clasping her hands on her lap, and ignored the stares of the women in the typing pool who worked just on the other side of the partition window.

Instead, she focused on the view outside. From her vantage point, she could see that the Mittlere Brücke—one of Basel's three bridges that spanned the Rhine—was sparsely populated with foot traffic. Morning light reflected off the puddles from last night's rain and the sparkling reflections of booted footsteps disrupting it.

"Well, looks like we'll have a nice summer day outside," Dieter remarked, as if he was reading her thoughts. "Folks are getting a head start on our National Independence Day. You have plans for the First of August?"

"I'm taking the train tomorrow to the mountains to see my brothers. Andreas and Willy are guarding the American pilots interned in Davos. They complain there isn't much to do—just sitting around and learning American slang—so I thought I would surprise them."

"Good for you. I'm sure your brothers will enjoy a visit from their beautiful sister." Dieter's crisp blue eyes held her gaze.

She looked into her lap, not sure if she heard right. Was he calling her beautiful?

"Actually, they're mostly looking forward to seeing what goodies I bring from home. My mother's chocolate torte is the best."

"I'm sure you're wonderful around the kitchen as well. A lady of many talents." Baumann was clearly flirting.

Gabi tried not to imagine what it would be like to date someone such as him. Even though she judged him to be in his late twenties, just a few years older than she, he seemed so sophisticated, so . . . Gabi pursed her lips, refusing to let her mind go there. *Time to cut to the chase.*

"This is all very flattering, Herr Baumann, but I'm sure you didn't call me into your office to discuss my baking abilities."

"You're correct—Gabi. May I use your given name?"

"That would be fine, but I'm more comfortable with calling you Herr Baumann."

"Very well." He crossed his arms over his chest. "I called you in today to relay a message from Mr. Dulles, who is back in Bern. He told me to tell you 'Good job.'" Dieter used the English expression. "It was amazing the way you cracked open that safe. And the information you found is one more piece of the puzzle in our struggle against our common enemies. Mr. Dulles said you can expect to be called upon again."

Gabi felt her lips form a slight smile. She looked away, her heartbeat quickening from a mix of excitement and anxiousness. Not that the translation work wasn't interesting, but undercover work . . . well, she could really make a difference.

An awkward silence filled the air.

"Fräulein Mueller—Gabi—I was wondering if we could discuss your new role in a more informal setting, one without prying eyes." Dieter tilted his head toward the translation pool. Gabi glanced at a dozen women, each with their heads down, clacking away on their typewriters. One or two glanced Gabi's way, then quickly resumed her typing chores.

"Yes, I suppose . . ."

"Perhaps after work we could have a coffee. I promise not to take too much of your time."

Gabi nibbled on her lower lip and felt a slight tightening in her shoulders. His request seemed out of the ordinary, but then again, undercover work demanded such peculiar encounters, right? Perhaps this was one of those odd rendezvous.

A thought stirred. She let out a sigh as Eric's face filled her thoughts. "I just remembered. I'm meeting someone after work."

Baumann arched an eyebrow.

"He's just a friend. A good friend, I can assure you. He attends the church my father pastors."

"Oh, I see. I suppose we'll have to meet another time." Dieter's voice hinted of disappointment. As if turning a page, he continued, "Well, this can wait. Shall we meet after the First of August celebration?"

Gabi sensed there was no way she could say no. "That will be fine." She smiled. "In fact, I look forward to it, Herr Baumann."

• • • • • • • •

Gestapo Regional Headquarters
Heidelberg, Germany
2:15 p.m.

Bruno Kassler hated long lunch meetings, especially with obliging officials from the Heidelberg Gemeinde eager to stay in the Gestapo's good graces. *City Hall bootlickers, every last one of them.* He entered his office with a stomach leaden from too much Ruladen and Spätzle and set his gabardine hat with the National Socialist insignia on a wooden clothes tree. Before tackling a slug of new paperwork, he straightened the SS bolts on the lapels of his black dress uniform, knowing that with one glance of the Knights Cross with an Oak Leaf cluster on his left breast, any good German would recognize the high status of his position.

In just three years, steady promotions moved him from a lowly commander in Section A, investigating sabotage and assassination attempts, all the way to SS Brigadeführer, the most important—and fear-inspiring—post in the region. No wonder local politicos wanted to have lunch with him.

Although he was only twenty-eight years of age, men and women far older treated him with the respect his rank deserved. And for enemies of the Reich, a Luger held point-blank between insouciant eyes had a way of turning a smirk into a plea for mercy. And what of pulling the trigger? He had done it so many times he'd lost count.

The discovery—*his* discovery—of a Jew working on sensitive military research in his hometown portended all sorts of opportunities. How best to turn this to his maximum advantage?

He'd rounded up the last of the Jews in the Heidelberg region more than a year ago. Now, at least, he had something to focus his attention on. The cowardly attempt on the Führer's life netted a couple dozen arrests in his jurisdiction, but Kassler knew those troublemakers had no connection to Stauffenberg's plotters. They'd pleaded innocence in a rain of tears, right up to the moment ten-gauge piano wire was cinched around their cowardly throats at the courtyard gallows.

Now, a *grosser Fisch* was swimming in his pond. How best to reel him in? What made the most sense for his future with party leaders?

Kassler picked up the thin file marked *Engel, Joseph*. Nothing since Engel's adoption indicated he was even remotely connected with the loathsome Jewish race. No records of him belonging to a synagogue or joining a Zionist organization. His academic career had been exemplary. Single, with few close friends.

He's in love with equations. Kassler snorted. Engel, a physics wizard, exempt from being handed a rifle and told to go fight the Russians.

Kassler considered what a contact in Berlin had told him yesterday: Heisenberg's weapons project was cloaked in secrecy because the scientists were developing a bomb that could level a city the size of London.

A single explosive could do that?

If so, the Third Reich would renew its march toward global

conquest. The military setbacks of the last two years would be just that—setbacks. None of the battlefield defeats would matter, and soon the German Volk and the conquered lands would join together to provide *Lebensraum*, "living space" for the growth of the Aryan population.

But what about Joseph Engel?

The Jews were the source of evil in the world, political subversives who controlled world banking and international commerce. Maybe they had placed Engel there to make sure that Germany *didn't* succeed in building an atomic bomb.

Yet, to act unilaterally in a matter of national strategic importance might not benefit him if things went wrong. No, it would be better to bring Himmler into the mix—as cover. The Reichsführer had a way of becoming your worst nightmare when failure occurred, and Kassler could not take that chance.

He seized the phone's handset. "Becker? Come immediately. I have a letter to dictate."

7

A warm wind rippled across the Rhine and caressed Gabi's face as she strolled down the busy sidewalk. It was just a short walk from the OSS offices to the Globus, Basel's largest department store, where she was due to meet Eric.

Though pedestrians clogged the walkways, Gabi realized she'd been plodding several blocks without paying one bit of attention to the lively streets. Her mother could have passed by and Gabi wouldn't have known it. Instead, her mind was on Dieter's words.

Beautiful . . . he'd called her beautiful.

Gabi touched a hand to her face, hoping her flushed cheeks weren't too obvious. She could always blame her rosiness on her walk and the excitement of seeing Eric, yet Gabi doubted he would be fooled. He had a way of reading her gaze.

And she knew him just as well. In fact, as certain as William Tell split the apple perched on his son's head with a crossbow, Gabi was sure that Eric would be waiting for her at the Globus. The dairy farmer was as punctual as the Basel-Zurich Intercity train that departed at the top of the hour. And about as unpolished as a second-class rail car.

Gabi mildly rebuked herself, then chuckled. Actually, she liked Eric Hofstadler, who milked *Braunvieh* cows at dawn and stirred Emmentaler cheese in a copper vat the rest of the day. She didn't love him—much to her parents' chagrin—but she did admire the way he treated her like a lady. Eric had a chivalrous, salt-of-the-earth quality she found endearing. When she looked into his gentle blue eyes, honesty and compassion were captured in his gaze.

And more than that, love was captured there too. Not that she didn't already know that. Over the last year or so, Eric had made his feelings quite clear.

Gabi turned the corner and stood on her toes, looking for him among the dozens of shoppers rushing through the double-door entrance, including working women hurrying to pick up the last loaves of bread and other staples from the basement grocery.

There he was—Eric's red hair and ruddy complexion were unmistakable. The crimson flannel shirt was another giveaway, as well as the brown britches. He looked like a dairyman lost in the Big City, a hayseed among the sophisticated Basel burghers. At least Eric wasn't wearing his slop boots or sandals with socks. And even though he was good about washing up, she hoped he didn't bring the faint smell of the fresh manure with him.

When their eyes met, he flashed a smile and held up a fresh bouquet of long-stemmed white lilies accented with green bells of molucella picked from the fields of the family farm.

Gabi held her cloth hat with her left hand and skipped toward her friend. "For me?" She accepted the floral arrangement from his hand. "How sweet of you." Instead of offering a customary *bisou* on each cheek, she wrapped her arms around his broad shoulders and drew him close.

Eric stiffened slightly, as if startled by her unexpected affection, then quickly relaxed in her grasp, pulling her closer. "And to what do I owe this pleasure?" His words tickled her ear.

Her meeting with Dieter Baumann filtered through her mind. Gabi pushed out lingering romantic thoughts. How horrible to allow her peaked emotions to get the best of her. She gently stepped away and offered Eric a sweet smile. "Oh, I don't know. Maybe because it's a holiday tomorrow."

"Speaking of holidays, I have something for you." Eric reached into a rear pocket. He moved his hands for a moment, as if passing something between them, and then stretched out both arms with fists closed. "Which hand?"

Gabi liked playing games. She also liked surprises. "Let's see . . . I'll take the left."

Eric opened his left palm skyward and exposed two cardboard train tickets.

"Eric, did you plan an adventure for us, really?" She shook her head. "I'm so sorry, but I was already going to see my brothers tomorrow in the mountains."

"I know. These are a pair of Basel-Davos round-trip tickets. When your mom told me that you were going to spend the First of August on a train all day, off to see your brothers, I bought these so you'd have some company. I can't think of anyone who would want to spend the holiday alone."

Gabi felt warmth spread through her chest. "Mother must have told you about my trip when you dropped off some butter at the house." The whiff of the lilies and molucella in her hand rose to her nose. She had to admit that the aroma intoxicated her, and she felt her affections for Eric matching those she felt for Dieter earlier that day. If Eric only realized what the scent did to her. She was sure she'd have them on her doorstep every day.

"Yes. Your mother spilled the news two days ago, but joining you was my idea. I hope it's all right. I haven't taken a day off all summer since it's our busy season on the farm, but Papi approved. After all, we only get to celebrate Switzerland's independence one day a year."

Gabi didn't have to consider his offer for long. She enjoyed Eric's company. He could carry a conversation well and laughed easily. And the scent of the freshly picked flowers made the idea all the more agreeable.

"Of course, it's all right. We'll have a fun time." She took the tickets from his hand and tucked them into her purse, realizing that having a male seatmate on a long train ride into the mountains also had other benefits. Eric could be her protector—not from the enemy—but rather from all the young soldiers who were trying to find favor with the young ladies.

"I'll be thankful for your company. Are you sure it's okay? Will the cows survive without you?"

"Okay? Whenever I can spend time with you, I'm happy. Papi will make do just fine." Eric placed his right hand lightly on the small of her back. "Let's walk over to the Mittlere Brücke, shall we?"

The downtown sidewalk teemed with pedestrians. People getting off work were hurrying home to open their first bottle of Neuchâtel white wine to start the holiday off right. As they reached the bridge, the crowds thinned, and Eric guided her along the Mittlere Brücke.

"This is a beautiful evening for a stroll, but my bus is that way." Gabi pointed behind her.

"I know, but we can wait for the next one. There are some things I wanted to talk to you about."

A sense of alarm rose in Gabi's throat. She didn't like the way that sounded, and more than anything, she didn't want to break Eric's heart. Wasn't friendship enough—close friendship? "Is it about—?"

"About us? Yes, in a way. We've been spending more time with each other over the last several months, and I thought you ought to know how I feel about you."

"I think I have a good idea." Gabi good-naturedly folded her arms across her chest and stepped away from his touch. "They didn't give me a job with the OSS for nothing—"

"Gabi, don't say things like that. I think it's wonderful that you're working for the Americans, but please, you can't speak of such things."

"I was just teasing. You sound like my father. It's no big deal, really. It's not like I'm sharing secrets or anything."

They had walked about 100 meters on the bridge and were only a fourth of the way across the Rhine. Eric suddenly stopped and faced her directly.

"Listen, I know I may seem a simpleton to you. Some people think all I do is milk my father's cows and muck out stinky horse stalls. But that's the life God has given me right now. It's what I do. I know my days on a farm aren't as exciting as yours in the city, but we have a lot in common, including our trust in Christ. This war business will be over someday, and when that happens, I want us to be . . . together."

Gabi leaned against the stone wall overlooking the water. She rested her arms on the top of the wall and placidly tilted her head in the twilight breeze. She took a long look at Eric. Yes, beneath that red flannel shirt beat a heart of gold. Attentive. A hard worker. Surely a good provider. And he'd learned a few things about how to romance a girl.

She lifted the bright bouquet to her face again and inhaled the aromatic scent of summer. Maybe Eric was the one God had planned for her. *Unless* . . .

As quickly as the image of Dieter's charmed smile surfaced in her mind, Gabi pushed it from her thoughts. He was handsome, and she had to admit she was intrigued by his undercover work, but there was more hidden about Dieter than known. And with Eric nothing was hidden. Eric's heart was laid bare. Given to her alone.

While a part of her heart believed now was not the time to get serious, she didn't feel the Lord telling her to shut the door in Eric's face. *Lord, give me wisdom here* . . .

Gabi glanced up at Eric, peering at the whorls of pure white, trumpet-shaped flowers. She blew out a slow breath, hoping he could hear her heart beyond her words. "Maybe we will be together someday. It's just that right now . . . it's hard with all the uncertainty in the world. Who knows what the next six months, or a year, will bring?"

"Of course." Eric's gaze caught and held hers. "I just wanted you to know that I'm very fond of you." He sighed. "It's important to say it. You know, life can be so short." His eyes clouded over as if a memory filled his thoughts.

"And I'm fond of you." Gabi meant every word of her declaration. Guys didn't come much sweeter than Eric Hofstadler. She could see herself with him—she just couldn't imagine herself tethered to his family farm. Yanking on cow's teats for half the morning wasn't something she wanted to do the rest of her life.

Eric interrupted her thoughts. "Does this mean—"

The *clackety-clack* clamor of a horse-drawn carriage coming toward them drowned out Eric's voice. Gabi looked up and noticed a Swiss Army private, dressed in an olive uniform and garrison hat, working the reins of a single horse with blinders. The Army private was ferrying a black-bearded young man in a mud-stained black suit and what looked to be his wife clutching an infant to her breast. The fourth passenger was another Swiss Army private with a bolt-action Karabiner 31 rifle lying across his lap.

Must be Jews. While Gabi hadn't seen this before, she'd heard the stories. Many Jews had escaped into Switzerland only to be caught by local authorities and escorted back to the German border, where they would be handed over to the Gestapo. It didn't seem fair.

Gabi paused her steps and looked into the face of the woman, imagining herself in that position. The woman clutched her child tight, as if to protect her innocent loved one from the fate awaiting them on the other side of the border.

The mother's doe-like eyes met Gabi's and held her gaze. The woman's plea was clear . . . *Isn't there anything you can do?*

The look caused the muscles in Gabi's stomach to tighten in a ball, and a wave of emotion rose in her throat. Without warning, a tear escaped and rolled down Gabi's left cheek, and her knees trembled. Just when she thought she couldn't hold herself up any longer, a warm arm wrapped around Gabi's waist, holding her up.

"That's got to be the saddest thing I've seen in my life." Eric's voice broke. And though his voice hinted of sadness,

Gabi also noted something else—determination. But determination about what?

"What do you think will happen to them?" Gabi dabbed at her eyes. She knew the answer but hoped Eric would tell her different.

"I hear they are taken to relocation camps in the East. The conditions are sure to be brutal. Lack of food, no sanitation. Can you imagine the Germans locking up people like barnyard animals?" Eric's hand led her forward, encouraging her on.

Gabi resumed her steps. "Those have to be just stories, right? Things can't be that bad, can they? I mean look at them." She nodded her chin toward the couple in the carriage. "They look harmless. What have they done? They can't help what family they were born into, what blood surges through their veins."

Eric patted Gabi's back. "Yes, but others do not see it that way, and I'm afraid the truth, well, is probably worse than the stories we hear . . ." His voice trailed off, and she knew he wanted to say more.

The mother glanced one last time at Gabi, and her pained look pierced Gabi's soul. She made herself look away from the refugee mother. What could she do? How could she help? She was only one person, and any attempt to help these poor people could jeopardize her job—and hinder the greater work she could do for their entire race.

The carriage moved on, and Gabi focused on her footsteps on the bridge. She glanced at the flowers in her hand, trying to turn her attention back to Eric. With so much happening in the world, a few moments of carefree romance seemed appealing.

"Eric, I've been thinking—"

Commotion interrupted her words, and shouts filled the air.

They turned just in time for Gabi to see the bearded husband lurching toward the Army guard. Both toppled out of the carriage and tumbled to the pavement, with the Army guard taking the brunt of the fall and crying out in pain. The horse's whinny joined the tumult as the driver yanked on the reins and attempted to regain control.

The husband jumped to his feet, holding out his cuffed hands to catch his wife and child. She leapt, and the baby's startled cry joined the noise. The horse spooked from the pandemonium, and the driver snapped the reins as the other guard moaned on the pavement.

"*Halt!* Stop!" the driver yelled.

Gabi held her breath, feeling as if she were watching something from a nightmare. Everything moved as if in slow motion.

"No, don't!" she pleaded, but it was no more than a whisper.

What were they doing? The Jewish couple wouldn't get far. Surely they realized escape was impossible.

Quickly, the husband lifted his wife and child and set them on the bridge's ledge. Then he jumped onto the ledge and helped his wife to her feet. The injured guard struggled to aim his rifle at the family, but he was too late. The Jewish couple took one step together and fell into the Rhine ten meters below.

"Stay here!" Eric sprinted toward the horse-drawn carriage as the soldier ran to the wall with his carbine.

"Don't shoot!" Eric tackled the soldier to the ground.

Gabi closed some of the distance and looked over the ledge to the water below. The husband was nowhere to be seen, but the mother—who wasn't handcuffed—bobbed to the surface, holding the crying baby aloft.

Eric scrambled to his feet and raced to the wall, just in time to see the woman struggle, then sink beneath the surface with her infant. With one motion, he whipped off both boots and jumped into one of the few placid eddies in a wide, swift-moving river.

Gabi gasped, losing sight of the mother and child just as Eric's body knifed into the water and disappeared.

"Save them!" she screamed. Ten seconds passed, then twenty . . . thirty seconds . . . Finally, Eric resurfaced. His eyes lifted in Gabi's direction, searching the bridge for her.

"You couldn't find them? Aren't they down there?" she called to him.

Eric shook his head, then dove toward the murky bottom again. He did this four more times and then finally surfaced for good, shaking his head. Without a word, he quietly stroked to a nearby dock.

Gabi buried her face in her hands. The Jewish couple wanted to die—together. Maybe they had decided that drowning was a far better fate than whatever awaited them across the border.

The rumors had to be true.

```
Gestapo Regional Headquarters
Heidelberg, Germany
5:15 p.m.
```

"Read me the last couple of paragraphs, Becker."

The young aide-de-camp glanced at his legal pad and cleared his throat. "'According to my investigation, Engel is a Jew who was raised in a Protestant family that attended a free church in Spandau.'" Becker looked up. "Sounds complicated, sir. Do we need to explain to the Reichsführer what a free church is?"

Kassler suppressed a flash of annoyance. "My dear Becker. Of course our great leader understands the differences between free churches and state ones."

"Then, uh, can you explain it to me?"

Kassler frowned, wondering just what they taught in Nazi Youth. "The free churches act independently and receive no government funding, and state churches like Lutheranism and the Roman Catholics receive a sizable portion of their budget from tax monies. The former accepts no discipline and has been a thorn in our side, while the latter has acquiesced—even been supportive—of our great cause. The Episcopalians and Catholics haven't issued a peep of protest regarding our handling of the Jewish problem. I see you still have some things to learn, Corporal." He cleared his throat. "Carry on."

Becker's Adam's apple bobbed once again as he slowly read the rest of the letter in a clear and concise monotone. "'Thus, Engel has two areas of suspicion. One, he is aware of his Jewish ancestry and is acting like a clandestine fifth columnist against the State, waiting for the right moment to show his true nature and fight for his people. Or two, he is a willing dupe of the Zionists, who have successfully planted him in a sensitive military research project. Sooner or later—probably sooner—Jewish interests will see to it that Engel successfully sabotages years of painstaking research by Professor Heisenberg's team. Furthermore, the fact that Engel was raised by Christian cultists who have not bowed their collective wills to the Führer's sure hand leads me to believe that Engel is a dangerous mole who must be rooted out.'"

"I like that," Kassler interrupted. "Makes our case, if I dare say so myself. And the last paragraph?"

"Here's how you ended your letter, Major. 'Because of the critical nature of Engel's work with Dr. Heisenberg, I humbly seek the Reichsführer's direction on how to handle this delicate matter. Until I hear from you, I remain in your service'—signed, Major Bruno Kassler, SS Brigadeführer, Sektor Heidelberg."

Kassler smiled at his own devotion and humility, certain it would bring pleasure to the Reichsführer. He left his desk and paced to the window. "What's the fastest way we can get this letter to Berlin?"

"We have a courier service on the 7:23 night train. Your letter will be on the Reichsführer's desk first thing in the morning."

"Very well. I would imagine his office will be calling sometime before the afternoon. I want you to be ready for that phone call, Becker. You understand its grave importance to the Reich, *ja*?"

"Yes, and thank you for your confidence in me." Becker's lips curled up with a hint of a smile.

Kassler glanced down at the people hurrying along the boulevard, realizing they had no idea how their fate rested in his hands. His chest swelled with well-deserved pride. He wouldn't be surprised if Herr Himmler himself called.

The pleasure of receiving such a response paled only in comparison to another truth: Engel was in for the surprise of his life.

* * * * * * * * *

Basel, Switzerland
5:24 p.m.

Dieter Baumann cocked the bill of his tweed hat and joined dozens of Baslers crossing the busy Thunerstrasse, weaving amongst the confluence of streetcar and bus lines. Without looking up, he darted into the entrance of the Globus department store.

This line of work never ceased to amaze him, he thought, as he energetically took the stairs two-by-two to the fourth floor. Gabi Mueller had a boyfriend? The strait-laced church girl whose idea of a wild night on the town was playing a game of *jass* with three girlfriends? And that was no peck-and-go embrace, either.

Dieter didn't recognize the guy holding the flowers like an embarrassed grade-school suitor. From his vantage point across the street, Dieter could smell the manure oozing from the skin of the poor sap. What was she doing with a simple farmhand who stood in cow dung up to his ankles all day long? He made himself a mental note to find out more about this cheese farmer after the First of August holiday.

Dieter reached the fourth floor landing and turned to his right, walking through the glass doors leading to the Globus coffee shop. The restaurant, which overlooked Basel's main shopping district, was lightly populated this late afternoon. That was fine with Dieter, who took a good look at the half-dozen patrons sipping their café au laits or nibbling their slices of *Aprikosen Torte*.

That's right, apricots were in season . . . for those who could afford them, that is. Everything for a price.

He settled into a two-person table next to the window, and

a waitress took his order for Aprikosen Torte—with a dollop of whipped cream—and a cappuccino. "Please hurry." He drummed his fingers on the table, as if shooing her away.

Within three minutes, the waitress set the late-afternoon snack and cup of coffee before him, along with a bill for two francs. The apricot pie, coated with syrupy glaze, would hold him over until dinner. After the last forkful, he set a two-franc piece on the table and regarded his watch. *Two minutes to go.*

At precisely 5:45 p.m., fifteen minutes before closing, Dieter set his hat on his head and departed the restaurant. Instead of turning left to return to the elevator, he continued straight and strolled into the men's restroom.

An older gentleman was scrubbing his hands at the wash-basin. Dieter ignored him and kicked open the first stall. Satisfied no one was there, he slammed the next door with his right boot and peered inside. When Dieter had finished checking all four toilets, he directed his attention to the older man, who was drying his hands with a pull-down towel.

"You had me scared with that tire iron." The older man smirked as he extended his right hand in greeting.

"Sorry to be so dramatic." Dieter shrugged his shoulders. "I guess I wanted to impress the girl."

"I'm sure you did." The man gave a low chuckle. "Then again, you've always had a weakness for the skirts."

Dieter ignored the mild rebuke and plowed into business. "Those code words she found in the safe really gummed up the works in Bern. The cryptologists are pulling their hair out trying to match those codes with the latest intercepts."

"Good. That'll keep them busy for a while. But your girl has a good set of fingers. I didn't think she'd be able to crack the safe."

"Gabi Mueller is a young woman of many talents. For all her naïveté, she cannot be discounted." Dieter glanced at his watch. They only had a few moments left. "You have something for me?"

"Yes, and it's important. It's been nearly two months since the Allies stormed the beaches in France, but Panzer divisions have managed to keep the American and British invaders bottled up on their beachheads. A few days ago, though, Patton's Third Army broke out west of St. Lô. Berlin wants to know where the Americans are headed."

"And you think I can find out that easy? As if a simple snap of the fingers can present this closely guarded information?" Dieter glanced at his reflection in the mirror over the sink, pleased with his comeback—pleased that they needed him more than he needed them.

"No, but you usually manage to find a way. That's why that Swiss bank account of yours is so healthy. A numbered account out of a bank in Zug, right?"

Dieter turned on his heels without answering.

• • • • • • • •

University of Heidelberg Apartments
7:14 p.m.

Joseph Engel dropped his leather satchel on the tiny dining table and slumped into a well-worn settee.

"Back so soon from work?" a male voice in the kitchen called.

Joseph couldn't decide whether his roommate was being combative or good-humored.

"I still have some things to do tonight." Joseph stood and took several paces toward the kitchen. "But admit it, Hannes. You can't turn off your brain at the end of the day any more than I can."

"That's why I unwind with a beer." Hannes Jäger raised his pewter mug in a mock toast before imbibing a long draught of Pilsner. "I've got to salute you, though. Impressive display of chalk work this afternoon." Jäger glanced at him with sincerity.

Now Joseph was really confused. Jäger was usually so

71

sarcastic. If Joseph asked a simple question, such as "What time is it?" Jäger was apt to reply with "Do I look like a watch?"

"Seriously," Jäger said again. "I was impressed."

"Thank you," Joseph mumbled. "That's not really neces-sary—"

"This is no time for false modesty. Unless you have a great desire to live in Siberia the rest of your life, writing equations for the Russians. What you described today about iso-tope separation may help the Reich stave off the Mongolian hordes. I also thought your mathematical insights regarding the perplexing problem of separating U-235 were brilliant, absolutely brilliant." Jäger's voice rose with excitement. "If Heisenberg can get even a small-scale reactor built in time, we could generate enough plutonium to build a bomb without parallel in man's history—and you'd be famous."

Joseph's chest filled with warmth at the flattery from his usually cynical colleague, who was pouring on praise like uncorked champagne at a wedding party. "Famous? You really think so?"

"Listen to me." Jäger settled into the loveseat, leaning forward. "You'll go down in the history books as the man who correctly theorized how the world's first atomic bomb could work. But before we can level Moscow or London, the bomb has to be tested. Maybe we could pack all the Jews in Warsaw and send a Messerschmitt in their direction. Wouldn't that be a surprise? The joke would be on them, *ja*?" Jäger slapped his thigh and took another swig of beer.

Joseph forced a laugh, but he failed to see anything funny about incinerating tens of thousands of innocent people, even if they were Jews. As a youngster—before Hitler came into power—he had several Jewish friends in school, including his best buddy, Caleb. It was Caleb who had worked as his lab partner in his first physics class when he was fifteen years old. After that, when the Austrian corporal was elected German chancellor, things changed . . . nearly overnight. Joseph never forgot how the newly installed Führer declared that Jews were *Untermenschen*—"sub-humans"—at one of his first rallies. Caleb had moved away after that, never to be seen again.

Joseph bit his lip, refusing to argue. But still, his silence didn't mean he agreed. The Jews he'd grown up with weren't sub-humans. In fact, it was his parents who taught him the Jews were "God's chosen people."

That seemed so long ago.

"Yes, some joke," Joseph finally conceded, glancing out the window to the cobblestone street below the second-story apartment. Like he had every day since Hitler took power, Joseph stuffed down Jäger's words—and his true sentiments. Papi and Mami hadn't raised a fool. To say *anything* deemed supportive of the Jews could cost him his job—or his life. He wouldn't put it past his roommate to denounce him before the Gestapo, even if he did make the history books.

Joseph forced a smile. "So, are you going to offer me a beer?"

9

The compact train, with a green locomotive and a half-dozen red passenger cars, had previously been known in tourist brochures as the Rhaetian Railway. That, of course, was before the war, when the popular line ferried English and German tourists high into Switzerland's Graubünden country for holiday. That was no longer the case.

As her body swayed with the train's rocking, Gabi reflected on the fact that England and Germany were now dire enemies focused on each other's destruction. All because of a madman bent on global conquest. When would the world return to normal again? Would it ever?

She and Eric sat across from each other in a second-class car as the single-gauge train huffed and puffed over viaducts, through winding tunnels, past raging mountain torrents, and across grassy meadows speckled with an array of alpine flowers. Her father had told her that since the turn of the century, Graubünden's healthy climate and picture-book charm had attracted guests of rank and class. Being American, her father never lost his appreciation for such information. He collected facts about Swiss history like one collected stamps or coins.

"I can see why these mountains were popular with the English," Gabi said. "It's as if I'm being transported into a time of knights and princesses. Looking out at all those

74

wildflowers it makes it easy to forget there's a war being fought just over those mountains."

"Ever read any of the Sherlock Holmes books?" Eric lifted his arm, resting it on the back of the empty seat next to him.

Gabi nodded. "One or two. Not my favorite author."

"The author of the series, Sir Arthur Conan Doyle, moved to Davos in the 1890s because his wife had been diagnosed with tuberculosis. He thought the mountain air would be good for her. At any rate, Sir Arthur is credited with popularizing skiing in these parts. I read somewhere that he had skis shipped from Norway, and that's when he introduced skiing to the locals. Do you ski?"

"Just cross-country. Dad made us some wooden skis a few years ago. We tramped around the snow a few times, but I've never skied in the mountains. Those ski lifts look a little dangerous to me. What about you?"

"I had to learn to ski in boot camp. The Swiss Army wants all soldiers to at least know how to stand up on them."

Gabi turned her gaze from a pasture of goats. "I'd forgotten you were in the Army."

"I'm not full-time like your brothers. Switzerland doesn't produce enough food to feed all her citizens, so they're keeping us farmers close to the soil." He chuckled. "Or in my case, close to a three-legged milk stool. Anyway, I've heard even the city parks in Zurich, Lucerne, and Bern have been dug up and planted with vegetables and fruit."

"If Germany attacked though, would you return . . . ?" She leaned forward slightly, cocking her eyebrow.

"Yes, well, if Germany invaded, I would be expected to report to my mobilization point within twelve hours. I would trade my stool for a gun."

Gabi knew better to ask where that meeting point was. All Swiss soldiers in the citizen army knew where their mobilization points were located. She also knew, when needed, the soldiers were required to get there by any means—on foot, if necessary. Her father, though he was in his early fifties and a naturalized citizen, was also expected to bear arms in case of an invasion. Like Eric, he kept a rifle and a knapsack in the cellar, along with forty-eight bullets. She'd counted them once, out of curiosity.

The train suddenly turned dark as it entered a series of tunnels. After ten minutes of darkness and light, the train chugged into bright sunshine, prompting Gabi to suck in her breath at the first glimpse of glistening snow in the couloirs.

Gabi looked at her watch. Within a half hour, they'd arrive at the Davos-Platz rail station. She opened her mouth to point out the cumulus clouds circling the highest peak like a halo. She closed it again when she noticed Eric resting his eyelids. A soft snore escaped his lips, and she held in a giggle.

Poor man, those cows keep him busy. It had to be hard providing for the nourishment of his needy countrymen.

Gabi soaked up the scenery outside her window. She studied the wooden farmhouses, each draped with flowerboxes overflowing with red geraniums. One sturdy farmhouse they passed also sported a distinctive Swiss flag—a white equilateral cross established on a red field, a banner derived from the Holy Roman Empire.

In the fields, shirtless men and their wives in ankle-length cotton dresses rhythmically swung long wooden scythes to cut the hay. Following behind them, older children hand-raked the hay into piles.

Poor highlanders, straining to wring the bare essentials out of lean soil, Gabi thought. It didn't seem fair some had so much while others had so little. *And having to work on the First of August, such a special day.*

Her active mind returned back to her second-grade class when she learned about how a handful of men representing three cantons—Uri, Schwyz, and Unterwalden—had gathered in a grassy meadow next to the Lake of Lucerne on August 1, 1291. They swore an oath of confederation and signed a self-defense pact that fateful day. For nearly seven hundred years, Switzerland had repelled invaders and endured many dark moments, but none as serious as the threat being posed by neighboring Nazi Germany.

Eric woke from his nap and rubbed his eyes. Then he sat up straighter and pointed to two dozen black-and-white cows, each with a cowbell hanging on a wide leather band around its neck, yanking at clefts of chewy grass in a well-fenced pasture.

"Amazing. Holstein cows in this part of Switzerland," Eric said. "They are said to give half a liter more milk per day than the Brown Swiss. I talked to Papi about bringing a bull and seven females to the farm and breeding them because of their high protein-to-fat ratio, which makes for especially good cheese."

Gabi rolled her eyes in a mocking manner. "You and your cows. You still sleeping in the barn?"

"No." Eric diverted his eyes. "Sorry to go on about these things. I guess I've been having too many one-sided conversations sitting on a stool as the sun comes up."

"No, don't worry about it. I like teasing you." She glanced at her watch. "It seems like we should be there already, don't you think?"

Gabi looked outside the train window, as if she could gauge the distance that remained. Instead, her eyes spotted a mother holding a toddler in front of their two-story farmhouse. She giggled at the sight, knowing the cows took the first story and the family lived above them. The mother held the baby's tiny arm and waved at the passing train.

Gabi solemnly waved back.

A mother and her baby. So sweet. So innocent.

Images flooded Gabi's mind—fresh memories of the Jewish family drowning before her eyes. The pain cut through her chest like a knife. The sad intensity of the mother's forlorn look met her many times, even in her sleep. Without meeting Eric's gaze, she tugged a white-and-red-bordered handkerchief from her pocket and dabbed her eyes, sucking in a deep breath.

"What's the matter?" Eric reached forward and placed a hand on her knee.

"I can't put that poor family out of my mind." Gabi lightly blew her nose. "The desperate mother holding her baby above the water. If only someone could have saved her baby."

Eric shifted in his seat. "I swam as deep as I could. The water . . . it was too murky."

Gabi dabbed at her nose again, and then she patted his hand to show him she didn't think it was his fault.

"What do the Nazis have against the Jews anyway?" She frowned. "More than that, what are the Nazis doing to them?"

Eric pursed his lips. "It should come as no surprise what Hitler is doing to the Jews. He's out to exterminate them like pests."

"How do you know that?"

"If you read *Mein Kampf*, you know that the Führer alluded to exterminating the Jewish race from the face of the planet. He put it all down in black and white. The way he views the world, the German people—the 'Aryans'—are at the top of the heap. The Jews are at the bottom."

Eric sighed. "The dirty Jews, Hitler says, are conspiring to stop the 'master race' from ruling the world by diluting its racial and cultural purity. It's really scary stuff. Hitler believes that Aryans are superior intellectually, culturally, and athletically."

"My papi says Jesse Owens put Hitler in his place during the Olympic Games in Berlin."

"You're right. Jesse Owens beat Germany's best. Hitler left the stadium so he wouldn't have to shake hands with a black American. But that was eight years ago. Things have just gotten worse since then."

"You seem to know a lot about this stuff." Gabi tilted her head, looking at him with renewed interest. He wasn't an uneducated farmer—not if he was reading dense manifestos like *Mein Kampf*. "When did you read Hitler's book?"

"Back when the spring offensive started in May of 1940. Now that was a terrifying time. Remember all the rumors that Hitler's armies would sweep into Switzerland to get around the Maginot Line? Or after the fall of France, when we heard the Nazis would invade Switzerland next?"

Gabi shuddered. During the summer of 1940, their family expected to be evacuated at a moment's notice. After all, only two areas in Switzerland were north of the Rhine River and shared a land border with Germany: the heavily forested city of Schaffhausen, eighty kilometers to the east; and her hometown of Riehen, located in the so-called "knee of the Rhine" five kilometers east of Basel. Add to that the fact their house in Riehen was only several hundred meters from the border, which left them extremely vulnerable.

"I remember after the fall of France how Papi got everyone on their knees after dinner. It was a tradition we continued for weeks. All we could do was pray."

"We did the same at our house. Hey—" Eric pointed— "there's the train station!"

Gabi felt the train brake as it pulled into Davos-Platz. The platform was filled with travelers waiting to take the Rhaetian Railway back to Landquart. From there, one could transfer to a fast intercity train to Zurich and Basel. She ignored those traveling for the holiday and instead scanned the faces of those in uniform.

"There they are!" Eric pointed, spotting Andreas and Willy first. They were dressed in woolen pants and gray short-sleeve shirts. Each packed a pistol on their belts.

"Who's with them?" Gabi noticed the soldier chatting with her brothers. He was dressed in khaki pants, light flight jacket, and cap with a U.S. Army Eighth Air Force insignia—the number 8 with scalloped wings and a five-pointed star.

She glanced at the handsome American again and couldn't help but allow a smile to form.

79

• • • • • • • •

18 Toblerstrasse, Apartment 4
Heidelberg, Germany
1:20 p.m.

Bruno Kassler, dressed in a white undershirt and black flared breeches, sat in his apartment bedroom less than two kilometers from his office. A sleeping form curled up in his bed, but he ignored her for now. There was a time for pleasure and a time for business. Now was a time for business. Kassler had told Becker to patch through any calls to his apartment until he returned to the office later that afternoon.

He tapped the wooden desktop with his fingertips as he watched the black phone. Its sudden jangling startled the Gestapo chief, even though he had been anticipating a call since mid-morning.

"Hello?"

"Major . . . Major . . . Kassler. Berlin is on the line." The young corporal sounded as if he would faint from asphyxiation at any moment.

"Stay calm, Becker. Exactly who's on the phone?" Kassler expected Himmler's personal assistant, or perhaps a major general.

"The . . . the . . . Reichsführer himself."

Now it was Kassler's turn to feel his face go pale. "Put him on, quickly now."

Kassler heard a click and then his name.

"Sturmbannführer Kassler?"

He'd recognize the voice anywhere. It *was* Himmler.

"This is Sturmbannführer Kassler, mein Reichsführer."

"Thank you for taking my call," said the oily voice from Berlin.

"Yes, sir." Kassler straightened up in his chair. As if the Reichsführer needed his permission to continue the conversation by phone.

80

"This is in regards to the letter that you sent by overnight courier."

"Yes, my Reichsführer. If you will allow me a moment to explain—"

"There's no need. Your letter outlined the situation in Heidelberg well. You were wise to seek counsel, but I can only hope you are not poking your nose where you shouldn't."

Kassler felt his heart boom inside his chest. "Reichsführer, that was not my intention. I was merely investigating possible collaborators working inside our local university. I thought making a couple of phone calls would help me root out these traitors, and when I came across something unusual—"

"You should have gone through channels with the Berlin office instead of calling the Spandau SS."

Himmler knows I called the SS?

"Fortunately for you," Himmler continued, "we were able to confirm that Joseph Engel was born to Jewish parents in 1917."

Kassler blew out the breath he'd been holding. "How would His Excellency like me to proceed?"

"Sturmbannführer Kassler, may I remind you of the sensitivity of the situation. Normally, the Jew Engel would be arrested for questioning, but at the moment, he's working for the Fatherland on a very important military project—one I cannot disclose over the phone. Nonetheless, we cannot let our guard down. I want you to pick up Engel, for safekeeping, until we decide what to do with him. He is to be taken alive, do you understand?"

"Yes, sir. How soon would you like my men to arrest the Jew?"

"He doesn't appear to be a flight risk; still, this matter cannot wait. You have twenty-four hours and not a minute more. Call me when he is safely in your custody. I expect no problems."

"Of course, Reichsführer. You can count on me."

Kassler heard the phone click, and then he set the handset

gingerly on the cradle and reached into his breeches for a handkerchief. Himmler didn't suffer fools—or unwise mistakes—gladly.

He dabbed his perspiring forehead and willed himself to calm down. After all, Engel had no idea he was a hunted man. Kassler still had the element of surprise in his hip pocket.

The Gestapo chief reached for the phone and dialed his office number. "Becker! Who's leading the night brigade this evening?"

He heard a shuffling of papers until Becker had an answer. "Frisch, Sergeant Frisch."

"Find him. Send him to my office. It's urgent. I'll be there shortly."

After he hung up, Kassler heard a soft moan and the rustling of bedsheets beside him.

"Problems at the office, sweetheart?" The voice was slightly hoarse from sleep.

Kassler turned and regarded the raven-haired beauty, Sylvia Neddermeyer. She rubbed her eyes and yawned, as if she had awakened in the middle of the night instead of the early afternoon. She rose from the bed and slowly gathered his silk bathrobe around her nude frame. Her high cheekbones, model skin, and hourglass figure were hard to overlook. And the fact that she was one-sixteenth Jewish was a technicality he was also willing to ignore.

As long as she maintained her end of the bargain.

"Come back to bed. I can't sleep when you're not here to warm me." She pouted for his benefit. "Besides," she purred in a sultry voice as she loosely tied his robe, "I can tell you've been working too hard."

Kassler smiled as Sylvia approached and slid into his lap, wrapping her arms around his neck.

Kassler nuzzled his face into Sylvia's neck, breathing in the sweet, musky scent of her. Sergeant Frisch could wait. He had twenty-four hours, after all.

10

Dieter Baumann stared off into the half-empty train yard as the iron brakes of the IC Express squealed, signaling its arrival in Bern—Switzerland's capital city and seat of the national government.

A festive mood filled the second-class railcar, with every seat taken by families anxious to visit loved ones on Swiss National Day. As the early afternoon train leisurely rolled underneath a massive cupola, men dressed in black stovepipe pants, pressed white shirts, and thin black ties reached for satchels in the overhead compartment. Their wives, adorned in embroidered blouses and bright dresses in various shades of crimson red—in homage to the predominantly red flag of Switzerland—gathered their children's belongings and picnic baskets. The outfits worn by their offspring were pint-sized versions of their parents' celebratory apparel.

Dieter regarded his olive-colored dungarees and simple dress shirt. No party clothes for him, or *wurst* and potato salad that afternoon. Instead, Dieter focused on the job he had to do. He exited the Bern Hauptbahnhof with a leather briefcase in hand and smoothly passed harried parents reining in hopped-up boys and girls sprinting for the exits. Within fifteen minutes, he arrived at the United States Embassy on Jubiläumsstrasse 93 where a pair of serious Marines studied the contents of his scarlet passport before phoning the office of Allen Dulles. Inside of two minutes, Dulles's secretary—

83

an American—arrived at the front door to escort Dieter into the inner sanctum.

"Mr. Baumann, it's good to see you again," the secretary, Priscilla Taylor, declared in a businesslike manner.

"And you as well, Mrs. Taylor."

Early forties, unadorned in a navy blue dress skirt and matching jacket, and not bearing a wedding ring, the frumpy Frau Taylor was married to her work. As per Swiss custom, Dieter couldn't bring himself to call an old maid like her a "miss."

"I thought you'd be taking the day off," Dieter breezily remarked as the pair walked along a granite-floored hallway toward the rear of the embassy.

"I doubt the Germans are on holiday today," she replied, businesslike.

"True, but we are in Switzerland."

"We didn't take the Fourth of July off either," she said curtly.

The ensuing silence told Dieter that Mrs. Taylor was in no mood to verbally spar with a Swiss operative from the Basel office. They remained mute as she ushered him into Dulles's office.

"Ah, Mister Baumann, thank you for coming on such short notice," said the angular Dulles, rising from a burgundy-colored, padded leather chair. "Have you eaten lunch?"

"I had a croissant on the train."

"Well, help yourself to some cheese and fruit if you're hungry." Dulles, dressed in a tweed jacket and matching tie, waved his right hand toward a silver platter overflowing with red grapes, ripe peaches, and a rectangular block of Appenzeller cheese.

"Maybe I'll have something before I go." Though Dieter's stomach growled, his physical needs weren't important at the moment.

"Very good." The six-foot, two-inch American spymaster, of medium build and impeccably groomed gray hair parted to his right, stretched his arms as he stepped up to a window overlooking a small courtyard. "Mr. Baumann, our cryptologists in the basement are having a devil of a time cracking intercepts from German operatives inside Switzerland these days. After four days of no matches, they've abandoned those prefix codes that Miss Mueller pinched from the safe last week. Disinformation, I'm afraid."

Dieter had been told to expect this by his Nazi contact. "I'm sure you're right, Mr. Dulles. We had to leave the apartment in a hurry, so maybe there was something we missed. You recall how—"

Dulles interrupted him with a wave of the hand. "I read the report. I know the mission was botched."

"Well, I wouldn't go that far, sir. But, perhaps in the rush to escape, Fräulein Mueller may have inadvertently overlooked an indicator sheet to launch the real codes." *Best to blame her.*

Dulles sighed and rubbed his forehead. "As you say. I may come back to that, but for now, let's move on to other things." The spymaster consulted a yellow legal-size pad, and for the next thirty minutes, peppered Dieter with inquiries about various field agents, what his contacts in the Swiss Army were saying, and the flow of refugees sneaking into Switzerland. The Basel station chief answered diligently, knowing his responses satisfied the curious cat.

Precisely at 2:30 p.m., a knock interrupted their meeting. Mrs. Taylor entered with a sterling silver set and a pair of chocolate éclairs. "Time for afternoon tea," she sang out as she set the service on a wooden side table.

"Where did you find the éclairs?" Dulles asked. "You must have paid a king's ransom for them."

"Actually, the bakery around the corner exhausted its monthly ration of chocolate. It's Swiss National Day, remember?" She winked at Dieter. "Please enjoy them, sir." Then she offered a slight curtsy.

Dieter accepted a chocolate éclair while Mrs. Taylor poured

him a peppermint tea. Then, as abruptly as she arrived, she exited.

With her out of earshot, Dieter thought about his next sentence very carefully before uttering it.

"I heard on the BBC shortwave last night that Patton's Third Army broke out of the Normandy hedgerows and is moving east." Dieter casually dropped a cube of sugar into his tea.

"Yes, very good news," Dulles said. "If anyone can kick the Germans' rear ends all the way to Berlin, it would be General George S. Patton and those pearl-handed pistols of his."

"Is Patton meeting much resistance?" Dieter probed, but ever so slightly.

Dulles pursed his lips, as if he was thinking how to word his reply. "The word from London is that two Panzer divisions have stalled the advance in the St. Lô region, but I'm confident ol' Blood and Guts will drive a stake through their lines. Patton doesn't stand still very often." Dulles sipped his tea before setting the hand-painted cup on a saucer. "I'm certain that Operation Cobra will be successful. In fact, I wouldn't put it past Patton to maneuver around the southern flank and surround the German defenses, which have bottled up Monty and the British Expeditionary Force near Caen."

Operation Cobra? Dieter hadn't heard that before. That meant Patton's Third Army wasn't racing for Paris but would come back around and strike German forces from the rear. A classic pincer movement.

"Is the Resistance helping out?"

Dulles finished chewing a mouthful of pastry. "I had forgotten how good the Swiss are with chocolate. To answer your question, yes. The French underground are bothering the Krauts like a nest of mosquitoes. Blowing up bridges, sniper attacks, that sort of thing."

Dulles seemed unusually chatty. This meant Dieter knew he had to reciprocate in some way. "Some of my contacts in the Swiss Air Force say that American pilots are dropping from the sky like unexpected drops of rain. Just in the last week, a dozen B-17 bomb crews limped into Swiss airspace after getting shot up over Germany."

Dulles didn't seem impressed. "Colonel Harris of the American Military Legation—he's on the second floor—has been keeping me briefed."

Dieter expected the American spymaster to say that. "Has the Colonel told you that Swiss Me-109s and anti-aircraft guns shot down four U.S. bombers last month?"

Dulles straightened up in his chair. "Why would the Swiss shoot down our bombers? Surely they know better than that."

Dieter shrugged. "Depends on your point of view. They see themselves as Swiss, defending national airspace. And remember, the Schaffhausen *was* bombed last month by the Americans—"

"Clearly an accident. The crew got confused. Schaffhausen is north of the Rhine—"

"Twenty Swiss, including women and children, were killed. That's why some of the Swiss"—Dieter barely caught himself from saying *our*—"flight crews have been, how you say, trigger-happy." He kept his voice matter-of-fact and unemotional. He knew whom he was dealing with.

"I see. What about the Swiss authorities handing Jews back over to the Germans—is that still happening?"

Dieter was relieved to change the subject. "Jews escaping into Switzerland, if caught by the border patrol or local police, are being escorted immediately to the Basel frontier. That's the official policy coming out of Bern. The Jews will do anything not to be put into German custody. I've heard about it all—bribes, sex, whatever. Yesterday a young Jewish couple and their baby jumped off the Mittlere Brücke rather than be handed over to the Germans."

"Ghastly. Did they escape?"

Dieter shook his head. "Their bodies were pulled out of the Rhine by firemen."

A buzzer sounded on Dulles's desk, followed by the entrance of Miss Taylor. "Your next appointment has arrived, sir."

Dieter took that as his cue to exit. He rose, and Dulles extended a hand.

"Mr. Baumann, thank you for coming to Bern on what should be a holiday for you."

"It's no big deal. Besides, the Germans aren't taking off today." Dieter shot a glance at Frau Taylor. He noted the smallest hint of a smile on her face, and he couldn't help but return a slight smile, understanding how even the most stoic often crumbled under his charm.

• • • • • • • •

Allen Dulles watched Baumann exit his office as a strange uneasiness settled over him. He tapped a plug of West Virginia tobacco into his cherrywood pipe. "Miss Taylor, do you trust him?"

His secretary hesitated for a moment. "Mr. Baumann's operational skills have been excellent, and he can be quite charming. He must be agreeable if he's cajoling that much information from the Swiss and German operatives here in Switzerland. But there's something 'off' about him, like he's trying too hard."

"Hmmm," Dulles muttered. He'd seen plenty of men like Baumann in his day.

When Allen Welsh Dulles joined the Secret Intelligence Branch (SI) following America's entrance into the war, he was taught to train case officers, run agent operations, and process intelligence reports. In the fall of 1942, Washington asked Dulles to set up shop in Switzerland because the neutral country was fertile ground for intelligence gathering—smack in the middle of Europe and surrounded by Axis countries. Since the Germans, Russians, and British were using landlocked Switzerland to spy on each other following the invasion of Poland, Dulles's nascent network was playing catch-up.

He found that sending Allied agents *into* Germany had scant hope of eluding the Gestapo, but travel between the Reich and neutral Switzerland was free enough to bring certain Germans to him. Hence the need for field agents with mother-tongue ability to speak German. Men like Dieter Baumann.

Dulles struck a wooden match and drew a puff. "He was curious about General Patton today—a little too curious." A wisp of smoke rose in the air. "Send a message to Jean-Pierre. Tell him I want Dieter Baumann put under surveillance. Very discreet. No reason to spook him."

Priscilla Taylor scribbled on her notepad, then looked up. "There's one more thing, sir. Our contact from Heidelberg sent this eyes-only message while you were meeting with Mr. Baumann."

Dulles opened the sealed envelope and scanned its contents.

"I have to contact Washington on this." Dulles felt the knot in his gut tighten. "Something must be done immediately."

11

```
Gestapo Regional Headquarters
Heidelberg, Germany
2:45 p.m.
```

"Are you sure Sergeant Frisch hasn't reported?" Kassler, back at Regional Headquarters, knew his question sounded accusatory, but this was *important*.

Corporal Becker, standing before his desk, deflected the critical tone. "I've yet to locate him, sir. His bunkmate said he slept until noon and then left on a walk."

Kassler exhaled. "When's Frisch due to report?"

"Six o'clock for dinner, unless we can locate him beforehand."

"Very well."

"One more thing, sir," the fuzzy-cheeked aide said. "It seems that Sergeant Frisch and the night brigade captured one of the Stauffenberg plotters last night. He was caught leaving a sheaf of anti-Hitler handbills at a local hofbrau. Frisch searched his apartment and found a hand-operated duplicating machine hidden in the attic."

"Where is the prisoner?"

"In the basement, where information is being extracted at this moment. The lead interrogator called. Says he needs to speak with you—in person."

Kassler reached for his short-brim hat and leather belt, which holstered a 9mm Luger P.08. "You know where to find me if Himmler calls—or if Frisch shows up," he said grimly to Becker.

Kassler descended three flights of stairs, each landing pumping more adrenaline through his body. He had long ago taught himself to ignore the wide-eyed looks of outright horror and inevitable shrieks of pain from his victims. Detached, emotionally remote—that was the persona he embraced whenever he approached the basement Interrogation Center. Kassler willed himself into a state of calm because he knew enemies of the Reich would slit his throat if given half the chance. Kill or be killed.

Still, there were always a few seconds of mental adjustment whenever he stepped inside the doors of the Interrogation Center, and this afternoon was no different. Kassler greeted the guard posted outside the entrance to the torture room. The guard acknowledged him, turned around, and looked through a peephole, then knocked twice. Sergeant Buchalter, a burly soldier in his early thirties, answered the door with a pair of pliers in his left hand. His blood-splattered gray tunic was half-unbuttoned, displaying a soiled white shirt.

Kassler entered. A single lightbulb illuminated a room that reeked of sweat, blood, and fear. In the far corner, a bony middle-aged man had been stripped to his waist. His arms were wrapped behind a post, and his wrists were bound by rope. Blood streamed from a gash on his left temple, flowing down the side of his face onto his chest. More blood dripped from his left hand. The prisoner's whole body quivered, as if seizures overtook him. His knees trembled the worst, and he struggled to remain standing.

"I told him if his knees touch the ground, I'll beat him to a pulp," Sergeant Buchalter said.

"So why did you call me?"

"Because the prisoner hasn't been giving me names. All I've gotten out of him is something about a church."

"Have you employed more persuasive techniques?"

Buchalter shrugged. "He screamed after I yanked one of his fingernails out, but didn't yield. There's something different about this one. That's why I called you."

91

"His name?"

"Vinzent something."

"Let's have a look."

Kassler knew from experience that interrogation sessions usually didn't turn out this way. Most men cracked at the mere mention of things getting "rough." Others sang like catbirds when nail-pulling pliers were produced. Sharp knives loosened tongues as well. Whatever the method, the vast majority of prisoners—under torture—blabbered everything they knew. Only a few were truly committed to keeping silent. Nothing moved them. In those rare cases, however, more stringent measures were required.

"Do you have a copy of the leaflet?"

"Right here." Buchalter removed a handbill from his shirt pocket and pressed it into Kassler's hands.

"Appeal to All Germans!" the headline shouted. Kassler read on.

The struggle for freedom of speech, freedom of religion, and protection of the individual citizen from the arbitrary actions of our police state is happening at this very moment in time. The tide is turning against National Socialist Germany. The Bible says, "'Vengeance is mine,' saith the Lord," and His vengeful sword of retribution will destroy the totalitarian regime that launched a global war and has killed millions and imprisoned millions of others, including God's Chosen People. Support the resistance movement!

Kassler's chest constricted, and he felt heat rising to his face. "He's given you no names?"

"Not yet, Major. He keeps mumbling something about the church of Jesus Christ."

Kassler balled up the leaflet and tossed it to the floor, sure he could turn this Vinzent character around. He approached the prisoner and grabbed a tuft of hair, jerking his head up. "You know what happens if you don't give us what we want." He tightened his grip.

The prisoner labored to speak.

"You want to say something?" Kassler demanded, shouting in the man's ear. "Don't you know what will happen to you if you don't talk?"

The prisoner nodded. "Yes, I know." It was no more than a whisper.

Kassler leaned forward.

"Victory," the man mouthed.

Anger coursed through his veins. "Victory?" He slapped the man's face. "Victory will be ours, not yours!"

Kassler unbuttoned the leather holster containing his Luger pistol and brandished the gun. He inserted the tip into the prisoner's right nostril and rammed the extended black barrel deep into his sinuses. The man—unable to resist—screamed in pain.

"You have it all wrong!" Kassler roared. "The Third Reich will be victorious in the end!"

"Something . . . different . . . victory . . . in Jesus." The prisoner groaned in obvious pain. "There is victory . . . in Jesus."

"No, there isn't!" Kassler's heart pounded harder. "Death is the end. It's over when you die!"

Kassler removed his pistol from the sinus cavity and planted the tip between the man's eyebrows. The prisoner strained against the ropes, but then—as if taken over by another force—he suddenly calmed.

"I am prepared," he said. "It is finished."

"Okay, we'll do it your way," Kassler bellowed. "At the count of three—unless you tell me who is helping you—you will find out if your Jesus is waiting."

"*Eins* . . ." Kassler toggled the Luger.

"Knees?" the prisoner begged. "I want to kneel to meet Jesus."

Kassler relaxed his grip and waved the gun toward the floor. The bound prisoner crumpled to the ground in a heap.

Buchalter seized the man's arm, pulling him to his knees and adding a kick in the man's side.

Kassler lowered the gun to the prisoner's forehead. "Where were we? *Ja,* I remember."

He held the pistol steady. *"Zwei!"*

The prisoner raised his head. His eyes looked above Kassler, as if he were fixated on something far beyond the clammy walls.

"You have five seconds to say more than 'church.' I want names!"

The prisoner shook his head, but now his piercing eyes locked onto Kassler.

A brave one, Kassler thought. *"Auf Wiedersehen,* Herr Vinzent."

The single shot to the forehead dropped the prisoner like a burlap sack of Alsace potatoes.

Kassler returned the pistol to his holster and turned on his heels with a twinge of regret. Not for killing the swine, but because the prisoner died without telling everything he knew.

• • • • • • • •

University of Heidelberg
6:02 p.m.

Joseph Engel heard the heavy footsteps and knew who would be rapping on his office door.

"The door's open, Hannes."

"Ach—put the Bible away." Hannes Jäger sneered. "Or is that silly book more important than reading the papers Heisenberg sent over?"

They'd been through this dance how many times before? Joseph's roommate had a habit of barging into his office after five o'clock—just as he relaxed by reading the Bible. This often prompted a cagey comment or a pointed question from Jäger, and tonight appeared to be one of those occasions. Joseph had been careful not to read his Bible back at the apartment or get dragged into discussions about religion, but he wasn't going to hide his light under a bushel, as he had read the previous day in Matthew 5:15.

"Listen, Hannes." Joseph beckoned his roommate to take a seat in the sparely furnished office. "You study papers by Fermi, Weizäcker, and Hahn, hoping to learn something more about the half-life of natural uranium after it's been bombarded with neutrons. I scrutinize those papers as well, but sometimes my brain needs a break, so I pick up my Bible. So much that is written here makes sense."

A stunned silence filled the office. "You must be joking, Engel. There are only superstitions in that book—medieval ones at that."

Joseph felt his face flush from embarrassment and hoped it didn't show. "You can blame my father." He crossed his arms over his chest. "He read the Bible to me every night as a young boy. Father said if I read the Good Book for fifteen minutes a day—plus one chapter of Proverbs—I would become a wise young man."

"A wise young man," Jäger repeated in a slightly mocking voice. "You're a Lutheran, right?"

"That's correct." Joseph considered himself a Lutheran— and a conflicted one at that. His parents complained that the Lutheran Church in the 1940s wasn't the Lutheran Church of their youth. After Hitler came to power, the Führer attempted to establish a German Reich Church, calling on all German Protestants to unite in the hour of national need. Although his effort was rebuffed, many Lutheran pastors—as well as Roman Catholic priests—remained silent or cooperative when Hitler enacted the Nuremberg Laws in 1935 that excluded Jews from public life, government, culture, and the professions. Nor did they offer a peep of protest after roundups of Jews and other "undesirables" gained momentum following Kristallnacht in 1938.

Joseph recalled sitting in the pews one Sunday morning

before the war and hearing the pastor repeat Martin Luther's anti-Semitic views that Jewish synagogues should be set on fire, prayer books destroyed, rabbis forbidden to preach, Jewish property seized, and homes vandalized—nostrums set forth in his tract, *Von den Juden und Ihren Lügen*—"On the Jews and Their Lies," published in 1543.

He remembered his father twisting the church bulletin in his hands and threatening to walk out, but his mother shook her head. Father relaxed while inside church walls, but when they walked home afterward, he could barely contain his rage.

"This country is headed for a terrible fall," his father had declared as they passed apartment buildings in Spandau. "Although Germany is the cultural and intellectual center of Europe, Hitler is persecuting the Jews horribly, and Germany will pay dearly for this mistake."

"What did you think when the pastor said the Jews are the 'natural enemies' of Christian tradition, or that part about secular government having authority over religious institutions?" Joseph asked his father.

His papi's face turned dark. "That's when I lost my temper, when he quoted the apostle Paul from Romans 13:1: 'Let every soul be subject unto the higher powers. For there is no power but of God: the powers that be are ordained of God.' I have never heard a man of the cloth twist Scripture in such a way."

After that, the escalation of anti-Jewish rhetoric and outright persecution of Jews never sat well with Joseph. He'd never forgotten the time when the Rosenberg family of six knocked on their back door, offering to trade two silver forks for a single meal. Within a week, the Rosenbergs were rounded up and shipped east to a "relocation" camp. Everything had been taken by the State: their house, their family car, their furnishings, and their clothes. Joseph shuddered at the thought of losing every possession and being forced at gunpoint to live hundreds of miles from home next to some armament factory.

The only light in the darkness, his father said, was a small band of Lutheran pastors, led by Martin Niemöller, who had formed the "Confessing Church" to oppose the Nazi regime. Their activities were covert, lest they be arrested by the Gestapo like one of the leaders, Dietrich Bonhoeffer. Joseph thought his father was involved, but he knew better than to raise the topic with him. It was too dangerous, especially in case the Gestapo asked questions. And now Jäger was inquiring about him being a Lutheran.

Joseph cleared his throat. "I consider myself a follower of Christ, and let me explain why. You know how you believe an isotope of uranium will produce a new element?"

His roommate nodded. "That's what we've been working toward the last year with Doktor Heisenberg."

"Correct, but so far that is a theory. It's a good theory and similar to the Bohr-Wheeler hypothesis that an uneven number of particles makes a good fissioner. But these are all theories that you and I are actively working to prove or disprove. Now this Bible"—Joseph patted his right hand on the brown leather cover—"is like a series of papers and proofs, but the same hand has written them all. And they are not theories but rather the thoughts and wisdom of a Power Source far greater than the atom. In fact, he created atoms and neutrons and protons, and he knows everything about them while we know so little."

His roommate only seemed to be half listening, but Joseph continued anyway. "Think of how far quantum physics has come in the last twenty-five years. Many hundreds if not thousands of brilliant minds have tackled unbelievably complicated equations on blackboards, but to the God of the universe, our knowledge of quantum physics is similar to the thickness of one of these pages in the Bible."

"That's nice you feel that way." Jäger smiled. "But it's rubbish all the same. I don't believe there's a God, and you certainly can't convince me that there's one in the midst of this global war. The stories I hear of the brutality, hand-to-hand combat . . . We can end that, you know, by building this bomb. Then the world will know peace."

The Bomb.

The office fell silent once again.

What looked possible on paper—building a wonder weapon—was proving to be far more arduous than originally thought. Heisenberg had told Joseph and the physicists that when Albert Speer, Hitler's Minister of Arms and Munitions, asked for an update on the bomb's progress, he downplayed the chances of exploding a Wunderwaffe before 1947, at the earliest.

"I think we're closer than what Doktor Heisenberg thought," Joseph told his roommate. He thought about saying, *I pray we will never have to use it,* but he knew such a public utterance could be used against him.

"You would be one to know," Jäger said, turning friendlier now that the subject was off religion. "Your theory about how to best start a chain reaction through the bombardment of natural uranium was a stroke of genius. If your assertions are correct, an atomic device could be feasible within a year."

"I didn't put a timetable on it, but yes, that was what I was thinking." Joseph couldn't help but return his roommate's smile.

"Good, because if we don't beat the Americans and their Jew scientists, we could be their first target."

Joseph hadn't thought of that. A year, maybe less. They could maybe even shave off a couple of months with another idea he had . . .

12

Davos Parade Platz
7:30 p.m.

Gabi Mueller brushed back her blonde hair and smiled at the boys and girls as the town's *kinder* proudly marched past her table holding up *lampions*—paper lanterns suspended on sticks—while an accordionist wheezed a peppy chorus of Ländlermusik. Hundreds of townspeople—along with several dozen American pilots—clapped rhythmically from their picnic benches, erected in Davos's town square for the holiday occasion. A distant sun settled behind the serrated Alpine peaks, and the paper lampions—which looked like miniature Swiss flags—glowed by virtue of small candles in this twilight hour.

"They don't celebrate Swiss National Day like this where I come from," said Captain Bill Palmer, assigned to the 351st Bomb Group, 509th Bomb Squadron, U.S. Army Eighth Air Force. "I mean, I've seen lampions before, but we don't have mountains like these back in Wisconsin."

"When did your parents emigrate from Switzerland?" Gabi inclined toward the American airman.

"Actually, it was my grandparents. They were among hundreds of Swiss who settled in the heart of Green County after the Civil War. They named their village New Glarus because the alpine farmlands reminded them of Glarus back in the Old Country. In fact, we call it 'Little Switzerland' because—"

"We know all about New Glarus, don't we, Willy?"

Gabi's younger brother flashed a knowing grin. "Dad grew

up there before he met Mom at a missionary conference in Amsterdam," Willy informed the American pilot. Then he directed his gaze toward his sister. "I told you, Gabi, that you should meet Bill since our families came from the same town back in the States."

Gabi turned to Eric Hofstadler. "Are you understanding this?" she asked in English.

"No, just a leetle bit," he replied sheepishly. "But okay. I learn English."

"Sorry, Eric." The Yankee pilot chuckled. "My parents only spoke English to me. I think they wanted us to be American, although my brother and I joked that they didn't teach us Swiss-German so we wouldn't understand when they were discussing how to punish us. I have to say, though, my Swiss-German vocabulary has picked up since I got here back in January, so be careful what you say."

Gabi brightened. "How did you decide to become a pilot?"

Captain Palmer let the kids and their lampions pass by before speaking up. "My interest in flying started in New Glarus when the crop dusters used to come through, so when the war started, I volunteered to become a pilot. The Army Air Corps shipped me to Maxwell Field in Alabama for basic flight school. There I got my first hours in a Beech AT-10 twin trainer. Those of us who didn't wash out wound up at McDill Field outside Tampa for training in the B-17, the Flying Fortress. After Thanksgiving in '43, I was shipped out to England, where I became part of 'The Mighty Eighth'—the U.S. Eighth Air Force, 3rd Air Division. We were stationed in East Anglia along the southeastern English coast. I was quickly put into the rotation, copilot in the right seat. Complete twenty-five missions over Europe, and you could go home."

Palmer paused and arched an eyebrow for effect. "On my *thirty-eighth* mission on January 18, we were given orders to bomb a munitions factory in Landsberg, a few miles west of Munich. The boys and I in our 'Lonesome Polecat'—that's what we named our bomber—dropped our load without incident, but as we turned around to deadhead back to the Channel, a swarm of FW-190s closed in tight. A burst of fire shattered the cockpit and just missed my head—and another caused a massive fuel line rupture. One engine stopped immediately. Our upper turret gunner hardly got out a burst before his hydraulics were hit, jamming the turret."

"You must have been scared out of your wits." Gabi leaned forward, her eyes focused on his.

"A lot more than that, I can assure you, sister. The fuel was leaking fast, and the captain and I agreed that we couldn't make it back to England. We talked with the crew, and we agreed that we didn't want to parachute into Krautland. We had heard about flight crews machine-gunned on the spot, so the only option was to limp toward Switzerland. That's exactly what we did, setting a course for Dübendorf, the military airport just outside of Zurich. Just before we entered Swiss airspace, German AA guns really fouled things up. Another engine took a hit. A fire started in the belly, and with black smoke billowing from the plane, we dropped our gear and dove for the Dübendorf runway. We managed to land in one piece, but a half-dozen Swiss troopers, rifles ready, were waiting for us when we rolled to a stop. I'll never forget what the squad leader said that day. With a K31 pointed at us, he said in English, 'Velcome to Sveetzerland. For you, ze vor ist over.'" Palmer mimicked the Swiss-German accent, which elicited smiles from the group.

"So now you're waiting out the war?" A cool wind brushed Gabi's face.

"You could say that." Palmer spread his hands wide. "You could also say that the Swiss stuck us in the middle of nowhere. Not much to do here. We play cards, read books. The Davos Kino has a movie in English every night, but they tend to show the same films over and over. Basically, we do our best to kill time."

"Great," Gabi said. "And now you're interned here in Davos until the war ends."

"Right," replied Palmer. "Officially, we are not prisoners, we are internees. We're staying at the Palace Hotel and several others, but don't get the wrong idea. We don't have maid service, and the food is horrible. Cheese, cheese, cheese! Yesterday we had cheese for breakfast, bread and cheese for lunch, and potato soup and cheese for dinner. And cheesecake for dessert! No wonder you have bidets over here in Europe, if you know what I mean."

Willy and Andreas nudged each other with a knowing look. Gabi had been translating snatches here and there for Eric and could tell from the look on his face that he wondered what he was missing. She stifled a laugh.

"Typsch Buebe," Gabi muttered to Eric, who would have to be satisfied with that. *Typical boys.*

"Hey, I understood that!" Palmer adjusted his flight cap. Like all the internees, Gabi knew he had to wear his standard-issue American uniform at all times.

"So the American airmen are allowed to walk around town." Gabi tucked her skirt tighter against her legs as a cool breeze stirred.

"Oh, yeah. Like I said, we get to talk to all the pretty Swiss girls. Some of the pilots have become quite smitten with the local ladies, so your boyfriend might want to keep an eye on a blonde bombshell like you." Palmer's eyes, filled with mirth, nodded toward the young man seated next to Gabi.

"Was ist passiert?" Eric interrupted.

"So Eric, your English is improving rather quickly." Willy laughed and elbowed his brother. "We have to be careful."

Gabi deflected the compliment about her looks. "What if you want to escape?"

"We've been told by the American Legation not to try," the pilot explained, "but the Army Air Corps drilled into us that we have to do everything we can to return to our units. It's not hard to try—all you have to do is walk out of town some night, but it's a long way on foot to the Rhine valley.

Most pilots who attempt escape are picked up in a day or two, and then it's bad news, right, Willy?"

"Correct. A trip straight to Wauwilermoos, a penitentiary camp between Bern and Zurich. Ninety days of confinement behind barbed wire, minimum, for escaping."

The lampion parade was over, and the accordion joined a quartet for a rousing musical celebration.

"Shall we dance before we have to get on the train?" Eric asked in Swiss-German.

Gabi looked at her watch. The last train would leave in twenty minutes and wouldn't get back to Basel until past midnight. She yawned, knowing she was expected to be at her desk in the translation pool at 8 a.m.

"Okay, but we only have a few minutes."

Gabi took Eric's hand in hers, and as she twirled, she caught Andreas and Willy watching them dance. They smiled and raised short-stemmed glasses of white wine, a signal, Gabi thought, that they approved of the young man leading her through an energetic waltz.

* * * * * * * *

Gestapo Regional Headquarters
Heidelberg, Germany
8:15 p.m.

"The Reichsführer is on the line," Becker announced.

The second time in one day. Kassler immediately stood at attention as he switched the black phone from his right ear to his left ear. He regarded the black-and-white headshot of his mentor on the office wall and held his breath, waiting for the phone call from Berlin to be connected. He had met Heinrich Himmler just once—at his installation as Sturmbannführer of the Heidelberg regional headquarters.

"My dear Kassler, I trust you are well since our conversation earlier today," the lubricated voice intoned over the scratchy connection.

"Very well, Reichsführer. It pleases me to receive your—"

"The Führer himself has been briefed about your discovery of Joseph Engel and is taking an active interest in the case," Himmler interrupted.

The Führer heard his name? Kassler felt a warm glow radiate through his body.

"And? Did the Führer provide input on how to proceed?"

"Yes. It is imperative that Professor Heisenberg continue his work on a secret military project that will assure final victory for the Fatherland. Because we do not know how vital Engel is to that effort, my previous orders stand. Engel is to be taken into protective custody and not harmed."

"I understand, Reichsführer. Our plan is to bring in Engel tonight."

"Good. I know this is very unusual—treating a Jew in such a manner—but with the weight of Heisenberg's project, I'm sure you understand."

"*Jawohl,* mein Reichsführer."

Moments after Kassler slipped the handset back onto its cradle, he buzzed for Becker, who arrived breathless in a matter of seconds.

"Has Frisch arrived?"

"He's going over assignments with the night brigade down the hall. He asked me to tell you that it felt good to be in the Jew-hunting business again."

"Excellent. When Frisch is finished briefing his men, tell him I need to see him."

After Becker closed the door, Kassler leaned back in his chair and ruminated on the phone call from Berlin. Himmler, he decided, was just checking up on him. But the truth couldn't be denied: it was he, Sturmbannführer Bruno Kassler, who'd discovered the Jewish mole working on the most secret military project in the Reich's history. And now Hitler knew that fact.

If everything went as planned tonight, Hitler would be apprised of that too.

13

Joseph Engel rinsed the dinner plate under a stream of hot water and handed it to his roommate to dry. "Last one." He pulled a rubber plug and watched the dirty dishwater run down the drain.

"Where did you learn to cook schnitzel?" Hannes Jäger ran his tongue over his lips. "Delicious."

"That was Mami's recipe. She taught me a lot, including a little horseback riding. I guess she doted on me because I was an only child."

"I had forgotten about that." Jäger set the dried dish atop the other plates in the cupboard. "Not common to have just one child. Your parents didn't want more—"

"Mami always told me I was a special gift to her and Father. But they never talked about why I didn't have any brothers and sisters. I never asked. In fact, I sensed they didn't want to talk about it."

"Maybe you should ask some day—" Jäger cocked his ear and quickly turned his head toward the front door. "Did you hear that noise?"

"What noise?"

"The car pulling up outside. Don't they know there's a curfew?"

"You're too nosy these days." Joseph finished wiping off the countertop. "Somebody is probably dropping someone off or picking someone up."

"I'm going to investigate." Jäger stepped out of the kitchen and approached their second-story window. "*Mein Gott im Himmel!* It's not possible!"

Joseph trailed behind him, wiping a glass with a hand towel. "What's going on?"

Jäger peered through the side of the drapes. "I think it's the Gestapo."

Joseph felt his knees go weak. He held a healthy fear for the *Geheime Staatspolizei*, the official secret police of the Third Reich. Laws passed in 1936 had given the Gestapo a blank check to operate without judicial oversight. So complete was their authority that Joseph couldn't recall having a single casual conversation about the Gestapo with someone other than his parents. Even the most innocent comment could be reported as a denunciation against National Socialism.

In fact, Joseph's only contact with the secret police happened three years earlier when the local *Gruppenführer* in Spandau interviewed him prior to accepting the research position with Doktor Heisenberg. Even though he'd nothing to hide, just being in their presence had intimidated him.

"I wonder where they're going." Jäger moved toward the apartment entryway and pressed his right ear against the front door.

"Do you hear what they're saying?"

"Nothing. Just footsteps." Then Jäger swore and took three quick steps back. "They're coming this way!"

Suddenly, without a knock, their front door burst open, and Joseph watched in horror as two of the three soldiers—each wearing black scarves to cover their faces—tackled Jäger to the floor. As bodies crumpled, Jäger yelped. His head hit the sharp end of their living room coffee table, inflicting a gash on his right temple. A thin rivulet of blood snaked down the side of his face. The third soldier pressed a black pistol to Jäger's forehead as he curled up into a fetal position.

"Don't shoot! Don't shoot!" Jäger screamed.

"Shut up! You're under arrest!" The soldier balled up his

right fist and swung at Jäger's midsection, landing a painful blow to the left kidney.

Joseph stood paralyzed. Without thinking, he allowed the glass he was holding to slip through his fingers and crash to the floor, causing three sets of suspicious eyes to turn his way. The scene before him was surreal—not possible.

"Don't hurt him," Joseph pleaded. "He's done nothing wrong."

"And how would you know that?" The voice came from a fourth person entering the room—a Gestapo agent wearing a black leather trench coat and hat. He, too, wore a black scarf to disguise his facial features. He casually reached inside the right pocket of his trench coat and withdrew a Luger, then pointed it at Joseph.

Joseph felt his knees grow weak. "I-I-I don't know." He thrust his hands toward the ceiling. His usually agile mind fogged over, and he couldn't make himself believe the reality of what was happening. After a moment, he managed to enunciate a sentence. "We're just scientists working at the University."

"And who are you?" the agent in charge asked.

"Engel, Joseph."

"And you?" The agent pointed his pistol down at Jäger.

"Jäger, H-Hannes. We a-are roommates." A pained cry escaped his lips.

The agent nodded his head toward Joseph. "He's the one."

Joseph felt the blood drain from his face. What had he done against the State? This had to be a huge mistake.

Before he could say another word, two soldiers lunged toward Joseph. He fell backward onto the sofa in a heap. They were on him like wolves on a carcass.

Joseph swung his arms and kicked his feet, attempting to push them off, but his efforts were of no use. One of the soldiers vise-gripped his upper arm while another latched on to his legs. Without warning, a heavy fist crashed into his temple. Joseph cried out as pain shot through his head. The room faded, but he fought to remain conscious. Again, he struggled against the men, but another sharp pinch pierced his shoulder as the Gestapo's nightstick found its mark.

"What are you doing?" he screamed. "I've done NOTH-ING!"

"Handcuff him," the lead agent directed.

One of the soldiers flipped Joseph over, pressing his knee into the small of his back, forcing him to struggle for breath as his face mashed into the thin carpet. The second soldier joined the first, pressing him down and cinching the handcuffs tight on his wrists.

With a loud curse, the first soldier rose and slammed his booted heel down on Joseph's backside for emphasis. Another stab of pain shot through him as his breath escaped, forcing him to gasp for air.

"Stop it! I'm cooperating!" he finally managed to wheeze out.

The soldier took a step backward, and Joseph relaxed. His eyes met those of his roommate, and he noticed fear in Hannes's gaze. Fear mixed with accusation.

"Get up," the Gestapo leader ordered.

Joseph struggled to find his legs. When he was fully standing, he felt a gun tip pressed into his lower spine.

"We need your identity papers. Where are they?" the Gestapo agent demanded.

"In my satchel. On . . . on the nightstand in the bedroom."

The Gestapo agent nodded toward one of the soldiers, who pivoted and marched into the apartment's single bedroom and returned with a well-worn leather satchel, handing it to the man in charge.

"Heavy. What's inside?"

"Physics papers and my personal notebook. My identity papers are in my billfold."

The Gestapo agent peered inside, fumbled around for a

moment, and then secured the silver clasp, tucking it under his arm.

Joseph's eyes met Hannes's again.

"Are you okay?" Joseph asked in no more than a whisper.

The left side of his friend's face was drenched in blood. Dark red dripped from his cheek, staining his white shirt in crimson.

Instead of answering, Hannes looked away.

"No talking!" The guard pressed the gun deeper into Joseph's back. He arched to ease the pressure.

"*Raus! Jetzt ins Auto!*" the Gestapo agent growled.

Joseph dropped his head as two of the soldiers and the Gestapo agent manhandled him out of the apartment. The fourth stayed behind with Jäger. Joseph couldn't stop his armed escorts from hustling him down the stairs and out the front of the building. There, a black Mercedes touring car waited with all four doors open.

One soldier jumped into the rear bench seat. The other grabbed Joseph by the scruff of the neck and shoved him inside the car, then remained outside awaiting orders.

"What should we do with the other one?" the soldier asked.

"Kill him." The Gestapo agent showed no emotion as he took the passenger's seat in the front.

"*Jawohl.*" The soldier turned on his heels and ran back into the apartment block. Within thirty seconds, a single shot rang out, followed by two soldiers sprinting out of the apartment block. One jumped behind the steering wheel. The other squished himself in the rear next seat to Joseph.

No, not Hannes . . . Joseph's shoulders trembled. His friend was dead.

The driver slammed the Mercedes into gear, and they roared away from the University apartment complex.

Joseph ached to turn his head for one last look. Instead, the man next to him removed a black scarf from his coat pocket and quickly wrapped it around Joseph's face, securing it with a tight knot.

"Where are you taking me?" he mumbled through the cloth.

"There's no need to say anything, Herr Engel," the Gestapo agent said from the front seat. "You'll find out very shortly."

"But—"

The guard to his left slammed his right elbow into Joseph's rib cage. The air from his lungs escaped in a fast whoosh, and he struggled to breathe.

Joseph moaned and then yanked at the cuffs, but they didn't give. His whole body seemed to protest the pain, and he wondered what he'd done to deserve this treatment. His mind searched for an answer, but he could think of nothing.

Something had happened, something beyond his control. Maybe it was a case of mistaken identity. Then again, these soldiers seemed certain they had caught their prey.

Maybe there was an explanation, but as each minute passed, the *why* no longer mattered. Joseph knew something horrendous was about to happen. Now he wondered *what*.

• • • • • • • • •

Kassler consulted his timepiece. It was after 11:00 p.m. when his Mercedes sedan, adorned with a pair of postcard-sized swastikas furling in the night air, jerked to a stop in front of the two-story brownstone apartments belonging to the University of Heidelberg.

Sergeant Rudolf Frisch stepped out of the front passenger seat, stiffened his posture, and opened the rear door for Sturmbannführer Bruno Kassler, who wore his black gabardine service uniform. A red swastika armband was wrapped around his left upper arm. Kassler nodded to Frisch, and then regarded the troop transport truck that noisily rolled in behind him.

From the truck's rear, a half-dozen soldiers energetically

jumped to the cobblestone street, each holding Gewehr 98 rifles. They quickly fell into formation before Kassler.

The Gestapo chief adjusted his leather cross-strap and jutted out his chin. "My fellow defenders of the Reich," Kassler pronounced solemnly. "Sergeant Frisch has outlined the action we will be taking tonight. The description I have of Joseph Engel is that he is 185 centimeters tall, weighs 65 kilos, and is slim in build with brown curly hair. Age is twenty-seven. He is a research scientist and not expected to be a physical threat. Nonetheless, none other than Reichsführer Himmler himself has ordered that he be captured alive. If any of you harm this man, I will personally court-martial you. I can assure you my sentence will be quick, harsh, and brutal. I can also assure you that you will not live to see your loved ones again."

Kassler turned to his left and paced a couple of steps. "The suspect lives with another University of Heidelberg scientist. Name of Hannes Jäger. They are not known to have many guests over to their apartment. Their sleeping habits are unknown at this time. Because of the sensitive nature of this arrest, I will be accompanying you tonight. I expect you to follow the orders and direction of Sergeant Frisch, but I will be immediately available if you have any questions."

Frisch reached for a Luger pistol and released the safety, an action that the six soldiers followed with their carbines. With a twitch of his head, they followed him into the apartment complex. The stairway leading to the second-floor apartment was lit with a bare lightbulb. Frisch crouched as he entered the second-story landing, and then stopped in his tracks.

"*Was ist los?*" he whispered, then held his hand up. He waited until Kassler joined the search party, then nodded toward Apartment 2, where the front door was left open.

"A trap?" Frisch asked.

Kassler peered toward the faint light. He wasn't sure, but what he did know was that a wide-open front door was unusual at 11 p.m.

"Maybe. Have your men storm the flat, but remember, Engel is to be taken alive."

The four soldiers nodded and readied themselves for the assault. Frisch led them closer, inch by inch, then raised his right arm and jerked it forward. One soldier sprinted past the door and knelt on the other side, his rifle ready. Another took a position next to the doorjamb.

Frisch pulled up beside him and held up his left fist. Making eye contact with each soldier, he mouthed *eins, zwei, drei* . . . and on the count of three, they poured into the apartment, guns ready to match fire.

Kassler was on their heels, and what he saw stupefied him. Living room furniture had been turned over, a bookcase toppled, and two pictures knocked off the walls. Sitting on the floor—his hands bound in handcuffs and a black scarf cinched across his mouth—a sandy-haired man looking to be in his mid-thirties struggled to free himself.

Frisch motioned to two soldiers to check the rest of the apartment.

"Take the gag off," Kassler ordered.

Frisch leaned over and untied the scarf. "Who are you?"

The prisoner devoured several gulps of air before responding. "Don't kill me! I'll tell you anything. Anything you need to know!"

"Who are YOU?" Frisch repeated.

The prisoner relaxed after a few seconds. "I'm Hannes Jäger. I work for Doktor Heisenberg at the University. I've done nothing wrong."

Kassler processed the information for a moment. "Put him in a chair." A sinking feeling came over him. He *would* find out what happened . . . but from what he could see, Engel was gone. He'd have to find the missing physicist, and soon. If not—well, he didn't want to think about that possibility.

14

After they blindfolded Joseph, none of the four men in the Mercedes spoke much except to say "Left here" or "Continue straight." They had motored just five minutes when he sensed the car slow down and veer sharply right. Judging from the reverberations, they were turning into some sort of voluminous building. Then the car parked, and the engine turned off.

Joseph's heart pounded so hard he worried it would break one of his ribs. His body ached, and fear caused his knees to weaken—and his legs to tremble. He was sure he was about to be tortured. The question was *how*. And why? His mind searched for answers. What did he do? Why did they drag him out of his apartment? Could his arrest be a grotesque case of mistaken identity?

He pictured the cold, hard steel of a muzzle pressed against his temple, and a shudder passed through his body. The truth was he could be dead *today*. His stomach lurched, and nausea rose in his throat.

Joseph heard the car door open and felt an arm squeeze his right bicep. "Out you go," one of his captors directed.

With his arms bound behind him, Joseph struggled to find his legs.

"Remove the blindfold," he heard someone say.

His eyes adjusted to the dimly lit warehouse with a cavernous ceiling. Swiveling his head to his left, Joseph regarded a half-dozen flatbed trucks, dirty and well-used. Bales of tawny hay were stacked in a corner, and truck parts were strewn haphazardly on the concrete. *So this is where it will end.* He couldn't believe everything—his own life—had come to this.

Three men dressed in workman's clothes strode out of the shadows, issuing greetings to his captors. He watched as the Gestapo quickly removed their hats and unbuttoned their uniformed shirts. Joseph noted smiles of relief as they shook hands with those welcoming them back. For a moment, their cheerful smiles seemed a worse greeting than if they'd approached with guns. At least then he'd know where he stood. But this . . .

These were not the Gestapo.

But who were they? Wartime Germany was not a place of safety, and Joseph knew enemies revealed themselves in many forms.

The reedy man in charge approached Joseph, unbuttoning his leather trench coat, and removing the scarf around his jowls. Joseph took a step back, tugging at the handcuffs holding his hands.

"Steady, Mr. Engel. We're not here to harm you." Under his coat, the man wore a frayed dress shirt that had turned beige since its last wash.

Definitely not Gestapo issue. *But who?*

"I'm . . . I'm afraid I don't understand what's going on." Joseph dared to lock eyes with the man.

The leader waved off Joseph's observation. "There are a lot of things you don't understand, Professor Engel, but there will be a time to explain everything later. We must move quickly because our situation is tenuous and very dangerous."

Professor Engel? The way his name rolled off the man's tongue caused the tiny hairs on the back of Joseph's neck to rise. Of course—the bomb. His work. His discovery.

"So you mean I'm not under arrest?"

"Not at all. But you were about to be taken in for questioning by the Gestapo. I can assure you, my friend, that they would not have been as kind."

"But why? What have I done?"

"So many questions, Professor. For now, the most important thing is your safety. Besides, the less you know the better. Information is life's most valuable commodity these days." He nodded his chin to a man standing nearby.

The "Gestapo" guard grasped Joseph's left elbow to steer him. "Right this way, sir."

The man led Joseph ten steps to a flatbed truck stacked with wire-bound bales of hay. At the rear of the truck, several bales had been removed, revealing a crawl space large enough for two men.

"Wilhelm will join you for the night," the soldier said. As if on cue, a man dressed in farm clothes joined them. "Now up you go."

"In there?" Joseph pointed to dark space.

"Yes." The leader pushed him forward. "You and Wilhelm will sleep there. It's too dangerous to drive past curfew. Roadblocks everywhere. We will wait until daylight before continuing our journey."

"Where are you taking me?"

"Surely, Herr Engel, you wouldn't expect us to answer that." The leader shook his head, and then he motioned to Wilhelm. "You have that extra handkerchief to gag Herr Engel?"

"But if I'm not a prisoner—" Joseph tugged again on his bound wrists.

"Please, Herr Engel. Standard operational procedure. It's for your own security."

Wilhelm reached for a cream-colored oversized handkerchief in his back pocket. "This is merely a precaution, Professor. Is there anything more to say before I bind you?"

"Yes. What about these handcuffs? And how do you expect me to sleep in such an uncomfortable place?"

"I apologize for the restraints as well as the accommodations, Herr Engel. But I suggest you accept the situation. It would be better for all of us."

Wilhelm tightened the handkerchief around Joseph's face, then boosted him onto the flatbed. Another soldier helped the two of them settle into their sleeping cave before closing off the entrance. Two threadbare pillows and blankets, both in grimy conditions, had been fashioned into makeshift beds.

"*Schlafen sie gut*," Wilhelm said. "*Bis Morgen.*"

Joseph, his hands shackled and mouth gagged, lay on his side and rested his head upon a blue-and-white-striped pillow that reeked of dirt and sweat. As he lay there, he listened to the other man's rhythmic breathing and wondered what the morning would bring. Thus far, he'd avoided the war—safely ensconced in university laboratories and classrooms, listening to lectures, participating in experiments, and sleeping in his own bed. His only disruption had been waking up with equations dancing in his head.

Now his shoulders ached from his hands being handcuffed, and the gag in his mouth pulled too tight—not to mention the ache in his legs from being unable to stretch out in the small space. With each breath, questions filled his mind, only matched with thoughts of escape. They hadn't tortured him . . . yet. But there was no guarantee it wouldn't happen. No doubt the knowledge he carried within him—information about the wonder weapon and the university's research—was of value to many.

Joseph breathed in the earthy scent of hay and considered the man's words, *You were about to be taken in by Gestapo, and I can assure you that they wouldn't have been so kind . . .*

Again, more questions. What did the Gestapo want with him? After all, he worked for the government. His work could help their cause.

Joseph's thoughts journeyed back to his apartment. Aching loss shot through his heart as he considered Jäger's death.

Surely, if they were trying to help him, they wouldn't have

killed his colleague. No matter what they say, they cannot be trusted. No matter what they do—

An aching sob escaped his gag, and his shoulders trembled.

Dear God, are you there? Do you see me even now? Are you with me even here?

His world of relative calm and safety, he feared, was in his past. What kind of future lay in store? He didn't want to try to guess. Still, he knew that Someone cared for him—Someone who did know exactly where he was.

Lord, show me what to do . . . and whom to trust.

With every worry that filled his mind, he offered it up to the Lord. Actually, "offer" was a weak term. Joseph imagined holding those fears in his hands and casting them at the foot of God's throne.

And as he lay there, wondering how many hours had passed, and how many still remained until morning, a Scripture came to mind. One his father had taught him as a young boy—2 Timothy 1:7.

God hath not given us the spirit of fear; but of power, and of love, and of a sound mind.

He could hear his father's voice in his thoughts.
A sound mind. It was what he needed most . . .
To know what to do.
To know how to keep his secrets his own.
To know whom to trust.

* * * * * * * * *

"Are we ready to transmit?" The Gestapo captain—as he was known on this mission—ran a hand down his dingy white shirt, aware that the recipient at the other end of the short-wave transmission waited anxiously for news about the abduction. Code name for this Swiss contact was "Big Cheese."

He regarded the message that would be tapped out in Morse code as quickly as his hands would allow. The problem wasn't his team's ability to send the information. The problem was not knowing if it would be intercepted in the process—or if *they'd* be intercepted.

Somewhere out there in the night, the real Gestapo had stationed trucks with listening devices in different Heidelberg neighborhoods. The purpose was to intercept clandestine transmissions and to determine where they were coming from. Was a truck parked around the corner? He had no way of knowing.

Package picked up. Will move in morning. Await instructions for final transfer. He regarded his scribbled words on a piece of paper. Concise, and to the point.

The leader sat down at a table tucked in the corner of the cavernous garage and set to work.

His fingers worked furiously to tap out the message. After the final sentence miraculously shot through the nighttime air, the leader hoped—prayed—that they would not be discovered.

* * * * * * * *

Brauhaus Vetter Restaurant
Heidelberg, Germany
11:47 p.m.

From the restaurant's rear dining room, Pastor Leo Keller ignored the din of drinking songs that rose in crescendo with the volume of beer imbibed. Instead, he focused on the earnest faces of those gathered around him, yet he still found his mind wandering more often than it should.

The proprietor had warned Pastor Leo that his restaurant had become the *Treffpunkt*—meeting point—for the local Swiss community. Though these Swiss worked away from home—most were employed in technical positions at the Krupp ball bearing factory and munitions plants in and around Heidelberg—their hearts proved near to their mother country tonight. Apparently, the emotional tug of the First of August, and a longing for their homeland, was a potent combination for letting wartime steam rise to the ceiling where hop wreaths hung in orderly rows from rough-hewn wooden beams.

In the main room, an energetic accordion player moved seamlessly from one Swiss folklore song to another as couples clacked silver spoons to the sprightly music. Numerous heavy-breasted waitresses, in low-cut dirndls, slung liters of thick ale and placed them before the male-dominated crowd, whose cigarette smoke wafted upward and created a blue cloud that seemed to dance and sway with the music.

In a curtained-off dining room tucked away toward the rear of the restaurant, the pastor in his late fifties, with tufts of gray hair atop his dome, wasn't about to complain. It was here that his underground church had been meeting thrice a week. On nights like this, the raucous music in the Brauhaus Vetter provided a convenient cover for a meeting.

Pastor Leo scanned the private dining room and regarded the three dozen members of his hardy flock. How their bravery touched him! His congregation probably numbered two hundred, but they somehow worked things out as to who would attend the church meetings and Bible study at the Brauhaus Vetter and who would stay home. Several took notes to share with the believers who couldn't make it.

With midnight fast approaching, Pastor Leo figured the party in the front of the restaurant would break up soon. He cleared his throat and prepared to bring his sermon to a close.

"As this meeting of the saints comes to an end this evening, let me encourage you with what Paul wrote in his letter to the Romans. Turn with me, if you will, to Romans 8:35–39. Beatrice, would you be so good as to read God's Word for us?"

The young mother, whose husband was listed as officially

119

missing in action by the German Army, took a second to find her place, then located the correct passage.

She stood and lifted her chin, her voice carrying over the music drifting through the thick, velvet curtain that separated the rooms. "'Who shall separate us from the love of Christ? Shall tribulation, or distress, or persecution, or famine, or nakedness, or peril, or sword? As it is written, for thy sake we are killed all the day long; we are accounted as sheep for the slaughter. Nay, in all these things we are more than conquerors through him that loved us. For I am persuaded, that neither death, nor life, nor angels, nor principalities, nor powers, nor things present, nor things to come, nor height, nor depth, nor any other creature, shall be able to separate us from the love of God, which is in Christ Jesus our Lord.'"

Pastor Leo allowed the Scripture passage to sink into the hearts of his flock. Then he nodded to Beatrice, who sat, seemingly unashamed of the tears that filled her eyes.

"Thank you, Beatrice." The pastor sought to restrain his emotion. His eyes scanned the group as he composed himself. "The verb *separate* is a translation of the Greek word *chorizo*, which is only used thirteen times in the entire Bible. The root of this noun—*choro*—carries the idea of putting space, or room, between two things. What Paul is saying is that no one can put any 'room' between you and your Lord. No one can 'distance' you from his love—the love that sent Jesus to die on a cross to save sinners like you and me."

Several believers murmured their agreement until he lowered his hands, asking for silence. *"Liebe Gemeinde,"* Leo intoned to the community of believers, "we are living in the midst of a horrible global war, the belly of the beast as it were, and followers of Christ who stand up for righteousness are enemies of the State. Be not afraid, however. Paul reminds that *nothing* can separate us from Christ, no matter how difficult our lives become or how much fear we live in." He felt his chest tense as he preached these words.

Then the pastor dropped his head before continuing, this

time with a voice thick with emotion. "And I have to tell you, personally, I live in great fear," he confided, glancing from face to face. "I fear for the sound of jackboots approaching my apartment door in the middle of the night. I fear that I will be stopped while walking on the street, minding my own business, and be taken in for questioning. I fear our meetings here at the Brauhaus will be betrayed to the Gestapo."

Again, his statements—not only as their pastor but also as their friend—elicited grunts of acknowledgment. The men stared at their shoes, and Pastor Leo knew their thoughts were not unlike his. Each German man, woman, and child found themselves contemplating their mortality with each passing day, especially as the Allies pressed in from all fronts. Though not all expressed their fears, he could read it on their faces. They could die today . . . or tomorrow . . . or next week.

"Excuse me, Pastor."

Pastor Leo looked up to see the restaurant's owner peeking his head through a velvet curtain hiding a French door. The genial owner, a fourth-generation proprietor of the Brauhaus Vetter, had prayed for Jesus Christ to come into his life a year earlier. Within two months after that life-changing event, he offered Pastor Leo a place for his flock to meet.

"Yes, Rudiger. I know we have to go."

"It's not that, Pastor. You can take your time tonight. I don't think my rowdy customers are going anywhere soon. The Swiss are duller than dishwater, but when they start singing those songs they learned in school, they can make a fest half the night and still show up ready for work on time." He laughed at his own humor. Then, as if remembering the true purpose for his interruption, his face fell. "Actually, Pastor, I've come here to inform you that I received a phone call."

"Is everything all right?" Pastor Leo's shoulders tightened, as if bracing them for another burden of bad news.

"Everything is fine. Someone would like to speak with one of your church members. Is Herr Becker here tonight?"

Benjamin Becker raised his right hand. "Present, sir." He

stood and swallowed hard, his Adam's apple bobbing up and down as if it hung on a string.

"Your mother is on the line. If you will follow me." The proprietor motioned to the front room.

Becker stood, his eyes meeting Pastor Leo's gaze. Yet he didn't blink, didn't show any hint of alarm.

As he strode out, others in the room offered him best wishes.

The pastor suppressed a smile. Benjamin Becker, he knew, was in a unique position, and his true identity needed to be protected at all costs. He and others had told Benjamin that . . . more than once: *"Never let Kassler ever doubt your allegiance to him. Never. Many lives are at stake if you do."*

Pastor Leo knew what the phone call was all about. No doubt Sturmbannführer Bruno Kassler had called Becker's home, stating the matter was urgent.

How Becker had come up with the uniforms, Pastor Leo didn't want to know.

15

Migros Market
Basel, Switzerland
Wednesday, August 2, 1944
8:08 a.m.

Dieter Baumann cradled the twined shopping basket and briskly walked to the rear of the grocery store where yogurt and other dairy products were stacked with smart precision in a refrigeration case. He peered at several of the plain yogurts, packaged in brown glass containers, then placed one in his basket.

"Shopping light, I see."

Dieter turned toward the voice he'd been expecting to hear, then looked over the man's shoulders to see if anyone else in the store had noticed their presence. The Migros Market was quiet this early in the morning.

"Just picking up something for breakfast. *Guten Morgen*, Ludwig," Dieter said, using the code name for his contact. Dieter, of course, knew his German counterpart's real name was Karl Rundstedt, but he would never let on that he'd uncovered such privileged information.

"What did you hear about Patton?"

Dieter knew all sorts of rumors regarding the Allied breakout of Normandy floated around the streets and offices of the city—no doubt fueled by BBC Radio. Dieter cleared his throat. "If I understood my American source right, the radio reports are true: the Americans have broken out of hedgerow country. Patton's Third Army will not race for Paris, though.

They will circle around and attack the German Seventh Army from the rear, attempting to surprise your military forces pinning Montgomery's troops at Caen. It's called Operation Cobra." He could see from Ludwig's gaze that he was digesting the information, which he had given without taking sides, as befitting the "neutral" Swiss.

"And, of course," Dieter added, "the French resistance is also doing their part to harass the occupiers."

"Good work. The knowledge is useful." Ludwig picked up a small jar of milk and tossed it back and forth between his hands. "Now can you find out what's happened in the last twenty-four hours?"

Dieter knew he'd pressed Dulles as hard as he could. But perhaps the American colonel with the legation in Bern would share some battlefield gossip. They'd become friendly when Dieter helped two American pilots who'd escaped from Davos meet up with French contacts in Geneva.

"Well, information is hard to obtain . . . unless I could propose a swap." Dieter let his voice fall, as if he were uncertain his idea would work. He'd discovered over time that the more unsure he acted, the greater the reward he was given for his work. "Unless . . . I could tell the Americans that one of my contacts in the Swiss Army wants information on Patton's movements in exchange for—" Dieter shrugged his shoulders. "You got anything worthwhile?"

"Well, there is something." Ludwig looked around the grocery store to see if anyone was within earshot. Then Ludwig pursed his lips. "I saw an urgent flash pass throughout the network this morning. Came out of the Gestapo regional office in Heidelberg. A prisoner has escaped. The Gestapo telegraph gave a physical description of the missing man. They mentioned a bonus of 1,000 Reichsmarks for help in finding him, so he must be someone the Americans would love to get their hands on."

"Why would the Yanks be interested in him?"

"Sorry." The German held his palms up. "The traffic didn't

say. But since Heidelberg is around 250 kilometers from the Swiss border, they must be worried that he could escape into Switzerland, where he could contact the Allies."

Dieter adjusted his shopping basket from the crook of his left arm to that of his right. "Maybe the American colonel will play ball with me, as they like to say in the States. I'll see what I can do."

"Fair enough."

Dieter spotted an older woman strolling in their direction. He quickened his words. "You'll have to give me a day or so," he said as he guided the German toward the bread aisle. "I'll be in contact." Dieter reached for a hazel-brown loaf of *dunkel Brot* off the shelf.

"Not so fast." Ludwig grabbed his arm. "There's something else that's come up. Something on the side that could mean a lot of francs for our pocketbooks."

"Oh?" Dieter cocked an eyebrow and studied the man's face. It was clear that Ludwig toyed with him, just as he toyed with Ludwig—both with their own interests in mind.

Ludwig looked both ways to be sure they weren't being overheard. "A high-level contact I've been developing just across the border told me they just picked up a Jew family who'd been hidden away in Weil am Rhein for the better part of a year. They apparently had heard about the—how can I politely say this?—unreceptive attitude from the Swiss authorities about Jewish refugees. *The boat is full* and all that."

"So they didn't want to chance sneaking into Switzerland."

Ludwig shrugged his shoulders. "You know how well-patrolled both sides of the border are. Listen. This contact of mine, who works for the local Polizei, said that he went back to search this villa where they picked up the Jews as well as the family hiding them. Behind an antique sideboard in the main bedroom, he found a safe—a heavy safe."

Dieter knew where this was headed. "And now you want

to borrow the little safecracker in my office. Her skill . . . well, I'll only risk it if you believe the reward will be worth our while."

"I know, I know. You want to protect the little beauty." Ludwig held his hands up. "But listen to this. Apparently the patriarch of this Jewish family was a diamond dealer in Berlin. He'd been able to avoid authorities because he paid people to hide them for years—like this winegrower in Weil am Rhein. Now that this Jew jeweler has been caught, his diamonds cannot help him or his family. A pity."

From the sarcastic tone Ludwig used, Dieter knew that he felt anything but sympathy for this *Juden* family destined for the work camps.

The Swiss operative checked once more over his shoulder. "I'm not sold on this. This would be a highly dangerous operation, Ludwig. We rarely operate in Germany because of the Gestapo's pervasiveness—"

"Dieter, please." Ludwig waved off his concern. "I'll provide you with valid work permits to cross the border. It's fairly routine, you know, since thousands of Swiss cross the border each day to work in our textile and war matériel plants. What's two more Swiss? You can cross the border in the morning, do the job, and return with the rest of the Swiss toting their lunch pails."

Usually Dieter would have jumped at the opportunity—after all, who knew how many diamonds a safe like that could hold? But he had to admit that while he valued Ludwig's help, he didn't completely trust him. No one, in fact, could be completely trusted, especially in their business. Furthermore, his concerns centered on Gabi. She was valuable—too valuable to risk.

The more time he spent with her, Dieter found his heart warming to her innocent trust . . . and her beauty didn't hurt things either. It was nice to have her around and would be even nicer to get to know her better. Dieter shrugged. "I'm still not convinced. I'll have to think about this one."

"Life's a risk, *ja?* But my contact and I agreed you would get half the diamonds because you're supplying the expertise. We'll split the other half."

"Honor among thieves?" Dieter chuckled.

"You could say that, my friend."

• • • • • • • •

Dieter paid for his breakfast—plain yogurt, a packet of honey, and a bread roll—at the Migros checkout stand and turned to stroll up the Thunerstrasse. His office was less than five minutes away.

As he bumped shoulders with Swiss businessmen and secretaries crowding the sidewalk on their way to work, he thought about how he had been playing both sides for nearly a year. His American handlers understood his methods were unorthodox and his contacts ran the gamut, but then again, he produced time after time. If his methods tipped the scales in favor of Nazi operatives in Switzerland on occasion, then so be it. He alone would be the judge of what was going too far. At the same time, Dieter also understood that "sharing" American troop movements or a classified document with the enemy—even though it sometimes garnered him *more* information for the Yanks—was a distinction often lost following an arrest for espionage.

He was playing a dangerous game. He had known his share of operatives, from both sides of the war, who were never heard from again. Like the French spy who'd been executed by a Nazi machine gunner poised no farther than five meters away. It was said the .50-caliber firepower nearly sawed his torso in half. But he wasn't the only one. Just a few weeks ago, a Russian double agent was discovered in a Zurich back alley with several amputated fingers stuffed into his mouth. The Soviet operative was also quite dead.

Dieter involuntarily shivered and willed his mind to fixate on happier thoughts—like glittering diamonds. Before him lay a new and different opportunity, a chance to cash in on a tip. A way to position himself well for post-war Europe.

As his thoughts progressed along the Basel sidewalk, Dieter knew his plan centered on Gabi Mueller. Thankfully, she trusted him completely.

He anticipated no problems selling his plan to this naive church girl.

• • • • • • • •

Gestapo Regional Headquarters
Heidelberg, Germany
8:12 a.m.

Bruno Kassler leaned back in his office chair and shuttered his eyes momentarily. It was his way of dealing with stress, but he didn't think there was a word that accurately encompassed the weight on his shoulders. Everything—his job, his position, his honor was on the line.

He regarded the telegraph that Becker had transmitted posthaste to Reichsführer Himmler an hour earlier.

Last night, 1 August, 1944, at 22:25 hours, Joseph Engel was kidnapped by four masked men. Suspect Jews or Zionist sympathizers. Will advise on future developments.

Kassler regarded the telephone, expecting it to ring at any moment with Becker announcing that the Reichsführer was on the line. He could save his career by finding the physicist and the perpetrators—maybe his neck too. Although that was questionable.

He had heard the story about Himmler's nephew, SS 1st Lieutenant Hans Himmler, who'd revealed SS secrets while drunk. Hearing this, his uncle demoted and shipped him off to the Eastern Front as a parachutist. Within six months, Hans Himmler was again charged with making derogatory remarks about the Nazi regime. The second time his loose lips resulted in a one-way trip to the Dachau concentration camp near Munich, where he was finally "liquidated" as a homosexual. In the new Germany, blood *wasn't* thicker than water.

Kassler shuddered as he pondered his fate for displeasing the Reichsführer. If he were a praying man, he'd pray for help to find those who'd kidnapped Engel.

For the moment, he'd ordered Becker and several other officers to review files of known subversives. Extra roadblocks had been set up within the city proper and all arteries leading outside of Heidelberg. Orders were to search every truck, open every car boot, scatter every load.

Within the hour, a half-dozen Gestapo teams would fan out to interview "suspicious" people in shops and restaurants. In addition, Kassler directed the Heidelberg Polizei to conduct a house-to-house search in districts home to academicians from the University of Heidelberg. Maybe one of their own had pulled off the heist of Engel, although he doubted the intellectuals could have pulled off something as audacious as what happened last night. Either way, it wouldn't hurt to poke around the elite class who'd never entirely warmed to National Socialism. But if they couldn't have done it, then who?

How did these impudent traitors pull it off? Where did they get the uniforms?

Kassler couldn't comprehend how four men dressed up as the Gestapo could brazenly snatch someone of interest just minutes before his arrival. It's like they *knew*.

The jittery roommate, Hannes Jäger, wasn't part of the plot, he decided. White with fear, the physicist insisted it was the Gestapo who'd taken his friend, and Kassler sensed no hesitation in Jäger's description of the abductors or what had transpired.

Jäger had even broken down crying as he described the gun that was placed on his forehead and then lifted into the air and fired into a painting hanging on the wall behind him.

The physicist genuinely believed the intruders would kill him. Either that, or Kassler had just witnessed the greatest acting job since Marlene Dietrich in *Blue Angel*.

Kassler rubbed his temples with his left hand. Bleary-eyed, needing sleep, he willed his weary mind to act . . . to do something more than just wait for news from those conducting the interviews or searching apartments and homes close to the university. He reached for the phone.

"Becker, who do we have in custody at the moment?"

"Let me look at the last report I received, sir," the youthful aide replied.

Kassler heard a rustling of papers over the phone line.

"Ah, there it is. This is surprising, sir. No one is being presently detained. The last prisoner was executed . . . yesterday."

Oh yes. That traitor who mumbled something about victory in Jesus. He deserved a bullet in the head.

Kassler rubbed his temples again. This was getting nowhere. Just when he thought he had exhausted all leads, however, an idea came to mind. A good idea.

"Becker, call the motor pool. There's someone I want to visit."

"Who would that be, sir? Can I make an arrangement?"

"That won't be necessary. I prefer to drop in unannounced."

16

Joseph's hands, bound by handcuffs in front of him, zipped up his trousers and yanked on the chain to flush the toilet. He nodded to his "guard" as he exited the single-seat WC.

After a night inside a boxed tomb on the flatbed truck, he was glad for fresh air. He lifted his arms and attempted to stretch the knot in his left shoulder that attested to the discomfort of sleeping on a heavy blanket of hay. The pain drew his thoughts to hundreds of thousands of men his age, maybe millions, who'd huddled in a ditch last night to the sounds of pounding artillery in the distance.

Through the night, as the peace of the Lord settled upon him, Joseph realized he didn't have it nearly as bad. Maybe these men wouldn't hurt him. Wouldn't kill him.

"Help yourself to an apple." One of the guards held a pewter bowl out to him. It contained a half-dozen Gravensteins, which were in season. "You can take two. We have a bit of a journey ahead."

By now, Joseph knew better than to question their plans. He cleaned both red-skinned apples against his shirt, a bit awkward with handcuffs, but not impossible. The first crispy bite of fruit released a burst of salivary juices. Then he ravenously devoured both apples.

"Hungry," he said after wiping his mouth with his left shirtsleeve.

The leader from the night before, dressed in dirty work-clothes like the others, stepped out of a side office. "Arrangements are made. We leave in five minutes. And take the handcuffs off. I don't think he's a candidate to run anywhere. Am I correct, Professor Engel?"

Joseph extended his arms to Wilhelm, who brandished a half-dozen keys on an oversized brass ring. He didn't want to lie, so he didn't answer. Instead, he smiled as the handcuffs were pulled from him.

"Thank you," he said, wringing his hands to boost blood circulation.

"Don't thank me yet. You can thank me when you're safe." The leader jerked his head toward the flatbed truck, and like a well-drilled team, four men sprang into action. One jumped into the cab and coaxed the engine to turn over, while another sprinted to the entrance bay to keep watch. Wilhelm beckoned Joseph, who eagerly went along to the rear of the truck. *When you're safe . . .* the words brought him some measure of comfort, but it still didn't relieve his mind of questions. *Who? Why?*

"Up you go." Wilhelm and a colleague lifted Joseph onto the flatbed. Wooden slats had been added to hold in the load of hay. As simply as if they were taking a hayride into the countryside, Joseph turned and gave his sleeping partner a hand up.

On the wooden deck, Wilhelm dusted his hands on the rear of his pants and then moved several bales around like oversized chess pieces. "I'm just doing a little rearranging in case the authorities start poking around. Got to make things tighter. Gives us a better chance to get through any checkpoints."

Joseph ran a hand down his face, feeling the pounding of his heart increase again. Even though he still had no answers, he was beginning to feel a measure of safety with these men. But the Gestapo . . . the real Gestapo. He doubted he'd ever feel safe with them.

"I thought random checkpoints happened after curfew." Joseph's voice cracked as he spoke.

"The fact that you're missing has the Gestapo swarming like hornets. We're expecting blockades on every route out of Heidelberg," Wilhelm declared matter-of-factly. "We do our best, but sometimes . . ."

Wilhelm let the thought hang, and Joseph's unease mounted. He didn't know why he had been kidnapped or by whom—but his fate was now tied to these enemies of the Reich. Which, by virtue of association, made *him* an enemy of the Hitler regime.

"So what happens next?"

"Herr Engel, we pray for God's protection. That's the only way I can explain why we are still alive today. But first, we have some work to do."

Wilhelm crawled into the hole to rearrange their hiding space. When he was done, Wilhelm exited on all fours. "Okay, in you go."

"Wait a minute—don't forget this." One of Wilhelm's colleagues had fetched Joseph's satchel—a satchel filled with papers, notebook, and personal identification—from the escape car. Joseph didn't know they'd grabbed it, but he accepted the leather valise with a smile. Then he got on his knees to scoot into the cramped cubbyhole.

Joseph inched on his hands and knees into the tight crawl space. There was just enough room for the two of them to recline side by side on the itchy hay.

Two colleagues neatly packed several hay bales at the entrance. "Stack it high," someone said before they wrapped the entire load with rope. From their entombed confinement, Joseph heard a solitary voice direct the driver to get going.

As the heavy truck careened into traffic, Joseph urged his active mind to go elsewhere. He forced his thoughts to turn to his parents . . . his work . . . even classes with Professor Heisenberg.

Yet each time the truck rolled to a stop, panic tightened in his throat. And he waited—almost expected—at any moment for a sharp bayonet to pierce the hay and tear into his skin.

• • • • • • • • •

University of Heidelberg
9:02 a.m.

The Mercedes sedan accelerated through a cobblestone street running parallel to the Rhine riverbank, and Bruno Kassler tossed Professor Werner Heisenberg's medium-thick file onto the seat between him and Becker.

Outside the car window, Heidelberg's Gothic architecture—which could trace its roots back to 1196—appeared untouched. For reasons unknown to him, Allied bombers had so far spared the city from destruction. Yet outside the medieval downtown proper, four-engine B-24 Liberators and RAF Lancasters, laden with 500-pound bombs, had issued a pattern of death and devastation in rail yards and factories. If only they'd known the scientific knowledge within the city—especially focused on the wonder weapon—they might have chosen their targets more wisely.

The University of Heidelberg was Germany's oldest university, founded in 1386, and had attracted scholars from all over the continent for hundreds of years. Known as a bulwark of the Reformation, the University provided for the studies of philosophy, theology, jurisprudence, and medicine. Its only dark days had been in the 1890s when the University became a repository of liberal thought—bitter seeds that sowed the Russian Revolution of 1917. As the Mercedes swung into the main courtyard, Kassler detected the faint whiff of Communism.

Kassler trusted the academicians perched in their golden sandstone towers as much as he trusted Jewish bankers. Yet the University had operated with a certain amount of local autonomy for reasons related to two factors: (1) propaganda minister Joseph Goebbels had earned his doctorate in literature and philosophy from the University back in the 1920s, and (2) the University was home to important military research projects, including the one headed by Dr. Werner Heisenberg.

The Gestapo chief opened the file one last time to review Heisenberg's curriculum vitae. Born in 1901 in Berlin, the scholarly Heisenberg netted the Nobel Prize in 1932 for his theory of quantum mechanics and the discovery of allotropic forms of hydrogen. He was most famous for the eponymous "Heisenberg Uncertainty Principle," which stated that it was impossible to determine at the same time both the position and velocity of the electron; therefore, he suggested, the laws of subatomic phenomena should be stated in terms of observable properties, such as the intensity and frequency of radiation.

Kassler stroked his chin. He had no intention of delving into subatomic particles with someone who could talk circles around him. He was here for another reason.

The black Mercedes ground to a halt in front of the Faculty of Physics, a four-story stone building a block east of the main student square, and Kassler noticed a handful of students walking purposely to their appointed rounds. None turned in his direction, but the Gestapo chief was used to people averting their eyes whenever he came into view.

"Becker, where am I supposed to go?"

Kassler's aide looked at his watch and consulted his notes. "Doktor Heisenberg's office is on the first floor. Room 124. If you'll follow me."

Within a few minutes, Becker led Kassler to Heisenberg's empty office. Becker waited just inside the door as Kassler quickly scanned the piles of papers, books, and research notes. Then Kassler turned his attention to an authoritative voice filtering in through an open door to the right.

"Let us review our calculations," the voice boomed. "For critical mass to occur under this model, the neutron cross-sections must travel a relatively long distance before striking another U-235 nucleus and triggering a new fission . . ."

Kassler pushed the door open with his foot, and then peered into a windowless classroom with walls of pale yellow. A gangly man, early forties with sandy hair combed straight back, wielded a piece of chalk. Around him, a dozen physicists jotted notes from their wooden desks. Kassler stepped into the room, and the sight of the Gestapo major in full military dress brought the class to a screeching halt.

"Doktor Heisenberg?" Kassler crossed his arms over his chest.

The man at the blackboard stared at Kassler. His frozen glare was one Kassler had seen a hundred times at least—a look that said, *What have I done?*

The Gestapo chief fully intended to play off the power of his office. He straightened his shoulders and slowly neared the professor. "Doktor Heisenberg, I need a few moments of your time."

The physicist set the piece of chalk on a wooden tray underneath the blackboard. "Excuse me for a moment." He nodded to the class and followed Kassler into his office.

Kassler grimly closed the door behind them, and then, spotting a radio in the corner, turned it on. The sounds of classical opera filled Heisenberg's office—an antidote to any eavesdroppers. Kassler didn't trust anyone, especially a pinheaded professor of quantum physics.

The lilting music immediately improved Kassler's countenance and offered him a chance to make small talk. He knew one of the best ways to get information was to build a rapport. And it was far less messy than the alternative.

"Ah, Richard Wagner." Kassler turned to the professor. "This must be from 'The Flying Dutchman.' There's something about Wagner's layers of texture, rich chromaticism, and elaborate use of leitmotifs that makes him one of Germany's most revered composers. Would you not agree, Doktor Heisenberg?"

Heisenberg walked around to his desk and extended his arms for Kassler and Becker to have a seat in the two wooden chairs. He then sat himself. "Wagner, revered composer, yes, if you insist," the physicist replied hurriedly. "Although I'm sure the reason for your visit is not to discuss the artistic merits of Richard Wagner. So if you would kindly get to the point. And you are—"

"Kassler, Bruno. Sturmbannführer of the Heidelberg region." The Gestapo chief returned to his feet and regarded a bookshelf crammed with volumes. Then he turned to the blackboard over the professor's shoulder. A rat's nest of consonants, numbers, and Greek letters was scribbled across the board, including the following:

$$|I,k_1 \ldots k_n\rangle = C_0 + \sum_{m=1}^{\infty} \int d^4p_1 \ldots d^4p_m\, C_m(p_1 \ldots p_m)\, |F,p_1 \ldots p_n\rangle$$

Professor Heisenberg noted his gaze. "That's an S-matrix equation, which is causing all sorts of fits these days. We think that removal of the divergent self-energy of the electron is accomplished with a hybrid version of the subtraction physics, but one of my colleagues here is paradoxically opposed to the finiteness of the S-matrix because the whole theory is built upon a Hamiltonian formalism with an interaction-function that is infinite and therefore physically meaningless."

Silence filled the professor's cluttered office.

"Yes, very well. For the good of the Reich, I hope you can untangle everything," Kassler dryly remarked. "I'm sorry, but my visit isn't to discuss your latest finding—however interesting that is. Instead, you've heard the news about one of your colleagues, a certain Joseph Engel?"

"Yes, I received a distressing report this morning: Doktor Engel was arrested by the Gestapo last night." Heisenberg leaned forward in his seat. "What has he done?"

Kassler stepped away from his chair as he contemplated the question. He pulled a book from the shelf and pretended to be transfixed by its title: *Physics Today* by Niels Bohr.

Kassler knew his movements were a signal to the esteemed professor that he controlled the space they were occupying. He also hoped the professor knew that no matter how many friends Heisenberg had in high places, they would never trump his superiors in Berlin. If he read Heisenberg's face correctly, the professor believed the Gestapo had abducted Engel. Kassler would do nothing to dispel the image of an all-knowing, all-powerful secret police network.

"You are correct about your colleague's arrest, but I'm not at liberty to go into the details. Rather, the reason for my visit is to ask you several questions about Doktor Engel. I expect your full cooperation."

"I'm listening." Heisenberg reached inside a desk drawer for a pipe, which he tamped with tobacco. "Although if you hold him in your care, I'm not sure why you wouldn't ask him yourself."

Kassler narrowed his gaze, yet he refused to give an answer. Instead, he continued with his predetermined questions.

"Doktor Heisenberg, has Joseph Engel ever said anything that would make you doubt his loyalty to our Führer and the great mission he has given our country on behalf of National Socialism?"

"Major, not only has Doktor Engel been faithful to the Fatherland, but he has done more to advance our research in the last six months than any of the physicists enlisted in our military research."

Kassler tilted his head in interest. "Military research?"

"Yes, and unless I have official notification that I can discuss our project with you, I'm afraid that's all I'm at liberty to say."

Kassler ignored Heisenberg's comment. He didn't need an explanation. He already knew what the esteemed physicist and his minions were working on—some sort of Wunderwaffe.

"What can you tell me about Engel's interests away from his work? Married? Girlfriends?"

"Doktor Engel is single, and like the rest of us, married to our important work. He lives with another scientist, and I have no idea about his personal habits. That sort of information doesn't interest me. His mind is what interests me, sir. His mind."

"Is there anything else you can tell me? Let me remind you that your cooperation could prove to be useful to your own personal safety." Kassler let the mild threat hang in the air.

Heisenberg rubbed his forehead for a moment, as if attempting to rub out the worry lines. "Well, he is quite religious."

Kassler straightened his posture. "Please explain, Doktor Heisenberg." Then Kassler even offered what he hoped was a warming smile.

"I know the family. They are lifelong Lutherans. Doktor Engel regularly attends services at Trinity Lutheran. He's the only one working for me who goes to church on Sundays—or at least most Sundays."

Kassler chuckled. "He must be the youngest person there. Everyone knows religion isn't embraced by the young these days. Is it because his mother goes to the same church?" The Gestapo chief couldn't imagine why any young, virile man would want to be in the company of a bunch of crabby old ladies on a Sunday morning.

"I've never met his parents. They don't live in Heidelberg. I think they're in Berlin, but that should be something easy for the Gestapo to find out." Heisenberg shifted in his seat, clearly uncomfortable. "Religion and politics—those are topics rarely discussed within these halls. If you want my opinion, and I believe you do, I would say Doktor Engel is a pious young man. On occasion, he spoke of his Lutheran upbringing by his parents, whom he seems to respect very much. I believe going to church is something he's done all his life, and in these uncertain times—"

Kassler stopped him right there. "Uncertain times? Do you question the wisdom of the course that our beloved Führer has set before us? Divine Providence will usher the Glorious Reich into a position of global supremacy for a thousand years, will it not?"

"Sturmbannführer Kassler, excuse my doubt. It's just that you hear so many rumors," Heisenberg said. "But I, for one minute, do not question the path set before us by our Führer. In fact, I've often wondered if our work will be the deciding factor in the struggle between National Socialism and the enemies who seek to destroy us. I'm just sorry that I'm not at liberty to say more . . ." Heisenberg adjusted his tweed jacket and shrugged.

Kassler nodded, then he shifted the topic back to Joseph Engel. "Anything else you can tell me? Does he have any likes or dislikes? Anything unusual?"

"Yes, I do remember something." Heisenberg struck a match and touched the flame to shreds of tobacco in his briarwood pipe. "He doesn't like to eat ham—even the delicious smoked *Schwarzwälder Schinken* from Bavaria. In fact, I've never seen him eat any sort of pork, including bratwurst."

Kassler cocked an eyebrow in surprise. "Did you ever ask him why?"

"No, but at last year's Oktoberfest, a group of us ordered the usual steins of Paulaner lager and enough bratwurst, fried potatoes, grilled onions, and sauerkraut to feed a battalion. When the food arrived, Engel stuck with the potatoes and onions. We all noticed he didn't touch the bratwurst."

A thin smile came to Kassler's lips. It was another confirmation.

Now to find Engel. The next twenty-four hours would be critical, but he still had a few trees he could shake.

17

Gabi suppressed a yawn as she fixed her eyes on the words she was supposed to be translating. Getting nowhere, she urged herself to focus. Perhaps the late-night train ride was the reason for her scattered thoughts this morning. Or her tossing and turning after trundling off to bed. Her father had been snoring loudly when Eric dropped her off near midnight, but that wasn't what kept her awake.

In truth, her mind mixed the memories of the ride home with Eric. With the clattering of typewriter keys around her, Gabi's mind took her back to the dimness of the train car as they sat side by side. The moonlight dancing through the window. The way Eric had protectively wrapped his arm around her shoulders during the journey. The combination had provided a dizzying effect.

She and Eric had talked of family, and country, and had shared simple dreams—like enjoying wildflowers on high mountain peaks once the war was over. Being with him seemed right in a way. Yet while one part of her appreciated the security of Eric's simple care, especially during times of war, the other part of her wanted something more. To experience life and to be challenged. To test herself—to test her heart—before settling into a relationship based on comfort and a farmer's simple dreams.

"Gabi, Herr Baumann would like to see you." Frau Schaffner, her supervisor, interrupted Gabi's thoughts, punctuating the remark with an icy smile.

Gabi ignored the frosty directive and gathered up her work, which, from what she'd managed to translate so far, involved troop movements along the Eastern Front. Even a military novice like herself could tell that the vaunted German Army was in retreat.

"I'll be right back, Frau Schaffner." Gabi locked her desk.

She couldn't help but notice that her heartbeat quickened just slightly as she neared Dieter's office. She also took note of the envious gazes of the others in the typing pool as they watched her quickened steps.

Enough, Gabi Mueller, she told herself. Dreaming of a thoughtful, devoted boyfriend was one thing, but Dieter was her boss. And that was that.

The last thing she needed was all the drama that would be wrapped around getting involved with the head of the OSS Basel office—drama from her co-workers, her parents, and most likely Eric too, who not only cared for her but also seemed wary of her work for the Americans.

She smoothed her skirt as she stepped into Dieter's corner office.

He offered her a grin and then held up his left hand. "I'll be right with you, Fräulein Mueller. Just let me complete this sentence." Dieter scribbled another line, then set his ink pen back into its white marble stand.

"Excuse me, but I just got off the phone with Frau Taylor. I wanted to make a note for myself before I lost my train of thought. Although this doesn't guarantee I won't misplace this note too—just like the memo I've been searching for half the morning." Dieter chuckled as he swept his hand over various piles of files stacked on his desk.

Gabi squinted her eyes, trying to keep on task. "Frau Taylor? I'm sure I haven't made her acquaintance."

Dieter nodded. "No, of course you haven't."

Perhaps it was the sunlight streaming through the window, or maybe the weariness of her own gaze, but he looked especially chipper this morning. His bright eyes and slight smile made him even more handsome, if that was possible. The truth was, Eric could never match her boss in the looks department.

"Perhaps an explanation is in order. Frau Taylor is the personal assistant to Mr. Dulles in Bern. She said that she needed a top-secret message translated right away." Dieter cocked an eyebrow and leaned forward. "She asked specifically for you."

"Me?" Gabi's right hand covered her heart. "But . . . are you sure? I've never heard of Frau Taylor."

"Apparently, you've gained favor with the Americans, seemingly overnight. They heard about your first mission . . . you made an impression. The message should arrive by courier in the next hour or so." Dieter looked down at his notes. "Yes, Frau Taylor gave me specific instructions. You are to translate the message at your desk with the courier seated in your vicinity. When you are finished, the courier will return by train to Bern."

"Isn't this unusual? I mean, doesn't Mr. Dulles have his own translators in Bern?"

"Well, on rare occasions, Bern *has* asked our bureau to translate messages or intercepts."

Gabi thought back to the last time such a thing had happened. The raw material had arrived via the Kleinschmidt teletype machine in the secure back room—and never handheld by courier. Still, what did she know? She wasn't here to question those who obviously knew more than she did about the workings of the OSS.

"But you're right. I, too, was surprised. Although I shouldn't be. Sometimes it's difficult to tell what the Americans are up to. It seems I can never figure them out." Dieter drummed his fingers on his desk, and she noted the tightening of his jaw. Just that quick he was all business once again.

Gabi pursed her lips, telling herself not to let his offhand comment bother her, even though she detected a "we versus them" edge to his tone of voice. Apparently, he had forgotten that she was half red-white-and-blue.

"The Americans?" she said nonchalantly.

"Excuse me, Miss Mueller. I meant no insult. That was frustration speaking. Yesterday wasn't an easy day. While you were playing tourist in the Alps, I had to drag myself to Bern to meet with the *Amis*. War doesn't take a holiday, remember?"

Next time just go ahead and share your true feelings—and hold nothing back. Gabi smirked. "I understand, Herr Baumann. We live in tumultuous times."

"Your graciousness is noted," Dieter said. "Now let me turn to another point of discussion. Remember how I asked you a couple of days ago if you were available to discuss your evolving role with this organization?"

Gabi leaned forward. "Yes, of course."

"Then how about lunch? After you finish your translation work, of course." He leaned back in his chair and threaded his fingers behind his head. "The courier will be here by 11 o'clock. Frau Taylor said it's just a couple of paragraphs, so it shouldn't take you long to type out the appropriate translation."

"Today? Lunch today?"

"Why not? You have to eat, don't you?"

She brushed her hair back from her shoulder, wishing she'd paid more attention to her appearance. Wishing she'd worn something other than the simple blue dress sewn by her mother.

"It's just a lunch between two colleagues. We'll keep it casual. Let's meet at the restaurant at the Globus department store. You know it? And don't worry about how you're dressed." Dieter's eyes quickly swept across her ensemble. "You look fine. Actually, better than fine."

Her cheeks reddened, realizing he'd read her thoughts but not sure how to accept his offhand remark.

"The restaurant at the Globus, of course." Gabi fumbled with her hands. "You're talking about the restaurant on the penthouse floor with a nice view of the Rhine."

"Exactly." He rose and led her to the door. "But let's keep this between you and me. I don't want Frau Schaffner getting wind of our meeting. She'd frown at such interaction within the office. Shall we say 12:30 p.m.?"

Gabi placed her hand on the door handle and glanced through the interior window into the translation pool, again noting the various looks from the others. "So you want me to meet you there?"

Dieter thought for a moment. "In this circumstance, prudence dictates that we walk there separately." He leaned his lips close to her ear. "We wouldn't want anyone to suspect anything, would we?"

* * * * * * * *

On the Outskirts of Heidelberg
10:19 a.m.

Joseph breathed in slowly and exhaled. The air was thick, and he tried not to let the tightness of his tomblike surroundings overwhelm him—or the worries that seemed to press on every side, equally constricting.

Even though he still didn't know who his captors were, or what their motives might be, a peace had come over him since they seemed to be looking after his best interests. After all, if they'd wanted to harm him—to kill him—they could have accomplished that deed by now. Instead, they'd treated him kindly. Or as kindly as one could under these circumstances.

And the peace that had settled deep in his chest seemed to be the same peace Joseph felt when he prayed with his friends from church. Maybe it was God's peace or the peace he felt when he tried looking for the good in people despite the pain of the war. Either way, he had an inner urging that they were transporting him somewhere for his own good.

It also helped his thoughts settle after he'd overheard the two men who transported him mention that his roommate had been bound up good. *That meant Jäger was alive.* Surely if they'd spared his friend, they'd spare him too.

The truck jostled its way through cobblestone streets and through occasional stretches of smooth macadam riddled with potholes.

"How long have we been traveling?" Joseph mumbled from the dark tomb.

"At least an hour," Wilhelm said. "Emil knows these roads well. He must be taking the circuitous route."

Joseph heard the truck downshift once, twice, and then a third time. "We're coming to a stop," he whispered in the dark. He focused on the noises from beyond the tomb of hay—the slamming of a truck door. Followed by footsteps.

"Willi, can you hear me?" It was Emil, their driver. "How are you doing?"

"No problems here." Wilhelm feigned cheerfulness. "Just a little dark and itchy, right, Herr Engel?"

"I've been more comfortable," Joseph mumbled. He tried to adjust, and he attempted to peek through a small opening that offered a faint ray of daylight seeping through the hay bales, but his effort did no good.

"Is everything okay out there?" Wilhelm asked.

"Yes and no," Emil replied. "We parked in the church plaza as ordered. Several hundred meters away we can see the road-block leading to Leimen."

From the rise and fall of Emil's voice and the slight movement of the hay around him, Joseph figured the man was pretending to check the load—tightening the ropes, making adjustments, retying loose knots.

"Two trucks are blocking the road," Emil's muffled voice continued. "We were told this is where the roadblock would be for all traffic flowing south out of Heidelberg. Looks like our information was correct. Still, I don't like it. Wehrmacht soldiers are stopping each vehicle—even horse-drawn wagons.

From the looks of things, they're turning everything upside down, giving it a good shake."

Joseph could tell Emil tried to share the information as nonchalantly as possible. No doubt he'd been schooled at keeping calm during stressful situations, but Joseph also knew they were in big trouble. To continue on would mean their sure discovery. And if they turned around, they'd most likely be followed. Fleeing, in fact, would simply delay the inevitable.

Dear God . . . Joseph wasn't sure if it was a plea or a prayer.

"So what do we do?" Joseph found himself asking.

"Our instructions were to park next to this church and wait. Hans is making a phone call to get some advice about passing through the checkpoint. Uh-oh—looks like trouble's coming our way. A couple of *soldaten* on a three-wheeler."

Joseph's ears caught the faint staccato sound of a motorcycle engine whining in the distance. "They've found us." Panic rose in Joseph's throat.

"Shush," Wilhelm whispered. "Emil and Hans know what they're doing. They're prepared to shoot if they have to. Just pray that . . . we won't be discovered."

"If they start firing, we'll be shot ourselves. Every soldier in this area will be after us—"

"Quiet. They're almost here." Wilhelm quit talking as the humming motorcycle engine drew closer.

• • • • • • • • •

Emil balled his fists to his side as he watched the three-wheeled motorcycle, with a passenger sidecar, careen into the cobblestone plaza and bear down on their parked truck in a cloud of dust.

Hans sidled up to Emil after making the phone call. "I don't like this," he piped out of the side of his mouth. "They are making a beeline right for us."

Emil's eyes remained on the motorcycle sidecar. "They'll be here any second. Quick—any news?"

"The message from the Americans is that nothing has changed. We are to continue waiting here until the appointed time."

"God help us." Emil continued to feign a look of disinterest, then turned around to eye his load. "Let's look busy."

Emil loosened one of the ropes binding the hay bales. With a practiced jerk of the head, he motioned for Hans to give him a hand. They clasped the fraying cord together and gave it a hard yank. Though Emil's stomach quivered on the inside, his grip was firm. There was no room for fear—men's lives were at stake.

Employing a practiced motion, Emil cinched the rope to a cleat on the flatbed truck and performed a figure-eight knot. His body was on full alert. Silently, he prayed that the approaching soldiers would believe that they had merely stopped in front of the church to resecure their load—something any prudent farmer would do.

Grant us calmness, Lord. Protection.

His eyes fixed on the pair of soldiers bearing down in their direction on a mud-splattered Zündapp Z22 motorcycle, painted in Panzer grey and sporting ammo boxes and jerry cans. Bushy gray sideburns sprouted from underneath the flared Nazi helmet of the driver. He looked old enough to be Emil's grandfather, but that didn't stop the fear clawing at his chest. On the other hand, the smooth-skinned soldier riding in the sidecar didn't look *old* enough to drive a motorcycle. Emil had heard the Wehrmacht was having trouble filling its ranks with able-bodied soldiers, and this pair's approach was further evidence of the tumbling of the Reich that began with the massive defeat at Stalingrad.

The motorcycle parked, and the grizzly looking captain stepped off and patted a sidearm that hung from a leather pouch belted next to his right hip. Meanwhile, his youthful sidekick jumped out of the cramped sidecar and jerkily pointed his Mauser carbine at Emil.

"Papiere!" The younger soldier's command sounded like he was practicing his unbridled authority.

Papers. Always papers. Emil reached into his back pocket, where he kept a well-worn leather wallet. Between several Reichsmark bills was his *Ausweis*—the official residence permit with his black-and-white photo, thumbprint, and the necessary stamps from Heidelberger authorities.

"You will find everything in order." Emil handed the papers over.

Hans produced his Ausweis as well.

"Privat Grüniger, search their load," the senior soldier ordered.

"*Jawohl,* Captain Hauptmann." The junior officer returned his rifle to behind his back and ducked underneath the truck, peering into the chassis with particular attention to the rear axle mount. Satisfied no stowaways were lodged beneath the flatbed, he pulled himself up and tugged on the driver side door. The door stuck for a moment before swinging open. He shoved the bench seat forward, but found nothing.

Emil watched as the teenage soldier next turned his direction toward the load of hay bales, stacked higher than normal.

"You have a pitchfork?" The youthful soldier glanced at Hans, who stood near the load with arms crossed.

"On top of the hay bales," Emil answered for his partner. Then he dropped both hands into his baggy pockets and fingered the Luger pistol in his right hand. His orders had been unusually specific: they were to get Engel out of Heidelberg at all costs, even if that meant killing fellow Germans.

Emil had never shot a man before, but he *had* witnessed death. In his mind's eye, he could see the small group of Jewish men being paraded across the Old Bridge to Heidelberg's main square. If he remembered correctly, they were the last of the stragglers rounded up in early 1943, but he had never forgotten how a firing squad meted out their deadly volleys.

He thought of that bloodbath often, and somehow the bleak image helped steel him for what he might be forced to do.

The young soldier walked around to the rear of the truck and climbed up a half-dozen wooden slats to scale the summit of hay. He freed the pitchfork and began probing between rows of rectangular bales, but the pitchfork's curvature failed to make much of a dent.

He swore in frustration. "You farmers usually stack five— what's with eight rows?"

"It was the first time we got petrol in a month." Emil shrugged. "Just trying to maximize our load."

Sweat built on the young soldier's forehead as he again tried to plunge the pitchfork all the way through the tall piles. Frustrated and uttering another string of obscenities, the private dropped the pitchfork and swung his Mauser rifle around to his front. He gripped his rifle in his left hand and deftly reached for his ammo belt with his right, unsheathing a bayonet. Then with one quick motion, he attached it to his rifle stock.

Emil saw Hans glance his direction, but he refused to acknowledge his gaze. The bayonet, they all knew, would go deeper. He just hoped it wouldn't travel deep enough.

Bending down to one knee, the soldier jabbed the space between the rectangular rows of hay, plunging as deep as he could.

Dear God . . . protect them. Shield them with your hand.

* * * * * * * *

Joseph willed himself not to move, even though he expected a steel tip to tear into his leg or back at any moment. One vigorous thrust just missed his feet. The next sliced through hay behind his torso.

Shafts of light entered their tomb, created by the soldier's poking between bales. Joseph looked across to Wilhelm, curled into a tight ball. Two times a sharp blade invaded their space. Two times the bayonet missed the pair by centimeters.

150

• • • • • • • •

The young soldier stepped back from the load. "Nothing so far. Shall I yank the bales off the truck?"

"Yes. Good idea." The older soldier ran a hand through his gray stubble. "This load is too tall and tightly packed. That way we'll be sure. You want to start throwing off bales?"

Emil took one step toward the older soldier, keeping his right hand in his front pocket. "Wait a minute—you're destroying my hay!" His hand tightened around the Luger.

"*Halt!*" barked the grizzled Army captain. He deftly unbuttoned his leather pistol holster and withdrew his Luger in one fell motion. "*Hände hoch!*"

Emil realized the older soldier had the drop on him. He hesitated, knowing that pulling a pistol out of his right pocket presented all sorts of problems. Releasing a breath, he eased his right hand out and raised open palms to shoulder height. "Listen, I'm not here to make trouble. I have cows to feed."

"You two, give him a hand. I want every bale removed—every one!" The older officer waved his pistol toward the truck.

Emil had just taken one step forward when the pitched whine of an air raid siren crackled through the air. The high-decibel tone rose and fell, alerting them that Allied bombers would soon be upon them.

They had only minutes to take cover.

Since D-Day, the Allies had stepped up massive bombing of German industrial areas along the Rhineland and Ruhr areas—places like Essen, Dortmund, Pforzheim, and Stuttgart. And where was the celebrated Luftwaffe? It was a question everyone wondered, but no one voiced. Their saviors weren't in the sky—that was for sure. There was no one to stop the waves of American bombers who released their deadly payloads during the daylight hours. No one to deliver them from their nighttime terror when British Lancasters and Halifaxes returned under the cover of darkness.

Emil looked up to see an American attack plane—with predominantly white U.S. Army Air Corps insignias on its tail and under its wings. The single-seat fighter screeched by at less than 100 meters overhead. *One of the new P-51 Mustangs!* The lone aircraft swooped past the church plaza, and Emil noticed farmers and civilians—including a mom with three children in tow—sprint for safety in a nearby building.

Gunfire sounded from the barricade, and Emil turned and observed three soldiers leaving their positions to fire at the approaching fighter. Emil knew the soldiers' effort would do no good. Unhindered by ground fire, the P-51 Mustang lost more altitude and let loose a hail of ordinance from its wing-mounted machine guns. A half-dozen lines of bullets ricocheted off the cobblestone plaza and bore in on the blockade checkpoint. Another deadly line of machine-gun fire closed the distance between the plaza and a German troop truck. Then, within seconds, the truck exploded into a ball of flames as the P-51 made its first pass.

Emil cheered on the inside.

"Grüniger, *raus!* Leave them!" the captain yelled over the commotion.

The surprised private high-stepped his way across several hay bales before grabbing the highest wooden slat and swinging his body over it. He descended two rows, then jumped to the ground and raced for the motorcycle sidecar. The white-faced captain was already kickstarting the Zündapp engine. On the second swing of the captain's leg, the 250 cc engine sprang to life. The *Motorrad* bolted out of the plaza, speeding to defend their comrades at the checkpoint.

Overhead, the swift American fighter circled and dove even lower on its second approach, relentlessly bearing down on the smoldering barricade that billowed with smoke and fire. A machine-gunner positioned atop a German halftrack suddenly slumped from a fusillade of bullets, and seconds later the halftrack itself exploded, knocking two soldiers to the ground, killing them.

On its third foray, the American pilot turned to the over-matched soldiers on the motorcycle speeding toward the checkpoint. The sidekick pointed his rifle at the pursuit plane and fingered several shots—none of which hit their mark.

Emil ducked underneath the flatbed truck with Hans and watched in fascination as the American pilot concentrated his attack on the German pair. Within seconds, a relentless hail of steel-jacketed bullets overcame the motorcycle. The old driver spasmed and fell onto the handlebars like a rag doll, and his younger charge toppled out of the sidecar in a heap. The motorcycle spun in several tight circles until the third wheel struck the private's inert body and flipped onto its side, dumping the older driver to the ground.

The P-51's final pass destroyed what was left of the checkpoint. Two military vehicles and a farmer's flatbed truck—the latter unlucky enough to be stopped at the checkpoint during the attack—had burst into flames. Billows of black smoke arched into the late-morning blue sky.

Then, upon his departure, the pilot dipped his wings, a signal that the coast was clear.

"Did you see that?" Emil straightened himself after crouching beneath the truck.

"Yeah, I did," Hans said. "This guy must be important to the Americans to have these types of connections."

"You got that right. Time to scoot out of here." Emil motioned to Hans to help him secure the load once again.

Minutes later, they swung onto Karlsruherstrasse. Emil didn't downshift when he pulled onto the shoulder, choosing to accelerate past the burning hulks and bloodied bodies. He barely glanced at the old soldier and his young companion as they passed, thankful he didn't have to be the one who pulled the trigger.

In less than a minute, the sandstone buildings gave way to countryside, and they made good time toward Leimen. Their safe house was a half hour away on a farm tucked away from the main roads.

Emil drove in silence and reflected on their close call. He wondered who the man they carried was, and why this scientist was so important. But their part of the journey was almost over.

The next leg to Switzerland would be far more difficult, Emil judged, and soon the *how* or *why* or *who* would no longer matter. Tomorrow he'd be given another equally difficult task, and Joseph Engel would become someone else's problem.

```
Basel, Switzerland
11:15 a.m.
```

The message was actually easy to translate. This time, there weren't any strange words like "radiation," "isotopes," or "uranium" in the communiqué.

Gabi peered at the original dispatch—in German Teletype—then at her legal pad, where she had written out a translation in preparation for typing. The memo's contents floored her, but in the presence of the Bern courier—and the omnipresent Frau Schaffner—she retained a professional coolness.

Gabi regarded her handwriting one more time:

Rescued Joseph Engel from Gestapo. Working on a "wonder weapon" project with Dr. Heisenberg at University of Heidelberg. Gestapo uncovered birth information showing that Engel was born to Jewish parents, but parents both died in 1918 from flu epidemic just after his first birthday. Adopted by a Berlin family and raised Christian. Life presently in danger.

Believe Engel has information vital for war effort. Must fall into American hands. Being driven to Location 3 this morning. Await your instructions for Switzerland insertion—Gideon.

The English word for *Wunderwaffe* . . . the literal, word-for-word translation was "wonder weapon." What did that mean? Did the Wunderwaffe reference have something to do with the "buzz bombs" slamming London neighborhoods?

The buzz bombs were the first set of futuristic "rockets,"

as Gabi recalled reading in the German press, and they'd devastated entire civilian apartment blocks during the month of June and portended a new way that war would be waged in the future. Or, at least, that's what Hitler's propagandists were predicting.

Gabi also noted the possible symbolism between the contents of the message and the name choice that the author gave himself. She searched her memory and recalled one of her father's sermons about Gideon—a man revered as one of the greatest judges in Israel. Since this Israelite warrior was a strong opponent of the Baal cult and conqueror of the Midianite oppressors, perhaps this modern-day "Gideon" viewed himself as someone standing up to National Socialism's oppressive regime.

Gabi turned to the courier, an earnest young man about her age. "Do you want this translation typed out in duplicate?" she asked in Swiss-German.

"No. I was told by Frau Taylor in Bern that wouldn't be necessary," he replied.

Gabi nodded and poised her forefingers above the home keys of her black typewriter. In less than three minutes, she finished keystroking the last sentence of the two-paragraph message. She advanced the carriage several times until the single sheet of bond paper gingerly released in her hands. After properly folding the sheet into thirds, she slipped the paper into a U.S. Embassy envelope and handed it to the courier. He, in turn, reached into his leather valise for his inkpad and rubber stamp. Then as Gabi watched, the courier turned over the envelope and stamped one time where the pointed flap met the envelope.

"Thank you, Fräulein. I have a train to catch."

"Any time." She smiled, hoping he couldn't see in her gaze any hint of the questions that filled her mind about the "wonder weapon."

. . . .

That didn't take long.

Jean-Pierre had been catching up on the latest war news from the *Basler Nachrichten* while hanging around the kiosk vis-à-vis the OSS office. Allen Dulles had asked him to meet the courier kid at the Basel SBB train station and keep an eye on the young charge.

"She was cute," the courier remarked to Jean-Pierre after exiting the OSS office. "Didn't catch her name, though."

"About 165 centimeters, straight blonde hair pulled back, apple-cheek complexion?" Jean-Pierre knew all the "girls" in the Basel OSS office—at least by sight—but this one . . . she was something special. "I imagine she caught your fancy?"

The gangly courier's nod was quickly followed by a mischievous grin that creased his face.

"So you were in the company of Gabi Mueller. She turns a lot of heads. Some farmer is sweet on her, but from what I've seen, I'm not so sure she's on board."

"Maybe she'll have a coffee with me the next time I have to make a trip."

"Take a number, my friend." Jean-Pierre looked at his watch. "Listen, if we get moving, you can make the 12:15 to Bern. No reason to wait around an extra half hour if we don't have to."

The Basel SBB train station was ten minutes away by foot, south on Schützengraben. Jean-Pierre deposited the courier into a second-class rail car, bid him off, and returned to the kiosk—just in time to catch Dieter Baumann leaving the OSS office building. *Perfect timing.* Allen Dulles had asked him to shadow the Swiss operative, and on this first day of surveillance, Baumann was already on the move. Since it was lunchtime, he was probably going out to eat like many Baslers enjoyed doing.

Jean-Pierre lost himself in the midst of hundreds filling the sidewalks during the noontime hour. Baumann, he noticed, never looked over his shoulder, never changed his cadence, and never stopped in front of window displays to glance sideways. *Sloppy fieldwork.* Jean-Pierre planned on noting these tendencies in his report to Bern.

He tracked Baumann to the elegant entrance of the Globus department store, where Jean-Pierre figured he was taking an elevator to the penthouse restaurant. That is, if he was having lunch.

• • • • • • • • •

"I would like the *Rösti* with onions," Gabi informed the waitress. Anything on the menu with meat—like the flavorful *Speck*—was frightfully dear and beyond her modest salary. She hoped the pan-fried potatoes would be cooked in butter rather than greasy oleomargarine, but even better restaurants like the Globus café were forced to deal with wartime rationing.

"I'll have the same," Dieter ordered. "And if you could cook our *Röstis* in butter, please."

The waitress finished scribbling the orders. "That will be an extra charge, sir."

"I understand." Dieter closed his menu and handed it to the waitress, who—in the same motion—set a checker-weave basket filled with chunks of *Pariserbrot* on the table. Dieter motioned for Gabi to take the first piece.

She opened the red-and-white-checked cloth hoping to find pats of butter along with the bread. Gabi sighed as she set a slice on a small serving plate.

"Disappointed?"

Gabi didn't want to sound ungrateful, especially since Dieter had asked that their Röstis be cooked in butter instead of that awful margarine. "I was just hoping for a dab of butter with my bread."

Dieter reached for a slice of Pariserbrot. "I'm fortunate that I like my bread natural. Unless, of course, I have a cream sauce or olive oil and pepper to dip it into. Maybe you should try that sometime. It's not half bad."

"You sound just like my father. And you're both right . . . I know I have nothing to complain about."

"Well, even if you do complain, perhaps the war won't last much longer." Dieter winked at her. "Things are looking better on a lot of fronts. From what the newspapers are saying, the tide has turned—the Allies are threatening to break out of the Normandy box any day. If that happens, the Germans might not be able to hold the Low Countries or even Paris. After that, who knows what could happen?"

Gabi chewed in silence, wondering if Dieter Baumann would continue to hold court. Instead, he posed a question.

"Have you thought about what will happen when the war is over? I don't mean in a geopolitical sense, but what will the war's end mean to you, Gabi Mueller? What will you do?"

Gabi wiped her mouth with her napkin, a reflex motion that gave her a few extra moments to collect her thoughts. "Actually, I've been thinking a great deal about the future. When the last shot has been fired, the world will be a different place, that's for sure. I think I want to find out what the world has in store for me. Maybe even go to America."

Dieter registered surprise.

"Maybe that didn't come across right," she said. "What I mean is that working for the OSS has opened my horizons. Given me more possibilities. Maybe I'll go explore them."

"You'd really move to America?"

Gabi sensed that Dieter was genuinely interested. "I've been to the States just once, when I was twelve. Dad was asked to speak at a couple of church conferences. It took us nearly two weeks to travel from Basel to Chicago, where Dad spoke, and then to Wisconsin, where we visited my cousins. They were so nice! Maybe if I were to go work in Washington or New York, I'd be able to see them again."

"Well, that U.S. passport gives you options that many people don't have, including me."

"That's what I was thinking. My dad always teases me that he won't be able to keep me down on the farm after working for the Americans."

"Like translating messages marked Top Secret. So, how did it go this morning?" Dieter cocked an eyebrow.

Gabi remembered the courier's explicit instructions not to discuss the contents with anyone—including those in her office.

"Oh, fine," she replied airily. "I can't discuss what was in the message, though."

"I wasn't expecting you to, Fräulein Muell—Gabi. Nobody understands better than me that there are certain things we have to keep secret from others, even those we work with." Dieter reached for a sip of Henniez water. "That's why what I'm about to tell you must stay between us. Do you understand?"

Gabi hesitated. The directness in Dieter's speech was a departure from their friendly colleague-to-colleague discussion. She opened her mouth to answer, and then closed it again, unsure of how to respond.

"Sorry—I didn't mean to startle you." Dieter smiled. "What I mean to say is that something has come up—an opportunity, you could say—that only Mr. Dulles and myself know about. In fact, he asked me to involve only you in this mission, should you choose to accept it. No one else in the office is to know a thing, which is why I asked you to meet me at this restaurant."

Gabi leaned forward to listen.

"All I can tell you is that this assignment would be danger-ous . . . it takes place in Germany."

"Germany? In the middle of a war? We have no protec-tion there!"

"I know. That complicates things if—how shall I say it?—the situation does not have a positive outcome. But don't worry, we've taken steps to minimize the risk. You and I would leave Switzerland in the morning and return to homeland soil before dinnertime. The only other thing I can tell you is that the mission is of vital interest to the Allied war effort. Lives hang in the balance."

Gabi reached for her Henniez and took a sip. Here was another chance—a bigger opportunity—to make a difference. Her chest warmed with the thought that Mr. Dulles thought she was up for the job—and Dieter did too. "So you're saying that you can't tell me exactly what's involved until I say yes?"

Dieter beamed as he fiddled with his bread. "I always knew you were a fast learner. That's why I like you so much."

Gabi blushed. "Does it involve breaking into a safe?"

"Yes. That much I can tell you."

"Then I'm your girl."

* * * * * * * *

University of Heidelberg Hospital
12:45 p.m.

Sturmbannführer Bruno Kassler, with Corporal Becker on his heels, walked past the nurse's station without breaking his stride. His hobnail boots clacked on the linoleum floor in precise military measure.

"Make a left. He's in Room 14." Becker pointed toward the long hallway.

The hospital corridor smelled of lemon-scented disinfectant and a trace of urine. Kassler involuntarily wiped his nose with the back of his hand, then set his mind on weaving through the steady traffic of white-coated doctors and nurses coming his way. He narrowly missed brushing shoulders with a studious doctor reading a clipboard in his left hand.

Becker stopped him in his tracks. "This is his room, sir."

Kassler rapped the white door with his knuckles, then entered without waiting for a reply. He did, however, remove his black cap and place it under his left arm—a sign of respect for a wounded soldier.

"Heil Hitler!" Kassler bellowed, his right arm slanted at the perfect, practiced angle.

161

Privat Grüniger lamely raised his bandaged right arm ninety degrees. The rest of his upper torso was swathed in gauze. "Heil Hitler," he mumbled.

"I see you got into a bit of a scrape with the Yanks." Kassler returned his cap to his head and crossed his arms over his chest. "The cowardly swine will pay, I can assure you. But first, a few questions about the air attack." The Gestapo chief nodded toward Becker, a signal for his assistant to take notes. "Can you tell me what happened?"

The private didn't hesitate. "Captain Hauptmann and I had been on routine patrol since 0700 in response to the red-alert security directive our commanding officer received during the night. We observed a farmer's truck leave the main road just before the last security checkpoint in southern Heidelberg."

"The Karlsruherstrasse leading into Leimen?"

"That is correct. Captain Hauptmann thought it unusual for a truck loaded with hay bales to pull over just several hundred meters before the checkpoint. We went over to investigate."

"What was the farmer like?"

"There were two, actually. Neither of them looked much like farmers. Their papers checked out, though. Maybe they were helping out an old lady who couldn't find farmhands."

"Could be." Kassler stroked his chin. Most able-bodied men had been either constricted into the army or forced into the factories, although some received furloughs during planting and harvest times. The Fatherland needed food since armies marched on their stomachs, as Napoleon famously said one time. "So you initiated a search?"

"Correct. It's common to hide fugitives in hay loads, so we followed standard procedure. I was probing between the rows of hay bales when the air raid siren blasted."

"How many planes?"

"Just one. I recall taking a few shots at the American fighter, but he wasn't too concerned about us."

Kassler cocked his head in interest.

"What I mean, sir, is he blasted the checkpoint. Came in real low. It wasn't until his third dive he attacked us. After that, I don't remember much."

"Let's talk about what happened before the raid. You mentioned you were on top of the hay bales when the attack occurred. Do you remember anything else?"

"I do, but I'm not sure if it's my memory playing tricks on me."

"What do you mean?" Kassler looked toward Becker, who was poised with his notebook.

"While probing the hay pile, I saw what appeared to be clothing through the hay. Maybe just a lost scarf . . . or maybe something else. Maybe it was someone. But like I said, I'm not sure."

One more clue, Kassler thought. One more clue.

* * * * * * * * *

"Type out the description of the flatbed truck and notify the local authorities," Kassler barked.

Trailing his superior officer, Becker struggled to keep up, scribbling reminders in his notebook. Kassler barely broke stride as he pushed his way through a set of glass doors that led to their staff car parked at the hospital entrance.

"A mid-morning, single-fighter raid on a security checkpoint in Heidelberg? Preposterous." Kassler paused beside the automobile, waiting for Becker to open the rear door for him. "Who do they think they are?"

Kassler sighed as he settled into the leather bench seat. Becker climbed into the front seat and mumbled something about a late lunch, but Kassler didn't respond. His mind replayed Privat Grüniger's report.

The fact that the Allies had owned the skies in the last year was one thing. But there was something utterly brazen about launching a midday aerial assault in broad daylight, with just a single fighter and no escort. P-51 Mustangs normally escorted the B-24 Liberator bombers to their missions, and while it was true that some rogue American P-51 pilots hung back to hunt for Luftwaffe ME-109s or strafe rail yards and supply depots, a single-seat sortie on an overmatched checkpoint was unheard of—unless . . .

Kassler balled his hands into fists. Those "farmers" *knew* the air raid was coming, which is why they stowed their truck in that plaza. And he had no doubt that entombed underneath a ton of hay was Joseph Engel—which meant the bandits and the Jew traitor traveled south.

Toward Leimen.

• • • • • • • • •

Dieter placed the folded napkin on the table and leaned back with a contented smile. He studied Gabi's face, watching her as she finished the last bite of her lunch. Although from the outside she appeared to be enjoying a comfortable meal, he noted a look of excitement in her gaze. He had her on a string—like a marionette at the Salzburg Children's Theater.

"I've got the check. I'll let you head back to the office first, Gabi."

"You don't have to. Here, let me cover my part of the bill." She reached for her pocketbook.

He lifted a hand and waved her offering away. "Don't worry. Lunch was on Mr. Dulles."

"Well, all I can say is thank you, Mr. Dulles." She stood and waved her hand in the direction of Bern. "I'll see you back at the office. Thank you . . . for thinking of me." She brushed a strand of hair behind her ear and hurried off with a smile.

Dieter kept his eyes on the lithe figure approaching the elevator. When Gabi was gone, he called over the waitress to pay.

"Two *Röstis*, two Henniezs," he announced.

The waitress, per custom, reached into her apron for a

black purse filled with Swiss banknotes and enough loose change to open a bank teller cage. *"Zweimol drüü macht sächs,"* she uttered in the local dialect, *"plus zwiemol eis macht acht Franke, bitte."*

Baumann counted out eight francs in coins and handed them over.

Instead of exiting via the elevator, Baumann turned right and pushed through the door leading to the men's room. His contact, Ludwig, waited next to the washbasins.

Dieter's eyes darted to the stalls. "Empty?"

"I checked. We're alone."

As habit, he walked over to the middle stall and bent over. No feet rested next to any of the three toilets.

Ludwig passed a comb through his thinning black hair. "What did she say?"

"She took it hook, line, and sinker, as the Americans say."

"Did you tell her when?"

"Not yet. I thought we should talk first."

"Consider yourself talked to." Ludwig tucked his comb into his front shirt pocket and then pulled two papers from a pouch he carried under his shirt. "We go tomorrow. Here are your papers for getting across the border."

Baumann fingered the two work permits. "Interesting that the Germans don't require a photo."

"They match this permit to your Swiss identity card, which has your photo, so you have to take both."

"I knew that. I was just making the observation that this seems out of character for our neighbors to the north."

"Could be, but consider that these work permits are for Swiss wanting to come *into* wartime Germany and work in their factories. They know what side their bread is buttered on."

Dieter tucked the documents inside his jacket pocket and then folded his arms across his chest. "You're sure the diamonds are in that safe?"

"I double-checked with my police source this morning.

You get your girl to work those magic fingers of hers, and when this war is over, we'll be sitting pretty. From what I hear, there are enough rocks inside that safe to open a diamond exchange in Amsterdam."

* * * * * * * * *

Jean-Pierre peered over the top of the newspaper as Gabi Mueller exited the busy Globus entrance. What was she doing here? She looked to her right and adjusted a white scarf over her hair, then turned to the left and walked past a series of department store window displays while he continued to track her progress from across the street.

At the third display—where two women were dismantling a First of August scene—she stopped and regarded their work. Jean-Pierre lifted the newspaper to cover his face. When a suitable amount of time had passed—fifteen seconds—he dropped the newspaper, but she was gone.

A minute or two later, Dieter Baumann departed the Globus, his right hand working a toothpick as he strode back toward his office. Jean-Pierre sized up the situation: this was an off-site rendezvous with Gabi Mueller. What was that all about?

Jean-Pierre didn't have an answer, but he was sure that Allen Dulles would be interested in *this* development.

He tried to ignore the knots that had formed at the base of his neck, and he hoped the anxious tenseness that surged through him was wrong this time. Gabi Mueller had a lunch meeting, nothing more.

Jean-Pierre told himself that was all Baumann was up to, but he was having trouble convincing the jury—himself.

19

A farmhouse outside Leimen, Germany
2:30 p.m.

At first, he believed he was still dreaming.

Joseph rubbed the sleep from his eyes and swept his gaze around the second-story bedroom, paneled in finished pinewood and fully furnished with an armoire, a small table, and chairs. He sucked in a deep breath, taking in the scent of lye soap and lilac—not unlike his mother's house when he was a child. He noticed a vase of lilacs on a small bedside table, and his lips formed a soft smile.

Sunshine flooded through a single-paned window, outlined with red-and-white checked curtains. He figured it must be midafternoon. From somewhere beyond his bedroom door, a chorus of baritone voices sung a familiar hymn—a muffled melody, he realized, that had awakened him. A song as sweet as an angel's hymn.

> Ein' feste Burg ist unser Gott,
> Ein gute Wehr und Waffen;
> Er hilft uns frei aus aller Not,
> Die uns jetzt hat betroffen . . .

Joseph closed his eyes and hummed along with the next stanza. The words flooded his consciousness, words as familiar to him as the Lord's Prayer. This didn't surprise him. After all, it was in Fräulein Ritter's second grade class when he first learned the lyrics to Martin Luther's seminal hymn, "A Mighty Fortress Is Our God." Luther's paraphrase of

Psalm 46, as well as the rhythmic isometric arrangement, reassured Joseph that no matter what he faced, God was a bulwark never failing.

After the fourth and final verse, muffled male voices rose from beneath his floor, but he couldn't make out more than a snatch of their conversations. Joseph stared at the ceiling as a peace settled over him. Even though this group of people had protected him, he still questioned whose side they were on. And he wondered what they wanted from him.

But now, waking to these songs, he had a renewed hope. Maybe it was God's people who'd protected him. Perhaps he was safe after all.

Two minutes later, a knock sounded on the pinewood door.

"Herr Engel, *darf ich herein kommen?*"

Joseph didn't recognize the voice, but the genteel request sounded courteous enough.

"Yes, you may come in." He rubbed his eyes once again and regarded the slim, tall man entering the bedroom.

Joseph quickly sat up on the low-slung twin bed, covered by a duvet with an ivory white slipcover. "Excuse me, but I don't normally nap in the middle of the afternoon."

"Well understood. The events of the last twenty-four hours would drain the reserves of any individual," the man said with an understanding smile.

Joseph swung his feet onto the hardwood floor, remembering that he'd slipped off his trousers before dropping into bed hours ago. He felt heat rising to his cheeks. "Excuse me. Let me put on some clothes."

The slender man strode over to the second-story window, peering out.

Joseph grunted as he plucked his black pants—still speckled with strands of straw—from the back of a chair. He dressed, and then approached the window, glancing out toward a dirt yard that separated the main farmhouse from a two-story barn whose stained finish had faded to a mellow burnish.

"I see that the chickens are finding enough to eat," the caller commented. "Lord knows how we need eggs around here."

The older man turned and extended his hand. "Please allow me to introduce myself. I'm Pastor Leo. I thank God Almighty that you arrived safely today."

Joseph regarded the visitor before him. The pastor looked to be the same age as his father—early fifties, clusters of wispy gray hair, and skinnier than a rail. His nose resembled a raven's beak, and his sallow cheeks spoke of his wartime diet. The way the pastor's blue eyes met and held Joseph's— warm, inviting—imbued the young physicist with confidence. He inspired trust, a sureness of mission.

"A pleasure to meet you, Pastor. You'll have to excuse me if I seem confused. I'm having a terrible time sorting this all out."

"I figured as much." Pastor Leo approached a pine table with a pair of arrowback chairs. Dressed in casual farm clothes—with no clerical collar—but wearing wooden clogs so as to not track dirt and mud into the home, Pastor Leo pointed to one of the chairs. "Here, take a seat. We need to talk."

"I would appreciate finally getting some answers." Joseph settled into the offered chair.

"You're probably wondering why you're here."

Joseph answered with a nod.

"To start, we aren't the Gestapo. In fact, I can assure you that if our location were betrayed to the local authorities, we would all be given one-way tickets to Prinz-Albrecht-Strasse . . . including you."

"But I broke no law! I . . . I've done nothing to instigate my arrest . . . kidnapping . . . capture—or whatever you call it."

"No, but you'd have a hard time convincing the Gestapo of your innocence."

"Why?" Joseph threw up his hands. "Surely they'll believe I had no part of this. I was taken by force."

The pastor pursed his lips, then reached out and took Joseph's right hand in his. He let out a long sigh. "There is no way to say this, but just to tell you plainly. The Gestapo—they won't believe you no matter what you say . . . because you're Jewish."

Joseph pulled his hand away as if the pastor's touch had scalded him. "No, you're mistaken. You must have me confused with someone else. This whole thing is a mistake. My parents' heritage is in accordance with the Nuremberg laws. I'm a God-fearing Lutheran. My background was thoroughly vetted before I joined Doktor Heisenberg's team at the University."

A sadness filled the pastor's eyes, causing the muscles in Joseph's shoulders to clench.

Joseph let out a coarse laugh to lighten the tension. "This must be some kind of twisted joke. My parents are *not* Jewish."

"You're correct." The pastor's eyes bore into Joseph's. His mouth opened and closed again as if he was trying to find the right words. "Are you . . . circumcised?"

Joseph's eyes widened. "How did you—what I mean is yes, I am. My father told me that my pediatrician—a Jewish doctor—recommended the procedure for the prevention of disease. When the Führer came into power, though, he told me never to show my privates to anyone."

"Your father was a wise man."

Joseph stood and strolled to the window, but his mind wasn't focused on the view outside. "Jewish? Impossible," he mumbled to himself.

Years of Nazi propaganda, he knew, had colored his view of the Jewish people. He didn't view himself as anti-Semitic, but he was naturally wary of Jews because of what he had been taught. In school he'd learned that the German defeat in 1918 was the work of Jewish and Marxist spies who had weakened the system from within. The financial collapse of the Weimar Republic was the handiwork of Jewish bankers. He couldn't be one of them . . .

A light breeze rattled the leaves of an oak tree outside, but he wasn't paying attention. Instead in his mind's eye he pictured the photographs of Jews held up by a social studies teacher during his "racial instruction" classes at his *Gymnasium*, or secondary school. Jews could be recognized by their puffy lips and their bent noses that resembled the number 6. Their eyes—predominantly black—were wary and piercing . . . and deceitful as well. Their hair was usually dark and curly like a Negro's, and their oversized ears looked like the handles of a coffee cup. A receding forehead was another giveaway, as well as an unpleasant odor coming off their bodies.

His thoughts took him back to a few weeks ago when he'd been passing by a schoolyard near the University. Elementary schoolgirls had been singing a little ditty that encompassed the shifty Jewish character:

> Once they came from the East,
> Dirty, lousy, without a cent;
> But in a few years
> They were well-to-do.

> Today they dress very well;
> Do not want to be Jews any more
> So keep your eyes open and make a note:
> Once a Jew, always a Jew!

He had always been a Jew? The thought failed to compute, just like incomplete theorems on a chalkboard. Joseph noted his reflection in the window. Hair: curly but brown, not black. Nose: fairly straight, certainly not a hooknose. Lips: neither puffy or protruding. Eyes: brown, but so was half the world.

Joseph turned back from the window and met the pastor's gaze. "But how do you know? I don't look Jewish."

Pastor Leo shrugged his thin shoulders. "Hard to say. But you are circumcised, and that can't be denied. Fortunate for you, your brown hair isn't that curly. Your nose, while generous, could go either way. You don't have the classic Jewish features, but neither do you look Aryan to me. Who's to say what God's chosen people should look like? I didn't know some of my neighbors were Jewish until they affixed a yellow star to their coats. Even though they looked like any other Germans, they were still transported. I'm sure that we have people in our church with Jewish blood who've kept that information out of official hands, or they simply don't know they're Jewish—like you."

"Well, if I am Jewish—which I am not—how would you know? How is it that you know more about me than I apparently know about myself?"

The pastor drew a long breath. "I'm not at liberty to tell you *how* we found out, but we did learn that you were adopted by Thomas and Eva Engel in 1918 when you were an infant."

"Adopted?" Joseph pressed his fingers to his forehead. "That is unimaginable. Surely my parents would have told me."

"Many adoptive parents are advised never to tell their children that they were adopted. In fact, I recommend this in my own counseling so that children do not experience the shame associated with the event." Pastor Leo leaned forward, threading his fingers and lowering his voice. "And in your situation, your parents may have saved your life. It's obvious that no one . . . neighbors, school officials, employers . . . knew that your real parents were Jewish—until now."

Joseph returned to the chair and allowed the pastor's direct words to sink in. He thought back to the few photographs of himself as an infant boy and realized that none of them included his mother or father—or rather the two people he'd always known as his mother and father.

He cleared his throat. "If what you're saying is true, then what happened to my . . . real parents?"

"They died in the Spanish flu of 1918. You were an orphan until a Christian couple took you in and made you their own. The secret of your Jewry remained deeply buried until the Gestapo ferreted out the information a few days ago."

Joseph struggled to mentally catch up to what he was hearing. "How did they find out?"

The pastor maintained a steady gaze. "After the attempt on the Führer's life, the Gestapo suspected treason regarding anyone remotely connected with the war effort. We hear thousands of lives have been purged. As for your situation, your important work with Doktor Heisenberg at the University warranted a second look. When the Gestapo found out about your ancestry, you were earmarked for pickup and transport to the camps. You've heard about the work camps in the East, haven't you?"

"Everyone hears things, but who knows what the truth is? Some say it's all lies. Some say it's not as bad as the rumors claim it is. Others claim it's worse. For the most part, I try not to think about it. Academic research has been my life since the war started. The people I work with are my friends. And even if the Gestapo did come, I'm sure that Professor Heisenberg would say something on my behalf—"

"Do you really believe he could convince them that you didn't know about your past? And that your true motives did not include sabotaging your important military research?"

The pastor's stark words gave Joseph pause. "So what you are saying is that no matter what I said, I'm a condemned man?"

"In the Third Reich, all Jews are doomed. Isn't that clear to someone as intelligent as you?"

Joseph thought back to the last time he'd seen any Jewish people in Heidelberg. How long had it been? One or two years ago? It was like they'd disappeared from the face of the earth.

"What's going to happen to me?"

"We're trying to get you into Allied hands."

The Allies? Until that moment when the American fighter plane burst out of the sky and saved them from discovery, Joseph had always considered the Allied forces to be the enemy. Yet now . . .

A sinking feeling came over Joseph again, and a battle waged in his mind. How did he know he could trust these people? How did he know if they were telling him the truth about being Jewish? About being chased by the Gestapo?

His hands rubbed against the seat of his chair and tightened. If the Gestapo knew, they would undoubtedly take away every bit of freedom he had. As important as his work was in harnessing the power of the atom, he was a condemned man. Like the pastor said: in the Third Reich, all Jews were doomed—no exception.

"Get me into the hands of the Allies? How do you propose to do that? The Gestapo must be looking everywhere for me."

"We're working on that. A plan is forming, but it'll take a miracle to pull it off."

"What sort of miracle?"

The pastor leaned in, and for the next five minutes, he outlined their strategy for Joseph's escape into Switzerland. Joseph listened and nodded at the right times, but he knew he would need time to process what the older man was saying.

If what Pastor Leo said was true, then everything about who he was had changed—forever.

• • • • • • • • •

"How did it go with Engel?" The pastor's brother-in-law, Adalbert Ulrich, who owned the ten-hectare farm, had been waiting downstairs. Actually, waiting and keeping his eyes on the single-lane dirt road leading to the farm.

"Very good," Leo replied. "I believe he understands the gravity of the situation. I asked him to stay inside the house. Perhaps at night he could get some fresh air, but we'll have to keep an eye on him."

"Did you tell him how we'll get him out of here?"

"Yes, I did. He was inquisitive, but he never asked me why I was telling him so much operational information."

"So why did you?"

"I'm not sure . . . maybe to ease my conscience."

"Conscience?"

"I haven't forgotten our last communication from the Big Cheese. The message clearly stated that if Engel's capture looks imminent or even possible, we're to shoot him. He cannot, under any circumstances, fall under Nazi control again."

"Because he's working with Professor Heisenberg."

"Precisely."

20

Sturmbannführer Bruno Kassler leaned over the topographic map of southern Heidelberg and ran his right forefinger along the main route—Rohrbacher Strasse—right into the heart of Leimen. He knew the region well, having grown up in nearby Sandhausen. Leimen was where the countryside started: rolling hills to the east, suitable for dairy production; flat, arable land to the south, where rectangular plots yielded rows of wheat, alfalfa, and corn.

"Everything points to right here, *ja*?" he said, jabbing a finger and tracing the contour lines that indicated an elevation change south of Leimen. "I can feel it in my bones. Nothing unusual turns up elsewhere, but an American plane shows up at the stroke of noon and smashes one of our . . . checkpoints? It doesn't make sense—unless it was a coordinated attack. Then Privat Grüniger swore he saw something move in that farmer's hay pile. You agree, Becker?"

The young corporal cleared his throat. "Grüniger's statement was convincing. I think you are on the right track, sir. It was genius of you to order more checkpoints south of Leimen . . . here . . . and here." Becker's finger also followed the Rohrbacher Strasse in a southerly direction toward Nussbloch. "I've circulated a description of the farmer's truck, so if the criminals are in the region, Joseph Engel will be captured."

Kassler stood and walked to the window overlooking the courtyard. "By now, the local Polizei in Leimen are fanning out, knocking on doors. They better turn over every—"

The jangling of Kassler's black phone interrupted his words. "Take it, Becker. We know who it is. I need another moment to gather my thoughts."

Becker picked up the phone and listened. He immediately stiffened and said formally, "Yes, he's right here." Turning to his superior, he announced, "Sir, the Reichsführer is on the line."

Kassler felt his shoulders straightening to attention as he cradled the receiver to his ear. "A pleasure to receive your call, Reichsführer Himmler. I regret—"

"I don't have time for excuses," replied the oily voice from Berlin. "I received your message that the Jew traitor has escaped capture, a serious lapse in discipline, unless you have more welcome news forthcoming."

Kassler felt his face flush. "No, mein Reichsführer, we have not located Engel, but we feel strongly he's making his way south in the company of the plotters. As I explained in my message—"

"But of course Engel's traveling south. Switzerland lies just 200 kilometers away."

Actually, the distance was more like 250 kilometers, but Kassler wasn't about to quibble with the Reichsführer. "Yes, sir, I've initiated several strike teams to comb the area. The fact that Engel and his cohorts are making it difficult to locate him prompts me to believe that our adversaries are more well-organized than previously thought."

Silence greeted Kassler's ventured opinion, and he wondered if he had overstepped his boundaries. Instead, he heard a voice of resignation. "It's becoming more obvious to me that traitors operate in our midst. First, the assassination attempt on our beloved Führer, then this betrayal. I was wondering why the High Command wasn't reporting more progress from those uppity intellectuals at the University of Heidelberg. When I briefed the Führer that a Jew had been working alongside Doktor Heisenberg and the other scientists for three years, he became hysterical, screaming that this latest example of Jewish treachery explained everything."

Kassler recoiled. The Reichsführer had discussed Engel's kidnapping with the Führer? "Sir, you can assure the Führer that every effort is being made to find Engel."

"Maybe I will," the voice replied. "Or maybe you can make the trip to Berchtesgaden and tell him yourself."

• • • • • • • •

Davos, Switzerland
4:30 p.m.

From a round white table parked in front of the Palace Hotel, Bill Palmer glanced one more time at the black-and-white photograph of him dressed in his Army Air Corps Service Dress uniform with his arms wrapped around a pretty strawberry blonde. His longing to hold Katie again caused his heart to ache. He missed her greatly, and her tender letters—which arrived in batches every two weeks from Wisconsin—were like salve to the homesickness that periodically gripped his heart.

On most days, Bill tried to pretend that he didn't mind being interned in Davos. Compared to the bunkhouses back in Britain, his accommodations at the Palace Hotel were fairly regal. There was enough to eat, if you could stand all the cheese and potatoes. His thoughts turned to his buddies back at the Mighty Eighth, stationed in England. Here he was, riding out the war in the cushy Alps while his buddies risked life and limb every time they climbed into a B-17 with their flight suits on. The load shouldn't fall on their shoulders. He needed to pull his weight in the effort to free the world from Nazi domination.

"Palmer, how ya liking life in this gilded cage?" The voice of J.J. Marx interrupted his thoughts, and Bill returned the photo of Katie to his breast pocket.

Bill stood and shook J.J.'s hand, then glanced at the Jakobs-horn, where fissures of snow filled its couloirs even in August. "Kind of like summer camp. Just a lot more rules."

James Joseph Marx, a bombardier with the 446th Bomb Squadron, 331st Bomb Group, U.S. Army Eighth Air Force, re-minded Bill of the kid in school who wanted to be friends with everyone but didn't really fit in with any of the groups. He'd been interned in Davos since German flak destroyed the right engine to his B-24 Liberator back in January. When the Yank bomber veered into Swiss airspace, they were inexplicably attacked by a pair of Swiss Me-109 fighters—Messerschmitts painted with a red square and a white cross on the tail as-sembly. Under a rain of .50-caliber fire, J.J.'s pilot buddy had managed to drop his wheels—a universal sign of distress. Then the crippled bomber successfully bounced onto the runway at a military airfield outside of Lake Constance.

Bill knew everyone's story, just like everyone else knew his. Those things were easy to talk about—the missions, the dogfights, the escapes. What they couldn't talk about so easily were their hopes of leaving this place. After all, they were in Davos "for the duration," an open-ended time that no one knew how long would last.

"This place isn't so bad . . . all things considered, although the hotel could use a paint job." J.J. jerked his head toward the peeling paint on the white colonnades fronting this grand five-star establishment as well as the faded red carpet leading to its lackluster lobby. The Palace Hotel, one of the village's fourteen hotels that had been transformed into lodgings for the interned pilots, had fallen into disrepair after Europe plunged into total war—and turned off the spigot of tourists.

"Yeah, I guess things could be worse. I'm not complain-ing." Bill adjusted his khaki cap against the afternoon sun. "We don't have to work. Three squares a day, my own bed, a bathroom down the hall. We even have some spending money in our pockets."

The American internees received their full flight pay, converted into Swiss francs, every ten days from the U.S. Legation in Bern. The $7 or thirty Swiss francs from each paycheck could be used to supplement their Red Cross packages or even buy something more frivolous—like Swiss watches, cameras, or a pair of skis. What the money could *not* be spent on was clothes. The Americans had to wear their regulation GI uniforms at all times so that Swiss authorities could tell them apart from the locals.

Beyond the cheese-heavy diet, their biggest problem was idleness. The Hague Convention of 1907 prohibited obligatory labor, so many of the internees turned to sports as an outlet for the constant ennui. The British pilots favored football, but not the American kind. Several teams of various abilities played against Swiss club teams that ventured into the high country to give the *Engländer* a good match on the soccer pitch. During winter, American airmen took to ice hockey since Davos had an outdoor rink.

Last winter, Bill remembered, *all* the Allied pilots were crazy about downhill skiing in Davos, where the world's first J-bar ski lift opened in 1934. Many pilots had never strapped on a pair of wooden skis and bear-trap bindings before arriving in Davos, but bombing down the hill seemed somewhat appropriate for this boisterous crowd. The Yanks and the Brits weren't interested in learning the stem Christie from their exasperated Swiss ski instructors—many of whom were their armed guards off the piste—but in schussing as fast as they could. Bill winced at the memory of broken femurs he had witnessed, but smiled at the reminiscence of Andreas and Willy Mueller helping him safely snowplow to the small warming hut situated at the bottom of the long Parsenn run. But it just didn't seem right—enjoying himself, snow skiing while his girl waited tables six days a week and his friends died in battle.

J.J. leaned close and whispered, "A couple of us guys are thinking of making a run for it."

"When?"

"Tonight. After the movie. You want in, Palmer?"

Bill paused. If you were caught escaping, it was an automatic ninety days in a Swiss penitentiary camp. There were several, but Wauwilermoos outside of Lucerne carried the reputation as being the worst of the worst. The drafty wooden barracks were populated with Swiss murderers, rapists, and robbers. Prisoners slept on clumps of straw. The outdoor privy was nothing more than a long plank of wood—with six holes—erected over a trench filled with effluent. The prison compound was surrounded by double rows of barbed wire, and guard towers stood sentry in each corner. Rifle-toting guards patrolled the perimeter with vicious attack dogs. Occasionally a Swiss guard released a Doberman or German shepherd on an unsuspecting prisoner for the sport of it.

Compared to *Wauwil*, as the pilots called it, life in Davos was a Roman holiday. The airmen were free to wander around the village, go window-shopping, even take tea with a local family. More than a few Swiss mothers angled to marry off their eligible daughters to an American pilot if romantic sparks kindled into a blaze. Bill recalled that J.J. enjoyed hanging out with Corinne Busslinger, whose beauty queen looks had won her the title of Miss Schweiz before the war.

The interned pilots were free to do pretty much anything they wanted—except escape. The Swiss military took a dim view of wandering beyond the chalk-marked boundaries at each end of Davos; the penalty for getting caught was swift and sure: extradition to one of the penitentiary camps like Wauwilermoos.

"Isn't tonight awfully quick?" Bill had heard the success rate was less than 20 percent.

"Didn't you hear the news, man? Patton's headed for Paris, and France is about to be liberated. All we have to do is get to the French border."

"Yeah, but what's your plan to get there?" Bill knew that Geneva, a likely jumping-off point, was 275 miles away.

"We walk to the valley and pick up a train near Chur."

"But that's more than thirty miles!"

"Okay, so we have to rough it for a couple of days. We'll be all right once we get to the Rhine valley. My buddy Sam speaks German like a pro, and I've been learning from the locals."

Bill shot a knowing look.

J.J. looked a bit embarrassed. "You heard about Corinne, I see. She told me the Swiss Army grunts thought someone would make a dash for it during the First of August celebration, figuring they were distracted. That didn't happen, so they've let their guard down."

"How much money do I need?"

"A hundred francs would do it. You have that?"

Bill nodded.

J.J. gave his buddy a light tap on the shoulder. "Then think about it. We're not leaving until the movie's over."

"What's showing at the Davos Kino?"

"Humphrey Bogart in *Casablanca*. I think I've seen it five times. Nice film and all that, but if I hear Bogey saying, 'Here's looking at you, kid' one more time, I'll lose my lunch." His Bogart impersonation was rather respectable.

Bill laughed. "Yeah, that might be enough to send anyone over the chalk line." He tried to act as if he wasn't intrigued by the idea—in case he didn't go along with the escape attempt—but the chance to rejoin his unit and perhaps receive Stateside leave to visit Katie and his family seemed more appealing by the minute. "I'll think about it."

"You think all you want." J.J. patted Bill's shoulder. "Listen, Sam and I are meeting up behind Heiz Bakery at the end of town. If you want to be a hero, be there."

21

Riehen, Switzerland
5:57 p.m.

Gabi's hands scrubbed the slightly oblong potatoes with a golden yellow skin under a stream of cold water, but her mind wasn't set on her task. Instead, she thought about her new assignment across the border in Germany and the fabricated identity card hidden under the red woolen socks in her dresser. Her stomach felt loaded down with rocks, but she hummed to herself as if she didn't have a care in the world.

Ernst Mueller, with a sheaf of papers in hand, breezed through the spring-hinged kitchen door. "I thought I smelled raclette. Good choice for dinner tonight."

"I'm glad you approve, especially since we had raclette two nights ago." Thea smiled.

Gabi watched her mother size up what remained of a half wheel of raclette cheese from the Valais region of southwest Switzerland. A small crescent of the firm, buttery cheese was all that remained—maybe 250 grams. "I think we can stretch another meal, don't you, Gabi?"

Gabi stopped washing the small, firm potatoes known as *charlottes*. "You're counting Eric, I hope." She dried her hands on a dishtowel. "Let's see . . . *eins, zwei, drü, vier, fünf* . . . ," she enumerated in Basler dialect. "We should have enough potatoes and cheese, and if we don't, we'll have to remember that millions on this continent are wondering what they'll eat tonight."

"Great perspective, Gabi," her father replied. "The fact that Switzerland has been protected from the ravages of this war is one of the points I'll be making in my sermon Sunday morning." He regarded the scribble of sentences on his papers, along with tangential notes in the margin. "It's like we're in the eye of a hurricane, surrounded on all sides by death and destruction. But God's protection doesn't mean we can turn our backs to what's happening around us. I haven't preached on the plight of the Jews since Bern announced 'the boat is full' earlier this year, but did you know that the Jews were kept at arms' length in this country for centuries?"

"Switzerland?" Gabi filled a pot with water and set it on the stove, glad to engage her mind on something else other than Dieter's assignment. "I thought it was only in Germany that they've had so much trouble."

"When the Black Death swept through Basel back in the fourteenth century, the Jews were accused of poisoning the wells because they didn't die in nearly the numbers as the Baslers did. The city fathers attempted to protect the Jews, but the local guilds demanded their blood. Six hundred men, women, and children were rounded up, shackled inside a wooden barn, and torched. Subsequently, Jews were banned from Basel—and just about everywhere else in Switzerland. Until 1879, Jews could live in only two towns: Lengnau and Endingen. The situation didn't improve until after the Franco-Prussian War when Switzerland loosened immigration laws relating to Jews. The great mathematician Albert Einstein, raised in a Jewish family in Munich, had no problem coming to this country in the late 1890s and was accepted at the Eidgenössische Technische Hochschule in Zurich."

"Andreas and Willy hope to start their engineering studies at the ETH when the war's over," Gabi interrupted, referring to the prestigious Swiss Technical University.

Her father smiled. "Yes, that will be nice when life can return to normal. Maintaining our neutrality hasn't been easy for us. Switzerland has had to go along to get along with Germany. There's a reason why Swiss newspapers don't criticize Hitler or the Nazi regime, and it's because our government pressures the press not to antagonize Berlin. We also do their bidding with this racial hatred they have against the Jews. When these poor wretches manage to escape into Switzerland with a J stamp on their papers, our official policy is to deliver them back into the clutches of the Germans or the Vichy government. Andreas and Willy said they heard that more than 30,000 Jews have either been turned back at the border or captured and escorted into Nazi hands. Shameful."

"But the Turrians at church said some Jews were allowed in." Thea glanced up as she scraped the skin off the half wheel of cheese.

Ernst moved toward the counter and leaned against it. "It's true that some Jewish families could stay, but that was in the early days of the war," he continued. "The cantons began charging a tax on each Jewish head for their upkeep. Organizations like the Swiss-Jewish Congress must support them, or otherwise they're handed back to the Germans on a silver platter—just like John the Baptist's head."

Gabi rarely heard her father pontificate like this—unless he was in the pulpit. "You're right, Papi. I'll never forget the flash of fear I saw in the eyes of that Jewish family on the Mittlere Brücke, or the sight of them jumping from the bridge."

"What the Swiss need is a reminder that God made the Jews his chosen people." Ernst regarded one of his notes in the margin. "It all goes back to Genesis 12:3, where the Lord God said, 'I will bless them that bless thee, and curse him that curseth thee: and in thee shall all families of the earth be blessed.' You can go down through history and point out what happened to civilizations that persecuted Jews as a matter of official state policy. The Assyrians, the Babylonians, the Phoenicians, and the great Roman Empire persecuted the Jews. All were destroyed. Spain hosted one of the largest and most prosperous Jewish populations before expelling the Jews in 1492 on the same day Columbus set sail for the New World. Within a hundred years, the defeat of the Spanish Armada signaled the decline of Spain as a great European power."

"So what are you saying, Papi?" Gabi lifted the pot cover to check the water.

"I fear what will happen to England when this war is over. Back in 1917, the British captured Palestine from the Muslims and offered the Jews a homeland. Within a year, England won the Great War, but once the hostilities stopped, the British broke most of their promises to the Jews. They've restricted Jewish immigration to the Holy Land, and during the 1930s, they turned their backs on Jewish families on this continent. I'm afraid we may have a holocaust on our hands."

Gabi wiped her hands on her apron and drew closer to her father. "Getting warmed up, I see. You've been doing your homework." She dumped a handful of potatoes into the stainless steel pot filled with boiling water.

Ernst set his notes on the kitchen counter and stirred the potatoes with a wooden spoon. "You've heard the popular saying around here: 'For six days a week, Switzerland works for Nazi Germany, while on the seventh day, it prays for an Allied victory.' We all know that thousands of Swiss cross the border daily to work in German factories. The Swiss need to work a little less for the Germans and pray harder for an Allied victory."

Gabi felt heat rising her to cheeks as her father spoke of crossing the border. He must have sensed her apprehension because he cocked his head, looking at her with a concerned expression.

"Gabi, are you okay? I—"

The sound of a brass door knocker interrupted her father's words.

"That must be Eric!" Gabi yanked off her apron and ran her right hand through her blonde-streaked hair, thankful for the interruption. "How do I look?"

Her mother tamped several strands of Gabi's loose hair behind her right ear, then patted her cheek. "Just fine, darling. You go answer the front door for your . . . friend."

186

Gabi's parents followed her into their living room. She opened the door and smiled at Eric, who was holding a wild-flower bouquet of daisies and foxgloves in his right hand. Gabi accepted them, pulling them to her face and breathing in their scent. Then she and Eric exchanged cheek-to-cheek busses.

"Look, Mami, a bouquet. How sweet of you, Eric."

"I'll fetch a vase," Thea said, retreating to the kitchen.

Ernst walked over and shook Eric's hand. "Almost harvest time."

"Our corn is just over two meters, so it could be ready any day now." Eric nodded and grinned, as if the height of corn was the most interesting topic in all of Switzerland.

"What's in the satchel?" Gabi playfully reached for the leather valise, which Eric swung behind him.

"Careful now," he said, as he sidestepped away from her second lurch.

"Don't tell me that you brought over some butter." Feigned excitement rose in her voice.

"Actually, I did—plus a dozen eggs."

Eric opened the satchel, taking out a small basket with a bundle of eggs and a porcelain jar filled to the brim with fresh-from-the-farm butter. "I churned it myself this afternoon. I got two kilos from today's batch, so I figured we could spare 100 grams for the pastor and his family." He winked at Gabi.

"How sweet of you. Butter the second time today."

A pair of heads swiveled toward Gabi, who wished she could retrieve her careless statement. Her father cocked an eyebrow at her.

"What I mean is that we . . . paid extra to have our Rösti potatoes fried in butter."

Her father shook his head. "Now Gabi, you know how hard it is for your mother and I not to ask too much about your work, but isn't a hot lunch in a restaurant a bit dear for your salary?"

"The lunch was work related. Dieter Baumann said he had something important to discuss with me, but he didn't want anyone in the office to know about it. He paid for the meal." She pressed her lips together, knowing she'd already said too much.

"Interesting." Ernst waved for Eric to take a seat at the dining table. From the kitchen, Thea could be heard moving pots and pans around in preparation for the dinner meal.

"Is it anything you're at liberty to discuss?" Her father took a drink from his water glass.

Gabi hesitated. Her father had always said he would understand that she couldn't talk much about what happened at work, and Eric had echoed the same thoughts in their private moments together. They certainly didn't need to know about the botched break-in a few days ago, which was no harm, no foul. But that incident happened on Swiss soil. If tomorrow's operation inside Germany didn't go well, she could be in danger. The worst-case scenario—

Gabi didn't want to go there.

"Does it have anything to do with breaking open safes?" Ernst reached over and patted his daughter's hands. "I'm pleased that you're carrying on the family tradition well. Your grandfather was one of the best locksmiths in Wisconsin, and I loved going out with him when some wealthy lady forgot her safe combination. But you and I both know that you don't have a lot of experience."

Gabi remained mute as she considered what to tell her father. She realized she had the freedom to tell him nothing, but at the same time, a new—and dangerous—twist had been added to the job: sneaking into and out of Germany, on forged papers no less. Like most Swiss, she hadn't visited the country since the Wehrmacht stormed into Poland and ignited a global conflict.

Then there were Eric's feelings to consider. She was definitely being pursued in a way that inspired confidence in him. He was attentive, caring, and she had the impression that he would volunteer to go in her place if he could pick a lock. Certainly, *he* needed to know about tomorrow's break-in. The push-pull came from the uncertainty she felt. At that moment, though, she sensed she should bring these two men into her confidence. Either of them might see something that she hadn't.

"Dieter Baumann had an interesting proposal for me," she began, making eye contact with her father and then with Eric. "He wanted to discuss it at the Globus penthouse restaurant."

"You've mentioned this Dieter Baumann before to me," her father said. "He's a Swiss who runs the Basel office for the American interests here."

"Yes, that's him. He's known for having lots of contacts. Bit of a wheeler-dealer, from what I see, but he gets results. Otherwise, he wouldn't be where he is."

"What was it that he asked you to do?"

Gabi drew in a breath after hearing the direct question from her father. "I'm not so sure I can—"

"Gabi, if you can't say anything, I understand, but I'm concerned about this Dieter Baumann," her father said. "You hear things, and I'm not so sure I like the scuttlebutt about this young man."

"Is this from someone in the church?"

Her father nodded.

"I heard the same talk," Eric said. "There's something about his eyes. They say you can tell he's hiding something. I guess what your father and I are saying is, be careful. Don't take any unnecessary risks."

"But Dieter said what's in the safe could change the direction of the war."

Ernst and Eric exchanged knowing glances.

"You hear that a lot these days." Her father sighed. "Listen, all we are saying is, think with your head before you follow the leading of your heart."

Ernst reached across the table for her hand. "Do you mind if we pray for you?"

"Of course not, Papi. Pray for the Lord's hedge of protection. I'm going to need it tomorrow."

189

22

Pastor Leo wasn't used to honest, backbreaking work.

Rivulets of sweat coursed down his temples, wetting an armless T-shirt caked with rust-colored dirt. He mopped his sweaty brow with a beige handkerchief and leaned against a wood-toothed rake. He and three bare-chested, sunburned men from his church—who'd taken time off from their factory jobs in Heidelberg—worked the latest alfalfa cutting under a relentless afternoon sun.

Pastor Leo scanned the nearly mown field, where red-winged blackbirds foraged for grasshoppers by inserting their bills into the soft substrate. He found it hard to believe that he was caught up in a cat-and-mouse game with the Gestapo, but for several hours that afternoon, he'd sought to forget about that. He pretended that the Ulrich farm, and the sweat of their labor, was all there was in life. He actually enjoyed losing himself in the ache of his muscles and the beauty of the countryside.

Even though prime farmland was now of much worth to the Reich, it hadn't always been so valuable. The pastor's brother-in-law, Adalbert Ulrich, had picked up the farm for a chest of sterling silver back in the early 1920s when the Weimar Republic's currency collapsed. Back then, paper money became so worthless that freezing Germans fed their stoves bundles of Reichsmarks to warm their homes.

Pastor Leo glanced at his brother's farmhouse two hundred

meters away and worried if they had hidden Joseph in the right place. Their talk earlier had gone as well as expected, but Leo had a hard time reading the mixed emotions in the young man's gaze—confusion, fear, and misgiving—all mixed with hope in God's protection.

After their arrival this morning, Adalbert Ulrich had pressed this unexpected source of labor into service. They'd arrived for the purpose of finding a safe place to hide their charge, but that didn't mean they'd sit around whittling sticks of wood. The seasoned farmer showed the makeshift crew how to rake the cutting into straight lines, which were then "rowed up" into tall, semi-round bales for drying. Since it looked like they would be around for a couple of days—until Joseph was safely moved—tomorrow they'd fork the hay into a horse-drawn trailer and haul the load to the barn. There the hay would be tossed into a stationary baler for compression into small, rectangular blocks. The hay bales would then be hand-tied with twine for storage in the second-story haymow.

"Pastor—look," Wilhelm called out, turning everyone's attention to the long, curved driveway leading onto the property.

Pastor Leo turned to see a black Opel Kapitän billowing a plume of dust as the sedan braked to a stop next to the Ulrich farmhouse. The pastor felt the rake slip from his hand, and he walked with quick steps in their direction even before he knew what he'd say or do.

Near the farmhouse, three men dressed in dark suits and felt fedoras stepped out of the dust-covered Opel. Even from this distance, Pastor Leo noted the confidence that exuded from their absolute authority. Leo's heart pounded, and his nervousness increased as he noticed them surveying the two-story *Bauernhaus*, whose siding desperately needed white-washing. Instead of approaching the farmhouse, though, the three men ventured toward the barn and stable. They walked cautiously, peering around the battered farm equipment in various states of repair and disrepair that littered the front of the barn. Meanwhile, Leo's footsteps quickened, and the other men kept pace with him.

"Who are they?" Wilhelm kept pace at Leo's side.

"From here, I would say some sort of Polizei, but I could be wrong." Pastor Leo slowed his steps. "Everyone maintain composure. We need the Lord's safekeeping, so I'll pray."

With his eyes open and feet moving slowly forward, Pastor Leo's voice turned somber. "Lord, we ask that our brother Joseph will be invisible in their sight. Keep these men from discovering his whereabouts. We know that thy Word says that thy hand will lead us, and thy right hand shall hold us. Keep thy hand upon Joseph and upon the rest of us. We pray also that if we are questioned, you will give us the right words."

Leo tilted his head skyward, and then he resumed his steps, leading the procession past head-high stalks of ripening corn on their left and Holstein apple trees heavy with russeted, deep-yellow fruit to their right.

Up ahead, Adalbert and Leo's sister, Trudi, engaged the three dark-suited visitors who had circled back and mounted the wooden stairs leading to their weather-beaten porch. Leo couldn't make out what they were saying, but he knew the unexpected callers weren't making a house call to sell Deutsches Reich war bonds.

Adalbert waved a beckoning hand, and Leo picked up the pace. A minute later, the pastor relaxed his balled fists and ascended the porch stairs. His brother-in-law appeared calm as he placed an arm around Leo's bronzed shoulders.

"Leo, this is Captain Stampfli with the Leimen Polizei. An important prisoner has escaped the authorities, and these men are searching for him."

The police captain held a black-and-white photo of Joseph Engel, cupped in his right hand. "Have you seen this man?"

Leo tried to appear disinterested. "No, I would have re-membered a face that distinctive." The pastor crossed his arms over his chest. "When did you say this criminal was reported missing?"

"Yesterday." The Polizei captain passed the photo around. The other farmhands feigned disinterest.

"I'm afraid we won't be much help. My friends and I have been in the fields all day, giving my brother-in-law a hand with the summer alfalfa cutting."

The captain regarded the green-golden swath of mown hay in the distance, with its undulating rows of raked alfalfa and two dozen "rowed-up" bales.

"Aren't you early? Most farmers wait until September—"

"You're right, Captain," Adalbert interrupted. "But my brother-in-law and friends weren't available then, so I took what I could get. I can't rake the entire field by myself, and reliable farm labor is impossible to find these days with so many of our men fighting for the Fatherland. If I had to rely on the strength of my back alone, the alfalfa would rot by the time I got it into the barn."

"Very well." The police captain motioned to his two lieutenants. "We have orders to search the house." The officer's tone was almost apologetic.

Leo knew better than to ask who issued the orders.

Adalbert stepped aside. "We understand. We'll just wait out here."

The captain rocked on his heels. "Actually, I'd prefer that you and your brother-in-law join us. The lady of the house as well."

Pastor Leo locked eyes with his brother-in-law for an instant, then looked away. Becker had told them that in situations like this, the authorities preferred to have house members accompany them when attempting to ferret out someone in hiding. People often unwittingly disclosed nonverbal clues that they were getting "warmer." Yet Leo also knew any attempt to deflect their request would be greeted by suspicion.

The pastor beckoned with an outstretched arm. "By all means."

The Polizei captain turned and ordered the third member of their search party to sweep the outside of the farmhouse.

Adalbert stepped around a rocking chair and opened the screen door separating the porch from the parlor. The captain and his lieutenant stepped inside, then Adalbert took Trudi's hand and followed. Leo tailed the others.

Pastor Leo scanned the room as if it were the first time he'd walked through it. A stuffed sofa covered with brown chenille velvet and two accent pillows was on their left, flanked by a loveseat with a floral gardenia print and a Kaiser-era rectangular coffee table constructed from an Engelmann spruce tree. Behind the parlor furniture, a black-and-white headshot of Adolf Hitler hung on the wall.

Nice touch, Ada. His brother-in-law had serendipitously replaced a scenic watercolor from Gerhard Richter with a portrait shot of der Führer's piercing visage and toothbrush moustache—an inch of hair that symbolized bottomless evil.

As he strolled behind the others, Leo felt as if his skin was being jabbed by a thousand needles, and he was sure that his pounding heart could be seen through his chest wall. Outwardly, he smiled and maintained an indifferent countenance, yet his mind raced with the knowledge that the next few moments could determine the fate of a young physicist who happened to live in the wrong place at the wrong time—as well as a half-dozen of Leo's closest family members and friends.

It wasn't just Joseph Engel in the Gestapo's pincer grip. The penalty for harboring a Jew—a *hunted* one, no less—was a one-way ride on the Jewish transport trains heading east. Too many of his flock had disappeared this way. *Not again, dear Lord . . . help us now.*

The pair of policemen stepped into the dining room. They glanced around but bypassed the canted china hutch and three rows of Baronet dinner and dessert plates displayed behind beveled leaded glass doors. They followed the house layout, moving into the kitchen, and opened a pantry door as well as a broom closet.

"Where are the bedrooms?" Captain Stampfli shot Adalbert a piercing glance.

"The master bedroom is around the corner, and we have three bedrooms upstairs," Adalbert replied in an even voice.

"Very good."

An inspection of the downstairs master bedroom yielded nothing. In the bathroom, the captain pulled back a shower curtain that partially wrapped around a porcelain tub and even lifted the toilet seat.

They moved to the stairs, and the ominous thump of hard-leather boots, pounding each tread, echoed throughout the wood-frame house. In the first bedroom, the junior policeman looked under the bed and opened an armoire, the only source of closeting in the room. Nothing warranted further inspection until Captain Stampfli approached the wooden nightstand and opened a small cabinet door, where a ceramic chamber pot was stored.

"That's for Trudi's mother," Adalbert explained. "The poor woman finds the stairs treacherous at night."

The Polizei captain scrunched his nose and quickly closed the door. After inspecting the second bedroom and finding nothing of interest, the group moved to the last room down the hall— a sizable bedroom that overlooked the driveway and entrance to the farm. Leo dared not make eye contact with Ada or Trudi.

The *Schlafzimmer*, like the others, was as neat as a pin. Two twin beds, each covered by a fluffy duvet, looked as though a Berlin chambermaid had made them up. The lieutenant got down on his knees and looked under the beds, then opened an armoire opposite the curtained window. A smattering of shirts, skirts, and pants belonging to both sexes filled half the wardrobe. Underneath the clothes were a stack of books and a leather satchel.

The lieutenant was about to close the door when he took a second look at the satchel, well worn from years of use. He grabbed the shoulder strap, yanked it from the armoire, and rummaged through its contents before pulling out one of the notebooks. The lieutenant thumbed through several pages and then handed the dog-eared notebook to Stampfli.

The police captain flipped it open, then his eyes rested on a random page.

"What have we got here?" Stampfli asked.

"Oh, that's my nephew's." Adalbert took a step closer to the captain. "Some old school notes. Wilhelm was studying math at the University of Heidelberg until he was called into the Army. He's serving the Fatherland on the Western front. Last I heard, he was driving a Panzer when the Allied hordes hit the Normandy beaches. We haven't received a letter from Wilhelm since the invasion, and the entire family is worried sick—"

Trudi choked back a sob and buried her face into her husband's shoulder. A silence fell in the room.

"I'm sorry," Stampfli said. "Maybe you'll receive good news soon."

"Captain, you may want to look at this." The lieutenant held up a black wallet he found in the satchel.

"Of course, Wilhelm's." Adalbert naturally reached for it, but the lieutenant pulled his hand away.

How did the wallet get in the satchel? Leo considered that question while sensing a change in mood sweep through the bedroom.

"I'll take a look at that." Captain Stampfli stretched out his hand and accepted the leather wallet from the lieutenant. He opened the billfold and found a pair of 10 Reichsmarks notes and several coins in a small pocket. He rifled through the rest of the wallet and extracted bits of paper and official documents, which he set on a pinewood nightstand.

His eyes alighted on a sepia-toned photo of a young man in his early twenties, black hair parted on the left side, dressed in a wool suit for some sort of formal occasion. The subject's face was small since the photographer had taken the full-length shot inside some sort of studio.

"That's Wilhelm at the Uni," Ada announced proudly. "His great desire is to teach math some day."

The captain grunted his acknowledgment. His fingers scanned the rest of the papers: a handful of receipts, a monthly pass to ride the Heidelberg tram, circa 1943, and an expired identity card with Wilhelm's photo on it. Stampfli took a second glance at the Ausweis before setting it down.

"Alles ist in Ordung," he said. *All is in order.*

The captain turned to the two brothers. "Meine Herren, here's my card. If you see anything suspicious, or come across this Joseph Engel, you are to notify me immediately. Any delay will be dealt with harshly by the authorities. Do you understand?"

Both men nodded.

"In that case, I bid you farewell." With a click of his boot heels and a Heil, Hitler! salute, the captain and his lieutenant pounded down the stairs and retreated to their black sedan, where the third officer was waiting for them. Leo and Adalbert watched the Opel Kapitän depart from the second-story bedroom.

It wasn't until the black sedan exited the property that Leo breathed a sigh of relief. "That was close. But tell me—how did that wallet get into Joseph's satchel?"

"When the Polizei's car arrived, I suddenly remembered that Engel had left his satchel on his bed," Adalbert replied. "I grabbed Wilhelm's wallet from where he laid it on the piano, ran upstairs, and made the switch while Trudi engaged the Polizei."

"Where did you put Engel's wallet?"

"Right here." Adalbert reached for his left-side back pocket and presented it to his brother-in-law.

"Were you crazy? You could have gotten us killed!"

"Leo, someone very close to me told me one time that all you have to do is ask and you will receive. I asked for God's protection, and I received it. See, I listen to your sermons. Aren't you glad?"

• • • • • • • • •

Pastor Leo found Wilhelm sitting on a low-slung fence rail as the burnt-orange sun hung just above the horizon. The sturdy farmhand had returned to whittling a piece of white birch when the pastor approached.

"Something has come up. Did you make eye contact with any of those policemen? Think hard."

"Just the third policeman who walked around the house. While you were tied up inside, I chatted him up a bit. I didn't learn much except the entire Reich is looking for Joseph Engel."

Leo explained what had happened in Engel's bedroom and his brother-in-law's swift action. "They saw your wallet—your photo. Ada and I think you should leave tonight. For all we know, the three cops could be putting two and two together right now. Sound like a plan?"

"This is awfully sudden." Wilhelm ran a hand down his face.

"I know. The times we live in, but we must stay one step ahead of the Gestapo. Listen, before you pack your things, do you want to say goodbye to Joseph?"

"Sure, that would be nice. We forged a friendship during our escape through the checkpoint. Normal, I think, when you come *this* close to capture." Wilhelm held up a hand with a small gap between his thumb and forefinger. "I think Joseph's come a long way in the last twenty-four hours. Lord knows what I'd be thinking or feeling after learning I was born Jewish."

"Good man. Let's go find Joseph. The rest of us have some work to do before it gets dark. We have to get that field cleared by tomorrow night."

Leo called out to the others, directing them to return to their work. They picked up their wooden rakes and returned to the alfalfa field, a rectangular plot that measured a half kilometer in length and 100 meters in width. Under a twilight sky, the pungent smell of the fresh-cut alfalfa greeted their nostrils. They returned to where they had raked the cutting—which was drying fast—into a straight line.

"The coast is clear," Pastor Leo said in no particular direction. "You can come out, Joseph."

From one of the tall piles, Joseph Engel pulled himself to his feet and brushed off stray strands of straw.

"They came, didn't they? Just as you predicted."

The pastor nodded, although he was not about to tell Joseph or the group that the information from Becker had been spot-on—door-to-door searches of the outlying farms south of Leimen.

"All I know is one thing, Joseph. We need to get you out of here in a hurry. But it's too dangerous to move you just yet."

23

The sizzling aroma of tangy, fresh-grilled bratwurst from an outdoor vendor caused Jean-Pierre's stomach to grumble as he paced back and forth under the weather canopy on Gleis 3, where he awaited the arrival of Allen Dulles on the 8:37 express train from Bern. Something dramatic must have happened for Mr. Dulles to leave Switzerland's capital city and request an evening meeting with him.

Beyond the Basel SBB Bahnhof, the sound of two distinct bells—marking thirty minutes after the hour—chimed from the Basler Münster, the fourteenth-century sandstone cathedral bathed in diffused rays of soft-amber light at this twilight hour.

Basel, as any local like Jean-Pierre knew, had two train stations. The Basel SBB south of the Rhine was the terminus for all intra-Swiss traffic as well as trains arriving from France. The Badischer Bahnhof north of the Rhine straddled the triangular border point—the Dreispitz—for Switzerland, France, and Germany and was the terminus for passenger trains arriving from the German state of Baden-Württemberg.

Tonight would be the first time Jean-Pierre would meet Allen Dulles without Pascal at his side. Since being recruited by Pascal nearly a year earlier, his mentor had been working with him on his English vocabulary, pronunciation, and sentence construction. For an entertaining way to speed up his learning, Jean-Pierre read Perry Mason books, the whodunit mysteries by Erle Stanley Gardner, that were gathering dust in Pascal's library.

A couple dozen Swiss businessmen in three-piece suits meandered about the train platform, studiously ignoring the rambunctious children trying to evade their harried mothers' attempts to control them. Jean-Pierre ignored the chaos and studied the bold face of the Mondaine clock hanging from a wrought-iron post. When the red second hand, with an exaggerated dot on the long end, reached 58 seconds, the minute hand jumped to the next minute—in this case, 8:37. After a half minute, the train's iron-red locomotive came into view and rolled to a stop.

The angular Allen Dulles, his graying hair topped with a Baldwin fedora and an unlit pipe stuck in his mouth, stepped off the first-class rail car, gripping a faded leather briefcase in his right hand and a compact travel suitcase in his left. He lowered his head and joined the stream of departing passengers. Jean-Pierre, dressed in a tweed business suit with his hands in his pants pockets, barely glanced at Mr. Dulles as he swept by. When the American spymaster had advanced fifty meters past his reconnoiter point, Jean-Pierre swung into the rear of the horde, marching toward the massive barrel-like roof above the train station entrance.

As he followed, Jean-Pierre occasionally stopped and concentrated on the masses headed for Schützengraben, the boulevard fronting the Basel SBB train station, to see if Mr. Dulles was being tailed. Satisfied that no one but himself was following the Big Cheese, he closed the gap, maintaining a respectable distance. Dulles quickly turned left onto Elisabethan Strasse. After two blocks, Mr. Dulles ducked into their meeting point—the Drei Könige, or Three Kings, restaurant.

Jean-Pierre pushed against the restaurant's heavy wooden door and stepped inside what had been a guildhall in medieval times. The restaurant foyer received natural light from a half-dozen stained glass windows that rivaled those found in the

Münster's Romanesque vaults. Ancient beams accentuated the ceiling trusses, and pewter plates and mugs adorned the ocher-colored walls.

As Jean-Pierre's eyes adjusted to the dim light, a waiter in a white shirt and black pinstripe tie hoisted an oversized tray covered with several entrées to his shoulder. The restaurant employee strode by, and Jean-Pierre's eyes—and nose—identified the saddle of venison accompanying a bed of dumplings and juniper berry sauce. Once again, his stomach expressed an audible complaint from hunger.

The maître d' escorted Jean-Pierre to a red-leather booth in the rear of the main salon, where Allen Dulles perused a boarded menu. The American stood to shake Jean-Pierre's hand as he offered him a seat.

"Thank you for coming on short notice," Dulles said. "Nobody followed us?"

"I don't believe so, sir."

"Excellent." Dulles handed Jean-Pierre another menu. "Feel free to order anything you want. Eat hearty. It's one small way my country can show its appreciation for what courageous folks like you are doing. Oh, which reminds me of something . . ."

Dulles reached underneath the table for his briefcase and set it on his lap. A side pocket held a padded envelope wrapped with a rubber band. "I normally handle this part with Pascal, but since you're here, you can pass this along to him. You'll find 5,000 Swiss francs and a thousand U.S. dollars—all cash. We know you have bills to pay, which is why we take care of our own."

"Thank you, sir." Jean-Pierre slid the envelope discreetly into his interior suit pocket. "I'll see that Pascal receives this right away."

Dulles resumed studying his menu. "I'm famished. I haven't had a bite to eat since Miss Taylor delivered tea and petits fours this afternoon. What's the house specialty?"

"The Drei Könige is known for its venison this time of year."

"That sounds like an outstanding choice." Dulles closed his leather-bound menu and set it aside.

Jean-Pierre took that as his cue. "If it's okay, I'll have the venison too."

The waiter returned, poised with a white pad and a pencil. "*Ich hätte gerne zwei Teller Wild, bitte,*" the American said in High German. Two orders of venison with all the trimmings.

"*Und zum Trinken?*"

The American ordered a liter of Henniez mineral water for the table.

Jean-Pierre unfolded his napkin and placed it in his lap. "I'm impressed with your German, Herr Dulles." Actually, there was nothing remarkable about the exchange, but Jean-Pierre wanted to put the American VIP—who was said to have the ear of President Franklin Delano Roosevelt—at ease.

Dulles deflected the compliment. "Just a little menu German, that's all. I'd like to learn your Baseldeutsch, but that will have to be another war, I'm afraid. Plus, all the intercepts are in High German, so I'm not sure what good learning Swiss-German would do for me anyway."

Jean-Pierre had heard from Pascal that Mr. Dulles didn't devote much time to exchanging pleasantries, and he expected the transition to happen at any moment.

"There are two things on my agenda tonight, but first, let's start with Dieter Baumann. I asked you to start surveillance on him just twenty-four hours ago. Anything happen today?"

Jean-Pierre considered his words. "The team will need more time to establish his routine, but this morning I watched him shop for breakfast before work. Normal for a bachelor, except that it took him twenty minutes to pick out a *Brötli*. Something even more unusual happened at lunchtime. He left the office shortly before 12:30. I followed him from a safe distance. A few blocks away, he walked into the Globus department store, which has a penthouse restaurant popular with the lunch crowd."

"And what was unusual about that?" Dulles struck a wooden match and held it horizontally as he drew several puffs from his pipe. A white ring of fragrant smoke lifted into the air.

"I noticed that forty-five minutes later, a young woman named Gabi Mueller—who works in the translation pool—exited the Globus a minute or two before Baumann. If I had to take a guess, they shared a meal together."

The waiter poured two glasses of fizzy water and set the bottle of Henniez in the center of the table. When the discreet waiter was out of earshot, Allen Dulles resumed the conversation. "You mentioned Gabi Mueller's name. I've been keeping my eye on her. She's been most impressive since she joined us last year. But what leads you to believe that Fräulein Mueller had lunch with Herr Baumann? And if so, what is there to make of it? Perhaps her entry into the Globus was coincidental, or maybe she was doing some shopping over the noon hour. I take it you didn't venture inside the department store."

"No, I stayed across the street, next to a kiosk. I think they ate together because they left at the same time, and both looked to see if anyone was following them. They walked different routes back to the office."

"Did anyone see you?"

"No. I didn't want them to discover my surveillance. But watching Herr Baumann, I definitely believed he was hiding something. I have this feeling about it."

Dulles took another draw of smoke from the pipe. "Why is that?"

"Because of what happened five minutes later. A German operative, code name Ludwig, stepped out of the Globus and looked warily in both directions before proceeding in the other direction."

"So Ludwig could be up to some mischief?" Dulles looked up as the waiter, with a white napkin over his left wrist, arrived with their venison entrées. The American waited a long moment before continuing. "If the two of them had a meeting at the Globus, this confirms some aspects about Mr. Baumann that aren't—shall we say—Charlie."

"Charlie?" Jean-Pierre drew a blank.

"Just another idiom. Listen, I want you and your team to increase your surveillance of his activities. He could be up to something."

Jean-Pierre nodded and smiled. Of that he had no doubt.

When the dining pair had set their knives and forks on their plates, signaling they were done with their meals, the Swiss waiter stopped by their table. "Anyone care for a dessert this evening?" The waiter set both dinner plates on his left forearm and picked up the bread basket with his right hand.

Both men shook their heads no. "Just the check, please," Jean-Pierre said in Swiss-German. "My colleague has a train to catch—"

"No, I'm staying at the Hotel Euler tonight," Dulles interrupted in English.

"So your Swiss-German is not so bad." Jean-Pierre flashed a grin. "I guess we must be careful in the future."

"No, no." Dulles waved him off. "I heard the words *miin Kolleeg* and *Zug*, and I know those words mean 'my colleague' and 'train.' A good guess, that's all."

After the waiter's departure, Dulles cleared his throat. "I said I had two items on my agenda, so here's the other situation I want to discuss. Any input that you and Pascal can give me will be greatly appreciated." For the next ten minutes, the American spymaster held Jean-Pierre's rapt attention as he spoke of a man named Joseph Engel who needed their help.

The conversation lulled as they both noticed their waiter approaching with his black leather purse that bulged with coins and paper money.

"You go, Jean-Pierre," Dulles whispered as he reached for a wallet in his briefcase. "Ask Pascal if he has any ideas on the best way to smuggle Joseph Engel into Switzerland. You can reach me at the Hotel Euler."

"Very good." Jean-Pierre set his napkin on the table. "If you'll excuse me, I have some phone calls to make."

• • • • • • • •

Gabi Mueller climbed a set of stone steps into the Hotel Euler, situated around the corner from Basel's SBB train station. With its Corinthian columns and black-and-white-checked marble flooring, the Hotel Euler exuded Old World ambiance. She regarded the life-sized statue of the hotel's namesake, Leonhard Paul Euler—a pioneering Swiss mathematician and physicist who lived from 1707–1783—dominating the expansive lobby. She had read in the *Basler Nachrichten* that the century-old establishment had recently lost its fifth star due to wartime austerity measures—an oversight the owners promised to rectify.

Precisely at 10 p.m., Allen Dulles stepped through the revolving door and immediately doffed his felt hat. "Miss Mueller, thank you for meeting me on such short notice. I apologize for the dreadful hour."

Gabi extended her hand, which Dulles took into his. "Nice to see you again. I know this has to be something important. I hope everything's okay."

"Yes, that's what I want to talk to you about." Dulles led her to the lobby fireplace, where several crackling fir logs created a warm glow. "Please have a seat."

Gabi settled into a dark brown leather chair trimmed with brass nail heads. She noticed that Dulles scooted his chair in her direction—an act conducive to good conversation. This relaxed her, but she still felt nervous about why he had asked her to meet with him at this unusual hour. Thankfully, he got right to the point.

"It has recently come to my attention that you're crossing

the border tomorrow morning with Dieter Baumann. Something to do with you breaking into a safe for him?"

Gabi's face flushed. "Are you saying you didn't know about this?"

"I'm afraid I just heard of this caper quite recently."

Caper? That didn't sound good. "Who told you?"

"I have my sources. Please understand I am not cross with you. But I do need to be informed about these things."

Gabi's mind scrambled to keep up with this blindside. "When Mr. Baumann asked me not to mention anything to my supervisor, Frau Schaffner, or anyone else in the translation pool, I thought that was because the mission came from *your* office. During our lunch at the Globus, Dieter . . . Mr. Baumann . . . said you and only you knew about the mission." Gabi watched Dulles consider this information.

Dulles leaned forward, his eyes locked on hers. "Tell me about the assignment Mr. Baumann proposed to you."

"Well, he said it was a mission of vital interest to the Allied war effort, and that he needed my help breaking into a safe." Gabi stopped. "Wait—am I right in assuming you didn't authorize it?"

Dulles nodded. "Listen, not to worry. What I need to know is what Mr. Baumann is up to. I will be quite frank with you. We've been suspicious about Mr. Baumann's activities for the last week or so. He could be playing both sides against the middle. These things happen in our world. Remember, when I arrived in Bern eighteen months ago, I started from scratch. I had to develop a network based on hunches. The stray contact. The odd recommendation. A year ago, Mr. Baumann was working on a freelance basis for Section Five—Swiss Intelligence. He caught my attention when he helped break up the Rote Kapelle spy ring—"

Gabi inclined closer.

"Pardon me." Dulles held up a hand. "I'm about to make you privy to more information than I normally share, but now you're on a need-to-know basis. What you've accomplished in the last three months has been remarkable, absolutely remarkable."

Gabi beamed. The long hours and willingness to take on any job were paying off. "That's very kind of you to say, Mr. Dulles, but wasn't the Rote Kapelle—the 'Red Orchestra'—a Soviet spy ring operating in Switzerland?"

"You've had your ear to the ground, I see. The Rote Kapelle scored great successes—until Mr. Baumann helped smash their cells in Geneva and Basel. That's what interested us in him. His anti-Communism, his contacts throughout Switzerland, and his excellent English skills fit the parameters of someone to join our Basel office. While he has performed well, I've operated on a trust-but-verify basis with him. He's Swiss, not American like yourself."

Gabi blushed again. "I appreciate your confidence in me, Mr. Dulles, but—"

"You're not like him at all. You'd never ask me nosy questions about the Allied advances on the Western Front, but when Mr. Baumann did recently, my antennae shot up. Then came information about this cock-and-bull break-in tomorrow morning in Germany. Listen, I think Mr. Baumann is cozying up to the Germans while staying in our good graces. We don't know what he's up to, but I want you to be my eyes and ears. If he is a double agent, we can use that information to our advantage."

Gabi was beginning to see the big picture more clearly. "So you want me to go tomorrow?"

Dulles hitched his trousers as he gathered his thoughts. "Listen, you're involved in a dangerous mission, but it's one that could help us know what Baumann has cooked up. In the end, though, it's your decision. There's little, if anything, the United States can do once you step on German soil."

Gabi drew a deep breath. "Let me reaffirm my commitment to you and the United States. I'm going tomorrow. This mission is bigger than me. Much bigger."

24

Davos, Switzerland
9:01 p.m.

As the house lights dimmed at the Davos Kino cinema, Captain Bill Palmer clutched an Army Air Corps–issue leather jacket in the crook of his arm and plopped into his usual red velvet seat—eighth row, middle section, fourth seat from the left aisle. He chose the empty row in the half-filled movie theater because the last thing he wanted was to strike up a conversation with other pilots, especially if the banter veered toward the topic of escape. One never knew whom he could trust or who would slip some information to the Swiss guards for a pack of Lucky Strike cigarettes.

At that moment, Bill would have given anything to light up, but smokes were hard to come by and extremely expensive. Even munching popcorn would have sufficed, but the Swiss hadn't adopted the American custom of crunching buttery kernels of popped corn in red-and-white-striped bags while engrossed by the action on the silver screen. Eating in a theater just wasn't done because the Swiss wouldn't dream of littering the carpeted floor with trash. They left the Kino just as tidy as when they entered.

Everyone in Davos knew that the Kino—the only movie theater within a seventy-five-kilometer radius—served two clienteles: the local Swiss and the Allied internees. German-language films were shown at 6 p.m., and English-language films screened at 9 p.m. The latest Hollywood films arrived in the Red Cross shipments—usually nine months after release in the States.

The nine o'clock show commenced with a newsreel from Germany, which immediately summoned Bill's interest and caused him to sit up in his seat. With sweeping martial music setting the tone, and a near-hysterical German narrator describing the action, the opening frames of the black-and-white newsreel showed Adolf Hitler—nursing an immobile right arm—escorting the Italian dictator Benito Mussolini through the rubble of Wolf's Lair, where the Führer had narrowly escaped death two weeks previously.

Bill remembered his keen disappointment after news swept through Davos that Hitler had survived an assassination attempt. The newsreel then cut to Hitler visiting a hospital ward, where German officers swathed head to toe in bandages received the Führer's best wishes for a speedy recovery. At least that's what Bill imagined the narrator—now sounding reverential—was describing.

How history could have changed, Bill thought. Maybe the German generals would have sued for peace after Herr Swastika had been successfully dispatched to the gates of hell. Bill winced at how close this awful war had been to a cessation of hostilities. His disappointment turned to revulsion, however, when the newsreel shifted to grainy footage of several uniformed men swaying from a wooden gallows. The next scene showed a blindfolded officer slumped against a wooden post, hands bound behind him. He caught the narrator pronouncing the name "Claus von Stauffenberg"—the mastermind of the plot. *Poor chap. God rest his soul.*

Bill glanced at his watch and tension rose in his throat. In a couple of hours, J.J. and his buddy Sam would be waiting for him behind the Heiz Bäckerei. Bill's hand involuntarily reached for the billfold in his back pocket. He had 115 Swiss francs and fifty U.S. dollars, more than enough for a train ride to Geneva and beyond.

Should he join their hastily planned escape attempt? He

certainly *wanted* to make a getaway, but a flashing caution light burned brightly in his mind. What if an itchy-fingered, inexperienced Swiss private took a shot at him? What if he and his buddies successfully escaped and met up with partisans outside Geneva, only to be turned over to the Germans for a case of Bordeaux?

Despite Bill's mental objections, J.J. had made a good point. Sometimes you had to go for it when the guards least expected it. He'd opined that the Swiss had probably anticipated that a pilot or two—fortified by liquid courage— would make a dash during the First of August celebration, when a third of the guard detail had received thirty-six-hour furloughs to visit their families or girlfriends. But the 128 Allied internees stayed put and raised a toast to the Swiss Confederation instead. Now that a couple of days had passed, their guard had to be lowered.

When was the last escape attempt? Bill had to think—yes, Harter and Buchanan made a break for it on the Fourth of July, another holiday occasion. He winced at the memory. Everyone knew the rules: if you stepped over the foot-wide chalk lines laid out north and south of the town, you were considered to be an escapee. The guards were supposed to yell "Halt!" three times before firing—at your legs.

When Harter and Buchanan slipped out of Davos after dusk, a Swiss Army private on patrol spotted them outside Laret, the next town. Fumbling with his K31 rifle, he yelled "Halt-halt-halt" in staccato fashion. Then he immediately triggered several rapid rounds without waiting to see if the two American pilots would become statues and raise their arms in surrender. One bullet shattered Harter's right shoulder blade, ending his career as a St. Louis Browns pitcher. Buchanan was luckier. He got nicked, where a slug tore into his left leg just above the ankle. After three weeks recuperating in a Zürich hospital, the boys began their ninety-day sentences at Wau-wilermoos penitentiary prison. Piles of hay on concrete slabs for their beds, bread and watery stew for their meals.

Bill's reverie was snapped when the main feature began. Tonight's film was *Casablanca*, a movie he'd viewed several times since his arrival. Despite his distracted mindset, Bill found himself lost again in the story of an American expatriate meeting a former lover in exotic Casablanca at the outset of the war.

Early in the film, intrigue filled the smoky, Moorish atmosphere of the nightclub belonging to Rick Blaine, but Bill wasn't fooled—that was his hero Humphrey Bogart. A stunningly beautiful Ilsa Lund, with husband Victor Laszlo on her arm, found a table inside Rick's Café Américain, where they believed the hard-bitten expat possessed two transit visas to escape Casablanca for Lisbon and eventually America.

Escape. Was art imitating life, or life imitating art? For nine months, he had been interred in Davos, tucked away high in the Alps, given nothing to do—and nothing to strive for. He and the dozens of other Allied pilots were expected to mind their manners, make no waves, and sit tight—for the duration. *Count yourself lucky* was the catchphrase around Davos.

Yet, if Bill could escape and eventually return to his Eighth Air Force Bomb Squadron in East Anglia, nothing would make him happier. He had a mission to complete, and with Allies breaking out of the Normandy beachhead, the Krauts were on the run. Bill wanted to be there to personally kick their butts all the way back to Berlin. Or maybe his superior officers would tell him that his dangerous days of bombing German factories were over and they were shipping him Stateside to fly some Air Force desk until the Krauts and Japs were beaten to a pulp. That would work for him too. Then he'd get to hold Katie in his arms again.

So maybe tonight was a good night. After all, there hadn't been an escape attempt in weeks. And fall was just around the corner, when nature's elements became your enemy. This might be his only chance.

Bill reined in his swirling thoughts as Hollywood's magic swept him to another world. Midway through the film, Captain Renault—the wonderfully corrupt Vichy gendarme—blew his whistle, signaling the start of a raid inside Rick's Café Américain.

"How can you close me up?" Rick pleaded. "On what grounds?"

"I'm shocked, *shocked* to find that there is gambling going on here!" Renault spoke with an imperious air.

"Your winnings, sir." The croupier handed Renault a wad of cash.

"Oh, thank you very much," replied the French captain, surprised.

Would the Swiss authorities be just as shocked that he skedaddled out of Davos? He knew the twins Andreas and Willy Mueller would be surprised.

Bill's thoughts returned to the screen as the film's denouement—the airport scene—began. Once again, Bogey was imploring Ingrid Bergman to get on the plane with her husband, Victor. If she didn't join him on the flight to Lisbon, "You'll regret it, maybe not today, maybe not tomorrow, but soon, and for the rest of your life."

Watching the cinematic DC-3 lift off in the darkness sealed Bill's decision. He didn't want to live a life of regret. He would journey to Geneva. He would rendezvous with the Resistance, where people like Victor Laszlo would help him. He would gulp draughts of freedom into his lungs.

The house lights went up, and Bill stretched his legs, determined more than ever to follow in the footsteps of those fighting tyranny.

* * * * * * * * *

Bill gathered up his leather jacket and fell into the small crowd exiting the theater. He kept his head down to avoid starting a conversation, then looked up and met the gaze of Jimmy, another B-24 Liberator pilot from Truth or Consequences, New Mexico, who was also quartered in the Hotel Palace.

Bill flashed a smile of recognition. "Like the film?"

"Isn't Bogart the best? When he told Renault that this was the start of a beautiful friendship—"

"Yeah, there's some great lines in that film, no doubt."

Bill stopped for a moment in front of the Davos Kino to put on his jacket. A light eastern breeze gave the moonlit night a cool bite. At 5,000 feet above sea level, summer nights in Davos often dipped into the forties.

"See ya, Jimmy." Bill took a step toward the north part of the village.

"Aren't you headed to the Palace?" Jimmy pointed the other direction toward their prominent hotel, which resembled a chalet fortress with its imposing block superstructure and colonnades.

"I told J.J. I'd drop by before turning in."

"The Park Hotel is that way." Jimmy jerked his head in the same direction as the Hotel Palace.

"Yeah, uh, right. He said he'd buy me a *dunkle* at the Yodler." Bill made another move in the opposite direction.

"Mind if I join you? Seeing Rick's Café Américain has wet my whistle."

Bill shrugged. "Actually, can you give me a rain check? J.J.'s having some girlfriend troubles. Said he needed someone to talk to—"

"I hear that Miss Schweiz has broken more hearts than Hedy Lamarr. Wait a minute—isn't the Yodler buttoned up? It's nearing midnight."

This scout doesn't give up. "They're still celebrating the First of August. I think a few tourists are making it a long weekend."

Jimmy seemed satisfied. "Maybe tomorrow. Tell J.J. I hope things work out with the beauty queen. She's no chunk of lead."

Bill waved goodbye and started down the sidewalk, hands thrust in his jacket. As the downtown square gave way to a series of gingerbread chalets with gabled rooflines, he found himself in an alleyway behind Heiz Bakery where J.J. and his buddy Sam paced back and forth under an amber-hued streetlamp.

"There you are," J.J. said. "I told you he'd make it, didn't I, Sam?"

"Yeah, and you also said if Palmer didn't get here in five minutes, we were out of here," Sam added.

"Shaddup, you moron." J.J. grinned. "Bill, here's your travel kit." He tossed a knapsack toward Bill, who deftly cradled it into his arms. "You'll find a change of civilian clothes, some rolls from Heiz, two apples, and a few toiletry items."

"Great. So what's the plan?"

"We'll follow the 'Heidi Express' rail line all the way to Landquart in the Rhine Valley," J.J. said. "Then we'll change into civilian clothes and hop on a train to Zurich and then Geneva. Getting caught out of uniform doubles your sentence, but we ain't getting caught."

J.J. looked at his watch. "It's a few minutes before midnight. Could be a patrol at this hour, but we're committed, right?"

Bill nodded, as did Sam.

J.J. continued laying out his plan, whispering low. "We'll go one at a time, sticking to the woods west of the rail line. Once you pass the chalk line, there's a rail spur about half a mile away—we'll meet there. After we reconnoiter, we'll make our way to Klosters. It's twelve kilometers or a little more than seven miles. I'm thinking a good three hours. From there, I'd like to make it as far as Küblis or Lunden before sunup. Maybe we'll go find some hay barn and get some shut-eye before one last push to Landquart tomorrow night. Any questions?"

When there weren't any, J.J. departed into the darkness, followed two minutes later by Sam. Waiting under the streetlamp, Bill suddenly felt exposed, even though within Davos proper, the Allied internees had freedom of movement—no curfew, no hassles—as long as they minded their p's and q's.

215

Bill reminded himself that he had nothing to worry about . . . until he crossed the chalk line.

He slung the backpack over his shoulder and headed toward the base of the mighty Schatzalp, the ski station where a half-dozen Allied pilots had busted their legs last winter. He followed the alleyway until he reached the Guggenbachstrasse. *Man, just saying the street names will break your jaw.*

Bill's senses immediately soared as the reality of attempting escape fell heavily on his shoulders. He could see his way fine—a full moon illuminated the stores and businesses lining the Guggenbachstrasse. He paused when a fluffy cat jumped from the window ledge of the tailor shop, startling him. When he heard only silence again, Bill continued past Davos's only gas station, which doled out its weekly ration of gas in drips to favored clients.

Bill strode along Guggenbachstrasse until he reached the Landwasser River, which was more like a bubbling brook as it meandered inside a concrete-lined channel between the town and the Schatzalp ski area. His feet left the asphalt and crossed a wooden bridge erected over the river. Once across, he made a right-hand turn onto a summer road cut through a forest of Norway spruce and silver trees.

The road lifted in elevation as it ran parallel to the Landwasser and the only rail line in and out of Davos. After several minutes along the road, Bill heard a branch snap. He turned and looked behind him, but he couldn't make out any human forms in the nocturnal landscape. He retreated several steps and peered around several large trunks. Again, nothing.

Bill resumed his walk along the dirt road, which made a slight right-hand turn and began descending toward the river. He traversed another wooden bridge—the last one across the Landwasser in the northern part of town. He could see the rail line, which paralleled a meadow, a little more than 100 yards away in the moonlight. The closed shutters on several chalets subdued any lights that might have still been on at this late hour. Behind those shutters, families slept soundly—and safely.

Was he risking it all? Should he turn back?

Bill had walked this area many times and knew that the streak of chalk—that precise line of demarcation—lay just ahead. He entered another woodsy area when he heard several footsteps gain on him. He stopped—and heard nothing. He took a few more steps . . . but the sound of trampled tree needles were audible again. Someone had to be following him. He immediately swung around—

"Isn't it late to be out for a walk?" a voice whispered.

Willy Mueller, dressed in Swiss Army uniform and topped with bucket helmet, allowed his rifle to remain shouldered. "And that wouldn't be a knapsack you're carrying, right?"

"Listen, Willy, I—" Bill stopped there. He hadn't prepared an excuse.

"Not so loud," Willy whispered. "It wouldn't be good for either of us to be caught. I'm here to let you know that you don't want to be crossing the chalk line tonight. There's an ambush waiting."

"How did you know?"

"Corinne Busslinger blabbed."

"Miss Schweiz? J.J.'s girl?"

"You got it. Late this afternoon, she was crying and carrying on at dinner, and her parents pried it out of her that her J.J. was escaping. She was worried sick that she'd never see him again. Amazing the lengths that love will follow."

"Thanks, Shakespeare."

"Actually, that's Willy Mueller and not Willy Shakespeare."

Bill forced a smile and glanced around. "So how come you're here?"

Willy leaned in close. "Because Andreas and I didn't want to see any harm come to you. That and the fact that if you left, we'd miss taking your poker chips every Friday night."

"What about my friends?" Bill looked in the direction they'd gone.

"Don't worry. Andreas is trying to catch J.J. and Sam before they cross the—"

The distant scream of "Halt!" punctuated the air, followed by another "Halt!" and another. Then a volley of rifle shots and yelps.

Bill felt his heart pound and his stomach lurch with fear for his friends.

Willy's eyes widened. "He didn't get to them in time. Rats. Looks like Miss Schweiz will see her beau again—in ninety days."

"Listen, comedian, those are my buddies out there—"

"Sorry. You're right, this is no joking matter." Willy grabbed Bill's arm and moved him back toward town. "Listen, if you really want to escape, I've got a deal for you. You'll have to sing for your supper, though."

"Meaning . . ."

"Meaning someone needs your expertise. Perform the favor, and you can write yourself a ticket home."

"Who's asking?"

"I can't tell you, but people in the know call him the Big Cheese. From what I hear, he can make just about anything happen in Switzerland. A driver will arrive in Davos sometime tomorrow afternoon, and you'll be told exactly what's expected of you. You can take the offer, or you can decide to stay."

"What about escaping Davos? Isn't that going to be a problem? I don't think I'll be able to wave to the guards as I'm chauffeured out of here, do you?"

"Don't worry about that. It's all been arranged."

25

Basel, Switzerland
Thursday, August 3, 1944
7:18 a.m.

Gabi alighted from the BVB #6 tram—painted the same spearmint green as other Basel streetcars—after it rumbled to a stop in front of the Badischer Bahnhof. Although the #6 had taken only fifteen minutes to complete the journey from the Barfüsserplatz downtown depot, Basel's "other" train station felt as foreign as dirndl and lederhosen to her.

Six years had passed since Gabi had last stepped through the imposing limestone edifice that resembled an elongated Noah's Ark. She was in high school when her parents took the family via train to the Schloss Neuschwanstein in Bavaria. Gabi chuckled at the schoolgirl memory of begging her parents to visit the fairytale castle after viewing the Disney movie, *Snow White and the Seven Dwarfs*.

She wished she could recapture those carefree days before the war, but on this particular morning she couldn't shake the feeling that all eyes were on her—as if *she* were wearing Snow White's satiny yellow skirt and navy blue bodice with puffy red-and-white sleeves. Today, instead of the princess's tiara, a plain felt hat hid most of her pinned-up blonde hair. With a sigh, she adjusted the broad brim of the unstylish headdress and ran her right hand down the front of her dowdy, gray two-piece wool suit to smooth any wrinkles. She had refrained from patting her cheeks with foundation and rouge that morning, hoping her plain face indicated that she was ready to punch a time clock and put in an honest day's work.

Gabi took a deep breath and refocused her thoughts. She reminded herself that when she walked through the German *Kontrolle*, she would be just another frumpy seamstress reporting for work at H&M Textiles, a Swiss-owned factory where two hundred employees—mostly her countrywomen— stitched military uniforms and wove army blankets for the German front lines and rear guard. At least that's what Dieter's forged work permit in her black leather handbag indicated.

Her shaky fingers tucked the handbag under her arm. *You can do this.* She struggled to control her nerves. *You need to do this. They are depending on you . . . and if Dieter Baumann turns out to be a lying, two-timing scoundrel, you can handle that.*

Gabi fell in with the early morning exodus marching into the Badischer Bahnhof station hall, which was architecturally punctuated by a five-story clock tower. Thanks to a long-standing treaty signed between Germany and Switzerland in 1852, the Basel train station was planted literally on the border between the two countries, placing the ticket booths, shops, and Three Corners Café on Swiss soil while the train platforms belonged to Germany.

Swiss commuters had to traverse a fifty-meter tunnel linking the Swiss station hall and the German rail platforms. Baslers working in German factories and businesses negotiated this no-man's-land by passing through separate identification and work permit checks performed first by the Swiss Border Control, followed by the Wehrmacht. Once in German territory, Swiss commuters exited the rail station and boarded buses and trams for Weil am Rhein and Haltingen.

The border arrangement was not reciprocal, however. The Swiss military had to approve all transit passes for Germans entering Switzerland, so there was very little foot traffic in the other direction, at least this early in the morning. Only Swiss citizens with proper identity cards—and a Basler dialect, as Gabi's friends joked—were allowed to reenter the Motherland.

Gabi joined the single-file queue descending into the tunnel beneath the station. The pungent odors of perspiring bodies nearly gagged her in the crammed space. She knew too many Swiss who believed bathing was reserved for Saturday nights only. For nearly a quarter of an hour, the line of people drew her along until Gabi finally reached an inspection table where three men dressed in olive Swiss Border Control uniforms perfunctorily checked official documents.

"Work permit, please." The youngest member of the checkpoint detail held out his hand while the other two Swiss border guards watched over his shoulder. "Along with your identity card."

Gabi reached into her handbag and produced the necessary identification. "You should find everything in order." She cast a warm smile but nothing remotely flirtatious. The Swiss border guard, a blond-haired, smooth-skinned Basler with glistening eyes, looked the same age as her twin brothers.

"Taking a job, I see. You must be new around here." The private's friendly grin revealed his dimples.

"That's correct." Gabi knew a flirt when she saw one.

"Maybe we can have a coffee after you get off work."

"Do members of the *Grenzpolizei* always make a pass while they're on duty?" Gabi punctuated her comeback with a brighter smile that turned the private's ears red and prompted his compatriots to stifle a laugh.

"Very well," he said dryly, waving her on. "Please respect the no-talking rule in the tunnel."

She was committed now. Gabi clutched another lungful of air to settle her nerves and queued up for the German checkpoint. The dark tunnel, packed mostly with Swiss women pressing to get to work on time, imbued a surreal eeriness. Nazi Germany certainly had to be another world, and this would be her first personal experience with the evil she had read so much about.

As Gabi advanced toward the end of the tunnel, a spotlight burned ever brighter into her eyes. She strained to see what was beyond the steel mesh fencing, which looked to be a transit hall leading to several rail platforms.

This queue, surprisingly, moved quickly, and she found out why when she reached the German customs control. A trio of Wehrmacht officers, flanked by a fourth brandishing a machine gun, waved through three or four at a time with barely a glimpse at the official documents. She assumed they were regulars accorded expedited treatment.

"*Halt. Papiere, bitte.*" A German officer, who looked to be in his early thirties, singled her out. With a square head larger than normal and a great beak of a nose, the officer personified rigid authority and a streak of ruthlessness.

Gabi's eyes moved from his angular visage to his gray-green tunic with four pleated patch pockets and a pair of silver twist, cord-piped collar tabs. What most caught her attention, though, was the insignia on the left breast pocket: a woven eagle and skull embroidered onto a matching gray-green wool trapezoid with a firm backing. She meekly handed over her work permit without a peep.

The officer studied the official German document. "How long have you been working at H&M?" His pronunciation of High German put her off balance for a moment, but she had rehearsed an answer to this question.

"Actually, this is my first day," she replied in High German.

The German officer next reviewed her Swiss identity card, eyes roving from her black-and-white photo on the document to her face. Gabi felt her neck muscles tighten and her stomach lurch, but she ignored her discomfort. She thought about distracting him by asking what bus line she should take, but she decided to remain as inconspicuous as possible. She lowered her gaze so he couldn't look into her eyes underneath the brim of her hat.

More seconds passed as a train whistle shrieked from a locomotive passing overhead. Heavy railcars sent a deep rumble through the concrete-lined tomb. The sound of squealing air brakes signaled that the train was coming to a full stop.

"Carry on." The officer returned her work permit and moved to the next person in line.

Just like that, she was in. Gabi accepted her papers and walked purposefully past the mesh fencing into the German side of the Badischer Bahnhof. Several concrete stairways on the right and left directed passengers to numbered platforms, but Gabi continued marching along the dimly lit hall strewn with old newspapers and trash. She noticed that a half-dozen shops were boarded up, save for a single kiosk offering a limited inventory of newspapers, magazines, and books along with several baskets of fruit. The price posted for her favorite fruit—apricots—looked cheaper than in Switzerland.

Dieter Baumann's directions were specific. Once in Germany, she was to walk to the bus depot in front of the train station, where the Swiss operative would be waiting for her. She set her sights on the bright daylight of a summer morning, but a hand brushed her arm, and someone sidled up to her. Gabi's footsteps slowed.

"I see you passed through with no problems."

Gabi turned toward the voice.

"Keep going. We can keep talking, but let's not draw any extra attention our way."

"I thought you were meeting me at the bus stop."

Dieter Baumann, dressed in a gray pinstripe suit, unleashed a broad grin. "I lagged behind just in case something tripped you up at the checkpoint." He winked at her. "I wasn't amazed that you made it. You never cease to surprise me, Gabi. I'm even awed by how gorgeous you look in those old-fashioned work clothes."

Nice try, Dieter. Her stomach churned as she realized how she'd let her emotions get the better of her in previous interactions with him. His intentions were becoming clearer. How he'd singled her out. Used his good looks to charm her.

Uttered compliments to disarm her. And now this operation in wartime Germany, which smelled like week-old perch from Lake Geneva. Gabi quietly balled her fists as her anger increased with each step, yet she could not give away her true feelings. Mr. Dulles counted on her. The Americans counted on her. And her compatriots counted on her to expose this weasel.

Gabi returned a flirtatious glance. "My mom said this Basque suit was quite the style back in . . . 1921, when she last wore it."

"You talked to your mother about—"

"Of course not. You have nothing to worry about." She ever so lightly brushed her fingers against his hand. "Have I ever let you down?"

· · · · · · · ·

Gabi and Dieter took seats close to the front of the bus where a farmer kept one arm draped over a tarp-shrouded wooden cage. Piercing squawks erupted each time the lumbering bus hit another pothole, an occurrence of increasing frequency.

Gabi thought the driver, a Frenchman in his sixties wearing a navy beret, wasn't too interested in winning the Bus Driver of the Month competition. When he wasn't driving straight into potholes, he forgot about double-shifting to the next gear, preferring to grind the gearbox as the dented bus lurched in response.

She touched Dieter on the arm and rolled her eyes, which elicited his grin. "I'll need to see a doctor for my lumbago after this bus ride is over," she said. "So where are we?"

"The Friedlingen quarter of Weil am Rhein. We're coming up soon on several Swiss textile factories, including H&M." Dieter pointed toward his left. "They were established before the Great War when Swiss bankers poured investment francs into German holding companies because of cheaper land and available labor. After the Nazi blitzkrieg in 1939, neither

224

side saw any reason to change the status quo. The Swiss had the law on their side because they owned the factories and the Germans needed their output to clothe their advancing armies as well as the home-front populace."

"That explains a lot." Gabi looked to her right through a grimy bus window. Beyond the leafy green environs, she caught the white steeple belonging to St. Franziskus Catholic Church—in Riehen. She found it hard to believe that her hometown—and freedom—were just a kilometer or two away as the crow flies. The double rows of three-meter-high fencing and barbed wire along the border were a formidable barrier, however.

"Is our stop soon?" she asked.

"Two or three to go before the main square. We'll walk from there." Dieter cradled a small leather valise in his lap as part of the Swiss businessman ruse.

Gabi turned toward her counterpart. "Have you been to this house before?"

"No, and I didn't want to risk another trip into Germany for reconnaissance. My source guaranteed the house is empty. A key is underneath the clay pot next to the back door. This place is on the edge of town and backs up to a vineyard. If we run into any nosy neighbors, I'll say we're acting on behalf of the Gestapo. That usually cuts short any conversations."

"Your High German is that good?" Of course, Dieter could speak *Hochdeutsch*. She was referring to his Swiss accent.

Dieter held up a hand. "Not as good as yours. Tell them you're my secretary on a mission that we're not at liberty to discuss."

When their stop came, they exited the bus. The deliberate walk through Weil am Rhein's modest commercial district passed without incident, and ten minutes later they found the house at Wittlingerstrasse 6, an upper-crust villa that had seen better days. The two-story mansion, painted in amaranth pink and as tall as it was wide, was set off from a quiet two-way lane with a circular gravel driveway. An unkempt lawn was green from summer thundershowers, and the scruffy grounds and straggly bushes hadn't been tended to recently.

Gabi adjusted her hat and glanced over her shoulder, scanning the streets for any signs they were being watched.

"Let's walk in the back door like we own the place," Dieter said. "In broad daylight."

The pair strolled around the sizable villa to an unfenced backyard bordered by several hectares of ripening green grapes, dangling in winged clusters from three-wire trellises. Within the backyard confines was a small garden plot overrun with weeds and field grasses. The unpicked tomatoes, zucchini, and squash were rotting on the vine.

Gabi helped Dieter move the clay pot, where the latchkey was waiting as promised. Dieter inserted it into the back door lock, which opened without protest at his quick, twisting motion. They stepped into a tidy kitchen, where a newspaper lay open on the breakfast nook table. Gabi peaked at the front page: it was a regional rag—the *Süddeutsche Zeitung* dated July 14, 1944. Just three weeks ago.

"We take the hall to the stairway." Dieter pushed open a kitchen door that swiveled in each direction. "Then it's upstairs and a right to the master bedroom. Next to a sitting area is a wall safe behind a credenza."

The wooden stairs creaked as they mounted to the living quarters. "Don't worry about making any noise," Dieter said. "No one's around."

The master bedroom, with a walnut-stained hardwood floor accented by a circular Persian rug, included two leather chairs and ottomans set in front of a fireplace. "Safe should be over there." Dieter pointed to the far wall and window that overlooked the driveway.

"Behind the French Country sideboard?" Gabi, the daughter of a furniture maker, pegged the chestnut sideboard with brass hardware to be from the Louis XIV era.

"I believe so." Dieter walked over and studied the antique

credenza for a moment. "Here, give me a hand." He directed Gabi to the other end of sideboard. She set her handbag down, and with the count of *eins*, *zwei*, *drei*, they lifted and moved the heavy furniture piece a couple of meters, revealing a secure lockbox set in the wall just above the floor molding.

"Right where the safe was supposed to be," Dieter said.

Gabi gathered her ankle-length wool skirt and crouched down for a closer look. "You're kidding me—a Rubin safe."

"Is something wrong?"

"No, just the opposite. Rubins are as easy as they come. Manufactured in Hamburg or Berlin. Jewish firm, if I remember correctly. This one looks to be 1870s vintage. Unless the components of the combination lock have rusted out, this should pop open in a jiffy. Maybe we're lucky and they left the combination lock on the factory setting—100, 50, 100."

Gabi dialed 100-50-100 in rapid sequence. The lock failed to click, however. "Well, I didn't think it would be *that* easy."

She rubbed her fingers and leaned her right ear against the combination lock. Then she rotated the dial to the right several times in quick succession before slowing considerably. Gabi closed her eyes and listened intently for the slight noise of the lever touching the tumblers. Nothing during the first go-around.

"I thought you said this would be a snap." Dieter peeked past the curtain edge at a window overlooking the driveway.

"Once you determine which of the tumblers the lever is touching, it's relatively simple to find the exact combination. Let me see . . ." Another rotation of the dial came up dry.

"It's going bad?" Dieter's eyebrows folded in concern.

"No, it's still early. These things require patience."

Gabi leaned closer again. Four, five minutes of listening passed until she heard something—actually, it was her fingers that ascertained a slight eccentricity in the tumbler. She memorized the number: 72.

She turned the combinational dial in the opposite direction, and her fingers detected the lever touching . . . 36.

227

"I think I got it," she said. People were creatures of habit, and if she were playing the roulette wheels at Monte Carlo, she'd push her pile of chips onto the felt square of 72—if the roulette numbers went that high.

She carefully moved the dial toward 70 . . . 71 . . . and detected the slightest indication of the lever touching the tumbler. Safe companies, she knew, always allowed a little bit of fudge on the combination numbers—plus or minus one—meaning that 71, 72, or 73 would work. The safe door unlocked with a satisfying thud.

"We're in."

Dieter hurried from the window to her side. Gabi reached in and pulled out a legal-sized brown manila folder, several centimeters thick, stuffed with papers. She didn't see anything else inside the safe—wait, in the back . . . her fingers touched something soft . . . and out came a royal purple velvet pouch with a gold-braided drawstring.

Gabi held up the fist-sized pouch to the light streaking through the window, surprised at its heft. "What's this?"

"I'll take that, please."

Both heads swiveled toward the deep voice's source standing under the transom—a voice speaking High German.

"Karl, what are you doing here?" Dieter sprang to his feet.

Gabi turned to see a shadowy figure whose fleshy face was partially obscured by a wide-brimmed hat, and her stomach somersaulted. She was in trouble. Deep, deep trouble. She stood to her feet and thought about making a run for it, but the menacing man with a bulbous nose blocked the path between her and the bedroom door.

"I see you know my real name, Herr Baumann. Quite a game we're playing. What else do you know about me?" The German chuckled, then quickly lost his smile when he reached into his jacket and extracted a black pistol.

Dieter held out both hands. "Karl—Ludwig—let's stick to the plan."

Suddenly, an eerie sense of familiarity came over Gabi. Her racing mind searched its memory banks until something clicked. The memory of the man's beefy hands wrapped around her throat came to the forefront, as well as the grotesque way he squeezed the last gasp of oxygen from her lungs until she bit into his sausage-like fingers.

"Wait a minute—you're the same guy as last week in Basel's Old Town!" Feelings of shock and betrayal swirled through her pounding heart. Dieter had set her up—

"Very perceptive, Fräulein Mueller. I'm running out of time, so if you'll just hand over the diamonds."

Gabi gasped. *Diamonds?* She turned toward her partner, anger pounding with every heartbeat. "So that's what you brought me into Germany to do—bust open a safe on a diamond heist?"

Dieter backpedaled. "Listen, we didn't know what was in that safe, did we, Karl?"

The German smiled. "You're right. It could have been anything. Jewish diamond dealers always keep German war plans in their safes, *ja?*"

Karl fluttered his free hand to Gabi, still keeping the pistol pointed in their direction. "The diamonds. I'm waiting."

She'd never had a gun pointed at her. The stakes had just been raised. The chances of surviving this encounter had dropped dramatically, unless . . .

Dieter dared to take a step toward the hefty man holding the gun. "Karl, we had an agreement, remember? Fifty-fifty."

"So? I lied. Now, Fräulein Mueller, my patience is fleeting."

Gabi knew time—as well as her options—were running out. She directed her wrath toward Dieter once again. "Why did you do this to me? Tell me, why!"

Dieter's eyes widened at her outburst. "Gabi, this wasn't the way things were supposed to go. I was always going to cut you in."

"Cut me in? You animal!" Gabi advanced on Dieter, furious. In one smooth move, she dropped the purple pouch and thick folder into her leather handbag and swung it in the air. "You tricked me, you traitor. Now look at what you've gotten me into!"

She whipped her handbag through the air, but instead of striking Dieter, she directed the blow across Karl Rundstedt's right forearm. His pistol clattered across the parquet floor and slid under the four-poster bed. The German dove for his weapon while Gabi secured the handbag's strap over her shoulder and lunged for the door. Forgetting his gun for the moment, Karl rolled over and grasped her ankle with his left hand.

"Dieter!" she yelped. "Get him off me—"

Dieter kicked the man's face once, but before he connected a second time, Karl used both hands to trip Dieter, then pounced on him like a raged animal, pummeling Dieter's back.

Released from Karl's grip, Gabi scrambled to the fireplace, grabbed the brass poker, raised it over her head, and swung with all her might, striking Karl's left shoulder.

"Ach!" Enraged by the blow, he swiped at Gabi's ankles, bringing her down hard. The poker tumbled out of her hand, and Dieter snatched it. He rolled to his knees and raised it above Karl's head.

"Run for it, Gabi! Take the diamonds and go!"

Gabi turned to the door, then paused as Karl lunged at Dieter, knocking the poker from his hand. They wrestled furiously for control of the brass weapon.

Dieter glanced her way. "Do as I say—now!"

Using this moment of distraction, Karl stretched out his left hand and retrieved the pistol from under the bed.

"Run, Gabi!" Dieter pushed to his feet as he grabbed the poker and swung it, forcing Karl to deflect the blow with both arms. Then came another blow and another . . .

Gabi sprinted out of the room just as a deafening gunshot splintered the air and the wooden doorjamb just centimeters from her shoulder. Hitching her skirt above her ankles, she scampered down the stairs, out the back door, and bolted across the driveway with a single-minded focus—returning to the safe haven of Switzerland as quickly as she could.

* * * * * * * *

Dieter knew he was in a fight for his life.

"You let her get away!" The German's eyes bulged with anger as he pulled himself up. "With my diamonds!"

"No, it was you who botched it! I had her perfectly under control until you came and screwed things up!" Dieter warily circled Karl, who stood in the center of the master bedroom, tracking him with the gun. He wondered for a scant moment if the German would murder him in cold blood. If only he had his ankle pistol! But he'd left the weapon back in Basel in case the Germans searched him at the Badischer Bahnhof.

Desperation turned his mind to a hidden weapon still at his disposal—a heavy blackjack in his right pocket. He switched the poker to his left hand and pulled out the blackjack to show he meant business. "Don't worry. I can get the diamonds from her." Then he faked a throw.

Karl feinted to his left and moved in a circle with Dieter, so as not to be outflanked. "Then you'd have all the diamonds. Do you think I'm stupid?"

Dieter regarded the pistol aimed at his torso, then locked eyes with the German. "Karl, we can work something out."

"If I let you go, I'll always have to worry about you. *Nein danke*. I like to sleep at night."

"But . . . but I can get to the girl. I know where she lives."

"I can find her too, and when I do, she'll give up the diamonds, all right. If she resists, I'll shoot her mother . . . then her father—"

"Don't do this, Karl. I left a file on my desk with your name on it in case something went wrong. The OSS knows about you, and if I don't come back—"

231

"All the more reason to kill you."

"No, Karl, please, don't. I beg you." Dieter sunk to his knees and raised his arms. "I'll take care of the girl so that no one will ever hear from her again."

"I don't believe you."

"You have to, please."

"Sorry, but I prefer to go this alone—"

Dieter flung the blackjack. It struck Karl hard in the stomach. The blow nearly buckled Karl's knees, and in a split second, Dieter leaped at Karl and knocked him off balance. Dieter rolled to the floor and seized the blackjack, then sprang to his feet. He reared back his right arm—

Then a gunshot sounded, and Dieter felt an explosion in his shoulder. His arms splayed, and his body hit the wall.

Dieter felt himself sliding to the floor as everything went black.

* * * * * * * *

A second shot rang out. A look of surprise came over Karl's face as his body crumpled. The clean entrance wound in his left temple leaked a thin crimson rivulet down the side of his face.

Jean-Pierre rushed to Karl's side and grabbed his jacket's lapels for a closer look. The German's wide-open eyes bore a hole right through him. He dropped the lifeless body to the floor and hurried to see how Dieter—lying in a heap—was doing. He hoped the traitor had survived the trauma, but when he rolled Dieter onto his back and spotted the bleeding wound that had ripped open his upper chest, he had his doubts.

Jean-Pierre grasped his left wrist and checked for a pulse. Dieter's eyelids flickered for a moment, as if in some sort of recognition. Then they quickly closed.

Dieter Baumann would not be double-crossing anyone else again.

* * * * * * * *

By the time Gabi reached the street, a gunshot reverberated through the neighborhood, followed almost instantly by another, but she didn't look back.

Instead, she looked up and down the street. No traffic, no pedestrians, no mothers hanging out their laundry. She turned and lowered her head, retracing her steps back to the bus stop. Gabi suddenly realized that she would have to give the Germans at the Badischer Bahnhof checkpoint a good excuse why she was getting off "work" before noon.

It better be a good one, or there would be a lot of explaining to do—in a German prison.

26

"Telegram from the Reichsführer." Becker handed the missive to his superior, then retreated one step and clicked his heels.

"I know what it's going to say." Sturmbannführer Bruno Kassler buried his face in his hands and rubbed his red eyes. "Read it to me."

Becker approached Kassler's desk and grasped a pewter letter opener embossed with the National Socialist German Worker's Party *Hakenkreuz*—the swastika symbol. With a flick of the wrist, he sliced opened the telegram and cleared his throat.

"Sturmbannführer Kassler to arrive at Berlin headquarters no later than 20:00 hours, 4 August 1944, with or without Engel. Accompanying escort to arrive Heidelberg Hauptbahnhof at 9:52 a.m. Reichsführer H. Himmler."

Becker set the telegram on the desk. "Sounds like he's giving you one more day, sir."

Kassler drummed his fingers on the wooden desk, then set his chin on his palm. "We've squeezed a twenty-kilometer radius like a lemon. Engel slipped through our fingers for a time, but he has to be holed up somewhere. He can't move, at least in public. He can't show his face within 500 meters of a train station. His picture has been distributed to the rightful authorities, printed on thousands of fliers. A reward has been discreetly offered to those we can trust."

"Have you thought about alerting the police and military ranks along the Swiss border?"

"Our assets working in Basel and Bern have been tipped off," Kassler replied, "but we should double-check with the border patrols and the local police. Around here, all roads lead to Switzerland."

"Duly noted, sir. I will make the necessary contacts."

"Have the next batch of reports come in? I'm talking about the house-to-house searches in Sandhausen, Nussblock, and Leimen. I haven't reviewed those yet."

"They're being processed downstairs at this moment."

Kassler shot Becker a cold glance.

The corporal backpedaled. "What I mean, sir, is that I didn't want to overburden you. Rothmund and von Meiss are gleaning through those reports at this moment."

Kassler unbuttoned another clasp on his tunic. "My dear Becker, what do you think I was doing all night? I read every report you set before me. I'm certain there could be an offhand observation, a stray clue waiting to be deciphered. Listen, my goose is cooked tomorrow night unless I find Engel dead or alive. I want the next batch of reports in this office in fifteen minutes." He pounded his desk for emphasis.

"*Jawohl*," Becker said without argument.

"And bring me some lunch from the canteen while you're at it. Weisswürst and potato salad will do."

• • • • • • • • •

Riehen, Switzerland
12:40 p.m.

Gabi stepped off the BVB #2 tram, her heart still pounding from the adrenaline rush that morning. After escaping, everything around her seemed more alive as she made the twenty-minute trek back home. Her heightened senses noticed the cracks in the sidewalk, the wind-whipped leaves on the poplar trees, and the mechanical sounds of light traffic on Baselstrasse, Riehen's principal route.

Inwardly, though, she seethed from Dieter's betrayal. He saw a way to steal riches that weren't his, so he used her. Something deep down told Gabi that if she hadn't struck the German with her handbag, it would have been only a matter of time before she'd been shot. Gabi involuntarily shivered and gathered her light suit jacket despite the 80-degree temperatures.

Her father and Eric had been right. Dieter Baumann wasn't trustworthy. Her boss—surely her *former* boss—had blithely said something in the safe was so important that lives would be at stake, but he didn't tell Gabi that it would be *her* life on the line. Mr. Dulles was right—this was a caper, and the break-in was all about a cache of jewelry, not military secrets.

Maybe Dieter's greed had cost him his life. She didn't know what the two gunshots meant back at the villa, but if Dieter had survived, she couldn't see him poking his nose in Switzerland unless he wanted to start a competition between the Swiss and the Americans for the right to hang him.

Her parents' home was around the corner. Walking along the rural road, Gabi peered inside her handbag one more time. Everything was there: manila folder, jewelry pouch, and her pocketbook. She was pleased with the way she passed through the German checkpoint at the Badischer Bahnhof without incident. At the guard's intimidating glare, she told him that H&M didn't have a sewing machine ready for her on her first day of work and to return tomorrow. The excuse passed without a challenge.

Gabi stepped through the unlocked front door and yoo-hooed. "Hello, I'm home!" Only the ticking of the mantle clock answered her call. Realizing the house was empty, she passed through the kitchen, crossed the backyard, and peered into the barn's open door. Inside her father wore a festive-looking painter's apron, decorated with colorful paint splashes and brush marks. He worked a paintbrush, staining a china hutch.

Her father looked up, and his rosy face broke into a wide grin that pooched his cheeks and accentuated his merry laugh lines.

"Gabi, you're back—"

She couldn't wait to embrace her dad and practically skipped into his bear-like hug. "Oh, Papi, it's so good to see you again."

Ernst Mueller gave her a squeeze and then pulled away. "Your mother and I were worried sick about you. She took Seppli on a walk, so she should be home soon. I'd ask you how things went, but—"

"You're right, I can't tell you, but Mr. Dulles said to come back here and call him at the hotel. I need to see him immediately."

Gabi heard footsteps and looked up to see Allen Dulles's lanky form, dressed in a gray suit and dark tie, approaching the barn from the driveway. He, too, looked delighted to see her.

"I called your father this morning and asked if I could await your return here," the American explained. "Thank God you returned safely. No father could agree with me more. Correct, Mr. Mueller?"

Ernst broadcast a wide grin.

"So how are you?" Dulles asked.

Gabi hid the emotions swirling inside her. "I'm fine, but something happened that I should tell you about. Could you excuse us, Papi?"

"Sure. I'll return to my staining while you two have a chat."

Gabi led the American spymaster back toward the house, her resolve strengthening with each step. For the next fifteen minutes, she explained everything—the border passage, the bus ride through Weil am Rhein, tiptoeing through the villa, cracking the safe, and a German named Karl or Ludwig seizing the initiative and demanding the velvet pouch of jewels. She described how she swung her handbag down on Karl's arm, which dislodged the firearm and ultimately allowed her to escape. She told him that Dieter yelled for her to run for it, even though from the back-and-forth she witnessed between Baumann and the Karl character, it was obvious that both were aware beforehand that expensive jewels lay inside the safe.

Dulles mulled the information for a moment.

"Why do you think Mr. Baumann told you to take the diamonds and run since he was working with the German?"

Gabi considered her response for a moment. "Maybe he felt guilty for the way the break-in backfired. Or maybe he thought if the diamonds were gone from the villa, he'd have a bargaining chip."

"I'll call my Swiss contacts and ask them to intercept Mr. Baumann at the border. Karl Rundstedt too."

"I don't think Dieter's alive. I heard two gun shots. If he would have made it, he would have caught me before I reached the Badischer Bahnhof."

"You're probably right," Dulles ran a hand through his graying hair. After a moment's reflection his eyes met Gabi's. "Have you looked inside the pouch?"

"No, not yet."

"Let's have a look."

She fetched the leather handbag she'd set on the dining room table and retrieved the purple velvet pouch. She opened the golden drawstring and peered inside.

"You have to see this . . ." Gabi gingerly poured the pouch's contents onto the dark walnut dining table. Dozens of diamonds . . . round, oval, and pear-shaped . . . spilled forth like a cascade. Many looked bigger than a karat or two—more than 200 milligrams or a fifth of a gram—but some were as big as pebbles.

"Oh, my word!" She covered her mouth with her hand. "Look at them!"

"There's a small fortune here," Dulles said. "Impressive enough to cloud one's judgment, for sure."

"And nearly get me killed in the process." Gabi picked up

the largest diamond, an emerald-cut stone that appeared flawless in clarity and color. The diamond had to be ten carats.

Dulles withdrew his pipe and squared up his shoulders. "Breathtaking, but the audacity! I don't know how Dieter Baumann thought he'd pull this off, but I'm impressed with your heroism. You can rest assured that Mr. Baumann doesn't have a very long future if he shows his face on this side of the border again."

"If I see him again, I'll kick him where it counts."

Dulles chuckled. "Now that's my girl." Then he turned serious. "Gabi, after all that's happened to you today, I'm hesitant to raise this topic, but something urgent has come to my attention."

"Would you like a seat?" Gabi beckoned toward the burgundy sofa in the living room as she put the diamonds back into their velvety pouch.

"Yes, perhaps that would be a good idea."

Gabi perched herself on the edge of a love seat upholstered by her father's hands from the same burgundy cloth. "How can I help?"

"Information has come from friendly sources inside Germany that an important scientist wants to defect to the Allied side." Dulles shifted his weight before continuing. "He may have information about secret military projects vital to the war effort. That's all I'm at liberty to say at the moment, but we have to safely courier him into Switzerland. Very soon, I hasten to add."

Gabi remembered the coded message she had translated yesterday for the courier from Bern. "Are you're talking about the message from Gideon regarding the scientist working at the University of Heidelberg on a wonder weapon? I think his name was . . ." Gabi searched her memory banks. Oh yes, his last name meant *Angel* in English. "Joseph Engel?"

"That's him."

"How soon?"

"Tonight, if possible. This is a strictly volunteer effort,

but I think you're the most capable for this mission. You have the English and German skills that we need. You're an American. You believe in what we're doing. And after what happened this morning . . . you've shown the ability to think on your feet. But more than that, I can trust you. And honestly, after discovering Baumann's true leanings, I'm worried about whom else in the office that I can trust."

"If we can spirit Joseph Engel out of Germany, do you think the tide of the war could change—or at least help our efforts?"

Dulles tamped his pipe on the glass ashtray set out on the coffee table. "I can assure you that the United States' interest in Joseph Engel and the wonder weapon extends all the way to the Oval Office. But I can't force you to go. Smuggling a German scientist into Switzerland will be exceedingly dangerous, and we're running out of time. We don't know how much longer he can remain at the safe house. It's imperative that we try—tonight."

Gabi's body ached from weariness. Her head pounded. She hadn't received much training. Surely there were others who'd do a better job. Yet Mr. Dulles believed in her. That had to count, didn't it?

She locked eyes with her boss. The urgency of this mission was clear. How could she say no? She'd always wanted to make a difference in this war. To be given more responsibility. And now was her chance. She straightened her shoulders. "I'll go. You can count on me."

"That's the spirit." Dulles reached for his briefcase and extracted a map of southern Germany and Switzerland. "For the first part of the plan, we need some help. Do you think your father would be willing to go on a drive for us? He'd get to visit your brothers for a spell before heading back."

"You mean drive to Davos? I'm sure he doesn't have enough gas ration coupons, even to get to Zurich."

"I anticipated that problem." Dulles extracted a thick envelope filled with beige ration cards from his briefcase, then continued outlining his plan to extricate Joseph Engel from Nazi Germany.

* * * * * * * *

The coded knock—two light taps followed by another pair of light taps—rang through the lightly furnished apartment.

Jean-Pierre pulled away from his fourth-story perch overlooking the Badischer Bahnhof, which afforded a bird's-eye view of the German rail yard. For the better part of a year, Jean-Pierre and Pascal had been counting German rail cars transporting war materials to the Wehrmacht and Fascist forces fighting in the Italian boot. Jean-Pierre had visual evidence that Switzerland received freight cars filled with Ruhr Valley coal and wheat stocks, no doubt an unofficial trade for looking the other way. On this particular day, rail traffic entering Switzerland from Germany had been light, which he attributed to the Allies' massive pounding by air.

"Welcome, Herr Dulles." Jean-Pierre motioned to one of the simple wooden chairs. "Good to see you again."

"Curiosity killed the cat . . . what happened this morning?"

A blank look came over Jean-Pierre's face. "What kills the cat?"

"Excuse me—another American saying. I just left Gabi Mueller's home, and she said after she escaped, there were gunshots."

"Yes, there were. Shall I start at the beginning?"

"By all means."

"From up here, I watched Herr Baumann, followed by Fräulein Mueller, enter the Badischer Bahnhof around 7:15 a.m. I quickly gathered what I needed and followed them through the *Kontrolle*. Once on the German side, I kept my distance, then saw them board a bus. I hired a taxi to follow and maintained my surveillance until they entered the big house. I hid behind a tree.

"Then a car approached, and Ludwig—Karl Rundstedt—got out. When he walked around to the back of the house, I followed him at a distance because I didn't think Fräulein Mueller or Herr Baumann were expecting him. After the German entered, I slipped just inside the back door into the kitchen. Then I heard—how do you say *Schlägerei*?"

Dulles shrugged his shoulders.

"Like a fight. Lots of noise, then a gunshot. I was about to leave the kitchen to investigate when I saw Fräulein Mueller running down the stairs. She never looked my way when she ran out of the house. I tiptoed up the stairs and heard another gunshot. I drew my weapon and looked into the bedroom. That's when the German fellow glanced in my direction. I shot him before he could do the same to me. I checked, and both were dead."

Dulles considered the new information. "Although I would have preferred finding out what Baumann was up to, you took the appropriate action. Certainly cleans up a frightful mess."

"Sorry, I had no time to think."

"You did fine." Dulles leaned toward Jean-Pierre. "We're on for tonight. I need you to get a message to Pastor Leo with the particulars. Do you have a notepad?"

Jean-Pierre approached a hardwood table with a wireless telegraph and several code books. He picked up a pad and a pencil. "Here you go, sir. Please write legibly."

27

Davos, Switzerland
6:30 p.m.

Bill Palmer didn't need to memorize the rendezvous point.

Head down, he listened to the cadence of his well-worn boots pounding the pavement as anticipation built in his heart. These steps were leading him out of Davos, he reminded himself. He retraced his route from the previous night to the empty alley behind the Heiz Bäckerei.

"There you are. Right on time." Willy Mueller, still in uniform, tucked his service cap into his waist belt and straightened up from where he leaned against the rear wall of the bakery.

Willy smiled and pumped Bill's hand, but thoughts of J.J. and Sam caused Bill to feel the weight of the world on his shoulders. He attempted to smile back but knew his attempt was weak.

Willy frowned slightly, then turned and knocked on a wooden garage door. When the door didn't open right away, he glanced at his watch. "We're a little early I suppose."

Bill glanced around. "Positive there isn't any problem?"

"Easy now. We're not doing anything wrong—just a couple of buddies hanging out like we have since you arrived here."

"I know, but now . . . well, everything's different." Bill pressed his fingertips to his temples.

"Still bothered by your buddies getting picked up? At least they didn't get shot."

Bill weighed his words. "Three months in Wauwil. They've probably been processed already and tossed into the general prison population. You hear all sorts of awful things about that slammer." He shook his head. "Hope they can survive on bread, water, and gruel."

"Yeah, makes our potatoes and cheese look like your New York steaks and California salads. Too bad Andreas couldn't warn them in time about the ambush. The Swiss like order, so when Allied airmen step over the boundaries, the authorities must act swiftly and surely. As an example to others."

"I see your point, but the thought of being stuck here in the mountains for another winter got to some of us. It seems useless to be here . . . useless waiting out the war." Bill looked at his watch. At this moment, in Wisconsin, Katie was gearing up for the lunch crowd at her parents' diner. He missed her horribly, but he reminded himself that after tonight, he might see her very soon.

Willy looked at his watch too. "Let's try this again." He knocked on the garage door firmly—too loudly for Bill's comfort. Yet as Bill scanned the streets, he still saw no one.

This time the paneled door rolled to the right side, revealing Fritz Heiz, the bakery owner, and the beaming face of Andreas Mueller, also dressed in uniform. "Great to see you, Bill, but hurry up," Andreas said. "We don't have all day." Bill and Willy stepped inside, and Herr Heiz moved quickly to close the garage door behind them.

Bill's eyes adjusted to the twilight inside the loading dock. An older man huddled over a roadmap draped across the black hood of a four-door sedan.

"Ernst Mueller," said the man with ruddy cheeks, dressed in a dark suit without a tie. "But you can call me Ernie. I'm the twins' father."

Bill noticed the family resemblance in the pronounced eyebrows and wide forehead. Just the way Ernie Mueller said his name told him that he was an American native.

"I guess I don't have to ask you who won the World Series last year," Bill joked.

"Baseball news travels slowly around these parts, but I'm aware the Yankees beat the Cardinals in the Fall Classic. What else do you want to know? That DiMaggio hit safely in fifty-six games in '41?"

Bill raised his arms. "Okay, you're an American. What exactly do you have planned for me?"

"You like to fly?"

"Sure. That's why I'm here in Switzerland."

"I'll tell you more on the drive. I shouldn't say too much around the boys anyway."

Ernie waved his sons over to his map. "I'm figuring four hours to Dübendorf. What do you think?"

"I've never driven there from here," Willy said. "Sounds right to me, though."

Andreas nodded his agreement. "Before you get to the Zürichsee, cross the lake at Rapperswil," he suggested. "You don't want to go all the way around the Lake of Zurich and through Zurich. Taking this shortcut to Dübendorf will save you a half hour or forty-five minutes."

Bill couldn't believe this was really going to happen, but when Willy and Andreas said they could get him out of Davos—in a matter of hours—he was willing to accept the risk inherent with an escape attempt. Whatever their father asked couldn't be too difficult.

"Very good." Ernie folded up the accordion-pleated map. "Time to go. Hop in, everyone."

Bill was puzzled. "The twins are going with us?"

"Following the escape attempt last night, the Swiss military set up a roadblock just outside of town. We're not leaving anything to chance, so you're going into the trunk and I'm taking the boys with me to the checkpoint. I need them to chat with the guards about their visiting father." Ernie Mueller dug into his right pocket for a set of keys and opened up the rear hatch. A pair of twenty-liter jerry cans took up half the trunk space.

"Gas for the drive back," Ernie explained. "Here, give me a hand."

Bill helped move the jerry cans behind the driver's seat. "What kind of car is this?"

"She doesn't look like much, but she's a '35 Peugeot." Ernie motioned a cordial invitation to the rear trunk. "Okay, in you go."

Bill removed his fleece-lined flight jacket and set it down where his head would lie. He scrunched his body into a pretzel to squeeze into the tight trunk.

Ernie tucked the airman's long legs into the cubbyhole. "Sorry. It might be a little snug, but—" He slammed the trunk door.

Flecks of light seeped through pinholes in the trunk, settling Bill's anxious stomach a bit. As they got under way, Bill learned that the shock absorbers were shot—every bump in the road jostled his kidneys and other internal organs.

Five minutes later, the Peugeot approached the checkpoint. Bill heard Andreas and Willy exit the vehicle, jabbering in Swiss-German. From the bantering tone, no one seemed too interested in searching the car belonging to the father of two Swiss Army colleagues.

· · · · · · · · ·

After fifteen minutes of bouncing on the soft axles, Bill heard the Peugeot growl through three downshifts before rolling to a stop. When the trunk opened, the late summer sun had set behind the towering Alps, casting shadows across highlands dotted with slate-roofed chalets and penned pasturelands.

"Where are we?" Bill asked.

"Just outside of Klosters." Ernie had parked the sedan on a dirt path behind a rustic barn adjacent to pastures surrounded by wooden fence rails. Several chestnut horses and brown cows occupied themselves with chewing moist Alpine grasses.

Bill sniffed the air. The faint odor of rotten eggs caused his nose to twitch. "What's that smell?"

"The sulfur baths in town. The medicinal springs were a tourist draw before the war. The locals swear by them for gout, rheumatism, and chronic arthritis. Jump in the front seat with me. We have a schedule to keep."

Ernie steered the car back onto the paved road that led to the valley floor. Once out of town, he confidently accelerated out of the downhill turns as the two-lane macadam hugged an outcropping two thousand feet above the Landquart River, a narrow sluice of angry white water that would eventually join the mighty Rhine. On the more treacherous curves, Bill noticed that the "guardrail" was nothing more than a series of stone blocks, each about a foot square, separated by a yard or two. About the only thing those blocks would do is rip off the engine's oil pan if they went careening over the cliff, Bill thought.

"Don't worry," Ernie said, as if he was reading Bill's mind. "I've been driving these Alpine roads for years."

"You always speed like this?" Bill asked.

"Just when there's a flight to catch."

Bill took his eye off the precipice and turned toward Ernie. "So that's what you do for a living—race car driver?"

Ernie laughed. "No. I make furniture during the week and pastor a church on weekends."

"Oh, yeah. I remember the twins mentioning something about you running a church. They asked me if I wanted to join their Bible study on Tuesday nights."

"Did you go?"

"I wouldn't receive a medal for perfect attendance, but yes, I showed up on occasion. All those 'thees' and 'thous' bored me before, but those boys of yours explain the Bible well, so I did get something out of it. They talked about Psalm 91 this week and how it relates to every soldier in the military these days. Willy even got us to memorize a few lines, like 'A thousand shall fall at thy side, and ten thousand at thy right hand; but it shall not come nigh thee.' I didn't understand what the last part meant until Willy explained that even though others will drop like flies around us, no harm will touch us when we trust in God."

"So have you placed your trust in God?" Ernie asked. "Sorry, the preacher in me has to ask."

"I'm working on it. Maybe I should with this cockamamie mission I'm volunteering for. What exactly will I be doing?" Now that the rubber was meeting the road, Bill's interest—and anxiety—about "singing for his supper" came to the fore. He operated under the maxim that anything too good to be true usually was just that.

"Well, I was told that plans could change, but here's what I know." For the next few minutes, the pastor sketched out the parameters of Bill's responsibilities. He didn't stop talking, not even when he came upon sputtering tractors and punched the gas to overtake them.

Bill nodded his understanding of the overall plan. "Sounds like the Mueller family is out to save the world. We have your sons talking me into participating in this daredevil rescue, you driving me to the rendezvous point, and your daughter waiting for me to arrive." He smiled to indicate that he shouldn't be taken entirely seriously.

"It's not what it looks like," Ernie said. "First of all, Andreas and Willy were asked who the best pilot in Davos was, and your name topped a short list. I happened to be drafted today to drive into the mountains and pick you up. As for Gabi, she's working for the same people you're working for, in a way. She was picked for this mission because of her language skills, because she's proven herself, and because she's trusted. You're in good hands."

Ernie flicked on the lights as the twilight hour merged into darkness. The switchback-heavy road gave way to longer straightaways as they dropped altitude. "Remember this route from when you arrived?"

Bill shook his head. "After processing, the interned pilots and I boarded a train in Zürich. Once we hit the mountains, a storm socked us in."

"Well, we're traveling through a part of Switzerland that hasn't changed much for hundreds of years, except for a couple of posh resort villages like Klosters and Davos. The farmers around here are a tough lot, scratching out a living."

"No doubt it's pretty around here, but this sort of life would be too simple for me."

After four more hairpin turns, they arrived at the valley floor, where the road leveled out and ran parallel to the Landquart River. Bill visibly relaxed. "So I've been thinking . . ."

Ernie accelerated into third gear as the road straightened out. "About the plan, right?"

"No, the plane. Just how am I supposed to get one?"

"Steal it."

Bill shifted in his seat. "Instead of trying to kipe a plane, why don't we ask the Swiss Air Force if we can just borrow one of our P-51s sitting on the tarmac?" he asked with a hint of sarcasm. "We can promise to bring it back."

"Listen, I wish things were that simple, but P-51s are single-seat fighters. We need something that'll carry three people."

"That's okay. I'm not checked out on the P-51 anyway. So that leaves us with something like a B-17, but I can't land a heavy bomber on German soil without attracting notice."

"Of course. That's why we're still working on that part of the plan."

"Where's the pickup again?"

"Just south of Heidelberg."

"How far is that?"

"Two hundred and fifty kilometers or around 150 miles each way. Not far at all."

"Easy for you to say."

Suddenly, the reality of the mission landed on Bill's shoulders. The preflight jitters that rumbled through his stomach during morning briefings reminded him that once again he was being called to put his life on the line. Bill hadn't experienced that uneasy feeling in months, but this time around, a blending of boldness and confidence calmed his nerves. What was that line from Psalm 91 that Willy made the class memorize?

I will say of the Lord, He is my refuge and my fortress: my God; in him will I trust.

Bill had the feeling he would be tugging on that trust before the night was over.

28

Bruno Kassler dipped the crunchy Bavarian pretzel into a
dollop of Dijon mustard and regarded the six piles of manila folders stacked on his desk. How many field reports had
he scanned for clues since morning? One hundred? Maybe
more.

Kassler took another bite of the pretzel and leaned back in
his chair. What he really wanted was a stein of Weizenbock—
a pale, sour wheat beer that matched his mood, yet he knew
he would need all of his faculties in the hours ahead. His
shoulders tensed at the dearth of information he'd received
from local Polizei bureaus. Even the smallest lead could point
him toward Joseph Engel.

Until something broke, however, all he had were the detailed reports arriving in dribs and drabs to Gestapo headquarters. Meanwhile, Himmler's deadline loomed: just twelve
hours until his departure on the Berlin Express. Once he
stepped into the first class compartment, it would be *his* turn
to travel on a one-way ticket. He knew the price for failure:
a choice between blowing his brains out by his own hand or
standing on the gallows' trap door with piano wire cinched
around his neck.

A distinctive trio of knocks rapped upon the door, and
Kassler welcomed the diversion from contemplating his de-

mise. Corporal Becker bounded into the office with a dozen manila folders tucked under his right arm.

"Rothmund and von Meiss say there's nothing worth following up on, but here you go," Becker announced, his young eyes hinting of disappointment. "These are the last reports we'll see today. I'm told more will arrive tomorrow morning, however."

Kassler rubbed his left temple. More than anything he wanted to take those files and hurl them across the room for the fix he was in. Instead, he motioned Becker to his desk with resignation. "Fine. Leave them here. File the ones I've read."

Becker returned to his post, and Kassler halfheartedly reached for the first file on top of the new stack. A paper clip held a note with a single hand-written word: *Leimen*. Kassler immediately sat up straighter in his chair. Leimen was several kilometers south of the P-51 attack yesterday— an attack on a blockade checkpoint too well-timed for his taste. There could be something here.

The file contained a dozen handwritten pages from Otto Stampfli, captain of the Leimen Polizei. The precise cursive script typified Stampfli's by-the-book investigations: paying attention to detail, keeping a checklist, sorting out leads, and reviewing his work for completeness and accuracy.

Kassler quickly shuffled through the papers inside the Leimen file—all comprised one- or two-page reports penned by Stampfli's hand—before he returned to the first one. He pushed aside his pretzel, no longer interested in snacking.

Stampfli offered an introductory sentence, stating his reason for searching farmlands in his district, and then moved straight to a narration of the facts.

Address: *Langer Farm off Massengasse*
Beginning of Search: *2 August 1944, 13:35 hours*
End of Search: *2 August 1944, 14:00 hours*
Description of Search: *Two lieutenants, Strassman and Wefel-*

mayer, and I arrived unannounced at the Langer Farm. Main source of revenue is raising chickens and milk production. Herr Langer was absent; he had gone into town to purchase more chicken feed. Frau Langer appeared nervous at our sudden intrusion but was cooperative. She escorted us to the chicken coops behind the main barn. There were ten coops in all. Inside the barn, she didn't react when we poked beds of hay with pitchforks.

In the main house, we conducted a systematic search of all rooms . . .

Kassler finished the one-pager and slipped it back inside the manila folder. While there wasn't anything worth following up, he appreciated Stampfli's thoroughness.

The second report proved more interesting.

At the Riezler homestead, one of Stampfli's lieutenants ascended a ladder into a cramped attic stacked high with household goods and suitcases. His nose detected something—a rotten egg smell. He tapped on a wall, then pulled away three wooden boxes, which revealed a half door. Couched behind the wall were two disheveled men—Jewish brothers, as it turned out. They lived and slept there in exchange for working in the fields. Stampfli summarily arrested the Jewish men as well as the Riezler family; the Leimen Polizei was detaining all until a transfer to the Gestapo Regional Headquarters in Heidelberg could be effected.

That would be my place, Kassler smirked.

In a better mood, he read a half-dozen more reports until he reached one that caused the hairs on the back of his neck to stiffen like a thousand needles:

Address: *Ulrich Farm off Landstrasse*
Beginning of Search: *2 August 1944, 18:00 hours*
End of Search: *2 August 1944, 18:30 hours*
Description of Search: *Two lieutenants, Strassman and Wefel-mayer, and I arrived unannounced at the Ulrich Farm. Main source of revenue is hay production and apple orchards. One*

of Leimen's largest farms, the owner is Adalbert Ulrich. We found him in his farmhouse with his wife, Trudi, who was starting to prepare dinner for the farmhands. Working the alfalfa fields were Ulrich's brother-in-law, Leo Keller, and several men, all older.

In the main house, we conducted a systematic search of all rooms, including opening closets and looking under beds. The only unusual circumstance worth noting is that we found a leather satchel containing scientific papers and a notebook in a bedroom armoire. I opened the notebook and saw strings of numbers with x's, y's, and Greek letters, but did not understand them. Ulrich said the notebook belonged to a nephew studying mathematics at the University of Heidelberg who's now serving in the army. Satchel also contained nephew's wallet and student identification, which was in order.

Kassler stopped right there. Strings of x's, y's, and Greek letters? He closed his eyes and imagined the jumble of letters, numbers, and symbols he saw on Heisenberg's blackboard. What was the esteemed professor's name for it? *The S-matrix equation.*

Those were equations that Stampfli had seen in the notebook . . . the notebook found in a satchel.

What had Engel's roommate, Hannes Jäger, said under questioning? That Engel had departed with a leather satchel containing research papers and his personal notebook, which undoubtedly contained similar strings of equations for his work in quantum physics!

Restraining his joy, Kassler allowed a slow smile to spread across his lips. "I've got him."

He immediately buzzed Becker. A few seconds later, the young man hurried into his office.

"Sir?" Becker asked, winded from the effort.

Kassler waved the file in the air. "Call Stampfli immediately. I don't care what it takes to find him. I must speak with him about the Ulrich visit."

"Which visit again?" Becker's brow furrowed.

"The Ulrich farm south of Leimen. Engel's hiding out there—I know it. After that, organize a detail, no more than two cars. I don't want a transport truck announcing our arrival from two kilometers away."

"Yes, sir, of course." Becker turned on his heels and practically sprinted out Kassler's office door.

Kassler slumped back in his chair and closed his eyes in thought. He knew not to let his emotions get the better of him, but he might have just saved his career—and his neck.

• • • • • • • • •

The Ulrich farm outside Leimen, Germany
10:18 p.m.

The carpenter's bench inside the Ulrich barn was a beehive of activity. Two men carried gooseneck flares, which resembled oversized watering cans with long-necked spouts, from a rear shed. Adalbert Ulrich inspected each one and made sure the main body contained paraffin with a wick placed in the spout. Once they were approved, Pastor Leo poured a half liter of kerosene into each gooseneck flare.

"How many do you think we need?" Ulrich asked his brother-in-law.

Pastor Leo stopped pouring, lest he lose a precious drop of flammable material. "At least one gooseneck flare for every fifty meters. I was told to prepare a landing strip five hundred meters long, so"—he performed the math in his head—"ten each side, times two, equals twenty flares. That should give the cowboy pilot enough of a target."

"An American flyer is coming tonight?"

"Believe so. Don't ask me how he's getting here or from where, but the message from the Big Cheese said to expect a landing a couple of hours from now—sometime between midnight and three a.m. If the plane doesn't arrive by three o'clock, we're to move Engel. Only God in *Himmel* knows where we'd go, though."

"How's Engel bearing up?"

"I gave him the news a half hour ago. Didn't tell him much, though. Just that he's being picked up sometime tonight." Pastor Leo set the empty kerosene bottle into a wooden crate and uncapped the next one. "I certainly didn't mention anything about the shortwave transmitter hidden in this barn. Yesterday, Stampfli's lieutenant must have been tired because he barely searched in here. Fortunate for us, although I don't think he would have found the transmitter hidden behind the muck buckets. You'd have to get your hands dirty, if you know what I mean."

Ulrich lifted another liter of kerosene. "Let me help you out, or we'll never get done in time."

"Be sure to top off each flare," Pastor Leo said. "This American pilot is going to need all the help he can get to find this place."

* * * * * * * *

En Route to Dübendorf
10:22 p.m.

Gabi thought about closing her eyes to give her racing mind a rest, but the Citroën's right headlight wasn't properly aligned, which diminished coverage on the winding two-lane road leading into Dübendorf. On some of the bigger curves, Eric threatened to outdrive his headlight beams, which kept Gabi concentrating on the strip of pavement beyond the darkness.

"You're going a little fast." Her fists clenched in two balls.

"Sorry, but we have to get you there on time." Eric gripped the wheel as the boxy vehicle plowed through another curve, then she saw him relax his grasp. "Just another five kilometers to Dübendorf."

When the next road sign said "Dübendorf 2 km," the knots in Gabi's stomach twisted even tighter. On one level, she couldn't believe she was actually going through with the operation, not because she wanted to back out, but because the experience seemed so surreal. Having Eric at her side, however, reassured her that she wasn't alone. When Mr. Dulles had asked her and her father who could drive her to Dübendorf, she was pleased that her father suggested Eric for the task.

Eric looked her way as incoming headlights brightened the cab. "You don't look so good. You feeling okay?" He reached over and patted her left knee.

Gabi stroked his hand and wished she could tell him how scared she was. Or share stories about how the Gestapo tortured spies within an inch of their lives to extract all the information they could before brutally executing them. But this was Eric, and she could tell him nothing. He had no ties to her work, and that's how things would have to remain.

Instead, she forced a smile. "I've never flown in an airplane before, that's all." She glanced out the side window, staring into the dark night and hoping the emotion in her words didn't betray her.

"I wish I could go in your place." Eric's voice caught. "I don't want anything to happen to you. I don't know exactly what you're doing, but it has to be dangerous."

She turned and scooted closer, then laid her head against his shoulder, letting the automobile's motion lull her.

Gabi moved her head so she could look up to him, then began speaking hesitantly. "I'm wondering if this is the right time . . . to share how I feel . . . how much I care . . . it seems all my emotions are heightened right now." She let her voice trail.

Eric kept looking straight ahead as a truck came from the other direction. "Go ahead. I'm willing to take that chance."

She straightened up in her seat and glanced at him again, noticing his strong jaw and handsome face. He was of good stock, as they said in Switzerland, a godly, kind man, and suddenly she wondered why she'd allowed herself to be dazzled by Dieter at all. Especially when she had someone like Eric so close.

She pressed her cheek once more against his right shoulder and wished she could stay there, in the car. Feeling the warmth of Eric's body. His soft breathing as he drove. Yet she knew she couldn't pretend this was an ordinary drive on an ordinary evening, not tonight. The thought of arriving in Dübendorf shortly shifted her mind back to the present.

"Let's talk about this when I get back. But do know that I find you to be a very special person, Eric Hofstadler." Gabi straightened up in her seat and met his eyes to demonstrate her sincerity.

Eric grinned like a schoolkid. "Thank you. Yes, to be continued when we meet again. But are you sure you want to do this, Gabi?"

"Maybe, but there are things we must do for a greater good, and we just do it without thinking." Her voice wasn't more than a whisper. "It's like when you dove into the Rhine to try to save that Jewish family. When it mattered most, you did the right thing."

"Jumping off a bridge was different, Gabi. There was no one else who could help . . ."

The Citroën passed a sign announcing their arrival in Dübendorf, and Eric slowed to 25 kilometers an hour. He steered the French car into the tidy town center located to the west and north of the military airfield and passed a whitewashed Reformation-era church and steeple. A left-hand turn took them into Dübendorf's commercial district, where darkened shops hid amongst vaulted arcades fronting a generous boulevard. Atop the covered shopping promenades were sandstone buildings that housed flats accentuated with decorative ironwork and flower boxes filled with flowing geraniums.

"I feel the same way about this mission," she said. "Mr. Dulles said I was the right person at the right time, and I'm confident in God's protection." She squeezed his arm. "Besides, if you were in my position, you'd do the same. I know you would."

Dear, sweet Eric. For the first time, she was thankful that he was a simple farmer who had nothing to hide—and would be waiting for her return.

• • • • • • • •

Dübendorf Train Station
10:25 p.m.

Bill Palmer regarded his U.S. Army Air Corps chronometer watch. "We made good time," he said as Ernie Mueller swung the Peugeot into the train station parking lot and extinguished the engine.

"Yeah, too bad you couldn't sleep," Ernie said. "I'm sure you could have used some rest."

"No way I was getting in forty winks—not tonight," Bill replied.

Ernie flipped off the headlamps, revealing a clear evening lit by a nearly full moon. "I told Gabi we'd meet at the train station since we can't risk a rendezvous in a public place like a restaurant."

"Mind if I stretch my legs a bit?"

"I'll join you. I could use some blood circulation myself."

Bill stepped out of the car and marveled how much warmer the Swiss Lowlands were compared to the Alps. It had to be close to 70 degrees on this warm, moist evening. He windmilled his arms to loosen up and was performing a set of knee bends when a powder blue Citroën carefully swung into the parking lot, still managing to kick up some dust.

Ernie greeted his daughter with a kiss, but formal introductions weren't necessary.

"Bill, you remember Gabi from the First of August celebration in Davos."

"I certainly do." Bill doffed his Eighth Air Force cap and shook hands with Gabi, who even in this low light still appeared to be a looker.

"And a good friend of ours, Eric Hofstadler, who's still learning English."

"You have to watch out for this one." Bill laughed. "I think he understands more than he's letting on, especially when you're talking about Gabi. I made a joke that Eric better keep an eye on Gabi with all the American pilots around . . ."

A dull rumbling in the distance grew with intensity as the source drew closer.

"What's that sound?" Gabi asked, and all froze.

Bill cupped an ear toward the propeller whine coming from the west. "I know those engines anywhere. That's a—"

An American B-17 bomber roared past, not 200 feet overhead, drowning out his voice. The bomber's tail was adorned with an equilateral white triangle and a black "C" painted in the center of the triangle. The wings dipped from side to side as smoke billowed out of the No. 3 and 4 engines.

"She's in trouble," Bill said. "Must have taken a hit over Germany. C'mon, guys, you're almost there." He didn't take his eyes off the stricken plane until it dipped below the tree line on its final approach into the Dübendorf military airfield.

"One of those guys can have my bed in Davos." Seeing the wobbly American bomber reminded Bill that he was back in the game. The war was still on, and there was a mission with his name written on the chalkboard.

He clasped his hands. "So what's the plan? We certainly can't fly that busted B-17 into Germany."

Ernie Mueller looked toward his daughter. "Mr. Dulles put you in charge of the mission tonight."

Gabi straightened her shoulders. "He did, and he said I could enlist your help with, ah, liberating a plane. Are you okay with that?"

Ernie translated for Eric, and they both nodded.

"Good." Gabi, dressed in khaki pants and matching jacket, caught Bill's eye first. "Here's a change of clothes," she said, handing him a leather satchel. "I don't think a U.S. military uniform is a good idea, not tonight. Once you get changed, we'll see if the Swiss Air Force has their guard up."

29

Bill Palmer hunched behind the bramble bushes, just meters behind a chain-link fence—topped with two strands of barbed wire—that marked the perimeter of the Dübendorf military airfield. He, along with Gabi and Ernie Mueller and Eric Hofstadler, had chosen to hide in the foliated overgrowth on the south side of the quadrilateral-shaped Dübendorf airfield, where the main runway ran east to west. The village of Dübendorf lay beyond the northwest corner.

From their concealed position, Bill could see the crippled B-17, with wisps of white and black smoke still rising from its engine cowlings, parked several hundred yards away at the east end of the military base. Ernie had told him on the drive from Davos that the Dübendorf airfield was considered the birthplace of the Swiss Air Force with the establishment of a *Schweizer Fliegertruppe* in 1914. Charged with policing neutral Swiss airspace from constant Allied and Axis intrusions, it looked like Swiss Me-109 fighters had escorted another banged-up American bomber to Swiss soil.

The B-17's final resting point was at the end of six rows of Flying Fortresses, B-24 Liberators, and British Lancasters positioned nose-to-tail with a precision that typified the Swiss desire for orderliness. Ten American crew members stood at attention under the floodlights' glare while Swiss military personnel rummaged through the grounded plane.

"Velcome to Sveetzerland. For you, ze vor ist over," Bill said, imitating his captor's Swiss accent that he had heard back in January. Gabi and her father exchanged glances, but neither cracked a smile because of the situation's seriousness.

"Just what we need," Gabi said. "The Swiss military on heightened alert at the same time we want to borrow one of their airplanes."

She raised a pair of binoculars and swept the airfield beyond the assemblage of American and British flying machines. "Most of the Swiss aircraft are buttoned up in the hangars"— she pointed across the airfield—"but there could be something past the B-17s and B-24s. Care to take a look?"

Bill accepted the binoculars from Gabi and peered toward the southeast corner. "Past the Allied boneyard, I see a handful of Swiss Messerschmitt 109s, but they're single-seaters like our Mustangs and Thunderbolts. They won't do—wait, I see a couple of . . . Schlepp 3603s. They're fast as greased lightning, two machine guns in the wings, and they're two-seaters. You might have to sit on someone's lap on the way back, but a Schlepp could do the trick."

Bill dropped the binoculars to his chest. "I forgot a couple of things, though. With these single-engine fighters, you couldn't assist me with the German words on the instrument panel. I don't even know the German word for fuel."

"That would be *Benzin*." Gabi adopted a teacher mode. "Just think of a Mercedes Benz—*Benzin*."

"Benzin. Okay, I think I got that. And magnetos for the ignition would be called—"

Bill's question was drowned out by the deep, steady thrum of radial engines on final approach.

"What's that?" Gabi pointed toward a slow, ponderous aircraft coming their way. A solitary landing light came on, and the pilot flattened out the silver-and-black plane for a two-point landing down the center of a grass runway. Under incandescent moonlight, a white cross against a square red background had been painted on the empennage of the *Schweizer Luftwaffe* airplane.

Bill peered through the binoculars. "Never thought I'd see a Junkers in real life."

"A what?" Gabi asked.

"It's a Junkers Ju-52—a transport plane. Made in Germany."

Ernie hid a laugh. "I don't think Bill knows it's pronounced *Yunkers*, which is the proper way to say it in German," he said, pronouncing the *Ju*-prefix to sound like *you*.

"Yunkers?" Bill said. "Back in the States, we called them 'Junkers,' because we thought they were junk. 'Iron Annie' was our other nickname. A decent enough bird, though, considering all the drag from the corrugated metal skin hanging on the fuselage and wings. Seats fourteen or sixteen, range of 1,000 kilometers. Three BMW engines top out at a speed of 265, 275 kilometers per hour. Junkers were workhorses for Lufthansa before the war, like our Douglas DC-3s back in the States. So where's she stopping?" He lifted the binoculars and tracked the Ju-52 until she came to rest next to a line of parked Swiss fighters at the main hut just to the right of their position. "Looks like big brass is aboard."

A dozen Swiss Army personnel sprinted from the operations building and formed a receiving line. A solitary officer positioned himself in front of the fuselage door—located on the port side, aft. As the first passenger exited, the receiving line stiffened and, in unison, presented arms. The attending officer offered a snappy salute to the uniformed man gingerly stepping down a four-rung ladder.

Bill squinted into the binoculars. "Lots of spit and polish. I wonder who the VIP is."

"Let me take a look." Gabi accepted the binoculars and studied the form addressing the officer on call.

The visitor was soon joined by three other passengers—all uniformed—making their way down the small ladder.

"I'm not sure—wait, I've got a profile. If I were a bettor, I'd say that's General Guisan."

"You can make him out from here? Who's he?"

"Henri Guisan is our General Eisenhower," Gabi replied. "They'll name streets after him when the war's over. General Guisan's done more to prevent the Germans from invading Switzerland than anyone else. When things looked their bleakest during the dark days of 1940, the general mobilized this country by invoking the medieval battle of Morgarten, where 1,500 Swiss peasants ambushed and defeated 5,000 Austrian knights. That happened back in 1315—way before our time."

"I'll say. So what's the general doing here?"

"Probably flew in for a meeting. Guisan's HQ is near Interlaken, and he flies around the country to keep in personal touch with his commanders. Makes sense that he'd fly in here if he had a high-level conference in Zurich."

Bill lowered his head, lost in thought. His idea could work . . .

"Got something?" Gabi asked.

He pushed up the bill of his nondescript beige cap. "I think I just figured out which plane to steal."

• • • • • • • •

Gestapo Regional Headquarters
Heidelberg, Germany
11:22 p.m.

Sturmbannführer Bruno Kassler, wearing a black leather trench coat and calf-high leather boots, stormed out of Gestapo Regional Headquarters onto Eppelheimer Strasse in a cranky mood. His eyes searched the darkness until he found Corporal Becker twenty meters away, standing next to a pair of Mercedes sedans, each flagged with swastika pennants mounted behind the headlights.

"Where have you been, Becker?" he shouted. "I was waiting ten minutes in the courtyard. Isn't that where our cars always arrive from the motor pool?" Kassler felt the steam building where his neck met his black tunic.

"I beg your indulgence, sir. Someone new in the motor pool just started the night shift and didn't know proper procedure. But we're ready to go. Except for . . ."

"Except for what?"

"The driver is unaccounted for, so I'll drive tonight." Becker moved to open the rear door to the sedan for his superior.

"Very well. You know the route?" Kassler couldn't afford an *aussichtslose Verfolgung*—wild-goose chase—on a night like this. Every minute, even at this late hour, could be the difference between capturing Engel or letting him slip away. The looming deadline to appear in Himmler's presence tomorrow night, with or without Engel, weighed heavily on Kassler's shoulders.

"I called the Leimen Polizei and got directions," Becker said. "They told me it can get tricky at night, but we'll find the Ulrich farm."

"The detail is arranged?"

"I have five men in the second car." Becker motioned to the black sedan idling behind them.

"Then let's go. Herr Engel is waiting for us."

• • • • • • • • •

Dübendorf, Switzerland
11:34 p.m.

Two hundred meters to Gabi Mueller's right, she and the others watched the Ju-52 pilots depart from the plane and enter the terminus building, where the lights inside burned brightly. The sticky evening air pressed around her, and her nerves tingled with crackling energy.

"What do you think they're doing?" she asked Bill.

Hidden behind bushes, the American pilot leaned close, even though it was doubtful any Swiss personnel were near enough to overhear him. "They're sitting down for a cup of coffee and getting briefed about the weather for the return trip," he whispered.

Gabi's eyes swept the grassy tarmac for any Swiss military patrols in the immediate vicinity. "Time to get the show on the road." She motioned to Eric, who sprang toward the cyclone fence clutching a pair of red bolt cutters that could handle the nine-gauge wire. Starting from the bottom, he clipped through link after link until he created a gap large enough for Gabi and Bill to pass through. She watched in awe as Eric sliced through the wire fencing as if he'd done it every day of his life.

Gabi regarded the Swiss soldiers who, with rifles leveled at the B-17 airmen, surrounded the American intruders a couple of hundred meters from her position. Although they were out of earshot, she worried an observant Swiss might turn in their direction.

Please don't look this way . . . Her eyes moved back to the operations hut, where she expected the Junkers pilots to return to their plane any moment. Either event would vastly complicate the plan that she and Mr. Dulles had devised that afternoon.

Eric sliced through the last link in the cyclone fencing and yanked on each side, opening a large gap.

She nodded at Bill. "You go first," she whispered.

Bill crouched and slipped through the fence, and Eric moved to Gabi, taking her hand. Even in the nighttime dimness, she could see concern in his gaze. When he moved her hand to his lips and kissed her fingertips, the gravity of the mission slammed home full force. The events of the morning—the confrontation in the villa in Weil am Rhein and the gunshot's narrow miss—still lingered, and she felt blood drain from her face. This really was the point of no return.

"Will you be okay?" Eric cupped both of her cool hands into his and rubbed them to boost circulation.

Gabi steeled herself. "Sorry . . . a lot has happened today. But I'll be fine. It's just a short trip, and then I'll be back. I promise."

Eric leaned over and gave her a light kiss on the cheek. "We'll see you in a few hours."

Her father drew close and patted her on the left shoulder. "Eric and I will be waiting here for you—and praying. You have some mighty protection behind you."

"Thanks, Papi." Gabi pursed her lips with determination as Eric yanked the cut fence aside so Gabi could scoot through on her knees. When she was through the fence, she motioned for her father to hand her the emergency radio.

Eric pulled on the fencing again so her father could pass her a heavy olive box with a pair of Bakelite headphones.

Bill intercepted the emergency radio from Ernie's hands. "Here, let me carry that." He cradled it with both arms. "That was nice of Mr. Dulles to spare one of these."

"I'm sure we'll be needing it." Gabi looked back at Eric and her father. "I love you both," she said. If she *didn't* return, she wanted Eric to at least have those words planted in his heart.

• • • • • • • • •

Gabi and Bill crouched and scuttled for the Ju-52. Gabi, with nothing in her hands, reached the rear door first. She scrambled into the cabin and extended a hand back to Bill, who, encumbered by a bulky radio, accepted her aid.

"Thanks, Gabi. Shut the door." Bill instantly switched roles from team player to pilot-in-command. He flipped on a flashlight. The Junkers was fitted with seven rows of leather seats, one seat per each side of the center aisle. He worked his way forward up the steep fuselage and into the cockpit while Gabi struggled to get the fuselage door closed. After setting the emergency radio behind him, he climbed over the cumbersome flap-setting levers and into the left seat.

The smells inside the cockpit—old leather, oil, gas, and sweat—stirred long-dormant feelings in Bill. He was a pilot again, back in his office, and it felt good to reclaim this part of his world. The first thing he noticed was that his Swiss counterpart had left his leather helmet hanging on a hook next to the captain's seat. Bill settled in and made himself comfortable.

Next, he extended his arms and grabbed the lacquered wooden control wheel, smooth to the touch. Comfortable with the arm extension, he set his feet on the rudder pedals. He recognized much of the instrument panel, although the controls and switches were written in German. The airspeed indicator, he reminded himself, was in kilometers per hour, not in knots or miles per hour like in American planes. What was the calculation? Oh, yeah. One hundred kilometers an hour was sixty-two miles per hour.

He was captain of the ship but had no time to appreciate it. He needed to get the battery switched on and get this lady ready to go. How that happened, however, would be inspired guesswork.

Using his flashlight for illumination, he first set the elevator trim about a quarter up. For the huge flaps that ran the length of the wings—which gave the Junkers its great short takeoff and landing capability—he wound down a quarter. He scanned the instrument panel for the electrical switches and followed a hunch by flicking a pair. A voltmeter flickered, and the cockpit lights came on. The earphones in the helmet next to him crackled as the ship's radio came to life. He was doing something right . . . but the rest of the cocks and spigots—what the Brits called the valves and switches back in East Anglia—looked like a plumbers' nightmare. He left them where they were.

Bill turned his attention to the engine controls on the center console. Three sets of levers controlled the throttles, mixture, and fuel cocks, he surmised, one set for each engine. If true, that simplified things a bit. Three guarded switches marked "Start"—the same word in English—looked to be for the electrical starter motors. A long lever marked *Tank* at the back of the pedestal—the fuel tank selector—had three positions for the separate fuel tanks in the right and left wings. He left it in the center *Alle* position, figuring *Alle* meant "all" and would siphon gas from each tank equally during flight.

Okay, back to basics. To start an engine, it needed fuel, ignition, and motion . . . he looked up and saw Gabi entering the cockpit.

"Sorry. I couldn't get the stupid door to close," she said. "The wind picked up."

"No problem. Sit here in the copilot's chair—duck!" Bill pushed Gabi into a hunched position and bunched himself into a ball as well.

"What's going on?" Gabi set her arms around her head.

"A truck full of soldiers just shot by. Let me see . . ." Bill peered over the cockpit coaming and immediately saw the source of consternation. A quarter of a mile away, the American airmen had scattered for the exits, and a dozen Swiss military personnel were running around, rifles raised, like a hornet's nest that had been upended.

"Looks like our Yank birdmen weren't interested in vacationing in Davos." Bill continued to peer toward the confusion around the parked B-17. "Something tells me they aren't going to get very far."

Gabi straightened up in the copilot's seat, a smile forming on her lips. "That was nice of Mr. Dulles to arrange a diversion for us, although I feel sorry for the pilots."

Bill's eyes grew wide. "You mean Mr. Dulles purposely diverted a B-17 to Dübendorf?"

"Yup. They were just waiting for a signal from my father to give us a little breathing room."

"Amazing." Bill couldn't imagine what league Mr. Dulles was playing in, but it had to be the majors.

"Not as amazing as what I'm about to tell you." Gabi looked directly at him. "Mr. Dulles asked General Guisan for a favor."

"You mean this Junkers?"

"It was the only way we could see flying into Germany, so the General offered to fly his plane here—into Dübendorf, supposedly for a quick meeting in Zürich. That's funny you had the idea to steal this Junkers when that was the plan all along."

Bill shrugged and set his right hand on the center console. "Brilliant minds think alike, I guess. Okay, it's flying time, so I'm going to need your help." The pilot applied himself to starting the right engine. He selected the right fuel cock lever and slightly opened the throttle. "This *Magnet* switch would be Magneto in English, right?"

Gabi peered over to the instrument panel. "Yes, that's correct."

"There's also this switch on the magneto panel that says *Haupt*."

"That's an old German word for *head*, but here it means 'main,' as in a main switch," Gabi said.

Bill selected the *Haupt* magneto switch. There was no time to vent the lower cylinders on the radial engines, but that was okay since not much oil would have gathered in the short time since the motors had stopped. He took a deep breath and switched on the No. 1 starter. There was an electrical whine, and the cockpit lights dimmed momentarily. Bill flicked the fuel switch . . .

A couple of bangs, and the No.1 engine on the left wing outside his window caught lustily. Exhaust smoke gathered around them. Bill reduced the engine speed with the throttle, and it idled noisily.

"Where's the fuel gauge?" Bill peered at the instrument panel. "Could this be it?" He pointed at a round gauge that said "Liter x 100." Below the heading, a numerical figure 12,6 was positioned at 11 o'clock on a timepiece, followed by markings of 12, 11, 10, 9, 8, 7, 6, 5, 4, 3, 2, 1, and 0—the 0 at 1 o'clock on a timepiece.

Gabi nodded. "That's the fuel gauge."

"Why the comma?" Bill asked.

"In Europe, we use the comma instead of the period for decimal points. Don't ask me why."

Bill studied the gauge. The needle rested firmly on the number 7 marking. "Looks like we're just over half full with around 700 liters of fuel."

"Is that enough to get us there and back?" Gabi asked.

Bill did some quick mental calculations. "Let's see. If a full fuel tank is 1,260 liters, and the plane's range is 1,000 kilometers . . ."

"Mr. Dulles said it was around 250 kilometers to the Ulrich farm, so that makes 500 kilometers round trip."

Bill closed his eyes and worked the math in his head. "I'm figuring we're good for 600 kilometers in the air, but that doesn't leave much reserve in case—"

"Soldiers are running toward us!" Gabi pointed over Bill's shoulder toward the operations hut.

"Obviously, they didn't get the word from General Guisan." Bill hurriedly repeated the same start-up sequence for the No. 3 engine, which roared to life and belched smoke from the exhaust pipes.

"Two are on a motorbike—coming right for us." Gabi strained to see beyond the view outside Bill's window.

"I have one more engine to start up." The Ju-52's No. 2 engine was mounted in front of the fuselage.

"But they'll be here any second!"

They couldn't wait any longer. Bill reached over to the center console and pushed forward on the throttles of the two engines. The Junkers shook and vibrated from the strain—but didn't budge.

"The chocks!" The fact that there were wooden chocks in front of the main wheels didn't surprise him since the Junkers didn't have a parking brake. He would have moved the chocks aside during a visual inspection, but there'd been no time for that—

The motorcycle's arrival on his left with two Swiss soldiers interrupted his thoughts. The soldier in the sidecar jumped out and shouldered his carbine—

Bill jammed the throttles to the firewall—full power—and the wing-mounted engines instantly responded to a fever pitch. The ship shook to the last rivet, then bounded over the wooden chocks and shot out like a rubber band from a kid's hand.

"Hang on!" The Ju-52 bounded through the grassy tarmac while Bill worked the compressed air footbrakes—and narrowly missed slicing a parked Me-109 fighter with his left wing. He turned sharply to the right and into the open field, where he finally had time to throttle down the engines and regain control of the aircraft.

"Like riding a bustin' bronco at the state fair!" Bill brought the Junkers to a stop and searched the airfield for the windsock. He found the red-and-white-striped conical tube up ahead and across the runway, and by its droopy angle pointing east, Bill figured on a light westerly or northwesterly wind. "Good, we're taking off in the right direction," he said. "We have to get the middle engine going, but that can happen when you windmill—"

"Wait! Another motorbike." Gabi peered out her window. Two shots rang out, and one struck the fuselage behind the cockpit.

"We're outta here!" Bill shoved the two throttles to their stops, and the Junkers fishtailed twice before he regained control. He aimed the aircraft for a departure to the west—and into the prevailing wind. The lumbering transport plane gained speed, and the pair of fully revved engines ate up runway.

At eighty kilometers per hour, the center prop started windmilling. Bill opened the center fuel cock, and within seconds, the middle engine roared to life in front of the windscreen. Bill pushed slightly forward on the control column to raise the tail wheel from the ground. The ship's speed steadily increased to one hundred kilometers per hour, which he figured was the "decision speed." Bill pulled the control column back gently. In just a few more moments, they'd be airborne—

"The fence!" Gabi screamed.

The fence? There should be more runway . . . The blood

drained from Bill's face as he suddenly realized that they must have taken a catty-corner departure *across* the grassy military airfield. They were running out of real estate. He regarded his airspeed gauge. They were past one hundred kilometers per hour, which should be enough to break the bonds of gravity.

"C'mon, c'mon," Bill said, his neck muscles taut as a bowstring. The engines whined at full RPMs as the fencing loomed . . . at the last moment, the Junkers lifted. The tri-motor plane cleared the boundary fence but remained desperately low to the ground.

Flight school training kicked in. He resisted the urge to climb until their speed built up and instead focused on maintaining a level course. As the airspeed nudged 110 kilometers per hour, Bill saw something up ahead that caused his neck muscles to flinch. Etched against a moonlit sky, they were careening directly into dimly lit Dübendorf. Bill couldn't risk gaining more altitude at this moment—or he would plant the nose of the Iron Annie into the middle of the town square. He held the steering wheel steady and let the Ju-52 zoom right through Dübendorf's main street, so close to the buildings that they were eye-level with the penthouse apartments in the buildings above the shops.

"The church!" Gabi pressed against the back of her seat.

"I see it," Bill said through clenched teeth. A medieval church and its steeple, fully five stories tall, anchored the end of the downtown district. They had driven by the church an hour earlier, but this time around, Bill didn't have enough airspeed to risk swinging right or left of the steeple—

"We won't make it!" Gabi squeezed the armrests.

"Hang on!" Bill kept the nose down, eased back on the control column ever so slightly to squeeze a little more altitude without losing airspeed, then wound down another quarter of flap. The Junkers bounded up thirty more feet of elevation, just avoiding the cross atop the church's statuesque steeple.

"That was close!" Gabi exhaled.

The landscape quickly gave away to pastureland, and Bill breathed for the first time in a minute. He watched the airspeed dial slowly rise to 130 kph . . . 145 kph, allowing him to wind in the flaps and turn her north. Bill decided to stay low in case a flight duty officer back at the Dübendorf airfield scrambled a Swiss fighter to chase him.

Bill's intuition proved correct. Within five minutes, a bright tracer flew past their cockpit, leaving a reddish flare afterglow.

"What's that?" Gabi pointed at the tracer leaving its mark.

"We have company." Bill looked to his left—and was startled to see an ME-109 so close that he could practically pass a cup of sugar to the other pilot.

The Swiss Air Force airman, his youthful face illuminated by his instrument panel, held up a radio microphone and mimicked a conversation.

"He wants to talk to us," Bill said. "No doubt to get us to turn around. You see the leather helmet hooked on your chair? Put it on like this—" He slipped on his leather helmet and listened in.

". . . and our Gracious Benefactor sends you his best regards and has asked me to escort you on this lovely evening," the voice said in excellent schoolboy English. "Do you copy, Roger?"

Bill's face registered surprise—not from the coded phrases but from the offer to help. He keyed his microphone. "Roger, hear you loud and clear."

"How much fuel do you have for tonight's spin around the park?" the Swiss pilot asked.

Bill scanned the fuel gauge, where the needle rested midway between the 6 and the 7. "Around 650 liters. A bit more than half a tank."

"You should have enough fuel," his aviator colleague said. "Our Gracious Benefactor had asked for more petrol, but there was a problem getting the fuel truck to the plane on time. He sends his regrets."

Easy for the Swiss pilot to say that he'll have enough fuel. Still, a thoughtful gesture by General Guisan. "Tell the Gen— Gracious Benefactor—thank you and not to worry. After we collect some Edelweiss, I'll bring his nice plane home in one piece. You'll escort us back into Dübendorf upon our return, right?"

The transmission turned to static, and Bill never received an answer.

He hoped that wasn't an omen.

30

Outside Leimen, Germany
Friday, August 4, 1944
12:50 a.m.

"I'm losing my patience, Becker!" Sturmbannführer Bruno Kassler slammed the leather bench seat with his left fist. "We've been driving around in circles for nearly an hour! Can't you find this place?" Kassler cursed under his breath.

"The Leimen Polizei fouled up, sir. According to their map, the Ulrich farm has to be on Landstrasse, somewhere around here." The corporal steered the Mercedes sedan along a narrow dirt lane flanked by boxwood hedges that hadn't been trimmed since Nazi columns marched on the Champs-Élysées.

"Turn into this driveway!"

Becker did as he was told, and the two-car caravan swung into a gravel driveway that led to a weather-beaten farmhouse with an attached barn. The corporal slowed the Mercedes to a crawl and extinguished the headlamps. On this cloudless night, bright moonshine lit the farmstead, but inside the main house not a single incandescent light or kerosene lamp shown.

"I'll go and see if anyone is home, sir." Becker killed the engine and set the parking brake.

"No, this time I'll take care of it." Kassler didn't wait for the corporal to open the car door. He charged out of the Mercedes and marched in double-time to the front porch.

Becker hustled after his commanding officer, and the five soldiers in the second Mercedes scurried to catch up.

Kassler pounded on a wooden door, as if each blow of his gloved fist would release the frustration building within his veins. How many fruitless roads had they followed in the last hour? Too many. If he didn't bring in Engel tonight, he might as well sign his own death warrant. Himmler's reputation for executing irritants who failed to perform stretched from Berlin to Baden-Wurtemburg.

A minute later, a disheveled man in his sixties answered the door dressed in a soiled nightshirt. Gray stubble covered his gaunt face. After rubbing sleep from his eyes, his mouth gaped when he noted the black leather trench coat of a Gestapo chief and the half-dozen soldiers circled behind him.

"What's the matter with you?" Kassler bellowed. "Lost your tongue?"

"Sir, I . . . was asleep . . . What—"

"I don't have time for this!" Kassler unsheathed his Luger pistol. "I must find the Ulrich farm immediately. You know the Ulriches?"

The old farmer nodded.

"Then where can I find them?"

"Simple. Go . . . go . . . go . . . out the driveway, take a left, and stay on this road for two . . . two . . . two-and-a-half kilometers." The man hugged his arms tight to his chest to stay warm. "You . . . you will see a driveway on your left . . . and a wooden sign posted on a tree. The sign says *Bethanien Haus*. The main farmhouse is 200 meters back."

Kassler turned on his heels. Anger seethed through his veins with every beat of his heart. "Did you hear that, Becker? We passed the Ulrich farm a half hour ago!"

The corporal held up his hands. "Sir, it's dark, and I didn't know about this sign."

"*Los jetzt!* We're losing time!" Kassler waved Becker and the soldiers back to the cars.

Kassler paused at the car's door. Then he turned and directed his attention back to the quivering farmer standing in the doorway. "If it turns out that you gave me the wrong directions"— he waved his Luger—"I will return and personally shoot you between the eyes." Kassler returned the pistol to his leather holster and patted his sidearm for emphasis.

And it would serve the peasant right. No one would betray him and live.

* * * * * * * *

Bill Palmer pointed the flashlight at the U.S. Army Air Corps Aeronautical Chart resting in his lap. Gabi had handed him the official U.S. air map for Southern Germany and Switzerland shortly after their chatty Swiss fighter escort had led them to the German border.

Mr. Dulles had used a ruler and pencil to indicate an air route to the Ulrich farm. He'd also provided a sheet of written directions and notes. To fly precisely, Bill was instructed to use the radio beacon at Basel. From Dübendorf, it was 120 kilometers to the beacon intercept point east of Strasbourg. From there, another 130 kilometers to the landing field outside of Heidelberg, but a note in the margin said this was an estimate. From his reading of the aeronautical chart, he was to track northwest toward Strasbourg on a heading of 200° magnetic, then turn right and fly north-northeast at 020° until they visually picked up a flare-lit strip south of Leimen. A hit-or-miss effort to be sure, since the Germans turned off their radio beacons at night to avoid helping Allied bombers.

"We're officially over Germany. See the Rhine River to my left?" Bill pointed out his window, and Gabi half stood out of her seat to grab a view. She was dressed in khaki dungarees and flight jacket to ward off the chill inside the unpressurized cabin.

"Pretty how the moon reflects off the river," she ventured.

Bill noticed Gabi shiver and hug her arms tight to her. From the look on her face, the shivering was as much from worry about their mission as from the coolness in the cockpit. "That's one of the advantages of being in the air—the great views," he said. "But I sure wouldn't mind a few clouds up here. I feel as if we have a bull's-eye painted on the fuselage."

Bill rechecked his instrument panel and reduced the manifold pressure for each engine as they leveled out at 1,800 meters above sea level, close to the Junkers' optimal altitude of 1,900 meters.

"Soon we can descend to 1,300 meters. That'll make our profile harder to pick out of the sky. Let's see that this mission *doesn't* include target practice for German anti-aircraft crews."

After sweeping past the church in Dübendorf, Bill had clicked the stopwatch button on his chronometer wristwatch. At an economy cruising speed of 200 kilometers per hour, it should take them forty minutes to reach the first beacon point outside of Strasbourg. From there, he figured another forty-three minutes to the landing strip.

"Okay, Gabi. Time to go to work." He took his left hand off the control yoke and pointed over his right shoulder. "Behind you, overhead, is a folding crank handle. To make sure we're on the correct heading, we have to set the frequency to the radio beacon at Basel. On my direction, turn that handle. Stand by—"

Bill held up his right hand and listened intently to the faint Morse code signals coming through his helmet earphones . . . *da dit dit dit*. . . . that was the letter B . . . followed by *da dit*, which was the letter N. Put them together, and you had the two-letter designation for the Basel Nord beacon—BN.

"Now slowly turn the handle."

Gabi did as she was told and turned the handle to the right.

"Nope . . . getting fainter. Try the other way."

Gabi turned the folding crank handle slightly to the left.

"Good. Getting stronger . . . more . . . more . . . back a bit—stop!" When the Morse code signals reached full volume, Bill checked the relative bearing on the dial. They were still tracking 200° on the BN beacon from Basel, but would wind-age blow them off course? Bill performed a radio compass check and saw that they were drifting right. He steered the Junkers ten degrees left.

"Are we okay?" Gabi returned to her seat.

"We're doing fine." Bill nodded. "Don't want to end up in Stuttgart, that's all."

The minutes ticked by without incident. After another glance at his chronometer, Bill turned to Gabi. "We're coming up to the 020° heading that will direct us toward the farm outside Heidelberg. Can you slowly crank the handle to the left?"

Bill swung the plane into a right-hand turn that set them on a heading of 020° magnetic. Then he restarted his stopwatch for the forty-three-minute stretch to the Ulrich landing strip. He strained to listen, but he could hardly make out the beacon on his earphones.

"We're too low to get the signal," he called out. "I'm going to climb." When he eased the Junkers past 1,800 meters, the signal came in strong again. "Okay, to the left a bit . . . left more . . . stop!"

"How will we find the Ulrich landing strip?" Gabi asked.

Bill straightened in his seat. "I'm afraid we're going back to the days of the barnstormers. This radio compass will steer us in the right direction, but it will be up to us to find the actual landing strip. Could be the proverbial needle in a haystack, unless they light it up well."

"I know that some type of spotter flares will be used." Gabi shrugged. "At least, that's what Mr. Dulles told me. When do we start looking?"

"According to the chronometer, I'd say thirty-five minutes from now."

Those flares better be visible right on the dot, Bill thought. They didn't have the fuel to futz around in the air.

• • • • • • • •

Kassler breathed a sigh of relief as the two black Mercedes sedans inched up the dirt driveway without headlights. Spotting something, Becker stopped their car. He stepped out and inspected a homemade wooden sign fastened to a leafy oak. Becker's flashlight revealed the etched words *Bethanien Haus*.

Kassler lightly punched the gloved fist of his right hand into the palm of his left. "We found him—and Engel is ours."

"What do you suggest from here, sir?" Becker switched off the flashlight as the Gestapo detail alighted from their four-door sedan.

"Leave the cars here. We'll spread out, cover the house, and make the arrest." Kassler unbuttoned his leather holster. "Remember, Engel must be taken alive at all costs."

The Sturmbannführer guided the group along a dirt road that eventually led to a circular driveway. The farmhouse, he noticed, was lit up like a Christmas tree. Every lamp in the house had to be turned on, and a floodlight illuminated the grassy patch between the farmhouse and the barn. The brightness obscured his view of the fields beyond the buildings. Kassler hand-directed the troupe to proceed behind the foliage, concealing themselves from view. They followed his directions silently, without question.

Kassler neared the house, shielding his eyes from the brightness, then stopped. Was he seeing what he thought he saw? He turned to Becker and pointed toward a grassy field beyond the main house.

The corporal stepped out from behind a tree and squinted into the distance. "Looks like a bunch of watering cans burning oil—and some sort of bonfire. I'm not sure what to make—"

"Let me fill in the blanks for you, Becker. That's a signal fire, and those burning flares are lining a landing strip! A plane is flying in tonight to spirit Engel away." Kassler regarded the faces of the men around him—and saw signs of disbelief, anger. No one could believe the audacity of the escape attempt. Not in the middle of wartime Germany!

"What's your plan of action, sir?" Becker's eyes narrowed.

"We'll circle around and take positions behind the house. On my 'go,' we'll storm the front door and take Engel by surprise, then round up everyone!"

Energy surged through Kassler's limbs. Not only would he capture Engel, but he'd also personally smash an underground spy ring that no doubt reached its tentacles deep into Switzerland.

And his reward would be great.

• • • • • • • • •

According to his stopwatch, Bill expected the Ulrich field to show up any minute. As the seconds ticked by, though, sweat beaded on his brow. The last bearing from the weak BN beacon had been barely audible. What if they had been blown off course—or had already passed the makeshift landing strip? Their fuel margin was already tight. Extra minutes in the air could prove costly.

The Junkers' three engines droned as he and Gabi searched the dark landscape. "Perhaps I should circle—"

"I see it!" Gabi leapt in her seat. "To the right—over there!"

Bill dipped the right wing, and a landing strip—unevenly lined with small dots of flame but punctuated with a generous fireball—loomed into view beyond a patch of woodlands.

"We're going in." Bill banked the Junkers to the right and reduced airspeed. Normally, he would have flown over an improvised strip before attempting touchdown, but tonight's circumstances didn't allow that luxury. Bill decided to land *toward* the bonfire or whatever that fireball was.

When the Junkers dropped down to 300 meters, he lined up his final approach. He maintained 100 kilometers per hour and set the flaps fully down. The muscles in Bill's stomach tightened. He knew the Ju-52 was designed for short landings, but he had only one chance to get it right. He squinted his eyes to get a better view, hoping to spot the ground.

"Strap in tight!"

Gabi pulled the harness across her lap and shoulders.

Bill concentrated on the smoky lights. He kept the ship on an imaginary center line and steady glide path angle. The Junkers reacted well to his constant corrections on the throttles and control column. He relaxed his feet on the rudders and only looked down into the cockpit to check his airspeed. As they came over the end of the field, he closed the throttles, and the constant thrumming of the past ninety minutes died to a whisper.

Don't float, he told himself as the field rose up beneath them. He deliberately touched the main wheels down close to the beginning of the lighted strip and raised the flaps to "load up" the airplane and significantly reduce the landing rollout. As the tail wheel settled, the heavy transport plane lumbered, bounced, and lurched along the field midway between the line of flare pots. The brakes squealed and hissed from compressed air.

Safely on the ground, in control, Bill taxied toward the bonfire, where a half-dozen men and one woman waved their hats in appreciation.

"Listen, we have to make this as fast as possible." Bill tromped on the foot brakes and brought the aircraft to a full stop, then released the right brake and goosed the right engine's throttle to swing the Junkers 180 degrees into position for an immediate getaway. "Hurry. I'll keep the engines running. You grab Engel, then off we go."

Gabi unbuckled her harness and seat belt. "This should only take a minute."

"I'll be counting the seconds."

* * * * * * * *

Gabi rushed past the seven rows of leather seats and swung open the passenger door. To save precious seconds, she left the four-rung ladder stowed and jumped to the ground, then raced toward the bonfire.

A half-dozen men scurried in her direction.

Gabi paused before them, catching her breath. "Which one is Joseph?" she gasped.

A skinny man with knots of gray hair approached her out of the darkness. "Fräulein, allow me to introduce myself. My name is Pastor Leo Keller, and this is Joseph Engel."

A gangly young man extended his right hand. "Joseph Engel. I can't tell you what a—"

"My pleasure too, but listen, we'll talk once we're in the air. We have to get over the Swiss border before dawn. One quick goodbye."

Joseph set down his satchel and wrapped both arms around Pastor Leo in a bear hug, then quickly embraced Adalbert and his wife, Trudi.

Gabi grabbed Joseph's arm. "Come on . . . we don't have a minute to spare—"

Out of the corner of her eye, she detected movement in the cornfields beyond the flare line. "We better make a run for it—now!"

Joseph threw his satchel over his shoulder, and he and Gabi set off for the Junkers, less than one hundred meters away.

"Run!" cried another voice.

Gabi glanced back and gasped as she watched a German soldier ramming a rifle butt between Pastor Leo's shoulder blades. He screamed in pain and crumbled to the ground. The other men held their arms high as the Gestapo detail surrounded them with raised rifles.

Joseph paused.

"Run as fast as you can, and don't look back!" Gabi shoved him hard. They *had* to get on that plane . . .

The pair set off as if they were jumping out of the sprinters' blocks at the Olympic Games. Joseph reached the Junkers first, slung in his satchel, and hauled himself inside.

Gabi pumped her arms for the final dash to the finish line. She had just another twenty meters to go when arms wrapped around her waist, and her body slammed to the dirt. Gabi's chin knocked the ground, causing her head to snap back. Pain shot through her chest. She struggled to rise. Struggled to breathe.

"Get up!" ordered a German voice.

Gasping for air, Gabi brought herself to her knees. She turned and attempted to focus on the man before her. Narrow eyes spoke of unrequited anger. A scrunched mouth that revealed gritted teeth. And then she saw it . . . the black trench coat—*Gestapo*!

The Gestapo chief grabbed her by the scruff of her neck. Gabi shrieked as he tightened his grasp. "To the plane!" He seized her left wrist, lifting and twisting until she complied.

Joseph stood in the open doorway, transfixed like a stone monument. The Junkers' engines suddenly increased pitch, and the plane settled against the brakes.

Gabi kicked the German's shins, diverting his attention momentarily. "Go, Joseph! Go without me!"

"Halt!" The voice sounded in her ear. Then she felt the cold metal of the pistol against her head. "Make one move," the Gestapo chief called to Joseph, "and she's dead."

Then, just as quickly as she was captured, Gabi felt herself free. She turned to see the Gestapo chief crashing to the ground. Another taller German officer lifted his fist, then cracked it flush against the right temple of his trench-coated leader. If Gabi hadn't seen it for herself, she would have never believed it.

"Run, Fräulein!" yelled the younger Gestapo officer as he pinned his superior to the ground. The Gestapo in the black trench coat, after a moment of disorientation, shook off the blow and landed his own right fist. The older one pawed for his pistol somewhere in the dirt.

Gabi scampered for the Junkers as the two Gestapo officers rolled in the grass. Joseph braced himself in the door, waving his arms at her in encouragement. She dove for the doorway, landing on the edge, half inside, half dangling outside. Joseph grabbed her jacket and left arm and dragged her inside.

"Close the door!" Gabi shouted.

Joseph swiveled the door shut, but failed to latch it.

"Here, let me—" Gabi scrambled to her feet and reached around Joseph for the handle. She shoved the door open about a foot, slammed it shut, and swung the handle to *ZU* with a resounding click. Instantly, the Junkers surged ahead, throwing her and Joseph to the floor.

She lay there, drawing in breath after breath as the transport plane lurched along the bumpy field toward the ebony sky.

• • • • • • • • •

Bill pushed the three engines to maximum throttle. If he had his druthers—or more time—he would've taxied to the other end of the field and swung the plane around for a southeasterly takeoff into the wind. Instead, he was forced to take off *with* a northwesterly tailwind, meaning the Ju-52 would need a longer runway and fifteen to twenty more kph to reach takeoff speed.

With a deafening roar, the groundspeed rose rapidly. He reached over to wind the flaps, which he had set at 1/4, down even further. As the Junkers thundered through the bumpy alfalfa field, the improvised flare path came to an end—and the field made a dogleg right! A hard right rudder slewed the Ju-52 to the right—just missing a chestnut tree and causing the left wheel to lift off the ground. They teetered several seconds, but Bill didn't reduce his takeoff speed. He couldn't if they wanted any chance of getting out of Germany.

Trees ahead! Bill quickly glanced at his groundspeed gauge, which had inched past ninety kph . . . too slow, but it was now or never . . .

He willed her off the ground, hoping the extra flap would help. The Junkers floated for a second, then settled hard, bouncing higher—airborne for about three seconds—then hit once more.

C'mon, c'mon.

Finally, the trimotor plane left the *terra firma*, climbing to one hundred meters—just enough to clear the oak trees lining the perimeter of the Ulrich farmstead. As he teased her up, Bill rowed through the treetops while turning to a heading of 200°, which he calculated would track them south directly toward the Dübendorf airfield.

A flushed Gabi, breathing hard, stepped inside the cockpit. "Nice work," she gasped.

"And nice work yourself," Bill replied, noticing Joseph standing just beyond Gabi. "Was I seeing things, or did one Gestapo officer fight off another so you could escape?"

"I'm not sure what happened out there. I'm still shaking."

She turned toward their new passenger. "Excuse me, do you speak English, Herr Engel?" she queried in High German.

"Not learn," he replied in English.

"Never mind," she continued in German. "I would like to introduce you to our pilot, Captain Bill Palmer with the United States of America Army Air Corps."

The German made a step closer in the cramped cockpit, and Bill momentarily diverted his eyes from the instrument panel and shook the proffered hand. "Excuse me for being abrupt, but I want the two of you to be on the lookout for German fighters. I'm sure we set off a three-alarm fire back there."

Gabi translated for Joseph's benefit.

"But our biggest concern is this—" Bill tapped his right index finger on the fuel gauge, where the needle vibrated next to the numeral 3, signifying around 300 liters of fuel. "We're just under a quarter of a tank since I burned extra gas while we were on the ground. The longer takeoff siphoned off more fuel too."

Gabi sat down in the copilot's seat. "Do we have enough petrol to make it back to Switzerland?"

Bill shrugged. "You seem to be a religious person. I'd start praying. A lot."

* * * * * * * *

As the Junkers Ju-52 slipped southward in the moonlit sky, Kassler's rage overwhelmed him. He turned the Luger around in his hand and took a step toward Becker, who was on his knees with his hands upraised.

"It was you! You were the treasonous vermin!" Kassler raised his pistol and struck Becker in the head once, then twice as he pistol-whipped the young corporal.

"I should shoot you now, but the Interrogation Room would be more appropriate—to make you suffer." Kassler took a deep breath as he fought for control. "Wait. I have a better idea. I will personally deliver you to the Reichsführer's office. I hear that Himmler has perfected the art of skin-peeling after finding the right technique with the Auschwitz prisoners. Get up and march!"

Kassler, with gun drawn, walked behind Becker toward the dying embers of the bonfire. Five underground members stood with their hands on their heads under the guard of the Gestapo contingent. As the men locked eyes with Becker, Kassler realized this personal aide had been in cahoots with these farmers all along. He would not wait for Himmler—nor could he wait.

"Halt!" Kassler walked around Becker, who froze in his step. "Everybody—kneel on the ground! Right here!"

With hands raised, Pastor Leo and the others approached Becker, and the six fell to their knees.

"How did you all work together?" Kassler demanded.

No one said a word.

"Were you responsible for intercepting Engel?"

Again, Kassler was greeted with silence.

"What's the matter, Becker? You lost your tongue?"

The corporal cleared his throat, and once more his Adam's apple bobbled. "Once I talk, you'll shoot me. I saw you do this a hundred—"

Kassler's nostrils flared in anger. "Do not address me in that manner!" He approached the kneeling Becker until he stood two meters away and pointed his Luger directly into the corporal's face. "My instincts tell me that I should kick your scrawny butt all the way to Heidelberg and wring every last bit of information out of you before putting you on a train to Berlin, but I don't care. You betrayed me, and the sentence I impose upon you is death. The rest of you"—the Gestapo chief waved his gun at Pastor Leo, his brother, sister-in-law and the others—"are next."

Kassler squared his shoulders and steadied his pistol to eye level. *"Auf Wiedersehen*, Corporal Becker. *Eins*—" Kassler's hand remained rock still.

"Zwei."

The clicking sound of a half-dozen bolt-action rifles diverted Kassler's attention momentarily. His mouth opened in surprise as he turned and saw the guns of the other Gestapo soldiers turned on him. And as he glanced at their faces, he knew they were not Gestapo at all . . .

Then several volleys shattered the tension.

* * * * * * * * *

Sturmbannführer Bruno Kassler, his skull and upper torso fractured by copper-jacketed projectiles, fell backward into the field, arms akimbo. A gusher of blood ran down his face, and starburst-like entrance wounds filled his black trench coat.

Becker hustled over, beating his friends from the underground church—the ones he recruited that evening to be part of his Gestapo detail—to see what happened. "He's dead—look at the eyes."

Pastor Leo worked his way past the scrum and reached for Kassler's left wrist. He pressed on the radial artery for thirty seconds before letting the limp arm fall to the ground.

"Brother Benjamin is right. It's Judgment Day for this monster."

31

Remember, the plane doesn't know it's dark outside.

Bill Palmer spun the pilot's proverb around in his mind like the ever-spinning propellers as he concentrated on piloting the Junkers Ju-52 through the black void beyond the Plexiglas windscreen. He stifled a yawn, knowing he would need all his faculties to return them safely to the ground—wherever that happened to be.

What kept him alert was the amount of fuel—or lack thereof—remaining in the plane's wing tanks. Fuel gauges were notoriously unreliable, but that thought did little to assuage Bill's concern with the fuel needle's steady march toward 0—or 0 x 100 liters. Time to make contingency plans.

"What did Mr. Dulles say about the radio?" Bill asked.

Gabi glanced over at the bulky radio box that she had set down next to the center console. "He said that it has a special frequency to reach him directly. The closer we are to Switzerland, the more likely we can establish radio contact. I couldn't drum them up ten minutes ago. How much longer do we have?"

"A good hour to touchdown in Dübendorf. We should see the Rhine in forty-five minutes if the prevailing winds hold." Bill looked over his right shoulder at Joseph Engel, who stood in the cockpit doorway with a pensive look on his face. Bill knew their German passenger would really have something to worry about if he realized they had no more than forty-five minutes of fuel, according to his reckoning. No way they would be landing the Iron Annie in Dübendorf today. Bill was shooting for any Swiss farm field south of the Rhine.

They told him in flight school that flying was the second greatest thrill known to mankind—and a safe landing was the first. Despite the chill in the cockpit, Bill felt damp patches forming under his armpits as he scanned the instrument panel one more time. The altimeter hovered around 1,500 meters—close to 5,000 feet off the deck. They needed the elevation since the Schwarzwald—the famous Black Forest—was coming up.

He glanced out the windows again, worried that the Krauts would unleash a fighter in their direction. Once a Focke-Wulf 190 had him in his reflector gun sights, they had bought the farm. Maneuverability was not the Ju-52's strong suit.

Bill was surprised that bogeys weren't already in the air since the Gestapo was part of the welcoming party back at that farmhouse. Surely someone in charge had radioed a nearby aerodrome and sent a fighter in pursuit. Maybe the rumors that Goering's *Luftwaffe* was a shell of itself—a paper tiger—were true. Maybe the Krauts didn't *have* a plane to send after them since the Nazis had their hands full on two fronts—and were losing on both.

Suddenly, a crimson flash burst several hundred yards in front of the plane, followed by the thud of its report. Then another . . . and another . . . like a sea of cherry-red umbrellas popping open from a sudden spring shower. The Junkers bounced and wallowed in the turbulence for several moments as more vivid explosions erupted in their vicinity. They were in a turkey shoot, and they were the turkey!

"What's happening?" Gabi hung on tighter as the Ju-52 shuddered from the shock waves.

Bill had experienced dozens of aerial attacks in the past. "An anti-aircraft battery is hammering us with flak!" Eerie whumping sounds carried over the engines' droning, and shards of razor-sharp shrapnel pinged off the corrugated aluminum skin like golf-ball-sized hail striking a car roof. Bill fought to control the sudden changes of pitch and yaw.

"They must have spotted the Swiss cross in the moonlight!" Bill pushed the ship down, then steered right to avoid the next flak barrage and make their profile more difficult to detect.

Gabi braced herself in the copilot's seat, but Joseph— standing in the cockpit doorway—fell in a heap from a sudden lurch and scrambled into a passenger seat. The ship shuddered as Bill continued to bank hard right. When he felt certain they were out of range, he leveled out the Junkers and resumed their original course heading.

Bill stared through the Plexiglas toward the barely visible southern horizon and wondered how much precious fuel the escape dive had burned up. That was the last thing they needed.

"Steady as she goes," he said, hoping his matter-of-fact voice would quell any panic inside the cockpit. "We should be fine—"

Another round of flak popped up around the aircraft like red Christmas lights, and a couple of loud bangs jostled the Junkers. This time when Bill took evasive action, the steering felt heavy and unresponsive.

"Look—the engine," Gabi shouted. "Fire!"

Bill couldn't see much more than the radial cowling and windmilling prop of No. 3 engine from his left seat. He peered at his instrument panel to make some sense—and sure enough, the oil pressure on the right engine was rapidly dropping.

"Flames! We're on fire!" Gabi cried.

Bill's damage-control training kicked in. He immediately closed the right fuel shutoff valve and pitched the Junkers into another dive, but this time at a much steeper angle.

"Everyone hang on! This is the only way to extinguish the flames!"

The bulky transport shuddered from the strain as Bill pushed the nose down farther, pointing her to the ground floor. The Junkers accelerated to 225 kph . . . 245 . . . 265, and the G forces squashed Bill into his seat. He dared a half-second glance toward Gabi, who was frozen in her seat. He squeezed the steering wheel with a white-knuckle grip to maintain steady control, and when he reached 600 meters in altitude, he leveled out the Junkers.

Audible gasps of relief swept through the cockpit.

"Gabi, how are we doing? Is the engine fire out?"

He saw Gabi tentatively look over her shoulder. "We're good! Fire's out!"

Bill whispered a silent prayer of thanks—and felt like he was getting more religious by the minute. Another glance at his altimeter revealed they were down to 500 meters. He immediately initiated a steady climb since the Schwarzwald foothills were coming up, then he checked the fuel gauge again. What he saw caused bile to rise in his stomach. Now the needle was clearly hovering below the numeral 2. Any reserve had evaporated in the last five minutes, and losing an engine meant that he had to run the remaining two props with more power—and burn more fuel.

* * * * * * * * *

Gabi didn't know how much more she could take.

Her stomach roiled from the plunge into the darkness, and her taut nerves put her on edge. If she survived this flight, she told herself, she would never board an aeroplane again in her life. But first, she needed to know where they stood.

She pursed her lips. "Will we reach Switzerland?"

Bill took his eyes off the instrument panel and made eye contact. "The good news is that we're still in the air. The bad news is that we may not have enough fuel to escape Germany."

Gabi felt her stomach spasm. "We're that low on petrol?"

Bill drummed his thumbs on the steering column. "I didn't want to worry you, but we left Dübendorf with a tad more than half a tank. It's too bad that your General Guisan didn't get us topped off, but in the confusion of getting out of there—"

Gabi took a look at the fuel gauge, which was fluttering between the 2 and 1 marks. "Is there anything we can do?"

"Not much except to stretch the fuel as far as we can." He reached over to the pedestal and set his right hand on the fuel tank selector, which had three positions: L, Alle, and R. "I'm taking it that L means left and R means right," he said.

"*Rechts* and *links*—yes, right and left."

"Instead of running both tanks down, we'll run the right tank bone dry and then switch over to the left tank when the engines start to cough. I want to make sure we use every last drop of fuel."

"But what if we run out of fuel before the border?" Gabi stole a look at Joseph Engel, who was standing in the cockpit doorway again. She could see worry written all over his brow.

"Then we'll glide across the Rhine."

Gabi motioned for Joseph to come closer and relayed their getting-dire-by-the-minute fuel situation. In the faint glow of interior lighting, she saw his face turn pale.

"I know this is a blow." She spoke in German. "There's not much we can do. How are you feeling?"

"I'm okay."

Gabi's eyes met Joseph's. "Really? I would think that you're scared out of your wits, just like me."

"Well . . . I must confess to a certain amount of unease."

"I do, too, but the Lord knows exactly where we are, even up here in a black sky."

Joseph shifted his feet as the Junkers swayed to the left. "You mentioned religion. Are you a spiritual person?"

Gabi thought how she should answer that question. "I'm a follower of Christ, if that's what you mean. I believe that we can have a personal relationship with Jesus Christ. I'm the daughter of a pastor, you know."

"Maybe that explains a few things."

"What do you mean?"

"After being rescued by Pastor Leo and his friends, and seeing how they've been protected from the Gestapo all these years, I'm realizing that God is orchestrating something, even in the midst of this madness."

Gabi glanced over at the American pilot, who was concentrating on the instrument panel. "God is at work in our lives and deeply cares about what happens to us." She patted Joseph's arm. "He knows us so well . . . right down to how many hairs we have on our heads."

Joseph folded his hands. "So what do you think is going to happen?"

"I think our friend here hasn't been very forthcoming on our predicament. Even a novice like me knows that when the fuel gauge needle sits next to zero, we're about to run out of fuel. I pray that we can get close enough to Switzerland for our radio to work. Maybe they'll have some ideas if we have to land in some German cornfield. But whatever happens, I trust we'll somehow make it to safety."

* * * * * * * *

Gabi pointed to the gathering tangerine hue outside Bill's port window. "Look—the sun's coming up."

Bill glanced at his watch—5:30 a.m. The sunrise was probably fifteen minutes away, but the faintest hint of orange-pink on the horizon presented another good news/bad news situation. "If we have to ditch, I certainly prefer landing this Junkers in the daylight," he said. "I don't like flying in German airspace in broad daylight, however."

He turned to Gabi. "You want to try to reach Mr. Dulles again on the radio? We should be getting close to the border."

"I see it—the Rhine!"

Bill looked for a sliver of river . . . and found the mighty Rhine. "Great eyes, Gabi!" All the excitement in the cockpit stirred Joseph out of his passenger seat.

Bill figured they were twenty-five kilometers north of the border, heading straight for Dübendorf. "At our slower speed, all we need is ten more minutes."

Gabi dragged the emergency radio to her side and fitted the Bakelite headphones over her ears. For the third time in the last half hour, she put the portable antenna in the window. "Maybe the third time is the—"

The Junkers's No. 1 engine coughed and sputtered twice before resuming its normal RPM cadence. The same instant, the center engine coughed twice but continued spinning. Bill wasted no time. He immediately reached for the tank selector and switched to L—the left tank. The fuel boost energized the remaining engines, but a sinking feeling in his stomach told them that they were flying on borrowed time—no more than five or ten minutes.

"If you can raise anyone on that radio, tell them it doesn't look like we'll make it into Swiss airspace." For Bill, the glass was suddenly half empty, and even though pilots were supposed to be supremely positive, he needed to square up with reality.

* * * * * * * *

Gabi hadn't given up.

"I'm giving it another try." She flipped the switch on the emergency radio and was greeted by static. "Come on, come on." She gave the tan box a good whack with the flattened palm of her right hand.

"Hello, Red Riding Hood?" The reassuring voice of her father carried through the headphones. Gabi's heart leapt.

"Big Bad Wolf, is that you?" Prior to leaving Dübendorf, she and her father had exchanged code names. There was a good chance that any radio transmissions would be picked up by German ears, which she assumed was the case at this moment.

"Yes—we've been up all night waiting to hear about your collection of Edelweiss. Did you find the big patch?"

Mr. Dulles must have heard from the Swiss Air Force escort to the border. "We found all the Edelweiss we were looking for, and now we're coming home."

She could almost hear her father's sigh of relief. "Excellent. Big Cheese is here too. I'll pass the news to him."

Gabi sucked in her breath. "Tell him we have a serious problem."

"What's that, Red Riding Hood?"

"We may not be home in time for breakfast."

"Where are you?"

"Wait a minute." She let off her microphone's transmit button and asked Bill for their location.

He looked at the Army Air Force map balanced on his knees. "We're on a direct approach to Zurich. Closest border town on the German side is . . . I hope I'm pronouncing this correctly . . . Waldshut."

She smiled. "*Waldshoot*, as in what owls do," she said, using the proper pronunciation on the second syllable. "Close enough."

She thought about how she could tell her father over the radio where they were—without uttering *Waldshut*. "Remember when the twins needed a cobbler who could make special shoes for their flat feet?"

There was a moment of silence. "Yes, and I know where you mean," her father said. "Let me speak with the Big Cheese."

Twenty seconds later, her father's voice interrupted the staticky transmission. "Do you still have that sheet of instructions with the chart Big Cheese gave you?"

"Yes, but wait a second while I grab it."

Gabi reached into her khaki jacket and unfolded the sheet of paper. "Got it, Big Bad Wolf." The single-sheet of paper contained ten lines of typed-out words that were gibberish.

"Look in the third line."

Gabi shined a flashlight on the string of words.

perdis xxos luthdaws ermnine annca cawth nosom dendser etors dumrat impleser muhelt . . .

"Copy down every third word, four words in total."

Gabi peered at her list again and wrote these four words in the margin:

luthdaws

cawth

etors

muhelt

"Done."

"Good. Unscramble those words and visit our mutual acquaintance there. You already know the first one."

Gabi wrote the word *Waldshut* next to *luthdaws* and double-checked that the letters matched. They did.

"Got the first one."

She began playing with *cawth*. With one vowel, that should be easy. *Tawch . . . hawct . . . wacht . . . watch!* The next one was even easier: *store.*

Now for the last, *muhelt*. Two vowels. *Tehmul . . .* no, that won't work. She feverishly wrote three-letter combinations to give her a running start . . . *leh, lut, meh, met, hum, hel* . . . Wait, a strike. *Hel . . . helm . . . Helmut!*

"Solved, Big Bad Wolf!" They were to go to a watch store in Waldshut and ask for Helmut.

"Excellent. When you get there, ask our friend to put you in touch with Jean-Pierre or Pas—"

Accordion-driven French music blotted out the words, cutting off the transmission. "Wait! I didn't catch all that!" Gabi slammed the side of the emergency radio, but now the chanteuse Édith Piaf was in her earphones. She gave up and committed the names Jean-Pierre and Pas to memory.

• • • • • • • •

The first rays of sunlight peeked through gaps in the saber-toothed Alps, bathing the Ju-52 in a soft orange glow.

"We'll stay up here until we run dry," Bill told Gabi. "Keep on the lookout for a field we can land in." The fuel gauge indicator was too depressing to look at since the needle was stuck on 0 like someone had nailed it there.

They had to be flying on fumes . . . then the two engines coughed again. Bill shut down No. 1; they would go as far as they could on the center engine. The Junkers shed altitude as the center engine labored to shoulder the load.

He hoped Lady Luck was sitting in A1 next to Joseph Engel. Just three minutes ago, they had left the Schwarzwald foothills and flown into an open valley that drained right into Waldshut and the Rhine River. Three, four more minutes in the air, under some sort of power, and they could glide over this border town and land somewhere in Switzerland.

Then Bill's ears detected a subtle lowering in the RPMs. Any second, the Ju-52 would become the heaviest glider in Southern Germany. A sinking feeling rose in his throat. They weren't going to make it to Switzerland. It was time to set her down now.

"Tell your friend to strap himself in," Bill directed. "Make sure you've got your harness on too."

On cue, the center engine sputtered and stopped spinning, and now the only sound was the wind. Bill pushed the rudder right away to counter any yaw that would send the Junkers into a death spin. While maintaining firm control of the craft, he trimmed the gliding speed to 100 kilometers per hour. Gabi, he noticed, gripped the armrests for all they were worth.

The Junkers' steering column felt as heavy as a dumbbell. Bill watched the altimeter drop steadily—1,000 meters . . . 900 meters . . . 800 meters. The ground, he knew from the map, was around 300 meters above sea level. He wound the flap lever down to slow their descent.

From his cockpit aerie, Bill saw a checkerboard of farmlands and pockets of ground fog. "There!" He spotted an open field that looked long enough to land on. Their altitude had fallen to 500 meters.

"We're going in!" Bill lined up the Junkers for the open field next to a beige farmhouse. Traces of wispy fog clouded his view, then a copse of firs lurched up at them, close enough to reach out and touch. The Junkers shook as Bill fought to maintain a level heading.

But they were coming in too high, too fast!

He extended the flaps fully and hurtled past the perimeter fencing. The front wheels slammed onto the grassy meadow with a savage groan, bounced heavily, then bounced a second time before gripping the ground surely.

Bill stood on the brake pedals, but the Ju-52 skidded like a rock skipping across a frozen pond. Without its power assist, the heavy transport plane barely slowed as the brakes shrieked.

"The trees!" Gabi's hands flew to her mouth as she screamed.

"We're not going to stop in time. Brace yourself!"

Bill aimed the ship for an opening—and the Junkers careened through a gap at the forest's edge. Solid tree trunks sheared off both wingtips, causing the Junkers to pancake into the soft forest ground and crumple like a cheap accordion. Amazingly, the steel fuselage remained intact.

Their seatbelts had saved them.

Bill sprang into action, figuring that he and his passengers had only moments before shock set in. "Let's go!" he shouted at Gabi. He wrestled with her seatbelt and sprang her loose. Together, they freed Joseph, woozy from the rough landing. Bill put one arm over Joseph's shoulder and dragged him toward the rear passenger door.

The exit door balked at opening. "You've been giving us trouble the entire trip." Bill raised his right foot and kicked the doorknob. The door sprang open. He jumped out first and helped Gabi and Joseph—who was now alert—jump out of the damaged aircraft.

"I'd say we have a minute or two before someone comes running out of that farmhouse with a shotgun," Bill said.

"*Ein Moment, bitte!*" Joseph called, then rambled on to Gabi in German.

"What's he saying?" Bill's eyes focused on the trees closest to them, expecting armed men to emerge any moment. "We don't have any time—"

"He forgot his rucksack in the plane, and it's very important." Gabi froze. "The radio! We need it."

"Then get going!"

Gabi and Joseph rushed back into the passenger cabin. Bill followed and watched the German quickly retrieve his backpack. Unfortunately, the crash landing had thrown the emergency radio against the cabin bulkhead and smashed it to smithereens.

Gabi's face fell. "We can't call for help now."

"Doesn't matter! Let's go!" Bill led the way back out the door.

Within a matter of seconds, the three ran deep into the forest.

• • • • • • • • •

Waldshut Polizei
3:15 p.m.

The local kommandant of the Waldshut Polizei reread the Teletype from Berlin because he thought his eyes betrayed him the first time he scanned it. Reichsführer Heinrich Himmler, no less, was loaded for bear; that much he could tell.

His message related to the phone call the Waldshut Polizei had received shortly after 9 a.m. that morning from a local farmer who said he'd walked an hour to the nearest phone. His report was startling: a Swiss Junkers had crash-landed on his property. Not so surprising was his report that the occupants were nowhere to be found.

The Waldshut police chief thought it was only a matter of

time before a Swiss aircraft strayed off course into Germany—but this was a tortoise-slow transport plane, not a lightning-fast Swiss fighter. Interestingly, the Junkers hadn't burned, and a lieutenant he dispatched to the scene confirmed that the aircraft had run out of fuel. So why were the Swiss flying planes around with no gas? And where were the pilots and passengers?

A riddle wrapped inside a mystery. He immediately reported the incident to his superiors at the Freiburg regional office. They must have tossed this hot potato to the Gestapo, who kicked it all the way to Berlin and the Reichsführer.

Himmler's message stated that underground partisans had stashed an enemy of the Reich onto a Ju-52 belonging to the Swiss Air Force very early this morning at a farm outside of Heidelberg. Apparently, some farmers in the Leimen area had been awakened by the racket of a Junkers roaring off a makeshift landing strip, and they looked out from the bedroom window in time to see a transport plane—the Swiss markings clearly visible in the moonlight—flying due south for Switzerland. Several farmers called the Leimen Polizei, and a detail was sent out to investigate a farm belonging to religious fanatics, the communiqué said. A Gestapo regional commander was found dead, and an aide and several soldiers were missing in action, probably kidnapped by the partisans. The farmhouse was deserted.

The Waldshut police chief thought whoever was in the Junkers that crash-landed was long gone—and probably racing for the border.

The police chief called in a pair of lieutenants and described what had fallen into their district that afternoon. A pep talk was in order. This was their chance to be heroes. A chance to get back in the good graces of Berlin.

Even though a week had passed, he still felt the shame of the recent ambush that resulted in a half-dozen prisoners making their escape. He had lost a couple of good men when partisans—one of them Swiss, according to a bystander who spoke with the man—overtook a truck loaded with traitors destined for the Gestapo firing squad. His only comfort was his men had killed one of the traitors—a woman dressed in a traffic cop uniform.

Finding the Junkers occupants would be one step closer to atoning for what happened last week. If this group of outlaws believed they could pass through on his watch, they had another thing coming.

32

Waldshut, Germany
5:50 p.m.

The rhythmic clacking of hooves on cobblestones echoed off the frescoed three-story buildings that fronted Kirchstrasse, a commercial street around the corner from Waldshut's courtyard plaza. A doddering farmer, driving a horse-drawn hitch wagon with a faded olive-green tarp stretched over the back, tugged on the bridle reins. A pair of powerfully muscled Fresian horses with thick, black manes whinnied and came to a stop just before the mercantile district locked its doors for the evening.

Wearing a tattered straw hat and denim bib overalls with one strap hanging down the front, the seasoned plowman climbed off the hitch wagon and stretched his back and arms while making a slow turn to surreptitiously study the neighborhood. He spit a stem of green hay into the street and yanked the free ends of several hitch-knots, releasing the ropes that crisscrossed the deteriorating tarp. The farmer then strolled to the wagon's rear corner and whispered to the three individuals balled up beneath the canvas covering, "You can go now, and may God be with you."

• • • • • • • •

Gabi's heart raced when Herr Beyer reined in the horses to a stop. Once the geriatric farmer lifted the tarp, she scooted to the back of the hitch wagon, where she looked in both directions to make sure no one was watching. The farmer

305

gingerly took her left arm and helped her jump to the quiet cobblestone street around the corner from Waldshut's main square. Then Gabi helped Herr Beyer assist Bill and Joseph from their shared hiding place just as a couple of passersby crossed the street at the corner, but neither looked in their direction.

Even though her heart pounded with urgency, she knew that acting too hastily would draw attention to them. She plucked a stray piece of hay from her hair and told herself to act like any other girl on a visit to town—just in case anyone noticed their arrival.

"Where's the watch store?" she asked in German. Before they left the farmer's house, she had stipulated that no English would be spoken in public, meaning that Bill would remain mute.

"Helmut's is right behind us." The farmer pointed his thumb over his shoulder.

Gabi's eyes darted to the gold lettering of "Helmut's Watch Sales & Service" painted on the storefront window. Underneath the gilded sign, a minimal window display featured gold and silver timepieces with leather bands and a dozen cuckoo clocks. A handwritten sign noted that cuckoo clocks were invented in nearby Schönwald in 1737.

"We have to get going." Gabi leaned over, and the old farmer lifted his straw hat to receive her grateful kiss on his leathery cheek. "Herr Beyer, I don't know how we can ever thank you."

The old farmer blushed. "Please, God brought you to my front door."

"No argument there. The tall wooden cross in the middle of your vegetable garden certainly seemed like we were led to your doorstep. You were so gracious to take us in."

After the Junker had crash landed, she, Bill, and Joseph had dashed farther into the heavily forested grove that had stopped the sliding transport plane. Shafts of sunlight had streamed through gaps in the trees' foliage, seeming to spotlight the fugitives wherever they ran. Gabi expected locals armed with shotguns and pitchforks to chase after them, following their spontaneous plowing of the nearby wheat field. But no one had come.

The threesome skirted a dense thicket of massive firs and towering pines until they found a foot trail dating back to Charlemagne. An hour later, beyond the forest's edge, Gabi spotted Herr Beyer's farm and his wooden cross. Surely God had been with them. She prayed he was with them still.

Gabi led the two men toward Helmut's watch store. Bill hustled ahead and opened the entry door for her and Joseph, which tinkled a bell. They hurriedly moved inside and away from the front window.

Within seconds, a gray-haired man with a walrus moustache and rotund girth stepped out from behind a burgundy curtain tucked away in the shop's left corner. He wore a white shirt and gray slacks, accessorized by a gray vest whose buttons threatened to pop off from his ample abdomen.

"Herr Helmut?" Gabi asked.

"Yes, how may I be of service to you today?" the proprietor replied.

"We're friends of Jean-Pierre and Pas . . . ," Gabi said.

The proprietor raised his eyebrows. "Pas . . . who?"

"I'm sorry. Our transmission stopped, and I didn't catch the full name. Sir, I was told that you could help us, and to mention Jean-Pierre's name."

The proprietor's gaze scanned the three persons, then returned to Gabi. "Your Swiss accent betrays you," he said with a smile. "And what's the story with your friends?"

"I'm a good German," Joseph Engel declared, which elicited raised eyebrows and a nod from the heavyset owner. Joseph shrugged his shoulders and gave a shy gesture toward Gabi. "I'm with her."

Gabi leaned over to Bill Palmer and translated what had transpired. Bill nodded and declared in English, "And I'm a good American."

"*Ach, ein Amerikaner!* That's a good one!" The jovial watch store owner rushed to the front door, turned over the *Offen* sign to *Geschlossen*, and pulled down the shade. "I think I can trust you. Quick, follow me."

He motioned them around a rectangular glass-enclosed display case to the burgundy curtain, which hid a wooden staircase.

When they arrived on the first landing, he pointed to a closed door. "These are my private quarters." Herr Helmut gestured forward. "I have a second flat on the top floor. You will be safe there. You can rest."

"Rest?" Gabi shook her head. "No, we need to get out of here. We must leave as soon as possible."

The German folded his arms over his broad chest. "We cannot act too hastily. There is a manhunt—I've already heard. I'll send a wireless message to Jean-Pierre and Pascal, telling them you're here."

"So the other person's name is Pascal?" Gabi tucked the name away in her mind.

"They're Swiss-Germans like you, but those aren't their real names. Operational security." The store proprietor hesitated before continuing. "I'm afraid you now know my identity, but Jean-Pierre wouldn't have sent you unless the matter was extremely urgent. The name is Helmut Emden." The watch store owner greeted each one with a hearty handshake, then beckoned them to follow him.

He escorted them up two more flights of stairs, which led them to a flat at the top landing. Helmut's beefy fingers fished for a key in his right vest pocket and opened the door.

The loft apartment with hardwood floors was minimally furnished. "There's a bedroom if anyone needs a nap." He led them on a short tour. "And here's the toilette. Try to flush when you hear Frieda or myself running water or the WC below. Just in case we have unexpected visitors."

Gabi nodded. "So what happens next?"

"I'm sure Jean-Pierre and Pascal will want to get you across the Rhine tonight. Let's plan on that. I'll return for you at twenty-two hundred hours and escort you to the rendezvous point, where they'll arrive with a skiff."

"How dangerous is the crossing?"

"Don't worry. We've done this sort of thing dozens of times. But it's dangerous."

* * * * * * * *

The Rhine River near Waldshut, Germany
11:47 p.m.

The sense of foreboding that gripped Gabi's throat refused to ease. Over the last hour and forty-five minutes, their group of four had stolen out of Waldshut's medieval, commercial district and worked their way eastward—on foot—along the Rhine River. As much as Helmut's genial personality diffused the considerable danger surrounding them, the fact that they were the object of a manhunt added to the pressure building in her stomach. At any moment, she expected a Wehrmacht soldier, a local Polizei, or a dutiful German to jump out of the shadows, and that would mark the end. Of her dreams with Eric. Of her mission. Of her life.

Eric Hofstadler had been on her mind ever since she waved goodbye in Dübendorf. He seemed so assured on the drive to the military airfield. The way he exuded confidence in cutting a hole in the perimeter fencing and the sureness in his voice as he waved her off spoke volumes to her. The guy was a rock, and if—or when—she saw him again, she would jump into his arms. She had straddled the fence far too long, and it was time to land on his side. She had told her parents that she always wanted to be pursued . . . that she didn't want to "settle" for a husband. Here was a solid Christian man who set the boundaries in their relationship, who matched her heart for God, and whose rugged good looks set her heart aflutter. Here was a godly man who wanted her.

Now, she wanted him—or better said, she wanted the chance to see if they were headed for the altar. The danger she currently faced stripped away all that she had used to keep Eric at arm's length and instead increased her desire to draw him close, to determine once and for all if God was bringing them together for his special purpose.

Gabi turned her attention to the task at hand as she tracked Herr Emden's footsteps through the riverside brush, thanks to a canopy of bright moonlight. Joseph followed with his leather satchel. Bill, who said he didn't mind playing the tail gunner role, brought up the rear, stopping occasionally to listen for anyone who might be following.

"Do you have the time, Herr Emden?" Gabi whispered.

"You're asking for the time from someone who owns a watch store?" The corpulent shop owner reached into his pants pocket for his gold pocket piece. Unsnapping the hunter case cover, he turned the face toward the moon. "I have 11:47. We're almost at the rendezvous point. Once there, we should get a signal from Jean-Pierre."

Bill sidled up to Gabi. "Ask him how well the Krauts patrol this riverbank."

Gabi repeated the question to Herr Emden, obviously not employing the "Krauts" pejorative.

"Not as much as you'd think," he replied. "Between here and Lake Constance, Germany and Switzerland share more than 100 kilometers of the mighty Rhine. That's a lot of riverbank to cover. But the Germans do a good job of preventing travel from the interior to the border areas, and the Swiss do a good job of preventing people—including Jewish refugees—from entering their country."

Gabi involuntarily shuddered, once again visualizing the scene of the poor Jewish couple jumping from the Mittlere Brücke in Basel and drowning in the fast-moving waters, along with their infant. Their looks of desperation.

"I've heard stories too," she whispered.

The watch store proprietor led them to a clearing on the

riverbank. "We're here. Should be any minute now," he said. "Look near that boathouse."

Gabi placed her right hand across her forehead. She judged the Rhine to be around 400 meters wide at this point. The water moved quietly, but at a good pace. Her eyes scanned the riverbank—then fifty meters east of the boathouse, she saw a light flash three times.

"Right on time." Helmut reached into his rucksack and retrieved a flashlight. He signaled back three times.

"They'll depart at midnight, at our signal. Jean-Pierre has a skiff with an outboard engine. Don't know where he finds the petrol to keep it filled, but he manages somehow."

In the moonlight, Gabi watched a winch lower a small skiff into the water across the river. Her mind was so intent on the shadowy figures positioning the boat on the river that a closer movement startled her.

"*Hände hoch!*" Three men dressed in black suits jumped out of the shadows. Gabi's stomach fell as she noted their rifles fixed on her group. She mutely raised her arms in surrender. Who were they? Certainly not soldiers. Her mind raced, trying to figure out a plan for escape.

"*Raus!*" one man yelled. "March! Keep your hands on your head! No talking!" Gabi felt a rifle press into the back of her shoulder. Her feet moved forward, and she dared not glance across the river, lest she give the boat away. Hands atop her head, she had no choice but to follow the path that led away from the riverbank.

When they approached a protected grove, Gabi's heart skipped when she noticed a Mercedes sedan with lights on waiting for them. They had been ambushed! It was like someone knew they would be waiting at this rendezvous point for Jean-Pierre.

A tall man, also dressed in a black suit, stepped out of the rear door, slapping a pair of leather gloves into one of his hands. Seeing this dark figure faintly visible in the moonlight prompted all sorts of anguished thoughts to swirl through

Gabi's mind. To come so far, to overcome so many hurdles, to be just 400 meters from freedom and safety . . . and now facing sure death. Feelings of anxiety and despair rose in her heart. The memory of her father's voice spoke to her heart—*Pray!*

She silently petitioned the Lord for a miracle and reminded herself that no matter what happened, she was God's child, and her Father would protect her.

Instead of approaching the four prisoners, the tall man—who was clearly in charge—reached back into the rear door and assisted someone too weak to exit the automobile on his own. The decrepit passenger wore a fedora that shielded his face from view. His gray slacks were worn through at the kneecaps, and a torn gray jacket with a ripped-out shoulder seam hung over his hunched frame, partially concealing the swaths of gauze bandages binding his upper left torso.

"Dieter?" she whispered to herself.

Shock and revulsion swept through Gabi's veins. So that's why they were trapped! Dieter Baumann was a modern-day Judas who had betrayed them to the authorities. She wanted to beat him with her fists. He had sold them out for the proverbial thirty pieces of silver—in this case, the allure of stealing a pouch of diamonds.

The tall man supported Dieter, who, in his weakened state, required his assistance to approach the prisoners. "I am Captain Aeschbacher of the Waldshut Polizei. Would you care to introduce our guests, Herr Baumann?"

Dieter remained silent.

By the glow of the Mercedes' headlights, Gabi saw several welts decorating his face as well as a black eye and bloody lip.

"What's the matter, Herr Baumann? You lost your tongue? When properly motivated this afternoon, you were much more forthcoming."

Dieter's knees unlocked, causing him to slump. The Polizei captain struggled to keep the Swiss on his feet.

"Take him back to the car," he said to one of his lieutenants. "He's served his purpose."

Gabi watched the lieutenant half drag Dieter back to the car.

Captain Aeschbacher stepped forward. "Time to get down to business. Which one is the American pilot? Or do we need a German vocabulary test?"

Gabi shivered, wondering how he *knew*. She looked over to Bill, and she could tell that he had picked out the two words: *Amerikaner Pilot*.

Since there was no way out, she motioned with her hand. "This is Captain Bill Palmer of the United States Army Air Corps."

"And who are you, Swiss Miss?"

Gabi considered not answering him, but his condescending tone told her that he already knew the answer. "Gabi Mueller, sir."

"And the others?"

"I'm Helmut Emden."

The Waldshut police chief advanced toward the portly German. "I saw your wife, Frieda, not more than forty-five minutes ago. Herr Baumann told us where we could find her. We had a friendly chat, and she told us about the visitors who arrived this afternoon. I admire her cooperation, especially in a short amount of time. She's waiting for you to join her very shortly."

Captain Aeschbacher's sarcasm sickened Gabi, and she wondered how Helmut was taking it—

"And you must be Joseph Engel." Captain Aeschbacher took two steps toward Joseph and stared into his eyes. "The most wanted man in Germany. You've been very difficult to find, Herr Engel. Very difficult."

Joseph remained mute.

The Waldshut Polizei chief allowed a satisfied smile to etch his face. "You were very clever to make it this far, but I'm afraid this is a case of so near, yet so far."

Captain Aeschbacher turned to one of his lieutenants. "Get on the radio and order a transport truck for the prisoners."

With a snappy *"Jawohl,"* the lieutenant retreated toward the headlights and slid into the Mercedes' front seat to call in the transport truck.

"Bind them."

With two rifles still pointed at them, a lieutenant approached with thin cords. He spun Gabi around, grabbed her arms, and held them behind her back. His practiced hands looped the cord around her wrists several times and gave the final knot an extra twist.

Gabi's knees trembled as pain coursed through her wrists and arms—although she'd never admit it.

The lieutenant had just finished binding Joseph's hands when a transport truck rolled into the open grove. Two Wehrmacht soldiers jumped out of the cab, leaving the driver behind.

"Into the *Lastwagen!*" Captain Aeschbacher barked his command, and the soldiers immediately herded them at gunpoint to the rear of the flatbed truck, enclosed on three sides by wooden slats. A soldier motioned Gabi to the rear of the truck, then grabbed her arms and tossed her in like a bale of hay. It took two soldiers to throw the rotund Helmut on board.

"Sit in the back!" one soldier barked.

Gabi peered through the slats and saw Captain Aeschbacher huddled with the driver, a Wehrmacht soldier. She only picked up snatches of conversation, but what she heard indicated they were discussing where to take the prisoners. When she heard something about picking up Frau Emden, driving to Freiburg, and then the dreaded word *Gestapo*, her heart pounded. Horrifying stories about cruel interrogation methods replayed in her mind, and she imagined that nothing would be out of bounds. First they would steal her dignity by stripping her naked, then they would inflict blood-curdling pain.

Even worse, her mission was a failure. Joseph Engel and whatever knowledge he possessed about a "wonder weapon" would remain in Nazi hands for use against the Allies. Her sad gaze met Bill's, whose seriousness reflected the peril they faced. Joseph appeared dazed, staring straight ahead.

She shifted her gaze to Helmut, who seemed passive—almost serene. He must have been a good actor to hide his feelings so well, since surely he knew that he and his wife were facing impending torture and death.

Two soldiers jumping onto the rear of the flatbed interrupted her thoughts. One whistled into the nighttime air, and the engine fired up. The transport truck executed a U-turn and soon found a frontage road that undoubtedly would lead them back to Waldshut and then on to Freiburg. The Mercedes followed in their dust.

As the truck bounced along, Gabi sat cross-legged with her hands tied behind her back. Trying to keep her balance, she pushed up onto her knees, which prompted an immediate glance from one of the soldiers. Bill did the same, followed by Joseph. Poor Helmut couldn't summon the strength or the agility, so he remained cross-legged on the wooden floor. Gabi winced at the pain of her pinched hands, and she turned her head to look at Bill. He appeared deep in thought, and she hoped he too was trying to come up with an escape plan.

The truck suddenly downshifted to lower gears and rolled to a stop. One of the guards standing in the back peered over the cab at the commotion over the unexpected checkpoint.

"What's happening?" Bill whispered.

Gabi eyed the soldiers, who also appeared confused. "I don't know. Pray. That's our only chance . . ."

"How come we're stopping?" one guard asked the other.

"There's a roadblock—"

The sharp report of several rifle shots split the air. Gabi instinctively hit the deck, and Bill landed on top of her. One of their guards barked out a stifled scream and fell hard next to Gabi. She craned her neck and saw his blood-drenched hand

315

clutching his neck as he struggled for a gurgling breath. The other soldier stooped quickly below the line of fire, his wild eyes taking in his dying comrade's condition. He jumped off the truck and took cover. Though he raised his rifle and fired off several shots toward the bushes, more gunfire erupted behind him, and he lurched forward against the truck and crumpled into a heap.

Pistol shots burst from the Mercedes sedan, but another volley of gunfire from the shadows shattered glass and tore into sheet metal, silencing the shooters in the car. A stray shot or two rang out, and then just as suddenly as it started, the shooting stopped.

Gabi found herself crushed under Bill's body. She could barely breathe—and her mind failed to comprehend what had just happened. She was just starting to regain her composure when she noticed—through the wooden slats—two German soldiers striding past the truck, approaching the rear.

German soldiers? Fear and confusion gripped her. All her mind could process was that there had been a firefight—an ambush—but the Germans must have beaten the partisans back.

The German soldiers nudged their fallen comrades with their rifle muzzles.

"Jean-Pierre?" Helmut cried out. "Pascal? You saved us!"

In the moonlight, Gabi felt detached from reality—out of sorts. She couldn't put this together . . . the soldier hauling himself onto the flatbed looked exactly like . . . no, this couldn't be, but there was no mistake. "Eric? Is that you?"

The soldier pushed back the brim of his German helmet, revealing a shock of red hair. "Gabi—you're safe!"

Eric Hofstadler gently untied the knots constricting Gabi's hands, stood, and pulled her up and into his arms. She kissed his face as tears blurred her gaze.

"Eric, it's really you." She touched his face. "I thought I'd never see you again."

Eric again squeezed her close. Then he leaned back and

wiped a tear from her cheek. "I can't tell you how good it feels to have you in my arms."

The watch store owner cleared his throat. "So, your real name is Eric." Helmut reached out to pat Eric's shoulder. "Although I'm sure I'll still be calling you Jean-Pierre ten years from now. And what's your real name, Pascal?"

All eyes turned to look at the second soldier boosting himself—with less agility—onto the back of the truck.

Gabi covered her mouth in surprise. "Dad! What are you doing here?"

"The same reason you're here." He grinned. "Doing my part to defeat Adolf Hitler."

Gabi dropped Eric's hand and embraced her father, allowing the emotion of the last twenty-four hours to flow from her eyes and wet his uniform.

After an appropriate wait, Helmut tapped "Pascal" on the shoulder. "I was hoping you'd set up a roadblock. But you old goat—you never told me a thing."

"Helm, listen, I couldn't, and now you know why. But one thing I do know is that Joseph Engel's disappearance has stirred up a hornet's nest."

Ernst Mueller let out a low birdlike whistle, and four partisans wearing berets came out of the foliage to approach the truck.

"Nice shooting, guys," Ernst said, removing his Wehrmacht helmet. "We have a boat to catch, but first, I need you men to go back into Waldshut. Frau Emden is being held at the store . . ."

* * * * * * * * *

The skiff—heavily loaded with six persons—touched Swiss soil at 12:42 a.m. The crossing had taken only three minutes. The welcoming party included some of Eric's buddies from the apartment overlooking the Badischer Bahnhof—as well as another American.

"Mr. Dulles!" Gabi exclaimed.

The American spymaster accepted her hand and held it. "Gabi, it's so good to see you. I can't tell you what it means to me that everyone returned safely. You are a remarkable young woman. And so is that young man next to you."

"Very kind of you, sir," Eric replied in Swiss-accented American English. He wrapped his arm around Gabi's waist and pressed his left hand on her hip. "When we heard the Junkers had run out of petrol, I didn't think I'd see the person I love more than breath itself, ever again." He smiled and leaned over to kiss Gabi—

"Wait one minute, buster." Gabi pulled away from Eric, feigning anger. "You're a fraud! You knew how to speak English all this time!"

"Well, I've been learning from your father. I guess that was part of my cover."

Gabi burst out with a laugh. "What else do I need to know about you?"

"That I can't live without you?"

"I think I knew that!" She gave him a quick hug.

Allen Dulles cleared his throat. "Can you introduce me to Joseph Engel?"

"Yes, of course." Gabi stepped over to pull Joseph away from Eric's friends and her father, who were swapping stories.

"Mr. Engel, it's a pleasure to meet you," he said properly in German.

Joseph dropped his leather satchel to the ground to shake hands with the OSS chief.

"A pleasure, sir. I can't believe I escaped."

"Indeed, you have. On behalf of the United States of America, I welcome you to freedom . . ."

Epilogue

Baden, Switzerland
Friday, May 18, 1945
5:05 p.m.

Inside the ornate chapel abutting the Schloss Bottstein castle, the jam-packed crowd rose in unison to the strains of Pachelbel's Canon in D.

"That's our cue," Ernst Mueller whispered as he extended his right arm to his daughter. "This will be the only time I get to do this."

"Daddy, don't start—" Gabi blinked back tears.

She took a deep breath and allowed her father to lead her down the aisle toward the man whom she had so badly underestimated for years. Her throat constricted slightly at the thought of the treasure she had in Eric Hofstadler, too long obscured by her immature naïveté. She drank in the sight of the one who had won her heart.

Her eyes shifted from Eric to Bill Palmer—back in Switzerland on a three-day pass—as the best man playfully nudged the groom. Eric's awestruck face broke into a broad smile.

When father and daughter reached the wedding arbor, Gabi slid her hand out of her father's arm as he straightened into his pastoral bearing. He took three more steps into the chancel and turned around to face her.

"Who gives this bride?" he asked, his chin lifted in formality.

Ernst Mueller immediately stepped down to rejoin his daughter, sliding her hand into the crook of his arm as he turned to face the empty podium. "Her mother and I do."

The audience tittered, and Gabi rolled her eyes, knowing the thoughts of every Swiss in the audience: *That's an American for you.*

As he motioned for Eric to accept Gabi's hand, he retook his place in front of the beaming couple. Together Gabi and Eric knelt beneath the flower-covered arbor.

Ernst cleared his throat. "*Meine Damen und Herren,* we are gathered here today in the sight of God, and in the face of this congregation, to join together this man and this woman in holy matrimony . . ."

* * * * * * * *

"How's my Swiss courier?" Allen Dulles, dapper in a top hat and silver-and-black vested suit, approached Gabi with a beaming smile.

"I really do think this is the happiest day of my life."

"My heartfelt congratulations. May I take a look?" The American leaned over as Gabi held out her left arm, adorned with a glittering diamond setting on her ring finger. The wedding reception—in a refurbished monk's cellar in the castle basement—was winding down after a delightful dinner for the wedding party.

"I still can't believe it." Gabi brought her left hand up to gaze at the ring, as if she couldn't believe such a beautiful diamond was hers. "Wasn't that nice of the Rosenthal family?"

"Yes, they were quite grateful to receive the pouch of diamonds that you 'liberated' from that safe in Weil am Rhein. Nice of them to include a diamond ring as part of your reward."

"How did you locate the family?" Gabi strained to remember the difficult morning of nearly nine months earlier.

"Remember that folder in the safe?"

Gabi nodded.

"Inside that folder was correspondence from brothers and sisters living in the States," Dulles continued. "It was a simple matter to track down members of the extended family, most of whom lived in New York City. They were in the diamond business too, as it turns out. Like I said, although the Rosenthals were devastated to learn that their relatives were murdered in the death camps, they were most appreciative of your bravery."

Dulles reached for Gabi's elbow and steered her away from other well-wishers. "They asked me to personally forward this to you." He extracted a letter-sized envelope from his inside breast pocket.

"What's this?"

"Take a look." The American spymaster maintained a face of equanimity.

Gabi slipped a lacquered fingernail under the envelope's flap. Her eyes widened as she withdrew a check made out in her maiden name containing more zeros than she had ever seen on a check.

"This can't be happening," she said, her face as white as her bridal gown. The amount on the green check drawn on the New York Bank and Trust: $50,000.

She threw her arms around Dulles and squeezed his neck, startling her boss. "How can I ever thank you?"

"Don't thank me," Dulles said. "I was told by the Rosenthal family that this represents a 10 percent finder's fee in recognition of your honesty and your good-faith effort to return the diamonds to their rightful owner."

"But this is a fortune!" Gabi shook her head in disbelief.

"Yes, it is, but I know you and Eric will use the money wisely."

Gabi examined the check one more time, as if she expected to awaken from a dream at any moment. "I don't know what to say, Mr. Dulles, except how incredibly blessed Eric and I are . . . for *everything* . . . at a time when the world is picking up the pieces after the German surrender. It's hard to believe V-E Day happened only ten days ago."

At that moment, her new husband returned with two long-stemmed glasses of white wine.

When Gabi spilled the joyous news, he nearly dropped the half-filled glasses of Dezaley.

"Looks like you'll be able to buy another dairy farm," Dulles said.

"Actually, I think I'm getting out of the milking business—thanks to the promotion you gave the both of us," Eric said.

Dulles waved him off. "Believe me, if anyone deserved to be put in charge of the Swiss section, it would be you and Gabi. Postwar Europe needs people like the two of you and Benjamin Becker."

Eric's face brightened. "How is Benjamin doing?"

"As you know, he remained undercover with the Gestapo and performed many valiant deeds on our behalf right up to when our forces liberated Heidelberg in March. I would imagine that he will be invaluable when the war trials start. In many ways, this is just the beginning for good people like you and Benjamin. Sooner or later, we'll have to deal with the Soviets."

"Thank you for your confidence in us." Gabi flashed a winsome smile. "Speaking of invaluable, have you heard from Joseph?" She remembered the letter she had received from him at Easter time. The return address was an APO military address, but the postal stamp said Los Alamos, New Mexico.

Dulles smiled. "He's doing well. I can't tell you where he is exactly or what he's doing because it's top secret, but you may hear from him—or about his work—very shortly."

Their boss let the thought hang in the air. "So where are you going on your honeymoon?"

Gabi and Eric looked at each other and smiled.

"We thought about some place in the mountains," Eric said. "You know, Davos sounds like a nice place to go this time of year."

Acknowledgments

We have many people to thank for their insight, advice, encouragement, and edits regarding *The Swiss Courier*. First of all, I (Mike) must toss a large bouquet of Edelweiss toward my wife, Nicole, a Swiss born in Basel and proficient in five languages. Nicole laboriously read version after version of each chapter, and she was a great source for the Swiss-German and German dialogue. And Tricia offers a mountain of thanks to her husband, John, for all his love, support, and showing her what love is all about.

Bill Palmer, an Englishman married to a Swiss (his wife, Andrietta, was our maid of honor), has flown planes for nearly forty years and was a Swissair pilot for twenty-five years. The Palmers live near Zurich, and Bill was especially helpful with the technical aspects of flying the Junkers Ju-52 plane as well as coming up with ideas for the departure from Dübendorf and the crash-landing in Germany, which is why we named a central character after him. Bill consulted with Hans Moser, who has actually flown the Junkers Ju-52. John Zublin, an American pilot whose grandfather was Swiss, also helped with the flight sequences.

J. L. Thompson dazzled us with his editing skills and deserves kudos, as did Amy Lathrop, Tricia Goyer's editorial assistant.

Dawn Saunders and her twelve-year-old daughter Sydney read the manuscript as it was being written and always asked where the next chapters were. Tom Anderson, the author of *Verdict: Jesus Christ Is Who He Said He Was*, also cheered us on. Tom, in his late seventies, said he'll never forget where he was when he learned the Japanese had attacked Pearl Harbor: he was a schoolboy delivering newspapers that Sunday morning.

Brenda Stoeker, wife of Fred Stoeker of *Every Man's Battle* fame, had eagle eyes for spotting typos. A pair of Swiss, Philip Dejaris of La Croix sur Lutry, and Carol Bieri of Geneva, gave us an "inside Switzerland" look, as did Stephan Stücklin of Basel. Rick Myatt, my pastor and my coauthor on my first novel, *By the Sword*, passed along timely advice, as did Jon Shafqat and Bill Farrington.

Urs Winkler, a longtime friend of mine who lives in Spiez, Switzerland, and heads up the World Vision office in Switzerland, organized an interview with his eighty-five-year-old mother, who was a teenage girl living in Riehen, Switzerland, during World War II. Martha Winkler described what it was like growing up within a few hundred meters of the German border, as well as wartime deprivations experienced by the Swiss.

Eddie Welch, whose brilliant mind was part of the Theoretical Division at Los Alamos Scientific Laboratory in Los Alamos, New Mexico, and who also worked on the hydrogen bomb, proofed the sections on Werner Heisenberg and the German atomic bomb project.

Anne-Marie Hämisegger with the Basel Tourist Office was especially helpful with the history of the Mittlere Brücke bridge spanning the Rhine River.

Finally, many thanks to the Revell team and their confidence in us, especially Vicki Crumpton, executive editor, and our associate editor, Barb Barnes.

Tricia Goyer is the author of eighteen books, including eight historical novels, two of which won "Book of the Year" from the American Christian Fiction Writers organization. She lives in Kalispell, Montana, with her husband, John, three children, one foreign exchange student, and her grandmother. She loves talking with World War II veterans, doing drama in children's church, and mentoring teenage mothers. Visit Tricia's website at www.triciagoyer.com.

Mike Yorkey is author or coauthor of more than seventy books, including the *Every Man's Battle* series and *By the Sword*, a thriller set in the Mideast. He lives in Encinitas, California, with his wife, Nicole, and they spend part of the year in her native Switzerland. They are the parents of two adult children. Visit Mike's website at www.mikeyorkey.com.